STUNNER

A Ronnie Lake Mystery

By

Niki Danforth

Publisher: Pancora Press

Book Design by Donnie Light – eBook76.com

Cover Design: KT Design, LLC www.kristaft.com

For Dan
who has cheered me on
through all the years

CHAPTER ONE

The fist explodes in a punch toward my stomach. Like most women, I would have folded in panic not that long ago, my only move to throw out my arms protectively in front of me, shielding myself from the blow while cowering like a trapped animal.

Not now. Even though this attack happens in a split second, time really does seem to slow down. First, I take in the whole of my opponent, never fixing my gaze on any one point. Without a doubt, this person means to finish me off.

As the strike travels toward my abdomen, I strategically move aside with a quick shifting of my feet, simultaneously grabbing my adversary's wrist, my fingers applying the force of a steel trap. With rapid speed, I turn my opponent away from me as if I'm opening a gate and swing this assailant right off balance.

Then I quickly step in and plant my feet close to one another while lowering my torso under my aggressor's center. I reach around my opponent's waist while turning my hips to load this individual onto the small of my back.

Hold that image! Hey, the decade of my twenties with my body feeling immune to injury was ages ago. So why would I even consider acting like Bruce Lee or Jackie Chan and stack an aggressive attacker onto my fifty-five-year-old aching back? Commmme onnnn.

The key is not to struggle and attempt to muscle this person onto my spine. It's all about the correct stance, the correct posture, and finally the correct hip turn from my core that together combine into a force of leverage powerful beyond belief. This set-up allows me to execute a flawless hip throw, and my attacker breaks a freefall through the air with an arm-slam onto the ground.

I hear a quick exhale of air and then a soft groan from the floor. Grinning, my attacker pushes up from the mat and tells me, "Good job with the *koshinage*, Ronnie. Your stance and core were rock solid."

"Thanks, Isabella. I think I'm getting better at *koshinage*." We use the Japanese name for the technique we've just practiced in the martial art of Aikido.

Isabella Romano is my *sensei*, or teacher, and she's a sixth-degree black belt. I'm just a humble first-degree black belt newbie, and I'm in awe of her. When Isabella performs that hip throw, well, I sure wouldn't want to be some idiot-guy in a bar picking a fight with her. I'd bet on this fifty-something, small brunette any day of the week.

We wrap up our weekly private lesson before Isabella's noon class starts at her dojo (a Japanese word that means *a place of the way* or, for our purposes, *training hall*). "See you in class on Friday?" she asks.

"Absolutely. Thanks for the lesson, Isabella." We bow out to *O'Sensei*, the founder of Aikido, whose picture hangs on the spacious front wall of the dojo (often referred to as the *kamiza*). I enter the dressing room to change into jeans and a tee-shirt and then head home.

Driving a little too fast, I glance down at the black belt neatly folded in the top of my Aikido bag on the front seat of my car. Not bad for an AARP broad, I muse. I feel the pride of recent accomplishment and love the time I spend at the dojo studying with Isabella *Sensei*. At least for the moment, my confidence and attitude register a one-hundred-eighty-degree shift from six months ago when my divorce became final.

The sun sparkles through a canopy of overhead branches as I maneuver the woodsy back roads close to home in my post-divorce, adorable red Mustang. With the top down, I fully enjoy this scenic route—although it still jars me to glimpse the flashes of trees tossed on the ground like random clusters of pick-up sticks, the result of a raging Superstorm Sandy.

I click on Bruce Springsteen, and his voice blasts at me through the car speakers.

…Glory days, well, they'll pass you by

Glory days, in the wink of a young girl's eye

Glory days, glory days…

It only takes a little Springsteen to remind me that being a Jersey girl, or better yet, a single Jersey *woman*, is not so bad.

My phone rings as I turn the Mustang onto the dirt road leading to the house. I press the button on my steering wheel and answer, "Laura? Hi!"

"Aunt Ronnie, where are you right now?" my niece asks on speakerphone. I hear an uncharacteristic tension in Laura's voice.

Concerned, I tell her, "Almost home."

"Can I come over?" She waits only a half-beat. "It's important, Aunt Ronnie." Her voice quivers. "An emergency."

She scares me with that. "Is everyone all right?" I ask.

"It's Daddy, Aunt Ronnie. You know he just got back, and he brought this girlfriend with him—I think they want to get married. Oh, Aunt Ronnie, I'm worried. Some weird things are happening here since they came home."

Oh well, if that's all it is… "Slow down, Laura—"

"All I know is my watch-out-for-Dad radar is on high alert and going off way more than usual since Mommy died. I'm not kidding, Aunt Ronnie. Something's wrong."

"Sweetie, get over here. I'll have coffee waiting for you." Maybe my niece has reason to worry.

CHAPTER TWO

My German shepherd, Warrior, rubs the soft coat of his head against my bare ankle as I search among a half-dozen opened but not-yet-unpacked dish boxes stacked on the kitchen countertops. I find two mugs, fill them with coffee, and then hear a car door slam. That noise is followed by the sound of a car engine roaring by, and I catch a glimpse of a van spewing gravel as it races up my dirt road. Metallic blue or grey, I think.

"Aunt Ronnie, I'm sure that guy was following me," Laura says as she dashes into the kitchen, a little out of breath.

I truly doubt it. "Probably just a delivery for the big house," I say and pour milk into both our coffees. "Hey, by the time I got the police over here, the guy would be long gone through the back gate, anyway."

Before Laura can manage another word, I give her the time-out signal. "Stop. Take a deep breath." I extend our filled mugs, and she takes them with a grateful smile.

"Follow me," I order. Holding the coffee pot and a small pitcher of milk, I lead her into my garden.

Warrior trots out behind us into the hedged enclosure that's backed up by fencing so my dog can be off his leash without my having to worry about him.

"Not working today?" I indicate a table with an open umbrella to shield us from the sun, and we sit down.

"Mrs. McCann doesn't need me to look after the girls this afternoon, but I've got some tutoring sessions later on." Laura is a recent college graduate working various summer jobs. In two months she leaves for Australia, a graduation gift from Daddy.

My niece is a welcome sight with her wild red locks flying out every which-way. While I usually brush my straight strawberry blonde hair into a quick ponytail, lovely Laura bounces out of bed every morning, long mane loose, looking nonhairdo perfect. We do have the same green eyes and toothy smiles, however, so there's no missing we're family. Today though, her beautiful, gentle eyes look panicked.

"OK. Tell all." I reach down to scratch Warrior's head. "Forget about that van. What's going on with your darling dad?"

"Well, you know it's already been four months since he went out to California." Laura puts her elbows on the table, steeples her fingers, and taps her mouth. I nod in agreement, remembering her oh-so-serious father gesturing the exact same way when we were in our teens.

I snap back to the present to listen to Laura. "…except for the weekend of my graduation a month ago, he's been out there the whole time, you know, working with his new CEO at that Santa Clara tech company he bought last year.

He was only supposed to be there a month. Remember?" She gives me a significant look.

"I do remember. All of us thought it'd be a great change of scenery for Frank." I adjust my chair so that it sits totally in the shade of the umbrella. Poor Frank. "How long's it been? Ten months, almost a year, since Joanie died?"

"Only nine months, thirteen days." Laura's eyes tear up, and she quickly blinks back the threatened drops.

Poor Laura, too. "Oh, honey, I know it's hard. To lose your mother is a very big deal, and it takes time to grieve and mend." I reach across the table and squeeze my niece's hand. "So tell me about this person your dad met. Does she work for his company?"

Laura shakes her head. "No. He met her at a country club out there. She's widowed, too, and they started playing golf and then *dating*..." Her creased brow broadcasts her distress.

Though I was somewhat wary, myself, on hearing the news, certainly Frank couldn't be expected to avoid eligible women for the rest of his life. "When did they arrive?" I ask.

"Two days ago." Laura picks up her steaming mug and inhales the aroma. "But you just came back this morning, Aunt Ronnie, and we haven't had a chance to talk. How was the Shore?"

"Great as always." I reach for my coffee. "Her name?"

"Juliana Wentworth. She's gorgeous, too. Long, dark, *perfect* hair. Great figure," Laura says, and I reflexively sit straighter and pull in my tummy as I lift my mug. She adds, "Late thirties. No way forty yet."

I stop mid-sip. Laura lowers her head and raises her eyebrows. "Isn't that a little young for Daddy, Aunt Ronnie?"

I ponder the reality. "Frank is two years older than I am, so that makes him fifty-seven. So, yeah, I might have to agree."

Laura now has a death grip on her mug and a faraway look in her eyes. "Laura?" Her head jerks slightly, and she looks at me. "I feel as if something else besides the age difference is bothering you," I say. "What is it?"

"Aunt Ronnie, I'm definitely picking up a bad vibe." She says that with both her voice and her eyes.

"I'm listening." Warrior nudges my knee with a ball in his mouth. "Not now, Warrior."

Laura sighs. "OK. Since they arrived, we've been getting hang-up calls at the house. When I pick up, no one answers," Laura says. "We never had those before. It's weird."

I'm definitely interested. "How many hang-ups have you had? And when?"

"Nine calls in two days, and it's any time of the day," she answers quickly. "Caller ID shows some of the numbers are blocked, and the rest of the hang-ups come from or around Scranton, Pennsylvania. Aunt Ronnie, I don't think we know anyone in Scranton, do we?"

"Don't think so, Laura," I say and slowly drink my coffee. Sounds like more than annoying telemarketers since if you answer, they—or their recordings—start their spiel. "That is strange, all those hang-ups."

Laura nods and sips her drink. "And then something even more bizarre happened. A box arrived for Juliana this morning. Daddy was out. I put it on the front hall table and noticed it had a funny smell. I told her about the box when she came downstairs."

"OK. What's so odd about that?" I ask.

"First, I saw her pick up the box and read the postmark," Laura says. "Right away, she got this very upset look on her face, like she wanted to cry, and then she rushed back upstairs with the box."

Well, that could be anything. "Laura, maybe you're reading too much into this."

"Come on, Aunt Ronnie. Usually if you get a box in the mail or from UPS or whatever, it's because you've ordered something you want, or somebody has sent you a gift. And that's a nice thing, right? You wouldn't look horrified, the way she did."

I drink from my mug. "Sweetheart, I'm sure there's a reasonable explanation. Maybe she got something for your father and was concerned he'd walk in before she could put it away." Is Laura being an alarmist, or do her worries warrant attention? I try to decide.

"Maybe," she answers. But my niece presses on. "What has me really worried is that Daddy's been dropping some funny hints..." Her voice rises in pitch. "...like maybe he's going to *marry* this Juliana. God, he barely knows her. It's way too soon."

She definitely has a point. "I would agree."

"And why would some *young* babe marry Daddy, who's almost sixty, anyway. No offense to Daddy, but come on."

I chuckle a little. "No offense, but your dad's a handsome, sexy guy—"

"TMI, Aunt Ronnie." Laura puts her hands over her ears, and I laugh again.

"Too much information?" I ask. "How so?"

"You do know kids don't think their parents are supposed to have sex." Laura now covers her eyes in mock horror. "But Juliana Wentworth would enjoy other benefits if she wants to become Mrs. Franklin Livingston Rutherfurd." Her fingers flick air quotes when she says her father's formal name.

"Yeah." I sigh. "There's the money…"

"It's not only the money, Aunt Ronnie. I'm worried that Daddy will make a terrible mistake the way Uncle Pete did." My niece once more looks as though she wants to cry. "And then we'll never see him again, just like Uncle Pete."

"Take it easy, Laura. This is about your father, not Peter," I say, but I also feel a wave of sadness wash over me. You'd think I'd be done with that after so many years.

That's when Warrior walks over and plops his big head in Laura's lap. I smile. "Hey, you need a dog. The world always looks better when you have a dog."

"Aunt Ronnie," Laura practically wails. "This is Daddy, your brother. I love Daddy, but he's gone head over heels for a woman who should be dating George Clooney, not *him*."

She clamps her hands onto her mug. "We don't know anything about her," Laura adds. "I tried to Google her. Not much out there. And I don't know what to do, because Daddy looks so happy for the first time since Mommy died."

"That's a good thing, Laura," I say firmly.

"But what if, like you said, she only wants Daddy's money?" Laura taps her mug against her chin, deep in thought. "...or I guess it's possible she might be a nice person. Oh, Aunt Ronnie, don't you think we should hire a private detective, the way they do in the movies, to check her out?"

The idea doesn't strike me as being a good one. Too many negative possibilities leap to mind—such as Frank finding out and wanting to disown both his daughter and his sister. "One step at a time. First I want to meet her." Definitely that.

"Done." Laura almost smashes her mug on the table to make her point. Horrified, she quickly examines the tabletop. "Sorry, Aunt Ronnie. I know how you like everything just so." She checks for scratches and apparently sees none. Nor do I with a casual, seemingly disinterested glance.

"OK," she continues. "Daddy's organizing a little get-together tomorrow evening, and I'm helping him. Six-thirty. Come meet her. See what you think."

"Sounds perfect," I answer. "Count me in."

I refresh our coffee, and we sit quietly for a moment. I breathe in the smell of fresh-cut grass, while gazing at a bed of astilbe perennials anchored on each end by blossoming white Annabelle hydrangeas.

Sitting in the garden of my old house always gave me great joy; the same now holds true in this smaller garden. I spot several weeds and can't resist hopping up to pull them out.

The sound of childish laughter distracts me, and Laura and I look in the direction of the dirt road. "Ah, those kids love riding their bikes back and forth," I say.

"You don't miss living in your big house?" she asks me. "I mean, you've really downsized, Aunt Ronnie."

"Nope. Don't miss it at all," I say, a little too quickly, remaining focused on the weeds.

She looks at me for any clues that indicate otherwise. "Come on. Even though you've only been here a couple of weeks, don't you wander up your road every now and then to check out your house? And maybe wish you were back there instead of living in your tiny guest cottage?"

I look up at my charming two-story stone cottage with its new split-shake cedar roof and smile. "No. Mostly I got tired of all those empty rooms, especially now that Brooke's working in the city, and Jessica's doing the internship out West. That big house needs people, and the Lattimores have five kids running around the place. Plus, they're good tenants, so it's great."

Laura looks at me skeptically. "Really?"

"You'll find out later in life, kiddo, once you're married, have children, and then one day, way in the future, become an empty-nester like me. You end up living in the same three or four rooms, no matter the size of the house."

STUNNER

I stand up straight and stretch my back. "Anyway, I always envied my guests who stayed out here. This cottage is heaven, and living here has simplified my life." I then add, "Plus, I'll be saving money, and that's always a good thing."

"You miss being married, Aunt Ronnie?" she asks, her tone rather careful.

"Truthfully? It was hard at first. But these days, most of the time, I like my life just the way it is." *Fake it till you make it*, I think to myself. I continue with the weed pulling.

Laura glances at her watch, and obviously surprised at the time, jumps up. "OK. Have to run." She comes over and hugs me. "Aunt Ronnie, thanks for listening. You're the best. I always feel better after I talk to you. See you tomorrow." She walks away and then stops. "Wait. What about that van that was following me?"

I shrug. "Like I said, that was probably a house repair up the road." I squint at my watch. "And by now he's definitely gone. Laura, I'm sure you'll be fine."

For the most part, fake it till you make it does seem to work, and I'm glad I could help Laura calm down. As for me, let's just say, at times since my divorce, I'm still on shaky ground. I tried to continue with life as it was at the big house before the split, but no go.

Too many rooms, too many memories, and too many spooky noises and shadows for me to be alone in that large space. My hope is that a new start in my cozy cottage will be a positive step toward me feeling in charge of my life again.

~~~~~

After my niece leaves, Warrior and I go inside and upstairs to the master bedroom. Warrior drops down on his dog bed to watch as I do some more unpacking. After placing linens and blankets in a closet, I open a box with framed family photographs.

The first one I take out is my favorite of Brooke and Jessica. It's a black-and-white of them sitting on the grass in the garden at the big house with our beloved Springer Spaniel, Cress, between them. The girls are about five and two, and it's a beautiful picture. I place it on the nightstand next to my bed.

Next I pull out a photograph of Frank, his wife Joanie, and their kids, Laura and Richard, on a sailboat, probably taken ten years ago. They look tanned, windblown, and happy. I put that frame on a shelf in a bookcase and sigh. *Oh, Joanie, we miss you so much.*

I reach into the box and find a photograph of my oldest brother, Peter, with his wife and their children. I study the young faces of Petey, Ben, Tim, and Jimmy. This picture must be twenty years old. Haven't seen them in, what? I do the math. It's got to be at least fifteen years, when the boys were still in their teens. Wonder what they look like today.

I tug at a frame that's jammed between several books in the box and shake it loose. It's a picture of my ex-husband and me with our children, taken outdoors during happier years. As a matter of fact, it was taken the same year as the picture of Peter and his family.

I reexamine the shot of Peter's family—a great picture of the six of them. I also remember that was the first year either of us sent out picture cards for Christmas, using these two family photographs, and neither of us knew that the other planned to do the same.

When his wife saw our card, she accused me of copying her and made a big stink about it. Wouldn't most people have just laughed and said, "Oh, how funny. Look. Yours is better than mine."

Peter was, is, our big brother. Frank and I looked up to him when we were growing up. We were in awe of him. I examine the faces of Peter's children in the photo. Not having him and his kids in our lives—this estrangement— still hurts, and all because of his wife's rigid insecurity.

Why did our brother go along with all her nonsense? Why didn't he stick up for his side of the family? Oh well, who knows what goes on in other people's marriages. I place the photograph of them on the end of a bottom shelf, where I'll hardly notice it. Then I tuck my family photograph back in the box. My ex will not be on display in this house.

Time to switch gears. I run downstairs, turn on my computer and Google Juliana Wentworth. She doesn't come up much on the Internet. A few party pictures at philanthropic events in San Francisco and San Jose. An obituary two years ago for her husband, Carleton Todd Wentworth, a successful technology investor twenty-five years her senior.

Hmm. This Juliana seems to like older men. Doesn't look as if she would need more money, unless she didn't make out very well in his will. No kids together, but he had three from his first marriage.

What does warm my heart is that the couple supported a number of animal and canine rescue organizations. "Hey, Warrior. I think Frank's new girlfriend likes dogs. And that's got to be a good thing. Right?" A snore answers me. He's fast asleep.

At first glance, this Juliana appears to be a private woman living a quiet life. But the phone hang-ups and the peculiar reaction to the delivery of the box are, I have to agree with Laura, at the very least, curious.

CHAPTER THREE

The phone in the living room rings, and the caller-ID shows Laura's number. She probably has last-minute jitters before the party for Juliana. "Hey, how's my favorite niece in the world—"

"I'm your only niece, Aunt Ronnie, and you've been telling me that forever." But she's ribbing me and doesn't sound annoyed.

"I know, I know. I need some new material. So, what's up?"

"Three hang-ups today," Laura announces.

Hmm. "How long does the mystery person stay on the line?" I ask. "Do you hear him, her, breathing? Making any sounds at all?"

"I *do* hear some heavy breathing, but it's all pretty quick," Laura says. "I try to reverse the call, but like I told you, it's either blocked or it's one of several pay phone numbers around Scranton and nearby Moosic over in Pennsylvania, and nobody answers. So weird."

"I guess so." I look around for my dog and call to him. "Into your mouse house, Warrior." Which is a joke, since I had to buy him a huge crate. He charges out of the downstairs bathroom where he likes the cool tile floor, skids around the corner into the hall, and heads for the kitchen.

"Warrior *loves* his mouse house," I say to Laura. "Are you all set over there?"

"Daddy's a happy camper, all smiling, laughing." My niece stretches out the first syllables on *smiling* and *laughing*. "He's helping Dino set up the bar."

"What about Juliana? Does she look drop-dead gorgeous?" I guess I'll find that out myself soon enough.

"Who knows. Juliana's been upstairs for almost *four* hours," Laura says. "Who needs *four* hours to get ready?"

Point taken, but… "Easy, kiddo. Maybe she's a little nervous meeting your dad's friends and family," I say. "Cut her some slack, OK?"

"I don't know why she'd be at all nervous. She's scary beautiful. Richard calls her a real stunner," Laura answers. "Aunt Ronnie, are you coming soon? It's almost six. I really need to show you something, before everyone else gets here."

"See you in ten." I'm as ready as I'll ever be and would need more than four hours to become scary beautiful. I grab the keys and head out the door.

~~~~~

I turn left off Hollow Road into Meadow Farm and drive up the long dirt road that winds among intermittent woods and fields. Split-rail and wire fencing surround many of the pastures containing the ninety-plus sheep that reside at the farm.

One more big bend in the road, and there, at the end of a lush green meadow among clusters of sugar maples, ash, and Chinese chestnut trees, stands the house where I grew up. I look over at the second floor, left-corner window, first my room and then that of my favorite-niece-in-the-world, Laura, during the last two decades.

My gaze sweeps across the fine-looking house with stone and stucco walls and slate roof. A textile factory owner built it in 1910, and I was blessed to grow up here from the fifties through most of the seventies, way before the hyper-rich and obscenely famous of the twenty-first century moved into the area. These days, this house would need a complete do-over to interest any hedge fund guy. Not over-the-top enough for that crowd—which suits us just fine.

I park, and Laura rushes out. We hug and walk inside to more greetings from my brother's son, Richard, and his wife, Susie.

My daughter Brooke walks through the dining room door into the foyer. "Mom!" We give each other a big embrace. She's here from Manhattan and incredibly grown up at twenty-four.

Laura tugs at my arm while saying to my daughter, "I'm stealing your mom for five minutes, Brooke."

"Be right back, darling," I call over my shoulder as Laura leads me through the kitchen door.

Then Laura scoots me past the breakfast table and outside to a grey trash bin. She flips open the lid, and I hear the rustling sound of garbage bags as she reaches inside.

I'm taken aback. "Laura, what on earth? Your guests are due any second."

"Aunt Ronnie, you're not going to believe this. I was out here a little earlier throwing something away, and I found that box I told you was addressed to Juliana in the bin. Daddy and Juliana were out, so I snooped."

I'm not happy to hear about this. "Laura—"

"I know, I know, but you've gotta see."

Reluctantly, I walk over to her, suddenly noticing the smell of rotten eggs and something else I can't put my finger on. Decay? I look in the bin, inside a black garbage bag on top, and see a white box. The lid is addressed to Ms. Juliana Wentworth, care of Meadow Farm.

I don't know what to say. The bad odor is now overpowering, and the sound of flies buzzing about causes me to step back. "Something in this garbage bag is rotten. The smell is awful—"

"It's inside the box, Aunt Ronnie." Laura gingerly pushes the lid to the side and motions for me to look.

On a bed of shriveled flowers lies the bloody carcass of a very dead bird. The sight takes my breath away. Dribbled raw eggs cover the mass. The eggs and the dead bird are the source of the rotten smell turning my stomach.

"This is super gross, isn't it? And pretty creepy, too." Laura fake-shivers as if she's watching a horror movie. "Those flowers look like they come from a cemetery. And is that a dead pigeon, Aunt Ronnie?"

"It looks like one," I answer, appalled. "Who would send such an awful package to Frank's friend here at the farm?"

"I don't know, but the box has a Scranton, Pennsylvania postmark, the same place that those hang-up calls are from. Look." Laura points at the corner of the lid. "It's dated the day before they arrived. I wonder who knew she was coming here."

So Laura's bad feelings really aren't unfounded. "This *is* alarming—the contents of the box and the fact that the sender knew she'd be here." Even though I haven't touched anything, I feel the desire to wash my hands.

"I wonder why Juliana didn't want anybody here to find out about the package," Laura says. "Maybe she knows who sent it, and that's why she was so upset before she even opened it."

"That's a good point, Laura. If it was a stranger who sent this, you'd think she'd want us to help and call the police to investigate." I glance down at the contents again. "Ugh."

"Exactly. Anyway, I took pictures of the box and the mess inside with my phone. You know, in case you hire a private detective." She closes the lid of the garbage bin and walks me back inside. "I'll send the photos to you."

As we enter the front hall, I notice goose bumps on my arms and rub them away. I'm truly disturbed.

From upstairs, I hear the sound of a man's voice. My brother is speaking soothingly to someone. Laura and I look at each other, and she gives me a small shrug.

A silky, melodic woman's voice answers, but I can't make out what they're saying to each other. I feel a bit guilty, even hearing that little, as though I'm eavesdropping on an intimate conversation between two lovers.

Then I hear footsteps move down the hall.

CHAPTER FOUR

Frank and Juliana walk down the stairs. Well, Frank walks. Juliana *sweeps* down, even though she stays right in step with Frank the entire way.

To be fair, if I were coming down our splendid stairway to meet a bunch of people for the first time, I would sweep down, too. I remember making the same show-stopping entry (or so I thought) on a regular basis in my teens at special family parties.

The stairs curve along the wall from the second floor of our high-ceilinged octagonal foyer and then descend gracefully to the ground floor. It's a staircase that calls for a big entrance, and I must say, Juliana is certainly worthy of such a grand introduction.

This lovely, tall creature is in her late-thirties with long, dark, perfect hair, just as Laura described. A flowy summer dress in vivid 1960s Pucci aqua colors does nothing to hide her amazing figure.

Even though some of my girlfriends proclaim fifty-five is the new thirty-five, and, OK, I look good in my simple Jackie-O-style shift, bejeweled sandals, and a pair of drop earrings, what I do miss about really being thirty-five is that it didn't require as much work to get myself together. I was also able to cheat much more on exercise, diet, and even sleep.

I bet Juliana rolls out of bed every morning pretty much the way she looks right now. She certainly didn't need four hours of prep for this party, as Laura had complained.

Something about her features is vaguely familiar to me—the high cheekbones, full lips, and inscrutable cat-like eyes. Is she simply an Angelina Jolie-type with a similar staggering beauty, or is my feeling of faint recognition something else?

Frank steps forward, and his lanky six-foot-two frame folds me into a familiar big-brother embrace. "I'm happy to see you, Sis, and happy to be home."

I pull back, look up into his handsome, weathered face and smile. "We've missed you, Frank." I affectionately mess his salt-and-pepper hair, an old habit from when we were little.

My brother, always so confident, seems a bit awkward now, like a schoolboy in the presence of a goddess. "Ronnie, you're the only one who hasn't met Jules yet." He quickly corrects himself. "I mean Juliana. Uh, I'm the only one who calls her Jules." OK. I try for a nonreactive expression.

Frank guides me to her. "Ronnie, this is Juliana Wentworth." He looks at her as though she's the only one in the room. Oh, boy, he's a goner. "Juliana, this is my sister, Ronnie Lake."

As we shake hands and smile, her sphinxlike eyes look straight into mine, and I see a momentary flicker of... what? A flash of something like repulsion and then maybe a question—or is the perception only my imagination? Her eyes are unreadable, even though her smile is responsive in a normal, polite way.

Before she and I can say much of anything except hello, guests begin to arrive. Pretty soon we're all caught up in the friendly chit-chat of our small cocktail party. The evening is beautiful and balmy. Two dozen of us mingle on the terrace off the dining room. Brooke, Richard, and Susie keep the finger food circulating, and the bartender makes sure everyone has a drink.

As I catch up with old family friends, I'm able to step back somewhat and watch Juliana. I have to hand it to her: She's doing all right. She has a laser-beam gaze that, while she talks with someone, I'm sure makes that person feel as if he or she is the only individual on the planet.

She listens, she nods, she ask questions, she offers a comment when that's appropriate—all the while picking the right moments for those special looks with Frank. I chuckle to myself. He never leaves her side, and she seems very relaxed.

The phone rings in the library, and I see Juliana flinch ever so slightly. Her eyes shift in the direction of the sound for a split second. Then she notices me looking at her, and she smiles, an unknowable, Mona Lisa-type of expression. I smile back and walk through the set of French doors that leads into the bookshelf-lined room. I cross to a desk and answer the phone.

"Hello?" Nobody responds. "Hello? Who's there?" I think I hear a slight breathing sound and then a click, and the line goes dead. Hmmm. It's most certainly another one of the hang-ups that Laura's been talking about.

I return to the terrace, where Frank and Juliana have moved over to a different couple, again deep in sociable conversation. Juliana has her gaze on the elderly husband and wife exclusively and doesn't look at me.

Fifteen minutes go by, then Juliana politely excuses herself to step into the house. I do the same a moment later under the pretext of helping in the kitchen. I step into the library and the phone rings, again. I pick it up, and, once again, nobody responds, and I hear a click.

As I walk through the foyer, I hear a cell phone ring upstairs and then Juliana's voice speaking to someone. I stop to listen. The only part I can make out is "stop calling—you'll ruin everything…" I can't understand the rest of what she's saying. Ruin what? Does she have some scheme in mind?

I think about these mystery hang-ups from Pennsylvania that Laura says started when Frank and Juliana arrived the other day. I mull over the disgusting white box in our garbage bin that Juliana wanted to hide, the one with the Scranton postmark showing it was mailed to her before she and Frank arrived. Who knew she was coming, and why does that person want to frighten her with the revolting contents of the box?

After catching her slight reaction on the terrace to the ringing phone, which resulted in another one of those hang-ups, and now hearing this cryptic conversation upstairs during our party—well, it seems pretty obvious that some connection exists between these calls and Juliana. The calls could all be perfectly innocent or reasonable, of course, but given the box, the circumstances do seem strange.

Her voice stops, and I hear footsteps above. I dash into the kitchen, now empty, waiting to hear Juliana go back out to the terrace and rejoin the party. When her footsteps tell me she has done just that, I make an immediate, rash decision. This concerns my darling, somewhat recently widowed big brother, whom I worship and adore—although he would go ballistic if he knew what I was about to do. But the nauseating white box has definitely upped the general creepiness factor surrounding Juliana's arrival at Meadow Farm.

I quickly run upstairs with pen and paper and stop at the bedroom that Frank shared with Joanie for almost thirty years. I stick my head in and see some of Frank's things tossed on the bed, but not Juliana's.

I continue walking a few steps further down the hall and push open a half-closed door to the main guest room, where I see her things. I'm glad Frank has given Juliana this room and not put her in his room, which belonged to Joanie. Of course, who knows what their sleeping arrangements are at night—and who cares since it's absolutely none of my business.

Juliana's cell is by her purse, and I hesitantly tap it with my finger. Then I quickly pull back my hand as if the phone's as hot as a cooktop burner. The idea of invading her privacy makes me hesitate, but then I think again of Frank. I check Juliana's most recently received calls and write down the last number from moments ago, 570-341-5772.

Scrolling down, I see that Frank's cell phone number shows up repeatedly, as do quite a few other area code 570 phone numbers, which I also write down. The small pad of paper next to her cell has the initials *BT* scribbled on it and an angry *X* scrawled over the letters.

I put down the phone and quickly give the room a visual sweep. I'm shocked to see Juliana's things in such disarray. The huge armoire is open, showing nothing on the hangars except a lonely jacket dangling limply by one shoulder. All her other garments are strewn across the bed, dropped on the floor, balled up in the bottom of the wardrobe, or piled on top of a chair.

Pairs of shoes have been separated and flung into different parts of the room. Jewelry and open, smudged cosmetics bottles are scattered on available bureau and table surfaces. Wet towels have been tossed on the floor and rug.

No wonder Juliana needed four hours to get ready. She must have tried on every outfit she brought in every possible configuration. And here I thought she effortlessly stepped out of the shower and into that marvelous dress and was good to go for cocktails. Silly me.

The chaos of this room also provides a striking contrast to her smooth, calm demeanor downstairs. It's as if she may have been in a frenzy as she got ready for this party, which seems extreme for a woman used to socializing among the same kind of people with her first husband. I wonder what that's all about.

I'm such a *neatnik*, so part of me wants to straighten up her things. But before I can give in to the stupid urge to tidy up, I hear a door slam somewhere downstairs and immediately dash out of the room, taking the back stairs down.

As I step into the kitchen, I come face to face with Juliana, who is filling a glass of water and looking toward the stairs to see who's coming. "Oh, it's you," she says and seems surprised. "I didn't expect to see you coming down from there." She hesitates a moment as if she has something additional to say, but changes her mind. "See you outside." She simply leaves.

That was close. And I'm horrified by my sneaky behavior. This isn't my ex-husband I'm checking up on, the only other time I've been so nosy. What's gotten into me? Well, I guess I wouldn't be so on edge about Juliana if not for the ongoing estrangement Frank and I have with our brother, Peter.

I come back to the terrace with a platter of food, my phone camera, and a new plan. The party carries on as I make the rounds taking pictures of our friends and family, including plenty of Frank and Juliana.

"Don't mind Ronnie, Jules," Frank says, and he holds Juliana close, surrounded by his children, Laura and Richard; daughter-in-law, Susie; and my daughter, Brooke. They all laugh and tease each other while I click off several shots. "She's been taking pictures at every family gathering and party in this house since she was six," he mock-complains.

I play my part as the loving sister and perfect hostess, welcoming this stranger who has quite apparently touched Frank's heart. I think back to my sister-in-law Joanie, a pretty woman but open and approachable. Not at all like this mysterious goddess, whose physical beauty is so perfect it makes her seem aloof and therefore intimidating and off-putting. She's the kind of super-gorgeous woman you're not sure you're going to like.

Plus she has those eyes, those unfathomable eyes that give nothing away. I've been watching, and Juliana has clearly demonstrated this evening that she's a master at keeping the spotlight on the person she's having a conversation with. That makes getting a fix on what she's thinking kind of tough. Does she do that because she's generous in spirit and truly interested in others, or does she herself have something to hide?

Even though I try to feel happy for him, I can't help wondering for the rest of the evening—who is this person Frank has brought into our midst?

CHAPTER FIVE

Once everybody leaves the party later, Laura slips me the list of Scranton phone numbers that she got off Caller ID after the anonymous hang-ups. At home, online, I reverse those phone numbers, plus those I got from Juliana's phone, to uncover the locations: a hotel, a diner, a baseball stadium, several bars. I still don't know who was making the calls, but these locales tell me the caller was probably a guy.

After my research, I doze off with my laptop next to me until the *ping* of a new email wakes me up. Laura has sent me her photos showing the contents of the white box. Looking at them reminds me of that awful smell. What kind of twisted person would create such a morbid display and then send it through the mail?

In one close-up, I notice a small scrap of paper hanging out of the dead pigeon's beak. I zoom in for a better look at the writing on the paper. The only words I can make out among the scribbles are *Teresa & Frankie*.

~~~~~

After coffee in the morning, I throw a canvas cover over the front passenger seat of my Mustang. My dog jumps in, ready for me to snap on his canine seat belt. He's excited, because he knows we're going on a road trip.

Warrior and I look for any excuse to take a drive, and we avoid the highways as much as possible. When you have the top down, the back roads are a whole lot more fun. I begin the twisty, scenic drive to Lambertville to visit an outdoor antiques market, where a leashed Warrior will walk around with me.

Car time is also good thinking time, and now that Frank is home, I have a lot to consider. Having seen firsthand how over the moon my brother is for Juliana Wentworth, I feel uneasy. I guess Laura's concern is contagious.

Driving into the nearby village this morning, I reassess my several meager clues. Hang-up phone calls from Scranton. A white box with a dead pigeon on a bed of withered flowers covered in rotten eggs, also from Scranton. Laura's photo showing a scrap of paper with the names *Teresa & Frankie* hanging from the dead pigeon's beak. Numerous Scranton phone numbers on Juliana's cell. Her pad with the initials *BT* scratched out. Finally, Juliana's *you'll-ruin-everything* cell call.

Before I hire an investigator to look into this, as Laura suggested, I've decided to see what I can find out on my own. After all, how hard can playing detective and snooping around a little be?

If Frank knew I was thinking along these lines, he would accuse me of overreacting, of being a way-too-interfering sister. And he would tell me to get a life. OK, maybe I do have too much time on my hands, freeing me to go on what is probably a wild goose chase.

What about a real job? Had one. For a long time. A year ago I was downsized from my corporate position and fancy title (both of which I loved) at a national cable network in Jersey City. The idea to leave wasn't mine, but theirs, due to the bad economy. And because I don't have money issues, I've been in no rush to find a new full-time occupation. But I do think it's time for a fresh chapter in my life.

What about a husband? Had one of those, too. Was married for almost thirty years until the lawyers finalized our divorce six months ago. The split didn't bring out the best in either of us.

As for kids—they grew up too fast. I have to admit the empty nest has been the hardest adjustment of all. Yep, the empty nest was the one that threw me for a loop, especially when it became emptier than I'd expected.

Don't get me wrong. I like my life just fine, even if at times I wonder if I've hit my sell-by date…you know, the moment at which dreams and life's exciting moments are mostly behind you. Still, I have plenty of worthwhile and pleasurable ways to fill my time until I figure out what comes next. And one of my enjoyments is road trips with my four-legged buddy, Warrior.

I make a split-second decision that will cause a slight delay, pulling over at the village café to buy coffees for the household at Meadow Farm. I've decided to drop by for a friendly visit and start the process of getting to know

Juliana a little better. Then I'll head off to Lambertville to look at antiques.

I turn onto the dirt road into Meadow Farm and drive along slowly. Since I have the top down, I don't want to kick up too much dust; but I also take my time because of the pleasant feeling of familiarity when I come down this road. I no longer live here, yet I still feel very rooted to this place.

Even though Meadow Farm became Frank and Joanie's house close to thirty years ago, Joanie always had an open-door, drop-in-anytime policy toward the extended family. This remained the center of our multiple generations as our children grew up. How fortunate we were to have Joanie, who was such an inclusive and lovely in-law. All of us miss her terribly. I can't even imagine Frank's heartbreak and sadness since her death.

As my convertible creeps along so that I can get a good look at a cluster of lambs in their pasture, I notice a black Porsche coming my way. It's my brother with Juliana as his passenger. I stop and wave. Then I hold up the cardboard carrier with the coffee cups.

He pulls over and leans out the window. "Hey, Sis! Breakfast at the Country Store?" Warrior woofs, and all of us laugh.

I hop out. "Mornin' Frank, Juliana! Sounds great." I hand them their coffees. "I'll follow you. Back roads or highway?"

"Highway," Frank answers. "It's quicker. Have to be at the lawyer's right after." He looks at Juliana with a twinkle in his eye. I look back and forth at the two of them, wondering why Frank is in a rush to get to his lawyer's office and why Juliana is going with him.

I take one more glance at Juliana, who only has eyes for my brother. There it is again. Her Mona Lisa smile, just for Frank.

~~~~~

Fewer than ten minutes later, we're on the highway. I give Frank lots of space, at least ten car lengths. It's late morning, and the traffic is light. Next to me, Warrior sits up straight in the passenger seat, harnessed in by his seat belt, staring out the window at the scenery.

The highways give the impression of vastness out here, because this area is mostly rural. I gaze at the farmland as we drive by, and suddenly a metallic blue van that took the on-ramp where we did moments ago races by in the left-hand lane. I catch a flash of a dark-haired guy behind the wheel. My speedometer reads sixty-five miles per hour, so he must be doing at least eighty.

The second he clears my car, he pulls hard to the right and veers into my lane with no blinker to warn me. His action is so swift, two of his wheels leave the pavement. Whoa! Is he going to tip over? I brake hard and let out a few choice words. He flips me the bird out his window. Who is this yo-yo? Warrior, now focused on the van, lets out a low growl.

Then the driver puts his pedal to the metal and the van speeds up, quickly closing the space behind my brother's Porsche. Everything seems to shift into slow motion as I watch this guy slam into the back of Frank's car and hear the loud crashing noise. Warrior barks.

I clench my steering wheel and tap the brake to stay a safe distance behind, horrified as I watch my brother's car fishtail from the impact. Frank struggles to regain control of the Porsche and slow down, which he does successfully. I realize I'm holding my breath and let it out. Frank's OK.

But blue-van doesn't go away. Instead, he does the same thing again, smashing this time into the left back corner of Frank's car, and Warrior barks even more. My brother's Porsche goes into a three-hundred-sixty-degree rotation. Fortunately, no other vehicles are near him, or the spin would be disastrous.

I can see Frank's face through the windshield, fiercely concentrating as he swings around and fights yet again to regain control. I also glimpse a terrified Juliana frantically turning in every direction to see if someone is still coming at them. Deeply shocked by the entire incident, I watch Frank pull out of the spin and then drive on.

This second smash can mean only one thing. Blue-van is crashing into my brother on purpose and not because the driver is drunk or high on drugs. His actions must be pure road rage. But I also wonder if this is the same van Laura thought was following her to my house the other day.

I note that the Porsche's rear is now scratched and dented and includes a broken left tail light. I call 911 and ask for help, trying to explain what's happening and where we are.

Why is the guy still on Frank's tail? Why won't he drive away from them? I watch the van pull up alongside the Porsche and quickly swerve to the right, this time crashing into the side of the car and producing a violent crunching sound. I scream into the phone as Frank's car skids to the side, sliding over the shoulder of the highway and down an embankment where I lose sight of it. The van finally speeds off. Warrior barks loudly and nonstop.

"They've crashed." I pull over and yell to the 911 operator, "Come now!" I'm breathless. "Warrior, stay." My barking dog obeys my command, even though he wants to go with me.

Leaving the car engine running, the phone still connected, and a noisy Warrior strapped in, I jump out, slam the door closed, and spot the car upright fifteen feet down in a gully. Thank god, it doesn't look as if it rolled, even though my brother's beautiful black Porsche is now a mass of scrapes and dents. I then feel intense relief as Frank unfolds his long-limbed frame from the driver's side and steps out of the car.

I scramble down the incline into the large ditch and get to the vehicle just as Frank runs around the front of the car to help Juliana out. They're both shaky and grasp each other in a desperate embrace.

"Frank, Juliana, are you OK? Any injuries?" I ask, my voice trembling. "I called 911, and the police should be here any second." They say nothing, and Frank squeezes Juliana's shoulders. She looks rigid, tense, her jaw clenched.

I walk away to give them some privacy. I wonder how far the van has gotten. He might not be going very fast right now. I look up at my dog, who watches my every move and begins to settle down. "I could maybe try to catch up with him, get a license, phone it in," I shout to Frank.

"Are you nuts? He's dangerous," my brother calls out to me. "Let the police handle it. Ronnie, stay with us. You're a witness, and the officer will want to talk to you."

I come back to where the two of them are standing. "I couldn't see the driver when he passed me, before he slammed into you. I do know he had dark hair." My voice cracks. "Oh my god, I've never actually witnessed road rage." Juliana's eyes flick toward me for a brief moment and then away, but I don't miss her total fear.

Frank looks up at the embankment. "It's a miracle, Jules, that the Porsche didn't flip, considering the angle of our slide." He still has his arm protectively around Juliana, and she shudders and stares directly at the ground. He glances at me. "Ronnie, it's an even bigger miracle that Jules and I walked away with no injuries."

"Did either of you get a look at the driver?" I ask. "Did you recognize who he might—"

"Frank, Ronnie, please excuse me," Juliana interrupts. She turns to my brother. "You're right. We're so lucky, my dear…" She kisses him on the cheek. "…but my nerves are shot." She rushes up the bank and walks around near the highway's shoulder. Frank and I watch. Warrior does, too, and then looks back at me.

"Jules is understandably pretty shook up. We're both shook up." Frank uses his fingers to massage the bridge of his nose.

"Did you see the driver of the van?" I ask again, my hands still shaking. The realization that they could have been killed is sinking in. I've already lost one brother more or less. I couldn't bear losing the other. "Did you see anything, Frank?"

"No. I was totally focused on maintaining control of the car." Frank shakes his head. "It all happened so fast, Ronnie. We don't know who it was."

Maybe you don't, Frank, I muse to myself, but I wonder if Juliana has any ideas. I hug my brother.

"Come to think of it," my brother adds, "I did see something, a flash of white with a blue banner on the top on the license plate. You know, Sis, it could have been a Pennsylvania plate. I'll let the officer know when he gets here."

I look up the embankment and see Juliana staring at us. Her brow is furrowed, and she looks away.

~~~~~

I stew. I stew while I give the police officer my report. I stew while I wait for the ambulance crew to check out Frank and Juliana to make sure they're OK. I stew while I drive them to Meadow Farm. In the car, everybody is quiet. I drop them off, go home, and stew some more.

I call Isabella Romano, not only my *sensei*, but also my friend, and give her the rundown on what happened this morning. "I need to look into this...figure out who this road-rage creep is," I say.

"That's for the police to investigate," Isabella cautions.

"I wonder if they'll find out who the guy is," I grumble. "Maybe having the police handle it isn't enough. Aren't the cops all overworked? I want to do something myself to help."

"Give the police a chance," she advises. "If after a while, you still feel that way, you can always hire someone privately."

"Funny, that's what my niece suggested." But honestly, I think if you want something done, you do it yourself. Am I wrong?

"You know Will Benson in the noon class?" Isabella asks.

"You mean the tall, gorgeous, new guy, who started a couple of months ago?" I ask. "He's pretty good." His Aikido does impress me. "What is he? Thirty-five? Maybe forty?"

"Forty, I'm pretty sure. He came out from the New York dojo," she says. "Are you aware he's a private investigator?"

"I heard that. Yeah. So?" Hire someone? Really?

"Hold it. Don't yeah, so, me, Ronnie. I know you," Isabella says. "You like to be in charge, and you're probably thinking you can do this yourself, but you have zero experience as an investigator." Her tone is stern. "You could mess it up and get in the way of the police. Plus, the road-rage guy sounds lethal, out of control." She pauses and adds, "What you could do is hire Will to look into things."

"Food for thought, Isabella," I say. "At the very least, if I hired him, I'd have an excuse to stare at him more. He's certainly a Triple-A hunk!" We laugh and sign off.

CHAPTER SIX

Fewer than twenty-four hours later, I'm still processing that my brother was almost killed because of road rage. My heart pounds at the thought of how close I came to losing Frank. I get into my car and take three long, deep breaths. It helps.

Random? Hardly. Too many coincidences have cropped up in the last several days since the mystifying Juliana arrived at Meadow Farm. I mull over the scene with Juliana and Frank immediately after the accident. Whether her nerves were really shot, who knows? Juliana is so guarded that I can't get a read on her.

My nervous fingers have a difficult time punching one of the hang-up-call addresses into the GPS, and I have to try several times before it comes up correctly. OK. Calm down.

Looking at Warrior, who's already harnessed in safely, I reach over and rub his sweet, velvety head. I then study a notebook with my list of clues. I add *beat-up blue metallic van with PA plates?* as #7, right after *#1 Scranton/Moosic hang-up calls; #2 dead bird in box from Scranton; #3*

Teresa & Frankie, the names on the scrap of paper in the bird's beak; *#4* Scranton numbers on Juliana's cell; *#5* the initials *BT* scratched out on her phone pad; and *#6* Juliana's *you'll-ruin-everything call.* OK. Time to go.

Warrior and I take off for Pennsylvania to see if we can learn anything more about the beautiful Juliana Wentworth via these phone numbers. I turn on the music. Oh, did I also mention that besides road trips with Warrior, I love classic rock, mostly from the 1970s and '80s. I turn up the volume on Blondie as my dog and I drive west, channeling some Deborah Harry attitude while I sing along with "Heart of Glass" at the top of my lungs.

~~~~~

A couple of hours later, I find myself south of downtown Scranton heading toward Moosic, where several of the hang-up calls originated. I spent time yesterday doing additional online research, and I now know that Moosic is an old coal-mining area that in the last decade has experienced a surge in commercial development. Although, this particular Moosic neighborhood where I'm driving looks a bit down on its luck.

Arriving at my first stop, Stan's Diner, I park in the shade. I fasten the top on my car and open all the windows enough for Warrior to get plenty of air, but not wide enough for him to jump out.

Once inside the diner, I choose a booth in order to keep my dog in view. It's eleven o'clock in the morning, and I'm the only customer, the breakfast rush no doubt having cleared out earlier. A bottle-blonde waitress with two inches of dark regrowth at her roots comes over carrying a pot of coffee and a menu. "I'll give you a minute to decide on your order," she says, as she pours me a cup.

"Already know what I'll have." I smile and hand back the menu, enjoying the aroma of the coffee. Her name tag says *Mary*. "Can you make me a two egg-white omelet and wheat toast, no butter, please?" She nods. "And, Mary, skim milk for my coffee?"

"Will do," she answers and heads behind the counter to place the order with the cook. Not exactly the chatty type.

I look around the place, which has a classic fifties interior. The red leatherette booths rest on a checkered black-and-white linoleum floor, while a vintage jukebox and old-fashioned enclosed phone booth stand over in the corner.

I go over and check out the jukebox and see that it's all music from the fifties and sixties. I drop in some change and select 1950s and early '60s heartthrob Ricky Nelson, and he sings "Poor Little Fool."

I walk into the phone booth and pick up the receiver to hear a dial tone. OK, don't laugh. The number on the phone matches the tiny numbers I wrote on the palm of my hand before I came in—from the list that Laura had given me. I now know someone called the farm from this phone on each of the last several mornings. I step out of the booth to full-on crooning from long-gone Ricky.

Waitress Mary watches me, and her gaze isn't friendly. "Hey, we're in a cell phone world," I say and laugh nervously. "Can't believe you actually have a phone booth here. Had to see for myself if it was real." She smiles a little. Might she be warming up a bit?

Mary brings over my food. I gaze at my health-conscious choices, imagining my favorite diner breakfast instead. "Truth be told, I'd rather eat two fat blueberry pancakes with hot maple syrup, four pieces of crispy bacon, and a creamy hot chocolate." I sigh and dig in. "Oh well. Mary, my heart doctor thanks you." For the first time since I've come into the diner, the waitress cheers up with a hearty laugh, and her tired looks turn pretty with a sparkle in her eyes.

"Mary, I'm Ronnie," I introduce myself. "Tell me, does *anybody* ever actually use that pay phone?" I pause as if my next question just occurs to me. "Like when was the last time somebody came in here and used that phone?"

"During my shift? Yesterday morning…" She looks at the ceiling and says, "Around nine." Inwardly I perk up. That's the time and date of one of the hang-ups on the list from Laura. Mary sits down at the table across from my booth. "I remember because he needed a lot of change, I guess for a long-distance call."

"You're kidding," I say. "Who makes a long-distance call these days on a pay phone? That's nuts." I steeple my hands and discreetly rub one of my palms with the thumb of my other hand to erase the phone number I'd written on it.

"I'll tell you who makes a call," Mary answers. "Bobby Taylor, that loser."

Bobby Taylor. I remember the *BT* scribbled on Juliana's pad—could he be the right guy? "God, Mary, you don't have an opinion about the man, do you?" I chuckle.

"Why's this Bobby Taylor a loser? Tell me all about it," I say like a co-conspirator. "Did it start in high school?" I cringe inwardly, flashing back on some of my own not-so-proud moments of bad high school behavior…and then quickly take another bite of wheat toast.

"High school? That guy and his big brother been getting into trouble since the first grade," she says. "And then their cousin Teresa moved here, and things got even worse."

Teresa? Like the name on the scrap stuffed in the dead pigeon's beak? I try to disguise my extreme excitement. Wahoo, I'm getting somewhere, the first time out. "Worse?" I say casually. "How so?"

"Oh, a lot of stealing, car chases," Mary says. "It was in all the papers. Called them the Scranton Gang, a teenage Bonnie and Clyde… Must have been, let's see, twenty-five years ago."

I finish my omelet. "Sounds like somebody could've made a movie about Bobby Taylor, his big brother, and Teresa."

"Yeah, what a show that would have been. Even heard something was going on between Bobby and Teresa. Like maybe he was after her." Mary hands me the check. "Anyway, first time I seen Bobby in years when he showed up here about a week ago."

"Where's he been?" I laugh. "Prison?"

She doesn't find the suggestion funny. "Probably. That's what I heard." Mary turns her head and coughs into the inside of her elbow—a deep, gravelly, smoker's cough. "Anyway, he's been having breakfast here every morning since. Funny, he didn't come in today. Maybe he took off again."

I settle up, leaving a quite generous tip. "What ever happened to Teresa Taylor and Bobby's big brother?"

"Joe Taylor? Who knows. The papers stopped printing the stories, and people lost interest," Mary says. "And her name was Gonzalez, by the way, not Taylor."

I get up from the table. "Mary, this has been the most entertaining breakfast I've had in a long time." I head for the door. "Great talking to you."

"Likewise, Ronnie." She glances at the tip and smiles.

Outside, I walk toward my car, and before I'm there, my dog pops up from his morning snooze in the back seat. I let him out on the sidewalk with his traveling water bowl, and he takes a big drink. "See, Warrior? How hard can this detective thing be?" As I empty the left over water in the gutter, Warrior takes a quick pee on the curb, looking at me as if I'm a fool.

CHAPTER SEVEN

Next stop—the Moosic Motel, the source of the second phone number on my list of mystery hang-ups at Meadow Farm. From my research, I know it's a fifty-five-dollar-a-night establishment about ten minutes from the airport. This part of town is dicey, or "sketchy," as my kids now say. Feeling a little ridiculous, I find myself automatically clicking the locks of my car.

When I reach the address, I park in front and sit a moment to take in the ambience. Maybe if they charged sixty dollars a night, management could sweep up the trash scattered around the building; give the place a new coat of paint to cover a disgusting faded turquoise color; and hang some shutters on the big, bare picture window framing a clerk on the phone at the front desk.

"Definitely not the Plaza," I mutter to Warrior, who's moving to the back seat of the car for his second nap of the morning. "This shouldn't take long. Be right back."

Armed with the information I gleaned during breakfast at Stan's Diner, I walk inside confidently and go straight to the front desk. "Good morning." I smile at the clerk, an unshaven skinny guy in his mid-twenties.

"Morning," he grunts, and then continues into the phone, "Have to go. Bye." He hangs up. "Uh, saw the dog in your car. We don't allow no dogs here."

"No, no. Don't worry about my dog," I say. "I'm not checking in. I'm looking for someone."

"Yeah?" A look of suspicion crosses his face. "Who?"

"Is a guy named Bobby Taylor still a guest here?" I ask.

"Never heard of him," the desk clerk answers a bit too fast.

I give this guy my sweetest smile. "Are you sure? I mean, you haven't even checked the register." I nod at the ledger on the desk. This place is such a dump, they don't use a computer to check in their guests.

"Lady, I don't need to check. We got a lotta empty rooms." He puts his hands together and cracks several knuckles. "I know everybody who's staying here."

"Come on. Give me a break. Was he here maybe yesterday?" I smile again. I'd like to get my hands on that register. "I'm trying to organize a reunion for my daughter and some of her former classmates." I'm a little concerned by how easily these fabrications—OK, white lies—come tripping off my tongue. "She and Bobby were in school together—"

"Like I said, I don't know any Bobby Taylor. Yesterday, today, or tomorrow." He grabs the register off his desk, stuffs it in a file drawer, and slams the drawer shut. "You sure are nosy, Lady. And a phony, too. I don't buy that reunion story."

Clearly, I've blown it. This guy's not cooperating, and I'm not getting my hands on that ledger. Guess my private eye skills need some work.

"How about two other classmates of my daughter's? Do you know a Teresa or a Frankie?" I ask.

"Never heard of them, either." He glances out the window at my car. I turn around to see my dog sitting up and looking through the window in our direction.

"Don't mind Warrior. He's a pussycat." I rummage in my bag and pull out a photograph of Juliana Wentworth. It's a blow-up from one of the pictures I took at the party two nights ago.

"Ever see her?" I put the photo on the desk.

He stares at me with suspicion and then looks down and studies the picture for a moment. "Nah, never seen her."

This time I believe him. Why, I don't know.

"What's her name?" he asks. I stare back at him and don't answer. "Sure is nice looking," he says and pushes the picture back toward me. "She supposed to know this guy, Bobby Taylor?"

"Maybe. Don't really know." I take the photo and stick with my story, while heading out the door. "Trying to find her for the reunion, too. Thanks for your help."

I let Warrior out for a quick water break, and he nuzzles me for a kiss and a neck scratch. I glance into the motel's picture window and see the skinny clerk on the phone. He looks at me and then quickly puts his head down as he speaks into the receiver.

"You think he's talking to Bobby Taylor?" I ask Warrior. "Let's go. This place gives me the creeps." We drive off.

"Well, that was a big fat zero." I click on the GPS. "Didn't get *anything* there, and that guy didn't buy my story at all." I wonder if I'll have the patience to roll with the dead ends that are probably normal for any detective on the hunt.

~~~~~

It takes less than ten minutes to drive five miles to PNC Field where spectators can watch the Railriders play minor league baseball. I already know this is the New York Yankees' triple-A farm team because my younger daughter, Jessica, who is a diehard Derek Jeter fan, told me so.

I park, read the third phone number on my list and look around at the empty stadium. At this time of day, few cars and even fewer people are in the parking lot next to the complex. Somewhere around here must be a pay phone.

I open the passenger door, take Warrior by his leash, and he jumps out for a little exercise. Looking around, I figure mystery-boy Bobby Taylor is a Yankees fan. Otherwise why did he call Meadow Farm from this stadium the first night Frank and Juliana arrived home? Probably a game that night that he wanted to catch.

Still, none of all this makes any sense. I mean, why doesn't the guy have his own cell phone? It's like he's still in the 1980s, using all these pay phones. Weird. Or he's broke and can't afford one, which is possible if he just got out of prison.

Warrior and I walk around the outside of the stadium. I finally locate a pay phone near a closed-up concession stand in the concourse behind the seats and check the number. Bingo. It matches another one of the hang-ups on my list. I guess Bobby Taylor could have come from the stands to buy a beer and then decided it was the perfect time to call Juliana. Why? I wonder.

As my dog and I return to the parking lot, I find two guys strutting around my car. Their beat-up green SUV sits sideways, almost touching the hood of my car and blocking me from driving forward. Big deal. I have plenty of room to back up.

Usually I'm the world's biggest scaredy-cat, but with my German shepherd at my side, I feel less hesitant than I usually would around two thuggish teenaged boys. Warrior and I walk until we get within fifty feet of the car. I signal Warrior to sit, and he is on alert. The two guys notice us, but they do nothing. I pull out my phone, zoom in and snap off a few pictures of their car right up against the front of mine.

My dog and I walk around the vehicle and take a few pictures of the SUV's Pennsylvania license plate. Then I shift my cell phone to the two guys and my car. They mock-pose.

"Hey, sugar," one of them purrs, stroking my Mustang. "This here's a hot car for a hot lady…" He pouts in a way that I'm sure he thinks makes him a sexy guy. He looks me up and down with hooded eyes.

They're idiots, one leaning against my car and the other now sitting on its hood. They're no more than seventeen or eighteen, and dirty in ragged tee-shirts and jeans. But strong. And one thing I'm not is completely stupid. With two against one, this is not the ideal moment to, say, try out my Aikido techniques.

Instead, my four-legged protector growls. "Easy, Warrior," I say in a firm voice. "Settle." I note his hackles are up from his neck to his tail, so my lovable doggy is a ferocious sight.

The grimy boys also take note of the German shepherd's low growl and the raised hair on his backbone, and the faux-sexy expression has disappeared from the first kid's face. The second kid stutters, "N-n-nice puppy dog. P-p-please keep him on the leash." They glance at each other nervously.

"I rarely see my dog act this way," I say with self-assurance. "But, oooh, I can tell that he doesn't like the two of you." They watch the dog and me, mostly the dog, not sure what to do next.

"Here's what's going to happen, so that Warrior doesn't attack," I say in a calm voice. "Understand?"

They quickly nod their heads yes.

"Once I tell you what to do, move slowly and not toward me," I instruct. "We don't want Warrior to think you're threatening me, now do we?" They quickly shake their heads no in agreement.

"What are your names?" I ask. "Only your first names."

"Jerry," says the one who called me *sugar* a moment before.

"T-T-Tony," answers the other on the hood of my car.

"Ok, Jerry. Tony." I stand still as a statue next to Warrior. "Slowly move away from my car, but not toward me." The boys comply. I look at them. They're pathetic, but perhaps I can use this situation to my advantage.

"Tony, reach into your SUV and toss the keys as far as you can over there." I point. "Away from Warrior here." He throws the keys toward a large sign, and they land on the gravel.

"OK. I've got a few questions for you." They stare at me like two deer caught in some powerful headlights. "Relax. Warrior may bite, but I won't." I smile a little. "Unless you piss me off." They're not laughing at my humor.

"OK, Jerry. Do you and Tony hang out here much?"

Tony jumps in. "Th-th-this is where we—"

"Did I speak to you, Tony?" I ask in a harsh tone that I hope makes me sound like one of their high school teachers.

"N-n-no, ma'am."

"Then, Tony, wait your turn." I motion to the other guy, Mr. I-think-I'm-so-sexy. "Jerry?" Warrior gives a low growl.

"We're here a lot, when we have time off from our jobs." The sweat circles under Jerry's arms are even more pronounced than when this encounter started minutes ago.

"Either of you ever run into a guy named Bobby Taylor?"

A look of pure panic passes between them.

"Yes? No?" I ask.

"Wh-wh-wh-we heard about him more than *know* him, ma'am." Tony shifts from leg to leg, and Warrior watches him closely.

"He was part of a gang a long time ago," Jerry pipes up. "There's lots of bad-ass stories about the guy. We been hearing, like, forever, that he's a mean dude." If this Bobby Taylor is the same guy who sent Juliana that repulsive box with the dead bird, then, yes, I would agree with them.

"Yeah, and now he's b-b-b-b—"

"Get it out, Tony!" Jerry snaps.

"Back!!" Tony says. "Since a week ago."

"And he's been hangin' here," Jerry says. "A guy pointed at him when we was here last night. But we don't talk to him or nothin'. We don't know nothin' about his business."

"Do you know someone named Teresa, who might be friends with Bobby Taylor?" I ask. They look at each other, this time seeming confused. "How about Frankie? Is he one of Bobby's friends?" Their eyes are blanks, and I realize they're clueless.

I click my key and unlock the car. "You two are going to walk toward the gate over there. When you see that I've left the stadium, Jerry, check your watch and wait five minutes with Tony before going over to the van. Don't even think about following me. If I see you in my rearview mirror, I will..." I gesture with my cell phone. "...email these pictures with your license plate to the police. Do we understand each other?"

They nod yes.

"Start walking."

They run.

Well done, Ronnie. But my own legs are a little shaky, too, as I walk Warrior over to my car.

~~~~~

After lunch, I sit at a microfilm machine in the reference room of the public library in Scranton, scanning through 1987 issues of the local newspaper. Taking off the red-framed drugstore magnifiers that I wear as glasses, I rub my nose, thinking how the nice surprise of my day has been my visit to this town. Here I had thought Scranton was in decline, only to discover a transformation of its once vacant but architecturally distinctive downtown due to extensive renovation.

Stay focused, Ronnie. Back to work.

An older librarian remembered the Scranton Gang story from back in '87, maybe late summer or early fall, and directed me to look at that period. Now I put my glasses back on and scroll slowly through the reel that includes August, September and October, 1987, finally hitting pay dirt in early September of that year.

Fugitive Family Arrested After Allentown Crash. And the subhead: *Scranton Teens Nabbed After Police Chase.* Front page, above the fold, September 9, 1987.

> *After a 25-mile chase and shootout in Allentown, police apprehended the so-called Scranton Gang. Officers took into custody two brothers, ages 16 and*

13, and a female cousin, 13. Following a bank robbery at a JNC branch in Stroudsburg three days before, the gun-toting, fast-driving teenage lawbreakers had invited comparisons to Bonnie and Clyde. Eyewitnesses reported the female gang leader fired shots...

This article and others I find in the microfilm archives go on to describe the girl as being a suspect for also shooting at a police officer as the gang fled Stroudsburg. The teen trio briefly went into hiding before heading south and showing up in Allentown in a beat-up, stolen, 1974 orange Ford Maverick.

An observant 7-Eleven employee called the police before the brothers came inside to buy snacks and three Slurpee drinks while their cousin filled the Maverick's tank with self-serve gas.

I continue reading and discover that when Allentown police approached the 7-Eleven, the 13-year-old female gang leader—had to be Teresa Gonzalez, of course—fired a weapon toward several officers as the three fled in the car. Fortunately, she missed.

The chase ended when the Maverick crashed and rolled on the highway. The 13-year-old male—and that must have been Bobby Taylor—jumped out of the car and fled on foot, but police quickly apprehended him. They arrested all three and took the juveniles to the hospital to be treated for minor injuries.

I study a bank surveillance camera photo of a gun-toting Teresa robbing a teller. She has on sunglasses while a baseball cap hides her hair and face, making it difficult to see her features. So young and already holding up banks—unbelievable. Was she really just a kid bad to the bone, or had something traumatic happened to her that led to such an early life of crime?

After their arrests, the story quickly went cold, because the Taylors and Gonzalez were juveniles with sealed records. But one comment from the police catches my eye—that the Scranton Gang was trying to get to Orlando, Florida to start a new life near Disney World. In addition to being bank robbers, it seems Bobby, Joe, and Teresa were also everyday kids who fantasized about visiting the famous theme park.

But what does Bobby Taylor have to do with my brother's girlfriend, Juliana Wentworth? And who is this Teresa? Then, too, what about Frankie, the other name in the beak of the dead bird in the box? Where does he fit in?

CHAPTER EIGHT

The class is spread out in pairs on the mat at the dojo, and I come at Will Benson with an overhead strike called *shomenuchi*. I attack him as if my extended arm is a sword and my hand is the blade (often referred to as *tegatana* or *hand sword*). My intent is to slice Will in half, starting right down the middle of his skull.

Actually, when practicing at the dojo, we aren't supposed to beat up or hurt each other, as that isn't the intent in Aikido. Certain types of attacks in Aikido, like *shomenuchi*, are based on sword movements, which may be a far cry from what happens on the street—but practicing in this manner eventually prepares us to deal with any type of attack. That's the plan anyway.

We also learn how to blend our energy with that of our attacker and apply techniques based on the physics of motion, using circular movements. Rather than forcing our opponent with football-player testosterone, we attempt to redirect our attacker's own power and throw him to the ground or immobilize him with joint locks.

So back to the mat. I attack Will with a *shomenuchi* strike, and he executes a technique we call *irimi nage* or *entering throw*. Often called the twenty-year technique, *irimi nage* encapsulates the essence of Aikido movement and, hence its nickname, takes a long time to master.

As I move forward and attack Will, he disappears by entering in behind me. Before I know it, he takes over my assault by grabbing my neck, controlling my spine, and redirecting me in the opposite direction. My body drops to the floor. Though I make an effort to stand up, while I'm doing so, he attaches me to his shoulder, and I feel as if he has made me a part of his own body.

While I struggle to get away from his firm grasp, Will follows my movement with a turn of his torso and his shoulder rotates and arm curves up and over me, pouring me yet again down to the ground. Lucky for me I've received this technique so many times I'm able break my fall safely and roll out of the way.

You'd think I'd be nervous practicing with a strong, muscular guy like Will, who's fifteen years younger than I am, about six-foot-four, and a third-degree black belt in Aikido, or *Sandan*. Especially since I'm a tall, small-boned older woman with numbers on my last bone density scan tipping into osteopenia. But I don't worry about accidentally breaking something when I practice with Will, because he's polite and doesn't muscle through a technique the way so many other guys can't help doing.

Back to *irimi nage*. When I first learned this technique, I thought it was way more intimate than I cared to be with strangers on an Aikido mat. After all, this technique makes everyone pretty sweaty and stinky, because it's so aerobic. Think about it. When your partner has you glued to his shoulder, you pretty much have your face plastered right next to his armpit, and it's often someone you barely know. The upside? All of us in the dojo are probably immune to every kind of germ by now.

After about ten minutes of Will and me throwing each other around using this technique, Isabella *Sensei* claps and finishes the class with breathing exercises to help us cool down. We bow then and thank our partners.

"Will, have a minute?" I step off the mat.

"Sure," he answers.

"I know you're a private investigator," I say, keeping my voice low while getting a drink of water from the cooler. "I may have a job for you…something I don't think I can do on my own."

"OK, let's meet in a few minutes at your car."

Once we're in our street clothes and outside, Will explains that most of his P.I. work is on the Northeastern Seaboard but at times takes him all over the country. He doesn't specialize and handles everything from marital-dispute and infidelity surveillance, to financial-fraud investigation and finding missing persons.

I give Will the broad strokes, describing the Scranton Gang and telling him that I'd like to know what happened to the three kids after their arrest in 1987. He says that even though records are sealed on juveniles, he may have a way of getting at that information and helping me.

"I tried Googling all three," I say. "I found millions of entries for their names, and still thousands when I narrowed the search to just Pennsylvania—but who knows if any of them still live there."

Will nods, understanding the problem. "Ronnie, let me start with the Scranton Gang and work forward from there," he suggests.

I hand him copies of the newspaper articles I found the day before. We exchange email addresses, and since I'm a new client, he says he'll send me some paperwork to fill out.

"Ronnie." Will shoves his hands partially into his jeans pockets, which I can't help but notice hang low on his narrow hips. I guess he probably has six-pack abs under that shirt… "Don't mean to intrude," he goes on. "But why do you want to know about these kids?"

"I'm interested because…" I hesitate and then collect my thoughts. "…because I'm concerned about a possible connection between these kids and a family member of mine."

"Just know, when you start an investigation, what you find may take you down a road you might wish you'd never traveled."

~~~~~

On my way home, I stop by Meadow Farm to drop off a couple of gorgeous heads of lettuce I'd bought at a nearby vegetable stand. I walk through the foyer on my way to the kitchen and glance into the dining room. There I'm surprised to see Juliana on her knees folding up a corner of an old Oriental carpet. Her fingers gently rub the pile where the shadow of an old stain barely shows.

"Someone, way back, dropped—oh, what was it?" I walk into the room. "Some kind of sauce?"

A startled Juliana drops the corner of the carpet. "I didn't realize you were standing there." She gets up quickly. "You caught me daydreaming." Her voice is smooth, not flustered.

"Sorry. I didn't mean to surprise you." I walk over. "Daydreaming about a spot on a carpet?"

"I love old carpets." She looks down at this one. "They have so many stories to tell about the people who've walked on them."

"Well, this one would have a lot of Rutherfurd stories to tell, since my great-grandfather gave it to my grandparents when they bought Meadow Farm." I look at the old stain and then at her. "And of course lots of stories about family friends and the wonderful people who worked for us over the years."

I see a momentary hint of something cross Juliana's face, and she says, "Well, it's a most beautiful carpet."

"Kind of worn around the edges." I use the toe of my shoe to rub the stain. "But that's how we like it here— nothing too shiny and new." I link arms with Juliana and feel her pull back slightly as I turn her toward the kitchen. "Now how about an iced tea?"

"Juliana." It's Frank, calling from outside.

"Ronnie, excuse me." She disengages from my linked arm. "That's Frank. He's taking me to meet a friend of his. Don't mean to rush off." But Juliana does rush off to go join him outside. I hear laughing between the two and then a car motor rev up and take off down the gravel road.

~~~~~

I walk into the kitchen and place the fresh lettuce in the fridge.

"Hi, Ronnie!" Meadow Farm's longtime cook and housekeeper breezes in, a petite bundle of energy with a pencil and pad.

"How are you, m'dear?" I respond. Rita Hendricks is adored by all our family. In fact, I don't know how this place would run without her organizational talents and general TLC. "Everything under control over here?" I ask.

"Yep. I'm heading out to pick up the mail and do some grocery shopping." She adds an item to her list on the pad. "Frank and his new lady friend are driving to Mantoloking and will be there until this evening."

"So, this must be serious," I say lightly.

Rita stops writing and looks up.

I go on, "Frank must be taking Juliana to meet his old Princeton roommate, you know, Dan Gardiner. He's usually at his shore house this time of year, but I know he's been doing a lot of rebuilding since Superstorm Sandy. Maybe Frank and Juliana want to take a look at Dan's place and see what kind of headway he's making."

"Meadow Farm was certainly fortunate compared to the Shore, Ronnie." Rita closes the pad and lays down the pencil. "Just some downed trees here. No damage at all to the house or any of the farm buildings except that one shed crushed by that pine tree. We do have a lot to be grateful for."

I nod my agreement. "Absolutely, Rita. A lot to be grateful for. Anyway, my brother wouldn't take her to meet Dan if this wasn't serious." I think back to the lawyer's appointment Frank mentioned before the road rage incident and wonder why it involved Juliana. The meeting with his attorney could be an indicator of how serious the two of them are. Things might be moving fast between them...perhaps too fast. It makes me uneasy.

"Well, it's easy to understand why your brother would want to show her off. She's very beautiful." Rita grabs the pad and heads toward the kitchen door. "Be back in a while."

"Bye, Rita." I walk into the foyer and look upstairs. No one's around, and my curiosity is killing me. Again.

I've rarely been a nosy person, but I sure have been turning into one ever since Juliana arrived. Oh well. This is my brother, and men can be so naïve about women. They need their little sisters looking out for them, don't they?

I walk up the stairs and into the guest room. This time Juliana's room is pulled together, with everything properly in its place. The sight is quite a contrast to that of the chaos I encountered the evening of the party, when it looked as though a hurricane had blown through.

I open the door to the beautiful old mahogany armoire that stands opposite the bed. Juliana's dresses, slacks, tunics, and jackets are neatly draped on cedar hangers. It's now easy to see a common theme here—elegant clothing and not fussy—as if each item had been carefully considered, or curated, before purchase.

Some of the pieces are classic with famous labels that telegraph *expensive*, and they're mixed in with several items from hip, cutting-edge designers. What surprises me most is that Pucci-like number she wore for cocktails a couple days ago. I can hardly believe it when I see the J.Crew label inside the dress. Not exclusive like some of the other clothing hanging in the armoire, which shows that Juliana has the confidence to mix it all up.

What catches my eye are her shoes, now neatly arranged in the bottom of the armoire—among them red-soled Louboutin high heels and apple-green suede Tod's loafers. The Louboutins are so sky-high that just looking at them practically hurts my feet. The days of wearing sexy black heels like that are long gone for me, but, oooh, those suede Tod's look so comfortable, and chic, too! My toes are almost wiggling with a desire to try them on, but I manage to control myself.

I walk into the bathroom, and my eyes sweep over the products she uses for skincare and her hair. All great quality, but not ridiculously expensive. I notice that this time the bottles and tubes are each wiped off, closed, and lined up on the shelf above the sink instead of scattered, smudged, and left open all around the bedroom as on the night of the party.

Her cosmetics are like everything else about this woman's outward physical appearance—clean, elegant and understated. The neatnik in me feels no urge to fuss over anything, because everything is where it should be this time around.

Leaving the bathroom, I spot two books and a Kindle stacked on the nightstand next to the bed. Turning on the e-book reader as I put on my glasses, I see Juliana is in the middle of reading *The Brief Wondrous Life of Oscar Wao*. I turn off the Kindle and sit quietly on the edge of the bed thinking about her choice of this Pulitzer-Prize-winning book.

At the end of the day, before the lights go out, Juliana chooses to spend her time reading about New Jersey ghetto-nerd Oscar instead of dipping into *Vogue* or *Vanity Fair*. I kick myself for stereotyping her simply because she's so beautiful.

I pick up the paperback book that was right underneath the Kindle—*The Sorcerer's Apprentice*—and I discover it's a well-used chess manual. So, Juliana plays chess? That I would also not have expected. I flip open the book and see the title page is inscribed *To a most talented future chess master! JP, 1999*.

The bottom book is another well-worn paperback with numerous folded page corners. *The Tender Bar: A Memoir* by J. R. Moehringer. I don't know this one. The cover says it's a bestseller, and an NPR review on the back reads:

A fierce and funny coming of age story about ambition and yearning...exquisitely describes every wince-making step of his class climb.

I may have to buy my own copy and read this one.

Even if she seems aloof, hidden, and not particularly warm, Juliana is turning out to be one very interesting lady.

I read an inscription on the title page of this book, too— *For the lovely Juliana, A little something to read and think back to your years at the Café Casablanca. It was always a pleasure watching my most gifted student develop her many talents and flourish into such a lovely woman. Warmest regards, Dragomir, Malibu 2007.* Who is Dragomir? What kind of a name is that? Whoever these people are who inscribed her books, she doesn't appear to be trying to hide this intellectual part of her life.

I carefully place the books and Kindle back on the mahogany stand and spot a partially opened drawer in a bureau. I head over to close it but see a red leather box inside next to an Hermès scarf. So, naturally I open the drawer more and stare at the box.

Lightly stroking the grain of the leather with my fingers, I notice a frail silver chain hanging out one side of the box, and I open the lid. Gorgeous earrings, cuffs, and cocktail rings, many using colorful semi-precious stones in their design fill the box. But it's a beat-up, tarnished silver locket attached to that thin chain that draws my attention, and I carefully lift it out, trying not to disturb the other jewelry.

I study the swirling design on the front. Flipping it over, I read

To MTG, with love, FEB

…or is it *FLB*? Hard to tell, because the letters are scratched and difficult to read. I run my fingernail down the side of the locket and open it to find a small cluster of dark hair inside. But then I hear the front door slam, and I snap the locket shut.

Suddenly voices echo from below, and I quickly drop the locket into the box and drape the chain over its side, hoping this is the same way that I found it. I put the box back in its place, quietly shut the drawer, remove my glasses and leave.

I come down the stairs and identify the voices of my niece, nephew, and my nephew's wife, who are all in the kitchen. Heading through the door, I greet them cheerfully. "Now what have you three been doing all afternoon?"

CHAPTER NINE

"So I talked to a friend I did a favor for a while back. She's a social worker in Stroudsburg, Pennsylvania," Will Benson says. He and I have made it official—he now works for me as a private investigator, though I haven't yet told Laura, my niece. I think it best to keep this secret for the time being. That way if Frank finds out, Laura won't get into trouble for knowing about my misbehavior.

It's the day following my further snooping among Juliana's things, and Will texted me to meet him, so we sit in a coffee shop around the corner from the Aikido dojo. "Won't this social worker get into trouble for sharing information about a juvenile case with you?" I take a bite of my grilled cheese sandwich.

"Look, it's true those files are sealed," Will answers me. "But the case is twenty-five years old, and the kids aged out of the system a couple of decades ago. Anyway, you're interested in what's happened to them more recently. So my friend called a colleague who's been a social worker up in Scranton for thirty years." He sips his coffee. "This woman remembered the gang, looked up a couple of things, and gave us a rundown of what happened to the kids."

That news excites me. "Are they still around that area?" I ask. I'm thinking about the dead-bird-box delivery and hang-up calls from Scranton and Moosic when Juliana and Frank first arrived at Meadow Farm. I'm trying hard not to think about the van with Pennsylvania plates that ran my brother off the highway.

"Even though shots were fired, mostly by Teresa, nobody was injured. Fortunately." Will pulls out a notepad. "So the court took mercy and placed all of them in juvenile detention centers. The oldest, Joe Taylor, appears to have turned his life around."

"How'd he do that?" I ask.

"First, Joe never fired a gun or was even found with one when arrested, so that helped. Plus the juvenile system worked for him, and it also seems he showed remorse and humility," Will says. "Joe kept his head down and worked hard while in detention up near Scranton. He made good grades and did community service during those years."

Will flips through the pad, stopping on one page and reading a bit. "Let's see. Once he was released, he went to community college and then Marywood University in Scranton. He has a criminal justice degree. Pretty amazing."

"Wow." I finish my sandwich and take a drink.

"Get a load of this," Will goes on. "Today Joe Taylor runs a school drug abuse program in Scranton."

"That's impressive." I'm truly surprised, even moved. "But what happened to his little brother, Bobby?"

"That's a whole different story. Since Bobby Taylor turned eighteen and was released from juvie, he's been in and out of prison numerous times. Mostly for smalltime stuff—burglaries, passing bad checks, conning money from old people. Until the last one," says Will. "That was a serious felony charge involving drugs where he beat up a guy so badly he put him in a coma. Plus he had a gun. That landed him a ten-year sentence."

Will flips through a few more pages of his notes. "His files say he's a psychopath. There were even rumors years ago that he went after his cousin Theresa a few times—you know, attacked her. But I couldn't find a record of any charges on that."

He glances at a page in his pad and drinks his coffee. "So, Bobby was released from prison three months ago, this time in Maryland, although he's pretty much dropped out of sight. Nobody knows where he is."

So why is Bobby Taylor calling Juliana Wentworth? My brother's elegant girlfriend and this smalltime violent crook couldn't come from two more different worlds. But what if there's a perfectly sensible explanation, such as... "Will, what happened to Teresa?" I ask.

Will checks his notes. "Her case was more serious, even though she was only thirteen when arrested—it's because she fired a weapon a number of times at the police during the gang's crime spree."

Will turns to another page in his pad and reads further. "Following two years at a detention center, Teresa was placed in a girls' group home when she was fifteen." He closes the pad. "But a year later, after repeatedly breaking the home's strict curfews, she ran away."

"Ran away?" My curiosity is further aroused. "What happened to her? Where'd she go? Did they bring her back—"

"Hold it!" Will laughs. "Let me finish, Ronnie. The Pennsylvania Juvenile Justice system was never able to find her—"

Wow. "You're kidding me. She dropped out of sight completely? How could they blow this? Who was in charge of her case?" I hate not having an answer to a mystery like this.

Will throws his hands up. "Time out, Ronnie. I don't know you except from class, but I'd guess this is a different world from yours. I get the sense from the methodical way you practice Aikido that you like to be in control of things in your life. For a kid like Teresa, a lot in her life was out of her control. So she could've easily slipped through the cracks at that point—because she wanted to."

Will finishes his coffee. "While Teresa was at the group home, it seems she talked a lot about Disney World, how she was going to live there one day." He waves for the check. "After interviews were conducted with other residents at the home, the thought was that she probably ran away to Florida. But they never tracked her down."

I shake my head. What a terribly sad story. "She was just a kid, Will. How could they lose her?" I practically spit out *lose*.

"Calm down, Ronnie," my private eye buddy says. "Lots of kids run away. Remember, Teresa was sixteen and apparently looked older. So who was going to stop her as she made her way South?"

Will closes his notebook and shrugs. "I've gotta be somewhere in twenty minutes. If you'd like, I'll run up to Scranton in the next couple of days and talk to Joe Taylor. You know, see what I can find out about Teresa."

"Thanks, Will. But let's hold off on that for the moment." I grab the check when the waitress brings it to the table. "I've got this one. You go. Get to your appointment." He tucks the pad in his pocket and leaves.

I wonder what Teresa was up to all those years after she left Scranton. Calling up the image of the dead bird holding the scrap of paper in its beak with the names *Teresa & Frankie*, I consider the bizarre trio of Teresa, Bobby Taylor, and Juliana. Or was it a foursome with that guy Frankie? OK, Bobby and Teresa were cousins. It's also clear that Bobby and Juliana have some kind of baffling connection, where he could *ruin everything* for her, I guess with my brother. But what exactly is Teresa's relationship with Juliana? Simply friends? Or how about... Nah. That's just too big a stretch. Or is it?

Whatever, the story has to be a fascinating one, at the very least, and more importantly, would help me further understand Juliana. I might even find out whether she could be the best or worst thing that's happened to Frank since Joanie's death.

~~~~~

I stop by Meadow Farm to drop off a book I think my brother would enjoy reading. That's my excuse anyway, should anyone ask. My real purpose is to dangle information on Joe Taylor in front of Juliana and gauge her reaction.

I breeze into the foyer ready to call out, when I hear a woman's voice speaking in low tones. The voice comes from the library, and the speaker is Juliana. I tiptoe closer and stand quietly beside the door, hidden from view.

"...oh, darling, don't cry. I'll see you very, very soon." Her voice is gentle and reassuring. A pause comes as she apparently listens. "Middle school girls can be so mean. Believe me, I remember."

Then I hear Juliana walk across the room and unlock a French door to the outside. "It sounds as if *Tía* Connie took care of it," she says to the person on the other end of the line.

I peek in and see my brother's girlfriend from the back, outlined against the open French door with the phone to her ear. Then she kisses into the mouthpiece. "Oh, darling, I love you very much, too." Her voice is surprisingly warm. Who in the world is on the other end?

Juliana continues. "Now please put *Tía* Connie on the phone." Who is *Tía* Connie? "Are you OK, Connie?" she asks. "Shall I send more money?" She listens. "OK. Love you, too." She clicks off and hangs up the phone.

I wonder if Frank knows who *Tía* Connie is. I go back to the front door and slam it as if the wind has blown it shut. "Hi! Anybody home?" I call out.

"In the library, Ronnie," Juliana shouts back.

Walking across to the door of the library, I stick my head in with a big smile. Juliana is sitting on a long white sofa flipping through a magazine. She looks up, cool as a cucumber.

"Hi, Juliana." Smiling at her, I march over to Frank's desk. "Found a book that my brother might enjoy." I place the book on top of his stack of mail and sigh, rubbing my forehead. "I thought when my kids left the nest, I would stop worrying. No such luck. You have kids, Juliana?"

First a long pause as she puts the magazine aside, then, "I have four stepchildren." She looks at me with curiosity. "Is one of yours giving you a tough time?"

"My youngest. Jess," I answer honestly. "We're working on financial responsibility...I remember it being much easier with Tommy and Brooke, but maybe that's my imagination." I scribble a quick note to Frank and tuck it inside the book.

"Frank and I love to read, and we're always trading books. You have any brothers or sisters, Juliana?"

"No, I was an only child." Her voice is even.

"Oh." I pause. "I can't imagine growing up as an only child. Frank, Peter, and I, well, we always had each other's back. Frank and I still do."

"When you're an only child, you learn to look out for yourself." Juliana looks neither sad nor happy, but merely neutral.

"How about cousins?" I then ask. "They can be like siblings."

"No, no close cousins." She volunteers nothing more.

The silence is deafening, and I'm eager to fill it. "So, how's your day going?"

"Great. Frank will be back in about…" She looks at her watch. "…twenty minutes. He's taking me to visit a farm that he says makes the most delicious cheeses."

I like that place. "Oh, that's Valley Farm Creamery. I only call them for special occasions, or I'd be eating their cheeses nonstop. You'll have a great time." I straighten some books on a shelf. "I also have a fun outing on the agenda."

Juliana smiles politely. "Where are you going, Ronnie?"

"Well, I'm on the board of a foundation that funds programs for kids. I just found out about one that I want to check out over in Pennsylvania." I sit on the corner of Frank's desk where I can look directly at Juliana to watch for a reaction. "So it's a little further than driving to the creamery."

"How interesting." Juliana's eyes say *tell me more*. She's giving me her full attention, the same way I watched her listen to our guests at cocktails the other night. "What do they do?"

"It's supposed to be a successful school drug prevention program up in Scranton, of all places." I give her my version of her laser-beam gaze. "And what's really interesting is that the guy who created it had a police record as a teenager. He used to be in a gang, was arrested, then placed in juvenile detention."

I watch Juliana's face carefully for any sign of recognition. Okay then, the moment of truth. "The man's name is Joe Taylor. He really turned his life around, and now he helps other young people do the same."

Nothing. I see no flicker of reaction when I say the name. Whatever Juliana may know, she gives nothing away. "What an amazing story, Ronnie. How exciting to go meet someone like that."

She's polite in a reserved way, but I don't give up. "If Frank deserts you for a conference call or unexpected meeting, would you like to come along? I'm probably going tomorrow and I'd love some company," I say. "It'd be fun."

"Thanks, Ronnie, but Frank says he wants to take me into the city tomorrow." She looks at her watch and suddenly gets up from the sofa. "He should be back any moment. I need to run upstairs now and get ready. Please excuse me."

She heads for the door but stops before leaving the room, turning back to me with that enigmatic smile. "Thanks for the invitation, though, Ronnie. Some other time." She leaves.

She's smooth. She's very smooth. Yep, Frank's got himself a real woman of mystery.

CHAPTER TEN

A funny thing happens when I pull off the highway halfway to Scranton. While waiting in line for a cup of coffee, I look through the window by the cashier and notice a nondescript Toyota idling off to the side. I wouldn't give it a second thought except this particular vehicle has a good-sized dent on the passenger-side front fender, very much like the dent in the nondescript Toyota at Meadow Farm.

I can't read the numbers on the license—too far away— but the car has New Jersey plates. Hard to see who's sitting behind the wheel. As I pull out my distance glasses to get a better look, the car shifts into drive, and all I see is the blur of a baseball cap and big sunglasses going by before the Toyota darts back onto the highway.

Wait a minute. Couldn't be. At any rate, isn't Juliana on her way to New York with Frank today? Strange.

Anyway, when I made the appointment with Joe Taylor soon after talking to Will, I told him I'd heard all about his successful drug abuse prevention program. And since I planned to be in the area, would he have time to tell me more about it? Of course I'm really interested in finding out what's become of the Scranton Gang.

Truthfully, some friends do have a small family foundation in New Jersey, and I'm on the board. Joe Taylor's program does actually fit the funding mission of this foundation. So he and I spend a half-hour discussing the challenges his nonprofit faces.

"Joe, this is all very intriguing," I say. "I'll bring it to my fellow board members at our next meeting." I leaf through the contents of a folder Joe has given me. "We'll see if we can be helpful and get back to you shortly for an official funding request." I stop when I get to his biography and read through it quickly.

"Thank you, Mrs. Lake," Joe then says. "I appreciate your interest and the possibility of the foundation supporting our work. With the economy so tough, outside funding dropped thirty percent last year, and, to be honest, we're scrambling."

"Please call me Ronnie," I say. "And I hope it's all right if I call you Joe?" He nods yes and pushes his thinning black hair off his high forehead. I refer to his bio page. "Your personal story is compelling, and I'm sure a big reason why you've been successful." Joe smiles modestly, leaning back in his chair and stretching out his khaki-clad legs.

I flip through other pages in the folder. "Before coming here for this appointment, I researched both your program and you." He looks at me curiously. "I even read up on the Scranton Gang."

Joe's dark, almost black, eyes become more guarded. "That's so far back. How'd you—"

"No, please, Joe. The way you turned your life around is an inspiration. And from what I've been able to learn, your brother, well, his life went in the opposite direction." I lean back in my chair, too. "What I want to know is how does one brother make his life work so well, while the other one blows it?"

Joe gives me a long, hard look. "Are you really here to consider funding my program? How'd you even hear about the Scranton Gang?"

"It's not so difficult to find out these things," I say, sidestepping the fact that it also helps to have a connected P.I. working for you. "I'm definitely here to learn about you and your program so the foundation can consider a grant."

His expression is now one of suspicion. "Is something else going on that I should know about?" He stands up. "I think we ought to wrap up this meeting." He walks to the door.

"Please, Joe, wait." Damn. Did I blow it, again, like at the Moosic Motel with the desk clerk? Am I coming on too strong, too direct? In a panic, I dive back in. "Joe, I mean no harm. You worked hard to turn your life around and have succeeded brilliantly in doing so. You're an inspiration. Please, I mean that sincerely."

He walks back to his desk. "Thank you."

But I can't leave it alone. "Why was it the opposite for your brother?"

Joe stares at me, sits down, and, I guess, makes a decision to play ball. "I believe in the power of one-to-one mentoring. In my case, a teacher early on took an interest and helped set me on the right path." He shakes his head. "Bobby never had that important advantage. Plus he didn't want to work very hard. I tried over and over to talk to him, but he never really wanted my help. So his troubles continued."

"What happened to Bobby?" I ask and try to relax. "Is he in the area, too?"

Having gone this far, Joe doesn't seem inclined to stop. "I don't know. About ten years ago, I finally gave up on trying with him. I don't keep track of my brother anymore and have no idea where he is these days." Joe's eyes look sad. "But I think I'd have heard if he was around Scranton for any period of time."

I decide to push things a little further. Maybe too far, but I keep my tone casual. "Whatever happened to Teresa Gonzalez? She was so young." I lean in on Joe's desk and steeple my hands. "From what I read, she sounded like the really tough one in the gang. Isn't it unusual for the girl to be the alpha in the pack when the others are boys?"

Joe's gives me a sharp look, but he does answer. "Teresa was our first cousin—our mothers were sisters. I don't remember much about her father, Uncle Tony— except he had homing pigeons. But he wasn't around much, so he gave the pigeons to Bobby and me when we were boys. Anyway, Teresa moved to Moosic with her mother, I guess when she was about ten or eleven."

"Where did they come from?" I ask without any particular emphasis.

"Her mother worked somewhere in New York or New Jersey. I don't remember where." Joe looks up at the ceiling. "Anyway, they were pretty broke when they moved here. Teresa's mom wanted to help her brother, our Uncle Marco, raise his kids after his wife died of cancer."

"How sad."

"Yeah, and two of those cousins got into a gang." Joe sighs. "Teresa started acting tough, wanting to hang out with them, but they wanted nothing to do with her."

"Did Teresa's mother try to help her?"

He shakes his head. "Not really. She didn't have the time. She got a job in addition to helping Uncle Marco with his boys. So Teresa was pretty much ignored. She developed real attitude."

"Then what happened?" I want to keep Joe talking now that we're getting somewhere.

"She decided to form her own gang and recruited Bobby and me." Joe gazes down at his desk as if he's looking into the past. "Teresa said we were going to be much tougher than our cousins' gang. And in some respects we succeeded, at least in the eyes of the press, who referred to us as the Scranton Gang." He rolls up the sleeves of his oxford shirt and appears to loosen up somewhat.

"Hey, was a guy named Frankie part of your gang?" I ask.

"Frankie? No," he says. "I don't know any Frankie."

"So where's Teresa these days? Did she turn her life around like you?" I hope my voice sounds suitably nonchalant.

"No one in our neighborhood has heard from her in a long, long time," Joe says. "She ran away from the group home where she was living when she was sixteen. Headed South." He snickers, and the sound isn't nice. "Teresa always wanted to live at Disney World," he sneers, "and be close to the Cinderella Castle—her favorite fairy tale. Hah."

He pauses, and the derision evaporates from his face. "I did hear she actually got a job down there, I think in housekeeping."

"How'd she make that happen?" I try not to sound overly eager. "I mean, she was on the run and underage."

"She probably changed her name," Joe answers me. "Remember, in those days, pre-9/11, employers weren't always a stickler for workers' papers. And maybe Teresa found a way to get fake ones." Again, he's in his own long-ago world.

I rub my neck. "How do you get started in a new place at such a young age if you just show up and don't know a soul?"

"First, Teresa wanted to grow up fast, and she looked older, so that helps. Second, I heard there was another kid from the group home," Joe responds. "Uh, Carmela. Carmela Suarez. She'd aged out at eighteen and moved to Orlando. Maybe they connected."

"Amazing how fearless these kids are." I wish I could ask Joe if Bobby ever attacked Teresa, but I'm concerned he'll get suspicious again and clam up for good.

"What's amazing," he goes on, "is that I heard Teresa worked her way up to a job as one of those fairy tale characters who interact with the kids visiting Disney World."

"Imagine that," I say.

"I remember she was great with children. Teresa was in big demand as a babysitter in Moosic before she created the Scranton Gang. And she was such a beautiful girl." Joe leans into his desk. He laughs and shrugs. "Hey, maybe she stayed in Florida and turned her life around, too, instead of ending up like my brother."

Oh, the hell with it. I'm going to ask. "Joe, this is a bit delicate. Do you think Bobby ever went after your cousin Teresa? You know, maybe attacked her?" I regret my question the minute the words are out of my mouth.

His eyes go hard. I almost flinch, the change is so extreme.

"What does that have to do with anything? And where would you get that idea?" His voice is measured and as cold as his eyes. "Come to think of it, I believe a grant for my drug program is the last thing on your mind."

Joe Taylor gets up from his desk again, walks around it and stands facing me. I'm frozen, entirely unsure what I ought to do next. He leans down, takes both arms of my chair, and gets right in my face. I smell coffee on his breath with a touch of some kind of booze. Whiskey? Not sure.

He never raises his now menacing voice. "One thing I don't like is being toyed with. Lady, really, what is your story?"

I don't say a word. I'm scrambling for a way to make a quick exit. He creates a way out for me, when he straightens.

"This appointment is finished. Show yourself out."

~~~~~

The entire drive home, I chastise myself for blowing the meeting with Joe Taylor. I'll never be able to call him again to ask any other questions. Man, I need to learn when to back off.

Will had offered to handle the interview, and I probably should have let him do just that. Still, I did learn a few interesting things about Teresa's life in Florida.

I pull onto the drive to my house and see another car come up behind my Mustang. Frank jumps out of a blue, not black, Porsche and quickly circles to the other side to open the door for Juliana, calling to me, "Hope you don't mind us dropping by."

"Never, big brother," I say, as he walks over to hug me. Juliana and I give each other quick smiles and wave. I nod to the car. "Loaner while yours is being repaired?"

"Yep," he says. "Have an admission to make. I wanted Jules to see where you live."

Noticing they're both dressed casually in jeans, I ask, "Hey, how was New York?"

"Change of plans. Meeting got rescheduled at the last minute, so we're going tomorrow." Frank winds his way back to Juliana's side and takes her hand.

I recall that blur in a baseball cap and sunglasses in the Toyota with the dent along the Pennsylvania highway. So that could have been Juliana.

"Sis, I told Jules all about Warrior. She loves animals and works with a couple of rescue organizations on the Coast," he gushes. Well, not really gushes. It's subtle, since Waspy guys don't gush.

"I'd love to meet Warrior," Juliana says, "but only if now is a good time."

"It's a great time," I say. "First, I'll let him out in the pen to do his business. You two go into the garden through the gate, and I'll bring him in to meet Juliana. Then we'll all go inside for a look around."

In a few minutes, Warrior and I walk into the garden, where he circles Frank and Juliana for several quick sniffs and then stops in front of Juliana. All of a sudden, he howls, issuing the most sing-songy noise I've ever heard come out of him. The three of us freeze. Then his tail wags, and we laugh, realizing he was just being goofy. Warrior then heads to his usual spot to plop down.

After we tour my cottage, I send Frank and Juliana again outside to my garden, while I open some beers in the kitchen. Frank pops back in. "Thought you might need a hand, Ronnie."

"Got it, Frank, but thanks for the offer." I stop what I'm doing. "Don't mean to be nosy, but why were you and Juliana in such a hurry to get over to the lawyer's office right before that guy ran you off the road?" I laugh nervously. "I thought you two were maybe intending to elope!"

He sidles over and squeezes my shoulder as he scoops up two of the beers. "Don't worry about me, Sis."

"What do you mean?"

"You know, about my so-called love life." He smiles at me. "You're a real mama bear, always worrying about all of us. She's good people, Ronnie. You don't have to worry about Juliana."

I smile back. "If you say so, Frank. Anyway, you don't have to be in a rush to get to know someone, do you?" Frank says nothing. "Do you?" I ask again. "Have to be in a rush, I mean."

He shrugs and smiles. "I don't have to rush, but, Ronnie, life is short. The older we get, the more we realize we shouldn't waste time. Anyway, Juliana needs a good lawyer for a confidential family matter she wants to resolve…"

My thoughts swirl as I listen to him. If you only knew my suspicions, Frank, but it's too soon for me to share what I've learned. "Just want my big brother to be happy. That's all." I take the bowl of chips and my beer, and we go out.

The three of us sit in the garden enjoying our cold beers, shooting the breeze. The most interesting aspect of our visit is Warrior. He's usually next to me no matter where we are, but right now he's practically glued to Juliana's side and flirting like crazy with her. I've never seen Warrior behave this way toward an absolute stranger. I remember though that my son told me some years back that

Warrior was first raised by a young woman. I wonder if my brother's girlfriend reminds Warrior of that person.

Juliana enjoys every moment of my German shepherd's attention. I can see that she's honestly a real dog person. She doesn't mind when Warrior pushes his wet nose against her rolled-up sleeve for more rubs between his ears. She doesn't scoot away when my dog wiggles his behind against her leg, shedding hair all over her jeans as he invites more butt-scratching. Juliana complies, which sends him into ecstasy.

Finally, Warrior lays his head in her lap and gazes up at her with his beautiful brown eyes. A deep look of understanding passes between them, and she leans over to whisper something secret into his ear. An audible sigh comes from my dog. He lies down at Juliana's feet and falls asleep.

It's not just Warrior who fascinates me. Watching Juliana meet my pooch, who usually makes most newcomers nervous, I see her being more open and down to earth than at any time since we've met. The wall is down, at least for these few passing moments. Animals have a solid sense of people, I believe. So is Warrior telling me that Juliana is a decent person—one I can trust is worthy of my brother?

~~~~~

They've left, and I stand in a guest room that I converted into a spacious walk-in closet, staring at endless hangars of clothes, cubbyholes of shoes, and overflowing shelves. I make a mental note to clear out what I no longer wear for the annual town rummage sale. Then I grab my favorite sweatshirt and almost fall over Warrior as I exit the closet. I kneel down to scratch his head.

My lovable seven-year-old German shepherd happens to be a highly trained bomb-sniffing dog that once belonged to my son. Tragedy arrived two years ago when the military notified my now-ex-husband and me that our twenty-seven-year-old boy, Thomas Livingston Lake, had died in combat in Afghanistan. Warrior, my dear Warrior, was next to Tommy when he died. He's a link to my son during his final moments, and for that, I more than treasure this 85-pound furry creature. I scratch his neck, which he loves. I scratch the top of his haunches, which he loves even more.

My son was a Marine Corps dog handler. He and Warrior stuck together like glue during their many missions. Unfortunately, Taliban sniper fire hit Tommy during a patrol. His commanding officer wrote me that Warrior climbed on top of Tommy to protect him from additional gunfire, but my boy still didn't make it.

The military granted Warrior early retirement because of canine post-traumatic stress disorder, and he came to live with me. The PTSD symptoms this four-legged veteran still exhibits are hypervigilance when it now comes to my safety rather than Tommy's and a strong reaction to sudden loud noises—a reminder of the gunfire that fatally felled his beloved handler.

My gaze falls on my favorite picture of Tommy as a soldier. I unpacked it yesterday, and it sits on the nightstand next to the photo of the girls when they were little. In the photo, Tommy, in fatigues, relaxes on a cot while listening to music on his iPod. Warrior sprawls out between his legs, which encircle the dog like a big soft nest. Oh, my precious son…he had so many plans for his life after the military.

I bury my face in Warrior's neck, partially to dry my tears. Even though my heart is slowly mending, I cry at the most unexpected moments.

Yes, the loss of Tommy does get a little easier with time. The pain doesn't go away, but the days very slowly become easier.

CHAPTER ELEVEN

"Daddy left for the city. He's got a business appointment this morning, and Juliana was supposed to go with him. But she changed her mind and asked to borrow a car to visit a friend in Pennsylvania," Laura says in a low voice over the phone. "Wonder if it's that mystery person who sent her the dead bird."

"Maybe." Who knows? But I'm thinking she's probably going to see Bobby Taylor. "Which car is she driving? Is it that loaner-Porsche your Dad got from the dealer while his is being repaired?"

"She wants to take the Toyota," my niece says, sounding puzzled. "I mean, who would take a Toyota when a sexy blue Porsche is sitting there practically calling your name?"

"Maybe someone who doesn't want to attract attention," I answer, thinking about the dented Toyota-sighting the other day when I drove up to Scranton to meet Joe Taylor.

I guess I have to let Laura in on one of my little secrets. So I tell her that I'm thinking of doing a little hands-on detective work. Today I plan to track Juliana. "Daniel's working around my place right now," I add. "I'll see if I can trade cars with him and use his van. How much time do you figure I've got to get on her trail?"

"Well, they're eating breakfast now," Laura says. "Half an hour maybe?"

I nod to myself. "Juliana will probably follow your dad out to Hard Scrabble Lane, where they'll split off in different directions. It'll be tight, but I'll be parked there waiting."

"Don't you think they'll spot you?" Laura asks.

"Not if I'm parked near the Smith cottage in Daniel's grey work van. Text me when they leave the farm." I hang up and signal Warrior to come with me.

~~~~~

I follow Juliana through the Delaware Water Gap, and forty-five minutes later we approach the outskirts of Scranton, Pennsylvania. So far, I'm pretty sure she hasn't noticed me tailing her.

Rather than heading into town, Juliana drives west toward, where else but good old Moosic. My van follows her in the dented Toyota, both of us trying not to stand out in our forgettable vehicles.

We drive through the more commercially prosperous part of Moosic and then transition into the shabbier section of town. She parks in front of the Moosic Motel. Why am I not surprised?

I get lucky and slip into a parking space a few yards from the hotel—the better to watch and listen from a reasonably unobtrusive spot. I unclip Warrior's seat belt, and he curls up on the front seat for a little nap. Soon I hear his baby snores.

Juliana finally exits the Toyota, wearing faded jeans, flip-flops, and a loose v-neck tee-shirt. Rather than showing off her fabulous long hair, she's opted to twist it into a sloppy bun and stuff it into a baseball cap. Strands have fallen loose and hang around her face and in her eyes. Still, it isn't easy hiding how beautiful she is. Juliana walks into a grubby-looking coffee shop next door to the motel, and I wait with Warrior.

Pretty soon a motorcycle roars up, and a guy with shaggy black hair and a leather jacket shuts down the engine and gets off. He removes the jacket, revealing a torn tee-shirt. His arms are loaded with tattoos all the way down to his wrists. His jeans hang low on his behind creating a sight that only a mother could love. Is that Bobby Taylor? If so, he and Juliana are like night and day. He also walks into the coffee shop, and I wait.

Thirty minutes later, still sitting in the van, I consider the fact that I'm conducting my first actual surveillance, and it sure is boring. I don't dare read and risk missing something happening. I can't nap like Warrior while I wait, and I forgot to buy the standard P.I. cup of coffee. I check my phone camera. I put the radio on low and listen to the news. Then I search the channels for some decent music. Unable to find any, I switch back to the news.

Another thirty minutes go by before Juliana and Mr. Butt-Crack come out the door of the coffee shop. I click off the radio and partially lower the passenger window in the hope of picking up their conversation. Fortunately, the van windows are tinted, so I don't think they'll notice me. To be on the safe side, I slide down a little more in the seat while remaining able to watch what's going on.

"…he even bought me a cell phone to help me get back on my feet. No more calling from pay phones all over the place." Bobby, if it's he, pulls the phone out of his pocket to show Juliana. "Hey, if he thinks I can do it, so should you," he tells her. She glances around what appears to be an empty street nervously, as if she's checking to see whether or not they're alone.

"Come on, say something." The guy looks as if he's close to Juliana's age, and he's got a swagger in his walk as they move toward her car. "This is a once-in-a-lifetime deal," he purrs. "If I don't show up with the money, he'll be really pissed and cut me out." His cocky purr turns into a whine. "You said you'd help me after I got out."

"What do you mean once-in-a-lifetime deal?" As she walks swiftly, Juliana's slightly raised shoulders and clenched fists at her side clearly reveal her state of tension. "I don't want anything to do with giving you money for a drug deal."

I stay low and discreetly snap pictures from the shadows of the van's interior. As Juliana's agitation increases, the volume of her voice goes up. "He always makes everything sound so easy. You know that. Don't believe him, or you'll end up back in prison."

I wonder, who is the *he* they're both talking about—the *he* who bought Mr. Butt-Crack a phone, and the *he* Juliana says makes everything sound so easy. Warrior moves to get up, and I slide my arm over his shoulders. "Stay down," I tell him in a low voice. "Quiet." I slide further down, too, to remain unseen.

Juliana opens the Toyota's passenger door and leans over as if she's pulling something from under the seat. She stands up holding a large brown envelope and slams the door shut, telling the guy in a firm angry voice, "You said you need money to go to school…get a fresh start. That I'm willing to pay for. This isn't for some hair-brained drug scheme. If it is, I can't give you this cash. Do you understand?"

"I promise," he says. "No drugs."

"I've had it with you, Bobby Taylor." So, that definitely is *BT*, the initials scribbled on the pad in her room, and a definite low-life. Juliana practically throws the envelope at him. "And no more phone calls and packages." OK, she's got to be talking about the hang-ups at the farm and the dead-bird box. She seems to have been in contact with this guy for a while, and that might explain how he knew she'd be at Meadow Farm before she'd even arrived.

Bobby opens the envelope, and as he partially pulls out a huge wad of money, other stacks of bills fall out. He quickly picks them up, stuffing them back in.

You've got to be kidding. Nobody I know carries around that amount of cash. Wonder if she brought it out from California in her carry-on. Or she could have stopped repeatedly at an ATM in town. Or both.

"I mean it," Juliana practically shouts. "We'll clear out. And I mean out of the country. You won't ever find us." Who is *us*? Bobby mumbles a response, but I can't really hear him. He flips through the bills, and I snap more photos as he mutters something else. I wish he'd speak more clearly.

Juliana cuts him off. "Stay away from Frankie, or the money stops. That's always been our deal." Her tone sounds ferocious. Who is this Frankie? Why is he the make-or-break on the money?

"Forget about us, Bobby." Does she mean my brother and her, or this Frankie guy and her? Then Juliana's voice drops to a murmur and she says something I can't hear. Bobby laughs, and she explodes. "You're going to spoil everything." I think back to her words the evening of the cocktail party. *You'll ruin everything.* Ruin everything, spoil what? Is something else terrible going on here that doesn't concern my brother? Or does it? She walks around the Toyota and opens the driver's door.

He follows her. "Oh, come on, sugar," he whines, and grabs her arm. She shakes him loose, but he moves in to grab her again. She quickly sidesteps out of his way. He stumbles and swears at her. Uh, oh. Should I call the police before this escalates?

Juliana hurriedly gets into the car, slams the door shut, and starts the engine. Bobby uses his fist to bang on her window and resorts to the vilest of language. She pulls away from the curb, and he bangs his fist on the car's trunk. Watching her drive off, he calms down, seems indifferent at this point, and walks into the Moosic Motel.

I start my car, fasten Warrior's seat belt on him, and pull out as Juliana maneuvers around two sets of double-parked trucks further down the street. I stay at a safe distance, curious to see if she makes any other stops.

I drive for twenty minutes, and once I'm sure Juliana is heading back to New Jersey, I reverse my course to return to Moosic. Think I'll check on tattooed-biker-man Bobby and see what's up with him.

CHAPTER TWELVE

Back in the dicey part of town, Bobby's motorcycle is still parked out front between the Moosic Motel and the coffee shop. I glide by at fifteen miles an hour and look into the big picture window of the motel. A different person is on duty, not the unshaven skinny guy I talked to during my first visit here.

I park further down the street and consider my next move. My heart is thumping so I reach for *The Art of Peace*, a little book that has some of the teachings of *O'Sensei*, the creator and founder of Aikido. I flip open to a quote of his that Isabella *Sensei* mentioned recently.

Do not stare into the eyes of your opponent: he may mesmerize you. Do not fix your gaze on his sword: he may intimidate you. Do not focus on your opponent at all: he may absorb your energy...

I take a deep breath. Am I really ready for snooping around among dubious strangers in a shady neighborhood like this? I could take Warrior, but that might arouse too much attention.

Lowering the windows partially for fresh air but not enough for Warrior to wriggle out, I then scratch his head. "You be a good boy. Stay here and guard the van. I'll be right back." I don't bother clicking the lock to the vehicle as I head for the motel. No need, with Warrior sitting inside, and I don't plan to stay longer than a few minutes, anyway. I glance back at the van, and my loyal companion is watching my every step.

Instead of going into the motel lobby, I make a quick turn down the garbage-strewn alley beside the building. The smell of rotting food in tossed-out containers almost makes me gag as I slowly walk along the narrow passageway. I realize I'm foolishly putting myself in harm's way and almost turn back to the van, but my curiosity pulls me forward, and I continue.

Every time I come to a window, I stop and peek past an old, humming air conditioning unit, carefully looking for Bobby Taylor. No luck. Maybe he's on the other side of the building. Of course, I'm not sure exactly what I'd do if I found him in one of these rooms.

I round the corner to the back of the building and unintentionally startle a scruffy, greasy-looking guy, causing him to stagger as he rolls a joint. His expression changes to one of anger when he sees my gawking expression.

"Lady, what are you staring at?" He staggers again and fumbles the half-rolled joint, almost dropping it. Instead, he recovers and quickly stuffs it into his pocket.

"N-nothing," I stutter, my knees now shaking. "Sorry, didn't mean to interrupt." I figure he's probably already high. "Hey, you friends with Bobby Taylor? I think he's staying here." I notice my voice is getting higher in pitch from nerves.

"Yeah, well, maybe we're friends…" he mumbles, and drool runs down his chin over a nasty sore. "What's it to ya?"

If Bobby Taylor looks like a low-life, then this guy looks like absolute gutter trash. His clothes are filthy and torn, his face is slobbery, and he stinks. He probably hasn't had a shower in many days. His stench, combined with the sweet smell of whatever he's smoking, just about overpowers me.

I snap to when he suddenly lunges at me, and I hastily step to the right. He crashes into some garbage cans and grunts as he lands on his side. Now he's really mad.

"You bitch," he yells at me, as he pushes himself up. He lunges at me again, and this time I physically freeze. He shoves me up against the building, grabbing me around the neck with a front choke.

All my Aikido techniques fly out the window while I go mentally blank. In my panic, I flail around, trying in vain to break his hold around my neck. I struggle for air and scratch at his face, but he won't let go. God, he's got a tight grip for someone who's stoned. My arms thrash even more at the thought of dying in this alley. I go lightheaded from a lack of oxygen, and that's when I hear a voice from inside the motel yell, "Hey, Jimmy, you outside?"

The man's hands immediately drop from my throat, and he looks in the direction of the voice. "Hey, Bob-beeee," he slurs. "Wan' some good weed?" That's all I need to break away.

I haul out of there as fast as I can to the front of the motel. Then, just as I come to the street, I hear a noise behind me. I turn to see the pot-smoking creep running after me and yelling, "You bitch. I'll kill ya."

I head for my vehicle where I see Warrior still on the alert, waiting for me. I jump into the van and jam the keys into the ignition. My dog's agitation is growing, and he growls continuously while he watches the bum—I guess Jimmy—run toward the passenger door. I hit the button to raise my dog's window and click the lock just in time, thank god. As the engine turns over, Warrior's growl evolves into ferocious barking.

Jimmy's eyes are filled with rage and he pulls on the door handle then spits on the window of the car. "You don't know what hurt is until I get done with you." He leers at me. "Me and Bobby are comin' for you." He pounds the window.

Warrior jumps at the glass on the passenger side, fully baring his teeth and snarling at my attacker. The guy totters back, hitting the fire hydrant and toppling over it to the sidewalk. "Holy shit," he sputters.

"Hey, you OK, Jimmy?" Bobby Taylor runs out just as I pull away leaving Jimmy still sprawled on his back. "What's goin' on, man?"

When I glance in my side mirror, driving the van down the street as fast as I can, I see Bobby helping Jimmy up. I also see them both look in the direction of my van. I keep moving and finally slow down a dozen blocks and three turns later. My breathing is still as rapid as if I'd run all the way here. Where I struggled for air moments ago, now I almost hyperventilate. My hands on the steering wheel shake.

What the hell did I think I was doing back there, going into that alley without Warrior? I'm not a professional private eye like Will Benson, just an idiotic, nosy amateur trying to look out for her brother. And an amateur who turned useless when the time came to defend herself. A coward. What happened to all my Aikido? Where was it when I actually needed it?

Once I enter a better part of Moosic, I pull over and look at my dog. "Thanks, Warrior." I kiss the top of his head and then fasten his seat belt as well as mine. Taking slow, deep breaths, I consider how I risked my personal safety going into that motel alley. "Really stupid move, Ronnie," I mutter.

I also think about Jimmy's threats. *You don't know what hurt is until I get done with you. Me and Bobby are comin' for you.* I'm aware that I don't have much experience with people like Bobby Taylor and that stoned, smelly wacko, Jimmy. I'm certainly naive, having always assumed these dark, harsh worlds would never touch me.

But all it takes is one person to crack through your false sense of safety or to connect with someone you care about. No matter how lovely that person appears to be, because of her past she may be the conduit into an ugly slice of humanity that spills dangerously into your own life and that of your family.

Didn't Will warn me that starting this investigation might take me places I wouldn't want to go? If it only concerned me, I'd slam the door shut on all of this right now. But what about Frank? He probably knows nothing about Juliana's questionable activities and wouldn't believe any of this. I'm also sure he'd be totally pissed at me for butting in.

I need to be rock solid about what's going on with Juliana before I talk to Frank. I can't risk endangering my relationship with my brother—my one remaining brother. I just can't handle any more loss right now.

I turn on my music, crank up the volume on Dire Straits, and head for home. Mark Knopfler's amazing guitar solo on "Sultans of Swing" helps wash all the pain and tension from my shoulders and neck.

~~~~~

"Are you crazy?" Isabella says to me at the dojo after I meekly tell her and Will about my encounter with the creep in the alley. Class finished twenty minutes earlier, and I was relieved to find the two of them still there working through some techniques. Guess I was more shaken up than I had realized.

"But Isabella—"

"Ronnie," Will interrupts, looking closely at my neck. "What are those marks? Is that where he choked you?"

"Wh-what?" I stammer and rush to the mirror. Sure enough, I see red hand imprints where Jimmy grabbed me around my neck.

"Are you OK?" he asks. "Does it hurt there?"

I touch the red marks carefully. "Well, it's a little bit sore, but I think I'm fine. My breathing's OK."

"Look, Ronnie," Isabella says. "If you didn't have your black belt in Aikido, would you have gone into that alley?"

"Definitely, not—"

"From now on when facing a decision like that, pretend you don't know *any* Aikido." She's emphatic. "Do *not* invite trouble."

"I was doing some investigating," I say. "And thought I could handle things." My tone is humble and my posture slumped.

"Ronnie, don't think that just because you now have a black belt you can go out into the world and channel Steven Seagal," Will scolds. "Why didn't you call me?"

"Like I said, I thought I could handle it myself," I answer.

"You should have Will help you when you go into the field to investigate." Isabella *Sensei* shakes her head in disbelief. "I would never have walked down that alley alone. Or at least take Warrior with you instead of leaving him in the car. No one would mess with that dog."

"I hear you, but why did my Aikido completely fall apart? It was as if I'd never, ever taken a class. I froze." This is the part that bothers me the most.

"That's because it was real this time," Isabella answers. "And Aikido class isn't about training to fight in the street."

Isabella and Will exchange glances and give me some lame excuses about having other things they need to do. Then they walk away. Ask me if I feel as though I'm ten years old and just got a scolding.

CHAPTER THIRTEEN

It's early evening, and Juliana and I sit on the small terrace off the kitchen's breakfast nook at Meadow Farm making polite chit-chat, drinking our iced tea. I wouldn't say we've connected, but we're being kind of friendly in a superficial way. I glance down at her feet expecting to see those apple-green suede loafers I found in her closet, but she's still wearing flip-flops, plus the faded jeans. She's changed the tee-shirt, though, to a loose oxford-blue "dress" shirt. Is it one of Frank's? Whatever. She looks great, of course.

Laura joins us and plops down on a chaise, feigning drama-queen exhaustion. She's just home from nanny-duty with the entitled, bratty McCann sisters, who aren't quite old enough for sleep-away camp.

"Juliana, Laura should be getting combat pay for this job," I say, chuckling. Every day my niece shares new stories of Lifestyles of the Hyper-Rich and Over-the-Top. "How'd it go today, kiddo?"

"Aunt Ronnie, they're worse than *The Real Housewives of New Jersey*!" she exclaims.

"Laura." Juliana leans forward. "I have to hear all about how your charges behave worse than *Real Housewives*." I observe warmth in her eyes as she looks at Laura. Am I witnessing a thaw in this goddess-beauty?

"Okay. Listen to this," Laura says. "Mrs. McCann found the girls some really cute fake Louis Vuitton bags from a street vendor when she was in the city today."

"How adorable," I answer.

"What a nice mother," Juliana adds.

"Wait." Laura holds up her hands. "You haven't heard the story part. Tiffany and Brittany grabbed the purses from their mom without saying thank you, checked them very closely, and then threw them on the ground."

"What?" Juliana and I respond in unison.

"Those princesses could tell the bags were fakes—they looked pretty good to me—and they demanded their mother give them the real thing." Laura shakes her head. "I wanted to strangle them."

"Laura, do they speak to you the same way they speak to their mother?" I ask.

My niece waves me off and sips her drink. "That's not the end of it, Aunt Ronnie."

"How could it get any worse?" Juliana smiles. She seems to like my niece. Or is that because Laura is Frank's daughter, and acting as though she likes Laura is strategically smart? *Don't be such a cynic, Ronnie. Control your inner bitch.*

"Well, it got worse." Laura rolls her eyes and says to me, "You know, Aunt Ronnie, how Mrs. McCann has been making plans to take the girls to Nantucket for a week—

you've heard me talk about it because I get a break then, too." She pumps her fist. "Yea!"

"Go on," I urge her.

"Well, she chats about it, and Brittany and Tiffany have another meltdown."

"Nooo." I smile at my niece's latest nanny war story.

"How could Nantucket be a bad thing?" Juliana asks, taken aback.

"Well, it is—if you're Brittany and Tiffany and want to go to Disney World," Laura answers.

"Disney World?" Juliana exclaims. "I always wanted to go there as a kid."

"Well, the girls recently went to a party and received a Disney World luxury guide by some expert as one of their party favors, and now that's all they want to do. They *only* want to stay in the best hotels, have a limo drive them around, and book the VIP Guide Service so they can do more things." Laura pauses to catch her breath.

"That's it?" I smile.

"Hardly." Laura's eyes flash disbelief. "They want their mom to book them the most expensive Castle Package of Princess Perfect treatments that turns little girls into princesses at almost two-hundred dollars each. They *told*, not *asked*, Mrs. McCann to take them on a Disney fireworks cruise. And they practically turned blue in the face demanding their mother make reservations for them at Cinderella's Royal Table."

"What's that?" I ask, trying not to laugh.

"That's a meal where they meet all the Disney princesses," Laura snaps. "Sorry, Aunt Ronnie. I get so mad at how spoiled those girls can be. Mrs. McCann lets them push her around."

"Wow," Juliana sighs. "You can do all those things at Disney World?" Her face glows. "Sign me up."

"Yeah, you really can do all those things," Laura answers. "I saw the luxury guidebook myself. Do you believe it?"

"Well, I understand. When I was ten, I wanted to go to Disney World more than anything." Juliana has a slightly dreamy look on her face. "But my mother said we couldn't afford it. It broke my heart."

OK. Wait a minute. Now I'm back to thinking about Scranton Gang member Bobby Taylor and all those hang-up calls, which seemed to have stopped today, by the way. Didn't the police say in one of the 1987 newspaper articles that the Scranton Gang tried to go south to Orlando, to Disney World? And didn't Joe Taylor tell me the same thing about Teresa?

I discreetly study Juliana's face for any sign of Teresa in the bank surveillance photo published in the newspaper. She's in her late thirties, and I subtract twenty-five years. She could have been thirteen in 1987.

Spit it out, Ronnie. Pay attention to your suspicions on this. It's really time to leave behind any delusions you've continued to entertain that Teresa might possibly be a friend or cousin of Juliana's. The truth has been staring you in the face the whole time, and you've known it deep inside. It's simple. My big brother has fallen head over heels for Teresa Gonzalez—the gun-toting Teresa Gonzalez of the Scranton Gang. Wow.

My heart pounds. I guess it's pretty obvious that this refined creature sitting before me and the teen Scranton bank robber I read about are one and the same. Still, I have nothing concrete to go on, yet. Again, I tell myself that I don't want to upset Frank with what he'll consider to be a wild theory on my part, especially since I don't really have any proof. My brother does deserve some happiness after Joanie's death.

Asking Juliana, who's pretty much a stranger, directly, "Hey, are you by any chance a formerly armed, law-breaking juvenile delinquent?" is also not an option right this minute. That would send her straight for the hills, and I'd never get to the truth. I'll have to push ahead cautiously until I'm sure of the facts.

~~~~~

I sink into my most comfortable upholstered chair with my tablet and view old 1990s commercials for Disney World on YouTube. Watching these ads from twenty years before, I imagine what it would have been like for Teresa Gonzalez to arrive in Orlando at that time. She may have been a convicted juvenile offender, but she was still a kid like any other. With Disney World at the top of her to-do list, she probably believed if she could just get there, she might change her life and make everything better. Am I a romantic, an optimist, or what?

Did Teresa thumb her way down to Florida?—a scary proposition that would make every mother shudder. Did she turn up unannounced on the doorstep of Carmela Suarez, her friend from the group home? Or did she first go to Disney World? Did she even have any money to get around? I think about Teresa navigating a new town at the age of sixteen in the days before cell phones, the Internet, and easy access to information.

I look at a school picture of Teresa that Will Benson got through his social worker contact in Pennsylvania. And even though her dark hair hides a lot of her face, from what I can see she looks like any other normal, pretty teenager at that time. Do I detect a resemblance to Juliana? Could be. Hard to say.

I navigate the online Disney World job site and click onto Housekeeping. I read the application page and think about Teresa wandering around Disney World to find the employment office. I imagine her filling out a paper application in the waiting room. Was she nervous? Probably.

I have to hand it to Teresa—or Juliana, if that's who she is now. It definitely took a lot of guts to run away from the group home, hitchhike her way south, show up on a doorstep to ask someone who was probably simply an acquaintance for a place to crash, and then talk her way into a job at Disney. If she made her way from there into the life that my brother's girlfriend has today, well, more power to her.

~~~~~

The dark-haired teenager sticks her thumb out from the side of the highway. A school-sized backpack, her only belonging, sits on the ground next to her feet. She nervously looks at the passing cars, biting a fingernail on her nonthumbing hand.

A metallic blue van slows down, but she gets one look at the two men inside, grabs her backpack and takes off as fast as she can, away from the van. She stays near the highway and runs against the traffic.

A greasy-haired guy leans out the van window laughing and yelling to her, "Catch you next time, bitch." They drive away. He looks like Jimmy, who attacked me in the alley behind the Moosic Motel.

Then another vehicle pulls up. The girl cautiously walks up to peek in, and the driver swings the door open. "Come on. You can't stand out here by yourself. It's dangerous." The voice is kind and familiar.

The girl looks in and I can see, too. It's Tommy, my son, smiling and beckoning the girl to safety. She climbs inside.

Then, out of nowhere, the blue van races up from behind and rear-ends Tommy's car, pushing him and his passenger off the road.

I bolt upright in bed. Another one of my bizarre dreams. They are definitely on the upswing since menopause hit five years before.

I look at my clock. Ugh. Three-forty-five a.m. My head drops back on my pillow. My eyes stay wide open. What a drag.

Next thing I know, I'm online booking a flight to Orlando. I need to find out more. Kind of nuts, I guess.

CHAPTER FOURTEEN

Strolling past the iconic Cinderella Castle in the Magic Kingdom, I think back fifteen years to bringing Tommy, Brooke, and Jessica to Disney World. Tommy, fourteen at the time, was almost too old to be excited about going on this trip, or so he thought. But Disney World seduced him just as much as it did nine-year-old Brooke and six-year-old Jess.

As I walk by a cluster of little girls showering Snow White with adoration, I envision a sixteen-year-old Teresa standing here, watching them. Did she imagine herself portraying Snow White, or better yet, Cinderella, also surrounded by adoring little girls? Her cousin, Joe Taylor, did say she was great with kids in her pre-Scranton Gang days. What exactly were Teresa's dreams once she landed at Disney World?

I look around and shake my head. What am I doing following this phantom girl all the way to Florida? Even my niece, who unknowingly started me down this road, would think I'm nuts.

Hey, professional P.I. Will Benson didn't think I was so crazy when I called him from the airport early this morning to share my suspicion that Juliana Wentworth and Teresa Gonzalez are one and the same. He did agree with me that I should gather proof before speaking with my brother.

I hop on the monorail for a ten-thirty meeting with an assistant manager at Disney's Contemporary Resort hotel. This happens to be where the kids and I stayed when we were here. We liked it because it's conveniently close to the Cinderella Castle, the gateway to the theme park.

Anyway, even though Will wasn't happy to learn that I was on my way to Orlando, he did get in touch with a former private eye pal down here who's now senior management in Disney World security. Will's buddy says this assistant manager, a Linda Alvarez, started out in housekeeping twenty-some years previously and worked her way up. He also told Will that everybody says she's friendly and always knew a lot of her fellow employees. The security guy made a call so that I could meet her. Maybe she'll remember Teresa.

I walk into Chef Mickey's, one of the hotel restaurants, and the hostess directs me to an attractive woman in a navy pantsuit with a brunette bob who gives me a small wave. We introduce ourselves and order coffee as Mickey Mouse, Donald Duck, Goofy, Minnie Mouse, and Pluto meander around the restaurant chatting it up with the guests.

Linda Alvarez is the epitome of low-keyed corporate confidence. She's sociable and professional, phrasing her words precisely. I've always been interested in the paths women take to succeed in life, so I ask her a few questions about herself and working in this fantasy world for children. Linda gives me the broad strokes—her start in housekeeping twenty-two years before and her hard work and steady progression through the ranks to her current position at this hotel.

I glance behind her as another sleek monorail whisks by. "Linda..." I shift my gaze back to her. "I'm trying to find someone who may have a connection to my family. She came to Orlando some twenty-plus-years ago, and she also got a job in housekeeping here at Disney World."

"OK." She looks at me for a long beat. "Any more details?" She chuckles. "Disney World was much smaller then, but a lot of us were still working in housekeeping at the numerous hotels at the time."

"She wanted to be close to the Cinderella Castle in the Magic Kingdom Theme Park," I say. "And Disney's Contemporary Resort is the closest hotel, so I figured I'd start here." I pull out the school picture and slide it across the table to Linda. "Her name was Teresa Gonzalez, but she may have changed it."

"Why would she do that?" Linda asks.

"Because she ran away and probably didn't want to be found." I add, "Plus she was underage and needed a job."

Linda studies the picture, and a slow smile plays around the corners of her mouth. "I'd already been cleaning guestrooms for about a year when Terry started. And you're right. She worked in this hotel. We both worked here."

A waitress refills our coffee, and I ask, "Terry? Teresa?"

"She was Terry Jones, not Teresa Gonzalez." Linda smiles.

"She changed her last name, too? She must have had phony papers." I shake my head. "And really wanted a fresh start."

"Sounds like it." Linda hands back the photograph. "How old was she at the time?"

"Probably sixteen," I answer. "How'd it go for her here?"

"I remember she was a tough kid, but she kept her head low and worked really hard. She had a great attitude—"

"Disney World was her dream come true," I say. "That's what I heard, anyway."

"So that may explain why this kid was so happy changing beds for two years," Linda answers.

"Where did Teresa—I mean, Terry, live?" I ask.

"She knew another girl who worked here, and I think she lived with that girl's family, at least in the beginning." Linda pauses, thinking back. "Carmela, Carmela Suarez in laundry services. Her family had an apartment in Orlando."

I nod in agreement. "I believe Carmela Suarez was Terry's contact down here—"

"You already seem to know a lot about this mystery person Teresa," she interrupts, "...who may have a connection to your family." Her amused expression tells me she's not exactly buying my story. I sigh and glance again behind Linda as another monorail whisks by. Damn, I've got to learn to hold back more of what I know as I talk to people.

Linda smiles. "Hey, take it easy. Dave in security says his friend in New Jersey vouches for you." Her voice is kind. "You must have a good reason." I look into her eyes with gratitude.

"Carmela still works at Disney World, by the way," she says. "Just like me."

"Hope she's not washing sheets and towels twenty years later," I quip.

"No." Linda laughs. "These days Carmela is a Disney's PhotoPass photographer. She often hangs out around the Cinderella Castle taking pictures of guests in the park."

"What about Terry Jones? Anything else you can tell me about her?" I ask. "What was she like?"

"What I remember about Terry is that she learned as much as she could from everybody around her," Linda says. "It was as if she was on a self-improvement mission."

I'm not really surprised. "What do you mean?" I probe.

"You know, trying to better the way she spoke, her manners, her grooming. Plus, she was really good with people," Linda adds. "She was a quick study and reliable. It paid off for her."

"How so?" I finish my second cup of coffee.

"First, she auditioned to portray one of the Disney Character Look-alikes—"

"You mean one of the fairy tale characters around the Cinderella Castle?" I think back to earlier, watching Snow White surrounded by a gaggle of girls.

"Yes. I don't remember which character, but she did that for a while. I guess a couple of years."

"After that, she must have been about twenty," I interject.

"I guess that would make sense. Then a spot opened up at the front desk of this hotel. Terry applied and got the job," Linda says. "I remember she worked at the desk for four or five years and did great at it."

I do some quick math and realize Teresa/Terry could have been working the front desk while I visited here with my kids and their friends. "So, Terry did that job until she was around twenty-five?"

Linda shrugs. "I don't really know much about Terry's life then, because I was in night school studying the hospitality business and working in reservations by day. So at that point I didn't see as much of her as I did during our years together in housekeeping."

I try to pay for our coffee, but Linda intercepts the bill and quickly signs for it. "I do remember a man once showed up at the front desk and started hassling her. He was bad news. Somebody from home, I think," she says. "Come to think of it, she showed up one day with several large bruises on her arm."

"You think he pushed her and she fell?" I ask.

"I remember they looked like hand imprints as if someone might have grabbed her," Linda says. "We were having lemonade, sitting outside in the sun during a break. She took off her jacket, and I saw the marks on her arm. You could see she had forgotten about them for a moment, but then she quickly put her jacket back on to cover them up.

"Did he get her fired?" I ask.

"No. I don't know how Terry got rid of him, but, as I said, she was tough. She figured out a way," Linda tells me. "After that I kind of lost track of her."

I'm dying to show Linda the picture of Juliana at the cocktail party, but then my story about why I'm here would totally fall apart. I'd have to explain too much, and she might caution Carmela Suarez not to talk to me.

I thank Linda for her help as we walk out of the restaurant. In the lobby, she pulls out her cell phone, speed-dials a number and asks if Carmela Suarez is working today and where. She clicks off.

"Just as I thought. Carmela's taking pictures near Cinderella's Castle. She'll be easy to find, and I'll call and tell her to expect you. Maybe she can fill in some blanks about what's happened to Terry."

We say goodbye, and Linda leaves. I stand a moment and watch two young women working behind the front desk of the hotel. They're dressed stylishly and professionally, and they're beautifully groomed, with understated make-up. One has her hair pulled back sleekly, and the other has a great shoulder-length haircut. Most importantly, they handle themselves well with the guests at the front desk.

I imagine Teresa Gonzalez, now Terry Jones, in their shoes more than fifteen years ago. In the span of four years, from age sixteen to twenty, she'd already substantially pulled herself up in life from the group home in Scranton as a juvenile offender. What a turnaround. Kind of like her cousin, Joe Taylor.

CHAPTER FIFTEEN

I stroll around the plaza in front of the castle and spot a stocky, jowly brunette in blue shorts, white shirt, and a khaki photographer's vest, snapping pictures of a family sitting on the castle steps. She finishes, and I call out, "Ms. Suarez." She walks over to me with her camera, looking worried.

"Hi, I'm Ronnie Lake. Linda Alvarez at the Contemporary Resort told me I'd find you here." I reach out my hand to shake.

She does so hesitantly. "I'm Carmela Suarez." Her face still shows concern. "Linda says you want to know about Terry Jones."

Well, OK, let's not waste any time with friendly get-to-know-yous. "Right," I say and come to the point. "I understand you two came down from Scranton twenty-plus years ago and that she stayed with your family in Orlando for a while. I'm hoping you might know where she is these days and can help me find her."

Carmela's body language is closed and tense. "Before I talk about Terry, who are you?" she asks. She's not hostile, just concerned. "I mean besides your name."

"I live in New Jersey, and there may be a connection between Terry and my family," I say, trying on purpose this time to keep things vague. Plus, I'd rather not concoct some farfetched story if I can avoid it.

I make sure my tone is friendly. "It sounds as though she turned her life around when she worked here at Disney—"

"I hope you did *not* go into detail with Ms. Alvarez about Scranton, you know, Terry and me," Carmela interrupts. "I've worked here almost twenty-four years, and I have a perfect record—"

"Hold it—"

"We both wanted a fresh start—"

I put my hands up to signal her to stop. "I didn't tell Ms. Alvarez anything about your history back in Scranton. That's in the past, and it seems you've been a good employee at Disney. Terry, too, when she was here." I smile. "Do you have time to talk for a few minutes?"

Carmela exhales. "I can take a ten-minute break." Her body relaxes noticeably. "First, Ms. Lake, Terry and I weren't friends or anything up in Scranton. We didn't do this run-away-to-Disney thing together. I left a month before she did when I aged out of the system there."

"Please call me Ronnie," I insist.

She sits on the castle steps and motions for me to do the same. "Terry heard me talking about my aunt in Orlando when we were still stuck in that group home. I moved down here the minute I turned eighteen, just wanting to stay out of trouble. All of a sudden she shows up one day at my aunt's apartment with a black eye and a fat lip."

"Oh my god," I say. "What happened to her?"

"The last ride she hitched, the guy who drove her into Orlando…well, it turned out it wasn't a free ride." Carmela shakes her head. "She resisted, and he beat her up, but she got away. Next thing, she's at our front door asking if she can crash with us until she gets on her feet."

Carmela looks at me with exasperation written all over her face. "Terry was just a kid, and she had no money. If she got picked up by the police, I was worried my name would come up, and that would cause trouble for my aunt. We took her in."

She fiddles with her camera and continues this amazing story. "Her beautiful face healed, of course, and she got a job at Disney in housekeeping. Actually, except for the attack when she first hitched down here and then Bobby Taylor turning up at the front desk some years later, Terry pretty much led a charmed life in Florida."

Carmela stops and quickly corrects herself. "Don't get me wrong, Ms. La—I mean, Ronnie. Terry worked hard. Even when they gave her the grubbiest jobs in housekeeping that everybody gets when they first start, she put a smile on her face and did what was asked of her. Terry earned every promotion she ever got."

"Carmela, you said *except for Bobby Taylor turning up.*" I lean in. "What did he want?"

"Money, and who knows what else," she says. "I guess he always tried to copy Terry. So if Terry wanted to live in

Florida, then he did, too. At least that's what she told me."
She pulls a cloth out of her vest and wipes a smear off the
camera's viewfinder. Then she looks at her watch. "In the
beginning, Bobby worked for a while on a fishing boat
until he got fired, of course. Then he disappeared. We
didn't see him anymore for years. Good riddance. What a
loser that guy was."

Not just a loser, but a bully, or so he seemed to me.
"She must have been shocked to see him turn up again," I
say. "How'd she get rid of him the second time?"

Carmela shakes her head. "Don't have a clue, but then
one day he stopped coming around. You know, in the
beginning she was a rough street kid, even the way she
talked. She scared most of us in the group home in
Scranton."

Carmela sort of snorts and giggles at the same time. "So
even though she was polished by the time she worked at the
hotel front desk, I'm sure she could still handle Bobby and
convince him to leave town."

She pauses a moment glancing away, and then she
looks back at me. "Even though I'm pretty certain he
knocked her around sometimes. But don't quote me. I
never actually saw it. And she never admitted it, maybe
because he was family—you know, his being her cousin,
and all."

"What do you mean—knocked around—and why do
you think that, Carmela?" I steeple my fingers and tap my
chin.

"Like when she first turned up on my aunt's doorstep
with that fat lip from the guy she hitched with—well, she

acted as if it was no big deal. She went straight for the ice for her lip and eye, as if she was an expert on getting beat up or something." Carmela's expression turns to one of disgust. "She made some comment that this guy wasn't any worse than Bobby. So, you know, it sounded like Bobby had hit her, too, but that was all she'd say."

"Anything else about Bobby that made you suspicious?" I sit back on the steps. Carmela was opening new vistas on Teresa for me.

"Well, after he turned up that second time, I remember seeing black and blue marks on Terry's arm." Carmela shrugs. "I don't know. He may have been physically stronger, but my impression was that she was mentally tougher than Bobby. You know, like she could apply some kind of psychological pressure and force him to leave."

I think back to Linda Alvarez's similar notion about Terry, and I nod. Then I look around the plaza in front of the castle and watch chance encounters between kids and Snow White and Belle from *Beauty and the Beast* turn into photo-ops for the parents. "I understand Terry first moved from housekeeping to working as a Disney character, so she must have done a good job cleaning up her act," I finally say.

"Yeah, she did, and she landed the Snow White job." Carmela smiles for the first time. "She really wanted to be Cinderella, but she was happy playing Snow White for a couple of years. She also moved out of my aunt's apartment and got her own place with two roommates. Then she applied for a front desk job at the Contemporary Resort, and she landed it."

"She did well working that new job?" I ask.

"She did more than well." Carmela gestures toward an adorable, tousle-haired three-year-old girl tugging on Belle's costume, and she quickly snaps several candid shots.

"Be right back," Carmela says to me and waves to the smiling parents of the little girl, who is now hugging Belle. The photographer takes a few more shots and then scans the parents' Disney's PhotoPass ID number so they can access the pictures later. As they scoop up their daughter for the next fun adventure, Carmela returns and picks up where she left off.

"What you have to understand about Terry—remember, she *was* the leader of the Scranton Gang—is that for such a tough kid, she loved this Cinderella Castle, because she wanted a Cinderella story for herself."

"How so, Carmela?"

"First, she wasn't waiting for any Prince Charming to come around. No, Terry was going to make her own Cinderella story. Second, she couldn't pay for school, but she read books and newspapers all the time and took classes whenever she could at the Disney World learning centers here."

Carmela's expression is now one of admiration. "Terry studied fashion magazines and changed her look to be more like a lady even though she didn't have much money to spend."

"That's quite something," I say.

"She even worked on the way she spoke by listening and copying other people, so that she would sound more polite." Carmela chortles. "To look at her and listen to her a couple of years after she got here, you would have never imagined her as some tough juvie kid out of Scranton."

An image of Juliana comes to mind. "I wonder where she got that urge to improve herself."

I notice an adorable set of toddler twins with their slightly older sister trying to herd them toward Minnie Mouse. I nod at Carmela. "Photo op," I say and gesture toward the kids.

She raises her camera, clicks away, and then walks over to the dad to scan his Disney's PhotoPass ID number. Carmela comes back and sits on the steps. "Terry told me somebody when she was very young inspired her to reach for a better life." She rests her camera in her lap. "She never told me who it was."

"Hmmm. An inspiring mystery person who changed her life." Who could that have been, I wonder. "So where'd she go after the front desk? Another job here?"

"No. After about five years at the front desk, Terry decided to move to New York." She catches my look of surprise and laughs. "I know. She grabbed me for coffee one day to tell me she was leaving. This woman who used to bring her kids here every year and always stayed at the Contemporary Resort was impressed by how well Terry did her job at the front desk."

"She offered her a job as a nanny?" I ask.

"No way," Carmela says. "Turns out this woman ran a private club in Manhattan that a lot of big-shot businessmen, athletes, and celebrities belonged to. She watched Terry handle a very difficult VIP one morning and noticed how calm she stayed." Carmela again checks her watch. I guess we're okay. She goes on. "This lady was amazed by how Terry turned around what could have been an embarrassing situation for the hotel."

Carmela then snaps a few more pictures of kids and Disney characters. "The lady thought Terry had a lot of potential, and with some training would be great at handling difficult celebrities. So she gave Terry her card and told her to call if she needed a job in New York City. And the rest is history. After giving two months' notice at the hotel, Terry went north."

"How old was Terry, when she left?" I ask, doing a quick calculation on my fingers.

"Twenty-five," Carmela answers. "I remember, because she said she was celebrating her quarter-century birthday by moving to the Big Apple."

I wish I could show Carmela the picture of Juliana at our party and definitively connect the dots between Teresa and my brother's new girlfriend. But Carmela might still be way too jumpy, and I need more information from her.

"Do you remember the name of the woman who offered Terry the job, or maybe the name of the club?" I pull out my phone to enter the contact information. "It might help me find her."

But Carmela shakes her head. "Can't remember the name of the club, just that Terry said it was exclusive and lots of celebs belonged," she says. "Don't know the name of the lady either—sorry—but she was definitely the boss."

"Let's trade emails and phone numbers in case you remember something later," I say, and she fishes out her card for me. I enter her information into my phone and text her my email.

"Did you and Terry stay in touch?" I ask.

"Like I said, Ronnie, Terry and I were never actually close." Carmela gets up from the Cinderella Castle steps. "She did send a couple of postcards from New York right after she moved, but I haven't heard from her or seen her since."

Now what? Is this Manhattan club even around anymore? Where do I start? I groan.

"Hey, Ronnie, are you OK?" Carmela asks.

"I ate something weird last night," I fib. "I have a little bit of an upset stomach." Which I do at the mere thought of all the work ahead once I'm back in New Jersey trying to track down a private club that was big during the dot-com era and might or might not still be around. But if I get stuck, thank god I can ask Will for help.

CHAPTER SIXTEEN

"I can imagine the three of you as kids running around this place, playing hide-and-seek," Juliana says. "You all had so many good places to hide." Her tone isn't exactly cozy, but she's OK.

She and I stand together in the Meadow Farm cutting garden next to some purple phlox and coral-colored coneflowers, looking toward the house. I ask, "And where would you hide if you had been a child here?"

Juliana gives me a funny look and glances around. "Let's see." She puts her finger to her chin and then points. "How about the tree house near the side terrace?"

I look at her, surprised. Frank must have told her about our secret tree house hidden in the low branches of that huge leafy sugar maple.

Juliana has a twinkle in her eye as she gazes toward the tree that now only holds broken boards, the last remnants of our childhood hideaway. "Growing up here must have been wonderful..." She returns to selecting and snipping the stems of several of the phlox and coneflowers.

I lean against the stone wall of the cutting garden. "Frank told you about us as kids, huh? Even Peter?"

"Well, not much about Peter. Only that you haven't seen him in years," she says. "That's very sad."

"Yeah. It seems every family has some kind of drama. How about you?" I ask. "Do you see any of your family often? I remember you said you're an only child…"

Juliana carefully lays the flowers she's cut in a large, flat-bottomed basket. "Not all of us are so fortunate to come from a family like yours, Ronnie. That's a gift of God." I hear a touch of sadness in her voice.

"Where does your family live?" I ask. "Where did you grow up—"

"Questions, questions, questions." Her tone becomes guarded. "Why do you ask so many questions? Ronnie, what is it you really want to know?"

"Just friendly curiosity—"

"Oh, look," Juliana interrupts. "There's Frank!" She beams and waves to him.

He signals us to come on over. "Rita just made this iced tea," he calls out, holding a pitcher.

"You go ahead," Juliana urges me. "I want to finish up here, and then I'll come." She moves to another section of the garden to examine the multi-colored cosmos and zinnias.

I walk across the small field and join Frank on the terrace. He pours a glass for me, and together we watch Juliana. It's a lovely scene, this graceful woman working her way through the flower bed with her shears and gently adding blooms to others already in the basket.

"She looks at home here." Frank sips his iced tea with an expression of, dare I say, bliss on his face. Uh-oh.

"She's the perfect guest," I throw in quickly.

"Ronnie?"

"Yes, Frank."

His voice is quiet. "What if Jules wasn't always a guest?"

"She's definitely a triple-A guest over there, cutting flowers in Joanie's garden." I'm trying to stall what I think may be inevitable, and I keep my voice soft, too. "You always loved when Joanie cut fresh flowers from her garden. So it's very thoughtful of Juliana." Okay, so I mentioned Joanie twice in my little speech, as a reminder.

"Juliana is thoughtful, Ronnie," my brother says.

"That's great, Frank." I suppose if I don't want to anger him, I should bite my tongue. But I just can't help myself. "This is such a nice, but *new* relationship for you. And given time, I'm sure the two of you will get to know each other even better."

"We already know each other well," he says, his tone taking on an edge.

I pick my next words carefully. "I mean *really* know each other, Frank."

"What are you trying to say, Ronnie?" my brother asks. I think he's struggling to keep it civil. "Just spit it out, Sis."

I do, spit it out. "Do you know her family? Her friends? What do you know about her world? Her history?"

"Well, she doesn't have children—"

"Are you making serious plans with Juliana?" I ask, managing to keep my voice low and glancing over at the woman in question, who is fortunately still focused on the flowers. "Like spend-the-rest-of-your-life-together plans?"

He laughs. "Ronnie, we're not there yet...but I can foresee a time—"

"Have you thought about the financial consequences of marriage?" I blurt out. "Have you talked to her about money, or a pre-nup—" Ouch. Nothing subtle there. I've really stuck my foot in it this time.

"Ronnie! Enough!" His voice is sharp. "You certainly know how to be a spoilsport."

"OK. Keep it down, Frank. You're right. I'm sorry," I answer. "But I'm thinking about your children, the kids you had with Joanie—"

"That's it. We're not discussing this any further." My big brother gets out of his chair. "I'm fortunate to have met Juliana. Why can't you just leave it alone? You've always been this way, sticking your nose where it doesn't belong. Now back off." He walks directly into the house.

I glance over at Juliana, who has stopped snipping flowers and looks toward our terrace. I toast her with my iced tea glass, smiling at her, and all I can do is hope she didn't overhear the exchange with my brother.

She nods and goes back to her flowers. Does the nod mean she heard Frank and me or she didn't hear us? But something familiar nags at the edges of my memory as I watch her. Just like the first evening when I met her at cocktails. I can't put my finger on it. Hmmm. I'm going to have to hurry my investigation so I can speak up, and then Frank will understand my caution.

CHAPTER SEVENTEEN

It's noon class now at the dojo. This time we practice with *tantos*, a word that always makes my mind flash on an image of the Indian character *Tonto* in *The Lone Ranger*. But no, this *tanto* is a wooden weapon carved to look like a dagger.

We spend the entire class working on disarming techniques. Since we switch partners every time we practice a different skill, I've worked with just about everyone in the room at this point.

Isabella *Sensei* demonstrates the next technique, *yokomenuchi gokyo* with Will Benson. When they finish, he turns toward me and bows. I smile as I return the bow, agreeing to train with him. His quiet charisma is appealing, making him way more attractive than any of the macho big-screen Hollywood martial arts stars out there. Focus, Ronnie!

I move toward Will with an attack intending to slice him diagonally across from one side of his head down the opposite side of his body with the pretend dagger. Rather than run for cover the way I myself would if someone came at me with a blade, Will quickly slides toward me and enters my space. As he does so, his arms come up as if he's beginning to raise a sword.

One of his hands nearly hits my face, but I jerk back in time to avoid being struck. At the same time, Will extends the edge of his other hand between the elbow and wrist of my knife-holding arm and stops my attack.

While I try to regain my balance, the hand that first went for my face now grabs the wrist of my hand grasping the dagger, so his two arms are crisscrossed. As Will turns his body one-hundred-eighty degrees, he continues to hold onto my wrist and then clasps his other hand securely behind my elbow. My body lunges forward and down from the force of his turn with my arm twisted and stretched out straight in front of him. Will continues to drive me all the way down to the mat face first and kneels beside me. Not so gracefully, I land on my stomach and just miss getting my face smashed in.

My outstretched arm holding the *tanto* now faces palm-up as Will lifts my elbow toward the ceiling to draw my arm upward, forcing the wrist he's gripping to bend at a ninety-degree angle, a position that can hurt like hell! I tap the mat as fast as possible, letting go of the *tanto*, which is obviously the point of the disarming technique, and he releases the pin.

I grunt and shake my wrist. "Need to talk to you after class, Will."

"Got more info for you, too, Ronnie." He smiles, and I try to smile also, still shaking my wrist.

At the car, he hands me a folder. "I've located the address of a woman on the outskirts of Scranton who may be Teresa Gonzalez's great-aunt. If you give me the go-ahead, I'll pay her a visit, try to find out more about Teresa. And Juliana."

"Let's wait on that." I quickly flip through the folder.

He eyes me suspiciously. "Ronnie, I hope you're not getting any smart ideas about checking this out on your own."

I widen my eyes in a way that I hope telegraphs *whatever*.

Will doesn't buy it. "Call me when you want to investigate or follow someone. You don't want to end up in another alley—"

"I may be thick-headed..." I put my hands on my hips and look at him, face to face, almost nose to nose. "...but I do try to learn from my mistakes, Will."

He raises his hands in surrender. "You're the boss."

"Damn straight, Will. Some things I can handle."

~~~~~

My GPS guides me to the address that Will gave me for the great-aunt, a Mrs. Consuelo Gonzalez de Torres. The street is lined with dilapidated clapboard houses on the hilly outskirts of Scranton—I'm getting to know this town way better than I ever intended.

Quietly sitting in the van I've again borrowed from Daniel, I reread Will's report on Mrs. de Torres. She's eighty-five, widowed for thirty years, and has been living in her tan house on this street for nearly fifty. She's the youngest sister of Teresa's grandfather, Manuel Gonzalez, who seems to have pulled his own disappearing act around the time Theresa was growing up.

Vanishing must be in the family genes—first her grandfather, Manuel; then her father, Tony, who, according to Joe Taylor, wasn't around as she grew up; later, her own runaway venture from the group home as Teresa; and now a possible vanishing act as Juliana with her threats of leaving the country if Bobby Taylor doesn't back off. I worry what that would do to my brother.

Warrior sits next to me, snoozing in the passenger seat. Suddenly his head pops up, and he alerts me with a whining sound. I look out to see an elderly, grey-haired woman locking her front door. Could this be *Tía* Connie from Juliana's phone call, the one I overheard in the library at Meadow Farm?

Mrs. de Torres carefully walks down the steps, grasping the banister with one hand and pushing something metal and flat with wheels ahead of her with the other. The metal shopping basket awkwardly clunks down, and when she gets to the bottom, she opens it up. She leans a little on the cart as she pushes it down the street. My guess is that she uses the thing like a walker to help her with her balance.

Telling Warrior to stay, I quietly exit the van to follow Mrs. de Torres at some distance. I hope my nondescript jeans and shirt plus hair stuffed under a baseball cap help me blend into the neighborhood.

The stooped octogenarian pushes her cart into a small bodega, and I enter, too, discreetly keeping an eye on her as she gathers provisions for the day. She chats warmly with various employees she seems to know well as she walks through the mini-mart, choosing bananas, grapes, and lettuce in the produce section, as well as sandwich meat at the deli counter. It doesn't take long for a small, friendly cluster of people to clog up the narrow aisle around Mrs. de Torres, eager to help her with her groceries.

The smell of fresh-baked bread permeates the air. Sure enough, as the group continues to advise her, Mrs. de Torres spends a little time selecting the very best loaf. I pull out my phone to pretend-read a text, and inconspicuously snap off a few pictures. A girl breaks away from the assembly and dashes through swinging doors to the back of the store, calling out to the elderly woman, "I'll check for you in the stock room, Mrs. de Torres."

I hear the girl yelling "Frankie!" in the back, as I tuck my phone again in my pocket and ladle soup into a carryout container. Wait a minute. Is she talking about the same Frankie as *Teresa & Frankie* on the scrap of paper in the dead bird's beak? The same as in Juliana warning Bobby Taylor to *stay away from Frankie*?

I wait impatiently while other people rush up, happy to see Mrs. de Torres. She asks them about family and whatever else is going on in their lives. They all treat her as a beloved friend.

Finally, the swinging doors fly open again and a gawky girl, all arms and legs, dashes through. My guess is she's twelve or thirteen, probably in seventh or eighth grade.

"Hi, *Tía* Connie!" she says to the old woman, and they hug. The girl takes Mrs. de Torres's arm. "Please let me help you."

Hold it. Is *this* Frankie? Well, she, not he (as I thought), and Juliana appear to be connected to the same *Tía* Connie. I quickly pull my phone out of my pocket again to supposedly read another text and cautiously snap off a few more shots of Connie, this time with the girl.

"My darling, I have everything I need, but thank you." Mrs. de Torres travels to the counter near the front and pays for her groceries while the budding teenager hovers around her *Tía*. I shuffle along, browsing. "Are you working hard, Francesca?" Mrs. de Torres asks, using, I'd assume, the girl's formal name.

"Absolutely, *Tía* Connie, and I love my summer job…" Francesca pushes Mrs. de Torres's cart out of the store for her while I quickly grab a newspaper and pay for it and my soup.

A man, probably the owner, calls out through the door, "Frankie, once you've helped your *Tía* on her way, please assist Jody with those boxes in the back."

I leave, too, as Francesca, I mean, Frankie gives her *Tía* Connie one more hug and says, "I'll be home in time for supper." She runs inside the store. "Coming, Mr. Sanchez," she hollers to her boss.

In a daze, I head in the same direction as Mrs. de Torres, continuing to shadow her. The whole time I've thought Frankie was a guy connected to the Scranton Gang twenty-five years ago. I've got to go somewhere quiet and process this discovery, and I've got to tell Will. In the meantime, I pretend to window shop whenever the elderly woman stops along the street.

I think about *accidentally* bumping into Mrs. de Torres, but I'm not sure what that would accomplish. What could I say that wouldn't trigger a phone call on her part to Juliana? And a call like that would (a) cause my investigation to blow apart before I'm ready; (b) motivate Juliana to grab Frankie and head for the hills; and/or, (c) even worse, really upset my brother.

Before I can do anything, we're back at Mrs. de Torres's house. I watch her struggle up the steps to her front door with the groceries and shopping cart and want to rush over to help the old woman. Fortunately, a neighbor steps in to give her a hand.

As I slide into the front seat of the van, Warrior gives me a huge yawn. I think about the gangly Francesca. What are she and Mrs. de Torres to each other? A niece who lives with her great- or great-great-aunt? And exactly how does Juliana fit into this picture, since Mrs. de Torres is her great-aunt, too?

This Frankie, or Francesca, could be the person I overheard Juliana speaking to in soothing tones on the phone in the library at Meadow Farm. As I drive away, I wonder why Juliana is so secretive about this part of her family.

I connect my iPod through the van's auxiliary jack and listen to a soulful Eric Clapton sing "River of Tears" in a sad, bluesy voice…and I think. And think.

The only thing I know for sure about Mrs. Consuelo Gonzalez de Torres is that she's the indisputable connection between Teresa's early years and Juliana's life today. It's more than a connection—Mrs. de Torres is just about proof that Juliana and Teresa are one and the same. Not quite, but almost.

Now an even more intriguing question. I absolutely saw a strong resemblance between the girl in the market and my brother's beautiful girlfriend, Juliana. Could Frankie be Juliana's daughter instead of just a niece or cousin? But she told my brother she has no children. Still, if the girl is her daughter, then I have to ask, who is the father?

Nah, not that slimy Bobby Taylor...couldn't be. At least I hope not.

CHAPTER EIGHTEEN

Has it already been fifteen-plus years since many of us thought we were so smart investing in those dot-com stocks? Then the bubble burst, and so much of that tech start-up paper-wealth amounted to very little in fact. We quickly learned we weren't so smart and could never know enough to avoid the downside. Fortunately, I'd invested only a little in that sector. These days, for me, a more realistic investment approach has become a part of my overall journey in taking charge of my life.

I stare at my computer wondering where to begin the search to track down Teresa Gonzalez, now Terry Jones, as she set out on the next chapter of her journey during that heady dot-com era—a journey I'm confident encourages her to evolve into Juliana.

I'm distracted though by my discovery that Frankie isn't a fellow Scranton Gang member from twenty-five years before. Also, that Frankie isn't a *he* (the way I assumed), but is a middle-school *she* living with a great-aunt in Pennsylvania. I call Will to update him on this salient fact and wind up leaving a message on his voicemail. Good. I'm happily able to dodge a dressing-down for following his lead into what could have been hazardous territory.

So back to Teresa, now Terry Jones. According to Carmela Suarez, Terry worked somewhere in the city at one of the high-end clubs where dot-com tycoons mixed with celebrities, athletes, and hedge fund managers. And I have one new piece of information since my trip to Orlando—an email from Carmela, who found an old postcard from Terry after she left Disney World for New York. She says Terry referred to her new boss as Adriana in the postcard and said that she loved her job. Carmela says she tried to track down Adriana's last name, but had no luck.

I spend considerable time online searching through the entries of high-end clubs in Manhattan and eliminate from my list any that opened after 1999. I wonder if the club where Terry worked is even in operation anymore. How many pages of Google will I have to comb through to hit pay dirt?

Finally, after three cups of coffee and a break with Warrior outside—bingo. A reference to an Adriana Cusco, the manager of Club Nucleus in Manhattan.

A different Google link leads me to an interesting profile on the club. Like many businesses servicing the new tech moguls of that era, Club Nucleus teetered on the brink of going under with the arrival of the dot-com bust—too many former tycoons could no longer afford the dues and services. Fortunately, one of its members, the CEO of a real company with genuine profits, came to the rescue and guided the club back to sound financial footing. The place has thrived ever since.

Switching to the club's website, I find a phone number to call for information on joining—how unusual. Rather than the typical hush-hush process of many exclusive clubs where you wait to be invited to join, here's one that reaches out for new members. Is it because the initiation and dues are so expensive that only a small number of people can afford to apply?

Instead of phoning the club directly, I call someone I know from the dinner party circuit out here who has the perfect profile to perhaps be a Club Nucleus member. Win Watson, an outrageously rich senior partner at investment bank Goldsmith Capital, is, I discover, actually a founding member of the club.

"Ronnie, my squash game just got cancelled," Win tells me. "You up for a spur-of-the-moment lunch at Club Nucleus? I'll even give you a tour."

Hmmm. Have to skip my Aikido class to make it, but yeah. "What time?" I say.

"How's 12:30?"

I check my watch. Just enough time to get ready and drive into the city. "See you then, Win! Thanks."

~~~~~

Club Nucleus comprises the first five floors of a sleek tower next to the High Line, an aerial greenway on the lower West Side that's my most recent favorite place in the city. The club's building is one of numerous architectural wonders that have popped up alongside this fabulous city park built on unused elevated railroad tracks. Its location near the also-trendy meat packing district almost makes me want to join Club Nucleus.

Turning off my phone and walking through the frosted glass doors of the building's entrance, I spot Win easily. He sprawls on a khaki-colored leather chair, texting on his phone, of all things. I raise my eyebrows. A lot of other members are also on phones, fingers flying. Oh well, different rules apply here.

Win looks up mid-text and motions me to give him a second. As I walk over, he quickly finishes and slides the phone into his pocket. "Ronnie, this works out perfectly!" He jumps up, wearing an elegant olive-colored bespoke suit, and engulfs me in a bear hug. "Marilyn sends her regards. Tried to get her to join us, but she's at a Met board meeting."

"Please send her my greetings in return." I can't help but glance around at the spectacular art hanging on the walls of the club's spacious entry.

We both turn to the clicking sound of tall heels coming down a floating stairway near one wall. There, we first see a pair of beautiful red-soled Louboutins descending the steps. Then, a black-haired woman with the perfect choppy haircut comes into full view. Exquisitely dressed in Armani, she looks like someone in charge and walks over to us in those amazing shoes, and I wonder if this club with this boss is where Juliana got her first yearning for these amazing black heels.

"Adriana!" Win calls out. "Come and meet my friend, Veronica Rutherfurd Lake." He turns to me. "Ronnie, I'd like you to meet the founding general partner and manager of Club Nucleus, Adriana Cusco." Her smile is spectacular, and we shake hands warmly.

Sitting in the dining room with Win and Adriana a few minutes later, I can't help but notice how many people around us are texting on their phones even right at their tables. A number of them are bold-face names who pop up regularly in *Vanity Fair*. At my club you'd get the evil eye from fellow members for breaking the no-phones-on-in-the-club rule, but the etiquette here appears to be different.

Win notices me noticing and grins. "Now tell the truth, Ronnie. This has got to beat the Colony Club."

"Well, it's very different from the Colony Club, but…" I emphasize, "…it's lovely here."

"Adriana, Ronnie's been a member of the Colony Club for years," he crows and turns to me. "Don't be shy, Ronnie. Now how many generations of Rutherfurds have been members? And isn't daughter, Brooke, a member, too?"

"Well, yes. But, Win, we're not here to talk about the Colony Club." I sip my iced tea and smile at Adriana. "I'd like to learn more about Club Nucleus."

She nods as I take another bite of my blood-orange salad. "Ah, Ronnie, I have so much to tell you about our special club."

"If this amazing salad is any indication of the quality of the club cuisine—"

"It is. Our chef, Danny Irvine, trained with the best in France, and came to us after five years at the Battery Park

Grill." Adriana tears a piece from her bread. "Need I say more?" She dips the piece in olive oil.

"I love the design of the place, from when you first enter the club to sitting here in this dining room." I put down my fork and gaze again at the walls. "It's the perfect backdrop for all these incredible paintings. That one over there of the flickering white candle—that's got to be a Gerhard Richter."

"Good eye, Ronnie." Win laughs.

I wink at him. "If I remember correctly, it's one of his photo paintings, similar to the one hanging in your screening room at home, Win." I drink my iced tea. "Remember? You gave me a wonderful tutorial on the artist not long after you bought it." He clicks my glass and laughs some more.

"And that's exactly the point, Ronnie," Adriana says. "Many of our members have multiple homes, and Club Nucleus strives to be similar to the one you prefer most, whether it references the paintings on the walls or your favorite tea or cocktail. And our members seem to feel we succeed. Plus they get to see all their friends, many of whom are at the pinnacle of their professions."

The three of us glance around the dining room, and Adriana continues, "It's a discerning crowd, and we offer many services."

"How about privacy and security?" I ask. "Why don't I see paparazzi camped outside this club? And why aren't there others, like, say, Occupy Wall Street-types, threatening to break down those frosted front doors—"

"That reminds me," Win interrupts. "Adriana, thanks for the name and number of the security firm."

"Glad to have helped," she tells him. "A number of our members have been happy with Elite Ops Protection."

"Hold it. Stop," I say. "Win, what are you talking about? A security firm? And who is Elite Ops Protection? Are you having problems at your office?"

"Goldberg Capital's got that covered," he answers me. "I'm having a risk profile drawn up for the house."

"In Willowbrook? You can't be." Despite a hike in robberies recently in my own neck of the woods, I'm genuinely taken aback. "You must be kidding."

"No, Ronnie," he answers. "It'll only be a matter of time before the ninety-nine-percent crowd discovers how many of us Goldberg partners have bought places in Willowbrook."

"But we're in the country, Win, living on farms." An arm reaches in to remove my empty salad plate. "Thank you," I say to the attractive young man who clears the table. "Win, we're not robber barons. These people don't care about us."

"Not so with us at Goldberg Capital, Ronnie. The ninety-nine-percenters and the old Occupy Wall Street folks hate us—a lot." His phone vibrates and he pulls it out. "Excuse me for a moment, ladies. Got a guy flying in for a meeting." Adriana and I watch him quickly answer his text.

Win looks up. "Ronnie, you know how the press has vilified Goldberg Capital." He catches my incredulous look. "I'm not saying that some of it hasn't been justified, but we're not as bad as they make us out to be," he says.

The corners of my mouth twitch, with me trying to suppress a grin. Even I've seen the headlines about Department of Justice fines handed out to Goldberg *et al*. A slap on the wrist, according to the *Times*.

"Whatever." Win chuckles and goes on. "If these people decide to visit the New Jersey countryside looking for us at home, then I need to protect my family."

"Win, that's astonishing." I shake my head. "I can't believe they'd travel more than fifty miles to bother you and other Goldberg partners in our area."

CHAPTER NINETEEN

Win dashes out because of a sudden emergency at the office, leaving me at the table with Adriana. The nice young man who cleared our table moments before now pours coffee and then disappears.

"Adriana, our waiter looks as if he could be a graduate student at NYU or Columbia." We're not that far from New York University, in fact, so I might be on target. I lighten my coffee by adding milk. I hope this isn't cream. Oh well.

"Good guess. Timothy's working on his MBA at Columbia." Adriana adds sugar to her own coffee, which surprises me. My reaction must show on my face, because she comments, "One of my, I like to think, few vices...sugar in my coffee. Anyway, Timothy is like many of our young wait staff. Here for a number of years, getting an elite education, building a professional network while serving our members. The arrangement works well for everyone."

Nice topic for what I want to discuss with her. "Your staff must play a huge part in why the club is thriving," I say, working my way to the subject of Terry.

"Our team is our number one asset." Adriana sips her coffee. "We offer many services to our members. Lectures, live music, a well-stocked library and wine cellar, personal training, and so on. Our people are key to the superb quality of service we offer the members. Now, Ronnie, how about a tour?"

Adriana walks me through the fitness area on the third floor and introduces me to the trainers, massage therapists, and a facialist. As we continue upstairs to see the rooms where members can stay overnight, I decide the time is right to dive in with my questions.

"Adriana, do you remember someone named Terry Jones or maybe Gonzalez? She may have worked for you years ago, when you first opened." I follow my hostess down a bright hall. "I heard she was terrific."

Adriana stops suddenly, and I almost crash into her. Her face lights up for a moment, and then she quickly shifts into neutral as we enter a bedroom. "You're right—it must be almost fifteen years ago that she worked here. How do you know Terry?"

I'm on tricky territory yet again. "Well, it's not that I know Terry directly. She's connected to a family member, so I've heard a lot about her," I fib and look around. "Are all the rooms quite this fabulous?"

"Yes, and they're all different." Adriana sits in a deep, cushy chair and signals me to do the same. "Terry Jones, now that's a name out of the past. You know, I first spotted her when she was working at Disney World. I was there with my children, and I knew right away that she had what it takes."

"You already had children fifteen years ago? You look way too young, Adriana," I remark. "How old are your kids?" I don't want her to think I'm just here nosing around for info about Terry.

"Sam is twenty and his big sister, Marissa, is twenty-two," she says with pride. "They're both in college and doing great." She gets up to straighten a picture hanging on the wall. "I remember watching Terry successfully handle a nightmare guest at the Disney Resort, and I knew she was special. I offered her a job on the spot if she ever came to New York. And guess what? She did! With just the money in her pockets, which wasn't much."

"How'd it work out?" I smile.

"Great! Terry was always one of my favorites. She started out a little rough around the edges, but that was OK. Many of our new members weren't much older than she was when we opened the club. You know, those geeky dot-com kids who had a lot of stock in all those companies, many of which eventually went bust."

"Did she start at the bottom, in housekeeping and work her way up?" I ask.

"Oh no. I wasn't going to waste her behind the scenes, when her real strength was people skills. But first she needed a Big Apple polish." Adriana smiles at the thought and then sees my surprise. "I know, I know. She was already so beautiful."

"Exactly."

"But her clothes were shabby, and not shabby-chic. Her hair wasn't at its best. She wore a little too much make-up." Adriana smiles. "So I put her in the hands of our pros here at the club—a good haircut for that beautiful long dark hair, facial, makeup, manicure, pedicure."

"That must have been great fun for Terry." I try to imagine my tomboy daughter, Jess, sitting still long enough for all of that. Older daughter, Brooke, would love it, of course, but definitely not Jess.

"I think the makeover was fun for Terry, because, as I would soon come to know, she was always trying to grow, learn, improve, evolve," Adriana says. "She wanted to be the best she could be. Then I gave my personal shopper a budget and sent her out with Terry to create an affordable wardrobe that was appropriate for working here. Of course, the finished results were fantastic."

I imagine Terry must have been in heaven. "So how did you use this charming vision of beauty at Club Nucleus, Adriana? What was her first job?"

"Come with me, Ronnie, and I'll show you."

Adriana's Louboutins once more click down the staircase to the ground floor entry. While my feet are comfy in my pretty ballet flats, I can't help yearning to wear a four-inch-high sexy shoe like hers.

"Adriana, how do you walk in those all day? They're beautiful, but my feet would be broken after five minutes."

She laughs. "I only wear them inside, which doesn't require a lot of walking. And mostly I use the elevators. Outside the club, I switch to flats."

Adriana ushers me into a spacious office furnished in the same minimalist style I've seen throughout the club. This is no cramped, cluttered work space. Three attractive people sit at computers—two women in their twenties working the phones and a man in his late thirties poring over a calendar.

"This is member services," Adriana says. "Besides meals, work-outs, haircuts, massages, and so on, we organize lectures on all sorts of topics, offer advance screenings of movies, present small concerts. You name it, we do it. We follow up most of those events with a lunch or dinner with the special guest and a small group of members."

Adriana motions to the two women on the phones and the man with the calendar. "This is Marie Dupois, Anna Brown, and David Spencer. David runs this office, plus he's the club's assistant manager. Club Nucleus wouldn't function so smoothly without David, who's been with me since the beginning." David, Anna, and Marie give us slight, friendly nods as they continue their work. "Not only do they handle the overall club schedule, but they book private events for members."

Adriana glances down at Marie's desk as she passes by on her way to a console, where she opens a cabinet and takes out a folder. "For example, Marie is booking a Bentley for tomorrow. An out-of-town member wants to take his girlfriend to a private dinner at the Blue Hill at Stone Barns in Pocantico Hills. I think he plans to propose, so Marie is organizing all aspects of the evening, also working directly with the restaurant to make sure everything is picture perfect."

I don't doubt that the services cost an arm and a leg. "And this is the job Terry had when she worked for you?" I ask. "How'd she do?"

"She was a quick study. Fabulous! All the members liked her." Adriana motions to David. "As a matter of fact, she and David started at the same time, and they became good friends."

David looks at us as he listens on the phone and types into his computer.

"So whatever happened to Terry? You said she was a name out of the past. Did she get a better offer?" I notice a shadow pass over David's face when he hears my question. He catches me noticing and quickly shifts back to his crisp professional demeanor.

"A better offer? Yes, well, you might say that." Adriana hands me the folder, and we leave member services. "Ronnie, this is a membership packet, if you're interested. It'll give you all the details. Please call me if you have any questions whatsoever. We'd love to add you to our membership."

I'm surprised by the easy invite. "Don't you have a membership committee that has to approve, once they meet me?" I quickly flip through the pages in the folder. "How many letters of recommendation?"

Adriana smiles. "I'm the membership committee and Win recommended you. So, you're in, should you decide to join. We'd love to have you."

"That's wonderful, Adriana. I really enjoyed meeting you today. I'll take a look at this and get back to you."

I leave through the enormous frosted glass doors, thinking I need another club like a hole in the head, even though this one seems like a lot of fun.

As I walk down Hudson Street in the meat packing district, I stop in front of a coffee shop. There, I pull out my cell, dial Club Nucleus and ask to speak with David Spencer. He picks up.

"Hello, Mr. Spencer. This is Ronnie Lake. Adriana just gave me the tour of the club, and she introduced us. May I invite you for a cup of coffee at your convenience? We could talk about Terry Jones—"

"Ah, yes," he cuts in. "It was nice to meet you, Ms. Lake. Oh, one moment, I have another call—" The line goes dead. Did he just hang up on me?

Hmmm. Guess my phone technique requires some work. Need to ask private eye Will at my next Aikido class for some tips on investigative cold calling...

CHAPTER TWENTY

The shadows from the trees are long as I drive up the dirt road at Meadow Farm. Having beaten the rush hour traffic, I made pretty good time coming from the city, and I soon pull up to the front of the house. I see Frank and Juliana on the side terrace talking, laughing, focused on something on the table. Are they playing chess? I think about the chess book on Juliana's nightstand upstairs.

They hear my car door slam, stop talking, and look up. When they see me, they don't say a word, but go back to looking at what I can now clearly see is a chess board. Why do I feel I've walked into the school cafeteria only to find the popular girl has just stolen my best friend?

I take a deep breath, walk over, and smile. "Hi, you two!"

"Hi." Frank doesn't look up from the board, and his greeting has a touch of coolness in it. Guess I'm still in the dog house with him.

Juliana looks up with a smile, but her eyes are neutral. "Hi, Ronnie. Don't mind Frank. He's figuring out his next move."

"Frank, I hope you're being nice to Juliana...saving some of those killer moves for another—"

"Ronnie, Juliana doesn't need any coddling when it comes to chess." Frank finally looks at me. "Jules is a superb player."

End of conversation.

"That's wonderful..." I drift into the house through the dining room terrace door.

Once inside, I think I hear Juliana ask, "Frank, does your sister just come and go at your house whenever she likes..." Her voice fades out while I walk across the dining room. Then I stand frozen in the doorway to the foyer, my heart pounding. For the first time I wonder if she could turn my brother against me.

The sound of footsteps behind me causes me to turn to see Juliana holding two glasses as she enters through the French doors. Her long, beautiful hair moves slightly in the breeze. She is something to behold, and I understand why Frank is smitten.

She shows a momentary surprise, perhaps wondering if I overheard what she just said to Frank. Then she makes a quick recovery. "I need to refill our iced tea—" Juliana stumbles as the heel on one of her shoes breaks off, and she loses her balance, falling to the floor. The two glasses fly out of her hands onto the carpet. I dash over to help her up.

"Thank you, Ronnie." She quickly disengages from me and hops over to a dining room chair where she sits and examines the black shoe. It's not the Louboutins—I see no red sole—and these are lower. "I can't believe this heel broke. Again..." she says of the shoe. "I had it fixed in

California. Three times. I guess I'll have to retire them, even though they're my favorites."

"Are you OK?" I ask, concerned.

"I'm fine." Still, she rubs her ankle.

"Juliana, what are you doing wearing these shoes around the house? You're so dressed up."

"Frank and I just got back from a lecture at Princeton. Part of an alum gathering," she says.

I pick up the two glasses that happen to have fallen near the spot on the carpet that I saw Juliana examining a few days before. I glance at her rubbing her foot and holding the broken shoe. Once more some long-forgotten thought flickers at the edge of my memory. I'm frustrated that I can't put my finger on what precisely that is.

Juliana takes off the other shoe and gets up to leave the room. "I think I'll trade these for something more comfortable."

When she leaves with the shoes dangling from her hand, the flicker at the edge of my mind grows stronger. The feeling is like déjà vu, but I still can't quite get to the exact memory, and it's driving me crazy. I sit on a chair and mentally reach way back. But before I know it, Juliana returns, this time with the green suede Tod's—god, do I absolutely love those shoes.

"You OK?" she asks. I nod, and she goes to the terrace.

She's forgotten their iced tea. So I get the refills for them and bring out the drinks.

Juliana looks up. "Oh, the iced tea. My broken shoe distracted me. Thank you, Ronnie."

Frank glances up and then back to the game. "Thanks, Sis."

At the French doors, I look back once more to see them lost in the chessboard and take a moment to watch. It's actually very intimate, this game between them.

I never got into chess, even though Frank tried to teach me when we were teenagers. I did have a fantasy for a long time, imagining myself as sexy Faye Dunaway playing chess with Steve McQueen in the 1968 version of *The Thomas Crown Affair*. For me, that scene is one of the all-time great movie seductions.

I'll have to see if I can stream the movie or order the DVD. That'd be fun to watch, curled up with Warrior and a bowl of cookie-dough ice cream—since I have no Steve McQueen stand-in in my life.

~~~~~

Rather than pig out on ice cream, I catch an evening Aikido class. Isabella *Sensei* has dedicated the entire hour to working on basics, something we never stop practicing in Aikido. After all, as Isabella always says, *advanced Aikido is basics done really well.*

We've been doing s*homenuchi ikkyo*, and my turn comes to practice this pinning technique. I walk away from my attacker, a young kid named Ben, who's getting ready to take his first test.

The sound of approaching footsteps causes me to turn just in time to see Ben rushing at me with the overhead strike that's like a sword coming down on my head. I try to get out of the way by entering into his space and extending my arms to blend with the attack, but I'm late and fall back, off balance. Not surprisingly, he reverses me, easily controlling my arm and pushing me forward and down.

Before I can respond, I'm flat on the floor, face down, with my arm out to the side in a pin that doesn't allow me to budge. I surrender. My free arm slaps the mat.

Ben releases me, beaming, and I congratulate him with a, "Good job, kid," even though, at his beginner level, his technique is rough and out of control. I'll remember next time not to turn my back on him (or anyone for that matter). His grin is huge, and I smile back. I catch a glimpse of Will, who it seems watched me being reversed, because I see a flicker of a smile at the corners of his mouth.

After class, Will and I meet around the corner at the coffee shop. Private eyes seem to drink a lot of coffee.

He hands me a folder. "Here's what I've been able to learn about Juliana Wentworth in California without actually going there. Her husband, Carleton Todd Wentworth, a successful tech investor, appears to have left her very well off. You can look over the report at your leisure. After reading this, I really don't get the feeling that she's a gold digger."

"Well, I'm glad to hear it, for my brother's sake." I quickly scan through the report. "I don't know...there's something familiar about her. I can't quite put my finger on it."

"Let me know if you want me to check into anything else regarding Juliana," Will says. "Now switching to her early years on the Terry-or-Teresa-Gonzalez front—since she was a minor, I'm having a tougher time finding out about her before her Scranton Gang days."

He sees my disappointment. "Why do you really have me checking into this?" he asks. "Your bogus family-reunion story is taking you much further in conducting your investigation than I ever expected, but what is it you really want to find out?"

"Part of me is just plain fascinated by her story. How did someone like Teresa start so far on the wrong side of the tracks and make her way over to the right side—so that she ended up as Juliana?" I ask. "That's the sixty-four-thousand-dollar question. More importantly I want to learn as much as I can, since she may end up marrying my brother. Plus there's the discovery of this new teenaged Frankie, or Francesca, and how she fits in."

I must look distressed at the thought because Will speaks up quickly. "Ronnie, can't your brother take care of himself?"

"Will, you don't get it," I say. "I have another brother, the oldest of the three of us. Years ago, he married a woman we all thought was nice enough. She turned out to be emotionally troubled and insecure, and she cut him off from the entire family. Our parents spent the last ten years of their lives without seeing my brother or those four grandchildren. It broke their hearts."

Will stares at me with a kind expression on his face. "How sad. Why did your brother allow it, though?"

I still wish I understood. "Who knows... sometimes it's easier to just go along rather than fight a difficult situation in a marriage. Still, to this day, it upsets me to think of it."

My eyes blink back the tears quickly as I finish my coffee. "Anyway, my niece, Laura, is terrified of history repeating itself when it comes to her father. I am, too."

I change the subject and bring Will up to speed on what I've learned at Club Nucleus and my failed attempt to get David Spencer to tell me about Terry Gonzalez. "He hung up on me. Plain and simple."

"Sounds like you need to practice your phone technique." He laughs.

"Not funny, Will." I do notice that he has a great smile.

"Ronnie, do you plan to join that Nucleus club? If you do, you could walk the application into the club personally, stop by David's office and try again," he advises.

"I already belong to a nice club in the city, so I don't plan to go back to the Nucleus offices any time soon."

"Then you have to phone David again. This time, right after you identify yourself, ask him to please not hang up and to hear you out. And write the script for what follows ahead of time," he says. "Keep it short and sweet, and use some charm. Got it?"

"Ten-four," I throw back. Heard that on some TV show, and it sounds very P.I.ish.

CHAPTER TWENTY-ONE

I go back to the drawing board and write a script for David Spencer at Club Nucleus. During the next call, I plead with him not to hang up. This time it works.

The next day, David and I walk down Hudson Street not far from the club. "What made you change your mind?" I ask while carrying two iced coffees from a nearby deli.

"How you told me that she's a part of your family," David answers. "And you're trying to get the family together for a reunion. And you want to make things right with her, even though she took off years ago. Well, all of that sounds good for Terry."

I wonder how many little white lies I will have told by the end of this investigation.

"So, the two of you started at the same time at Club Nucleus?" We walk onto a small plaza lined with benches several blocks from the club.

"Yes, and from day one, everybody liked her," he says.

We sit on a bench in the shade, and I hand David one of the drinks. "You've been at Club Nucleus a long time—you must really like it," I say, still trying to win him over. He nods. "And how'd it go for Terry at the club? Did she thrive, too?"

He shifts nervously on the bench. "Please don't let Adriana know that I've talked to you about this. She never discusses it. Are we clear?" His voice is firm.

"Yes." Must be job preservation that has David Spencer so adamant about this—and with member privacy a high priority at a place like Club Nucleus, my not saying anything would be crucial.

"One of the younger members fell for Terry and began to pursue her." David looks away as if he's thinking back in time.

"Why was that a problem?" I take a sip from my iced coffee.

"Adriana has always had strict rules about not fraternizing with members outside of the club." David also takes a drink of coffee. "Not allowed at all."

"Who was the member?" I ask.

He hesitates, but continues, "A dot-com guy, not much older than Terry. Probably in his late twenties when they met." David folds his arms, still holding the cup, and leans against the back of the bench. "John Palmer. I can still picture him in some quiet corner of the club playing chess with another member or off by himself playing online."

John Palmer. I'm mentally going through the books on Juliana's nightstand at Meadow Farm. I recall the inscription in her chess book—*JP, 1999*. Might well be this John Palmer.

"So how'd he go from chess to falling for Terry?" This has the makings of an interesting story.

"Oh, it was all innocent at first. He didn't set out to put the moves on her. You have to understand, Mrs. Lake—"

"Please, David, it's Ronnie."

"OK, Ronnie. John was geeky, you see." David chuckles. "Hugely successful, but geeky."

"Go on," I encourage.

"And Terry was just curious about, well, everything and always trying to learn new things. So, when she'd bring him a cup of coffee, she'd watch him play for a few minutes." He shakes his head. "Next thing I see Terry's reading beginner chess books during her breaks."

I give him a look. "So she put the moves on him?"

"Not at all. It wasn't Palmer she was interested in. It was chess. She wanted to learn how to play. She'd say to me, come on, David, why don't you learn, too. And I did. We'd play together outside of work."

We both drink from our coffees and contemplate the past. "So what happened? I mean, with John?"

"Well, when she'd bring him something to drink or, say, a message—he always turned his phone off at the club even though it wasn't a rule—she'd quietly cheer his move on the board or ask a question about strategy. John and Terry quickly developed an easy rapport."

"David, is that code for relationship?" I ask.

"Not yet. So, a couple months later, it's after work and I come across the two of them playing chess here, of all places, on this little plaza." He shakes his head. "The next day, I read her the riot act, tell her that if Adriana were to find out, Terry would be fired. I said she was a fool to be with him so close to the club, where maybe next time the boss instead of me would see the two of them."

"Were they involved?" I'm all ears.

"She said they were just friends."

David and I display similar cynical expressions at the same time and laugh.

"Whatever," he says. "Anyway, around the club, John Palmer seemed to come out of his tech-geek shell. He still played a lot of chess, but he was much more outgoing and friendly to everyone. I think it was due to Terry's influence."

"Sounds as if he was in love." I smile.

"Yep. He fell hard," David agrees. "And Terry was very happy, although she had to hide it, but I could tell."

"That's nice." Or was it, really?

David says nothing. I wait. Still nothing.

"What's the final chapter in their story, David? Did they run off into the sunset together? Did they live happily ever after?" He still doesn't respond.

David sighs. "They made plans to run off into the sunset, but they didn't live happily ever after."

"What then?" I'm always a sucker for a romantic story, but I prefer one with a happy ending.

"Four months or so after I first saw them playing chess on this plaza, I noticed Terry, at her desk, fussing with a ring on her finger. She had the stone turned down, and she was trying to take it off and put it in her bag. I'd just walked in, and she acted as though I'd caught her breaking the law."

"Was it an engage—"

"John Palmer had given her a beautiful ring. Terry was so happy. She said they were going to be married the very next week, nothing fancy. City Hall and then a small celebration for a few friends at a restaurant. She asked me to come, to be part of it. She didn't have any family around and didn't know many people outside of where she worked."

Hmmm. "What did Adriana do when she found out?" I ask.

"Adriana wasn't happy when Terry broke the news. First of all, Terry was involved with a member. Second, the boss was losing a valued employee. But Adriana was decent about it, since Terry had being straight with her and given her plenty of notice."

"Sounds as if they did live happily ever after," I offer.

"No." David looks sad and his posture sags a little.

"She wasn't in an accident or something—"

"No, no." His voice goes quiet. "She was a runaway bride."

My jaw drops open—literally. "Wha—"

"She took off the day before their marriage…just left him a note at the club…said it was better for him if they didn't marry, and that she didn't mean to hurt him. I saw the note, torn in half, on Adriana's desk." David finishes his iced coffee. "I guess Palmer tossed it, and maybe Adriana found it. Anyway Adriana quietly flipped out. You know, she originally discovered Terry in Orlando, gave her a start in New York. I don't think the boss ever got over it."

"And Terry? What happened to her?" I feel Teresa—Juliana—slipping through my fingers, again, in this early life of hers.

"She just disappeared. Something bad must have happened for her to bail. None of us ever heard from her after that." David gets up and tosses our empty cups into a container.

He returns and starts speaking again. "John stayed away from the club for about six months. Finally, one day he showed up again, back to his pre-Terry geeky self, playing chess all the time. A year later Hewlett-Packard bought his company, and he moved to Utah to start a new business."

David pulls a paper from his pocket. "Here. John Palmer's contact information in Salt Lake City. Never, ever, say anything to Adriana. I could lose my job for giving you this."

"I promise I won't." I look at the paper and then at him. "David, why are you giving me Palmer's address?"

"Because Terry had a heart of gold. I still miss her friendship. If she can reunite with family, then that's a good thing. Maybe John Palmer can help you find her."

"Thank you, David."

"You're welcome." He walks away, stops, and turns back to me. "Ronnie, were you ever really planning to join Club Nucleus?"

"Maybe. Haven't decided yet."

David smiles, gives me a skeptical look, waves quickly, and walks out of the plaza and up Hudson Street.

Me? I'm thinking of the chess-playing Juliana telling Bobby Taylor that she'll leave the country if he doesn't back off. I now understand this is no idle threat, since she's done this disappearing thing before. I've got to call Will.

Oh, Frank, you better guard your heart.

CHAPTER TWENTY-TWO

The crowd is screaming, and I have a headache. Inside an octagonal ring, two mixed martial artists, both with overly tattooed upper bodies, appear—in my nonexpert opinion—to be evenly matched. They come at each other with a combination of boxing, wrestling, judo, karate, and jujitsu. Every time one of them falls onto the mat, pinned by the other in some unfathomable joint lock, the decibel level in the place skyrockets. The fighters' stage names, which I hear repeated often by the announcer, are the Bronx Bulldozer and the Deadly Assassinator.

Will Benson and I sit on bleachers in a huge warehouse not far from the Wilkes-Barre/Scranton International Airport. I don't see many women in this crowd, so how in the world did I end up here? I think I agreed to come when I brought Will up to speed on runaway bride Teresa/Terry/Juliana, and he interrupted me to suggest we watch a mixed martial arts fight.

Mixed martial arts? I asked. What does that have to do with Aikido, which I love?

Nothing, he answered, except it was an opportunity for me to broaden my horizons.

When I told him I preferred to stay home and watch paint dry, he told me to stop being such a snob and come check it out.

Besides, he added, I might learn more about Bobby Taylor. It seems Will got a tip that Bobby Taylor is working security for one of the mixed martial arts companies that puts on events in this area. So we expect to see him here at this fight.

I'm surrounded by boisterous fist-pumping teenagers and back-slapping twenty- and thirty-something guys in the bleachers. I could be the den mother of most of the men cheering the cagefighters below, who one moment are on their feet punching each other and the next sprawled on the mat grappling.

Will nudges me. "Look to the left, Ronnie. The guy walking down the aisle toward the ring."

My eyes open wide. "Yep. Bobby Taylor. I saw him arguing with Juliana in front of the coffee shop in Moosic."

Taylor leans over to speak to a gruff-looking man in a ringside seat. Bobby's tee-shirt rides up, and I'm reminded that his tattoos are as ample as those on the gladiators in the ring.

"Hard to believe this is the guy who's been bothering your brother's girlfriend," Will says. "They're worlds apart. Whatever the connection, it must be an interesting story."

"She's paying him off to keep him away from the girl, Frankie. Or Francesca, to use her formal name." I say. "Sounds like blackmail to me."

"You never know. It could be more than that. Often something looks one way on the surface, but when you find out the back story… Hey, nothing surprises me anymore." Will sips his beer. "Ronnie, won't you let me get you a beer?"

"Thanks, but I'll pass." My throbbing head couldn't handle a beer at the moment. Is it my imagination or is the decibel-level of these screaming fans higher than it was fifteen minutes ago?

I shift my gaze from Bobby to the ring as the Assassinator jabs at the Bulldozer but misses. The Bulldozer responds with a strong left hook and connects. Then he follows it with a liver punch, and the Assassinator folds over in pain and staggers back.

"Will, if I were out there, I would have thrown up after that last punch—" Before I can finish my thought, the Assassinator, who has regained his balance, moves in quickly and tries for another jab, but he's slow. The Bulldozer moves to the side and kicks out the legs of his opponent, who goes down with a crash. The crowd jumps up and goes wild. They want blood.

I make a face showing my disgust. "Will, this is so not like Aikido."

"Yeah. It's a different world from the dojo, Ronnie."

I remember how I had wanted to study a martial art for the longest time. As I researched which one to study, I learned that Aikido techniques are especially effective for women, who in most cases don't have the same brute strength as men.

I had also read that Aikido is considered by many practitioners to be one of the most spiritual martial arts, sometimes called a *moving Zen*. Finally, at age forty-eight, I signed up for classes, and here I am seven years later, a newly minted black belt. But I wouldn't dream of going up against one of these mixed martial arts fighters, that's for sure.

Will nudges me again. "Looks like Bobby's stepping up to do his job."

A crazed, swerving fan tries to push his way over to the cage and yells, slurring his words, "Bulldosjher! Busht his head! Kill the Ashashin!" Bobby does his best to hold the gigantic guy back as reinforcements rush up to help. Three guys are needed to escort the screaming, tipsy—OK, drunk—fan from the warehouse.

Will grabs my arm and guides me down the steps of the bleachers. We exit through a different door and watch from a distance while they let the guy go. All the security guards go back inside, except for Bobby, who stays. Once he's sure they're all gone, he turns around and slugs the fan in his gut.

"Ugh!" The man doubles over and staggers. He appears to be drunk, which renders him unable to fight back despite his size. Bobby lands another blow, this time under the chin, and the man goes down. Then Bobby straddles the guy and strikes him over and over, the man's head whipping from side to side with each blow and slamming against the concrete surface of the parking lot.

Horrified, I can't stand it another second. "Stop!" I yell. Running with Will toward Bobby, I pull out my phone and snap some pictures. "I'm calling the police," I threaten.

Bobby looks up. "Mind your own business, bitch." He stands and moves toward me. I cringe, remembering the creep in the motel alley choking me not long ago.

"Hey, man," Will yells at Bobby and places himself in front of me. "That's enough."

The doors swing open and two other security guards come out. They quickly survey the scene, especially the beaten-up fan-man sprawled on the ground barely conscious and then notice Bobby's bloodied fists.

"You better get inside fast, before the boss sees this," one of them says. That guard guides Bobby Taylor by the arm, who continues hissing obscenities at me.

Then right before he goes through the door, Bobby takes his parting shot, staring straight at me. "Hey, bitch," he sneers. "You, I won't forget. I'm coming for you." I continue snapping photos with my phone. Bobby and the guard hurry inside.

The other security guard calls 911 and reports what he believes to have been a probable drunken brawl. He tells the operator that the guy needs immediate medical attention. The only witnesses to dispute his story are Will and me.

The security guard looks at us the entire time he speaks on the phone and walks in our direction as I continue taking pictures. He then surprises me and makes a sudden grab for my phone, but it falls to the ground.

Will steps in. Again. "Buddy, back off," he says in the guard's face. I pick up my phone and quickly move out of the way. The guy retreats and rushes inside.

"Let's get out of here, Will. I've seen enough mixed martial arts for a lifetime and enough Bobby Taylor until I decide my next move."

"Decide your next move? Ronnie, you need to watch your step," Will says as we hurry to our car.

"What do you mean, Will?" I ask. "We're fine."

"This rushing into the middle of things without thinking first is dangerous," he chides as he beeps open the car locks.

I'm indignant. "Bobby Taylor is a scumbag bully. You saw how he was slamming that guy's head against the concrete." I get into my side of the car and slam the door shut. "Someone had to do something." I glare at Will as he gets into the driver's side.

"OK, Ronnie. Look, we know that Bobby Taylor is one mean dude. And we know help is on the way for that drunk slob he beat up. So, calm down." He slams his door shut and glares back at me. "At the moment, that guy doesn't concern me. You do. The red marks on your neck the other day concern me—"

"The marks went away in a few hours," I interrupt. "See? No black and blues." I lift up my hair to show him my unmarked neck.

"The point is you came close to disaster *again* just a few minutes ago." Will slams his palm hard on the steering wheel, and I sit up fast.

"What is it with you?" he snaps at me. "You're like the proverbial bull in a china shop." Will goes on, his tone turning cautionary, "One of these days, you'll end up seriously injured if you continue acting first and thinking second."

CHAPTER TWENTY-THREE

Will and I stop for supper on the way back, even though we're giving each other the silent treatment. At the restaurant, things start out a bit tense as we order. But for some unexplained reason, Will and I don't hurry the rest of the evening along, and that turns out to be a good thing in terms of my getting to know him better.

Before I realize it, what we had thought would be a quick bite morphs into a leisurely two-and-a-half-hour meal. Mr. Hunky Third-Degree Black Belt Private Eye happens to be one very interesting man, and he and I talk about all sorts of things, none of them having to do with my investigation. Why am I surprised to discover that Will Benson is excellent company?

Once we're back in New Jersey, Will drops me off at my car, and I head home. As I drive through the EZ-Pass lane on the highway, the sign flashes *You Have Paid*, and my cell phone rings. My niece's voice shrieks through the earpiece.

"Aunt Ronnie. Hurry!" She breaks down sobbing and struggles to catch her breath. "R-R-Ronnie, please come!"

I shiver in alarm. "Laura. Easy. Calm down. Are you hurt?" I flip off the air conditioning in the car, which suddenly feels too cold.

"It's not me." She's crying. "I'm fine."

"Laura, what's happened?" I grip the steering wheel with fear. "Is it your dad? Please tell me." I push against the wheel, bracing for the worst.

"Please come," she sobs.

"Where?"

"To the hospital." I hear her blow her nose to clear out the stuffiness and tears. "It's Daddy. The ambulance brought him to the ER." She starts crying again. "Come, Aunt Ronnie, as fast as you can," she says through her tears. "I saw the whole thing."

"What do you mean, saw the whole—" *Click.* The phone connection goes dead.

~~~~~

I park and run to the entrance of the ER. Laura is waiting for me, and she's calmed down since our phone conversation. As we walk through the huge glass doors, she says her father is stable, much to my relief, and begins her story back at Meadow Farm.

"I was upstairs listening to my music and getting organized for some tutoring lesson for tomorrow. Dad was downstairs with Juliana in the kitchen, fixing supper." While she's telling me this, Laura and I walk down a hall, take a left turn, and head toward a bank of elevators. A nurse pushes a gurney past us.

"All of a sudden, I heard a loud crash and the sound of glass breaking. I ran to my window in time to see Daddy going out the front door to find out what was going on." She starts sniffling as we get to the elevator bank and hits the *Up* knob.

"As Daddy walked down the steps onto the gravel, this guy jumped out from behind one of our cars—" Laura breaks down crying again. "And I, and I, and I saw him hit Daddy over the head with a rock." She grabs me and buries her face in my shoulder.

"Oh, Laura!" I stroke her hair, and she quickly gets hold of herself as the elevator opens. It's empty, thank goodness. We step in and she hits a floor button. "Go on," I say.

"Daddy dropped to the ground unconscious. The guy— I couldn't see his face because he had his back to the house—he was yelling at Dad, something like, *That'll teach ya, that'll teach ya.*"

"Laura, did you see anything that might help the police identify him?" I ask.

"Nothing when it comes to his face, Aunt Ronnie. But he was wearing a long-sleeved shirt with the cuffs open, and it looked as if he had a lot of tats all around his wrists." Wait a minute, that sounds like Bobby Taylor, with those crazy tattooed arms. But I just saw him at the fights in Pennsylvania. How did he get here so fast? Well, Will and I did take our time at supper, so I guess it's possible the creep beat me back to Willowbrook.

Is Bobby Taylor hunting me down the way he threatened earlier in the evening? No way. Plus I'm pretty sure he doesn't know I'm connected to Juliana through my brother. This attack had to be about her and my brother.

We get to the seventh floor and another gurney rolls onto the elevator, this time with a patient. We go up one more floor and exit left down a long hallway. "What happened next, Laura?" I take her arm.

"He moved his foot back, as if he planned to kick Daddy, and I yelled out the window that I'd called the police," she says. "The guy stopped mid-kick and hightailed it out of there. The weird thing was he never looked up at me after I screamed at him. And he had gloves on. In the middle of summer."

"No fingerprints," I offer.

We pass a sign pointing toward radiology, where Laura slows me down. "They want to check Daddy for a concussion. Let's wait here a moment." We sit on a couch.

"So what happened to the guy with the tattoos?" I ask.

"Well, he ran over to a green SUV, and when he started it, he stepped on the gas so hard the car spit gravel. Then he went so fast, he fishtailed down our road trying to make all the turns. He slid all over the place! And you know the old apple tree at that sharp turn?" I nod yes, wondering where Bobby Taylor got this green SUV. "The car almost hit it," Laura says. "The guy missed it by a fraction and scraped the entire passenger side of his car. I bet he even left green paint on the tree."

I squeeze my niece's shoulders. "Where was Juliana during all of this?"

"I called 911 for real this time as I race down the stairs to go outside, and that's when Juliana showed up.

Something about being in the bathroom and hearing a loud noise? She saw Daddy on the ground unconscious and totally flipped out." Laura takes a deep breath.

"I felt Daddy's pulse, and it was strong," she says. "But Juliana kept on crying and wailing. I yelled at her to quiet down and not move Daddy and that the ambulance would be there soon. He came to while we both sat with him, but he was pretty groggy."

I just don't know what to think, not really. "It sounds as though you did a good job, calming Juliana and making sure your father was OK." I pat her hand supportively. Although outwardly I appear composed for my niece's sake, inwardly I want to scream and cry.

"Oh, Aunt Ronnie, it all happened so fast. Anyway, the ambulance arrived, and Juliana rode with Daddy to the hospital."

"And you followed in your car?" I ask.

She nods yes. "But first I talked to the police. They drove in right behind the ambulance. They looked at the rock that the guy used to hit Daddy over the head. You know, took pictures of it for the police report. Then we went inside and found the other rock. Well, that one looked more like a mini-boulder, and it had flown through one of the living room windows. That guy must be really strong. Anyway, it sat there on the carpet, and wait till you hear this, Aunt Ronnie—"

"What?"

Laura takes a deep breath before she tells me. "The word revenge was painted in black on this boulder. Only it was misspelled r-A-v-e-n-g-e, like *ravenge*." She pronounces the first syllable *rah*.

If not Bobby, then surely some old chum of Teresa's. "That's really weird, Laura. Either it has some other meaning, or this idiot can't spell or use a dictionary."

Despite the seriousness of all this, she laughs a little. "No kidding. And you may be right about the gloves," she says. "They were having trouble finding any fingerprints on the two rocks by the time I left."

At that moment, Juliana appears from a door further down the hall. With the revenge theme in this attack against my brother, I really have to wonder if she has a more sinister connection to Bobby Taylor than merely protecting Francesca. Laura and I get up from the couch, and meet Juliana halfway down the hall.

"What's the latest?" I ask.

"The CAT scan looks good, which means an excellent chance he doesn't have a concussion, thank god," she says, sounding quite relieved. "But the doctor wants to keep him overnight for observation anyway. They'll be moving him to a room in a moment."

Before we know it, we're on our way to the sixth floor and a room not far beyond the nurses station, where we sit by my brother's bedside for a short visit. He holds Juliana's hand tightly and gazes at her constantly.

Once again, just like after the road-rage accident, I ask, "Frank, did you get a look at the guy?"

"Not at all. One second I heard the crash and breaking glass. The next moment I glanced in the living room to see the broken window and then rushed outside. Next thing I knew I was flat on the ground with Juliana and Laura kneeling beside me, wondering how I got there." He puts his hand to the top of his head. "Man, my head is pounding."

"Daddy, that's hardly a surprise." And Laura recounts a shorter version of what she witnessed from the window in her room at the house. She finishes with the word *Ravenge* painted on the rock that crashed through the window in the living room.

"That word revenge is our only clue, and who would spell it that way?" Laura asks. "It's all got to mean something." She glances at everyone, but holds a beat longer on Juliana...or maybe that's my imagination. Do I see Juliana react with an imperceptible flinch? Or is that my imagination, too?

All of us say goodnight to a very tired-looking Frank and leave. Once in the parking lot, I split off from Laura and Juliana, who head for my niece's car. Halfway to my Mustang, I turn back and see Juliana staring at me while Laura walks the last few steps to her vehicle and gets in.

I go for it and walk back to Juliana. She stands still.

Once I reach her, I say in a calm voice, "Juliana, there's a lot I don't know. But I feel sure you know the person who attacked Frank."

She responds in an equally calm voice, "You're right, Ronnie. You don't know me or anything about me." As she walks away, I swear I hear her say, "You never knew me."

Now what the hell does that mean?

CHAPTER TWENTY-FOUR

Blending with the attack, I deflect the punch using a brush of my hand at my partner's elbow as I glide closely past him and grab his shoulder. My other arm raises up and across his neck and head as I continue my full-body entry displacing my Aikido classmate, Evan. With my body alongside his, I have the option of choking him or throwing him. I decide on the throw, and he falls onto the mat with a *thump*.

"Whoa, Ronnie," Evan grunts. "You nailed that one. Awesome."

"Thanks," I grunt back and repeat the *tsuki irimi nage* (rough translation is *thrust enter throw*). This time, as Evan comes at me, I imagine it's Bobby Taylor, not Evan, who is my opponent. *Don't you dare mess with my brother*, I think to myself, and I throw him down again, but harder.

Evan gets up from the mat, and it's still Bobby Taylor I see coming at me. As I execute the technique one more time, I mutter, "That'll teach you." I move with all my force and hurl him down again.

Evan takes a little longer to get up. "What did you say?" he asks. "Couldn't hear you." Watching him knead his lower back, I'm momentarily stunned by my power.

I walk away, in my mind working on my own revenge scenario against Bobby Taylor. "Hellooo, earth to Ronnie," my foe says.

My mind snaps back to the dojo and I turn to Evan. "Oh my god, so sorry. Are you OK?" I look at him meekly, as he nods. "Your turn. Please be kind when you throw me." I smile lamely, hoping he won't use the same amount of force that I just used with him.

After class, outside at our cars, Will Benson hands me yet another folder. "Here's everything I could find out about John Palmer and his Salt Lake City firm."

Evan walks by, and he waves. "See you later, Ronnie. Will, don't mess with her. She's tough!" He laughs and gets into his car to leave.

"Are you all right?" Will looks at me with concern. "I'm sorry about the attack on your brother." He sees my surprise. "A buddy in the department told me about it. I could tell in class that you're upset."

"Frank's better today. Thanks for asking." I put the folder in my car.

Will says, "It looks as if John Palmer hit a second home run with the Utah company. That guy must have the Midas touch. Anyway, you'll find addresses, contacts, phone numbers in the folder. I can follow up in the field or by phone for you—"

"Thanks, Will, I'll take it from here." The tone of my voice is sharper than I intended, and he looks at me funny. I try to soften it. "I'll let you know what I find out, and then we can decide what to do next." Yeah, I get it.

~~~~~

It's Daniel's day to work around my place, and we've traded vehicles yet again. First, I stop by the old apple tree on the road into Meadow Farm, and Warrior hops out, too. Sure enough, I see flecks of green paint on the gnarly bark from when the SUV tore out of here after the attack on Frank last night and sideswiped the tree.

Now I'm on a tear, driving as fast as I can to Scranton with Warrior next to me in the van. He sits up, attentive, eyes on me. He knows something's going on. I can't see straight I'm so mad at Bobby Taylor. First, for almost killing my brother on the highway, and second, for knocking Frank unconscious as the lowlife tried to break in yesterday at Meadow Farm. Well, I can see straight enough to drive.

Plus I have Pat Benatar blasting "Invincible" from the van's speakers, and that's just pumping my anger even more.

I head first to the Moosic Motel, but I see no sign of Bobby Taylor's motorcycle there. Putting my dog on a leash, this time I take Warrior for protection. We nonchalantly slip around the back of the motel, and I discreetly peer into all the windows. No sign of Bobby, and thank god, no sign of that stoned maniac, Jimmy, who attacked me last time I visited this dump.

I put Warrior back in the van and run into the café next door, where I order a cup of coffee to go. No Bobby Taylor here, either, among the several people sitting at tables and at the counter.

I slide back into the driver's seat and hit the button. You got it: more Pat Benatar.

I drive over to Stan's Diner and park. Walking in, I quickly see that my buddy Mary isn't on duty. The place is empty at the moment. I order another cup of coffee to go.

Back in the van I replay "Invincible," and the speakers thump as Warrior and I cruise up and down the streets of Moosic looking everywhere for Bobby Taylor. But no luck. We finally end up at the stadium, and I pull into the vast expanse of an almost empty parking lot. My head and heart are pounding. I turn off the ignition and take several deep breaths.

Ronnie, get a grip. What is it you're really trying to do here? Stalk Bobby Taylor the way he stalks Juliana? Still, he almost killed Frank, the only brother I have left. And that makes the situation completely different. But seriously, what would I do if I ran into him face to face here in Moosic or in Scranton? Confront him? Yell at him? Threaten him?

Get real, Ronnie. He's a maniac. He could physically hurt me. Especially because he'd probably recognize me from the confrontation at the mixed martial arts fight the other day. He'd try to make good on his threats to come after me.

I quietly sing to myself this morning's anthem. I wish I could wail the way Pat Benatar does when she sings. Hey, didn't she wear a lot of black leather? Could be a good purchase for all this P.I. work...

And then I spot it. Over in one corner of the parking lot. A green SUV. And I remember Jerry and Tony from my last visit to the stadium. I hadn't thought of their car when Laura told me about the attack on Frank and the guy driving off in a green SUV. The vehicle looks empty now, and I don't see the two punks anywhere.

I drive over and circle the car, spotting scrape marks on the passenger side. I hit the brakes, put the van in park and jump on out. I inspect the side of the SUV and touch the grooves from the scratches. Sure enough, it looks like wood slivers embedded in some of the paint. I shoot pictures with my phone.

I move around front to snap the license plate, and my anger grows. No way is this a coincidence. I take more photos.

I allow for the slim chance it wasn't Bobby Taylor who attacked Frank. Maybe one or both of these two kids did in retaliation toward me after our meeting here, and Frank was the collateral damage... But how'd they end up at Meadow Farm?

I walk back to my van and pull a metal fingernail file and small writing pad from my bag. "Pay dirt," I say to Warrior, who stares at me intently. I rip a piece of paper off the pad and go back to the SUV.

My file is the perfect tool to pick off samples of the paint and wood slivers in the scrapes, and I catch the flecks on the piece of paper. Folding it carefully, I slip it into my pocket.

"Hey, dude," a voice yells at me from across the parking lot. It sounds like the kid who believes himself to be god's gift to women. "What-cha doin' to my wheels?" I turn to see Jerry and Tony running toward me, each holding an open beer bottle.

I jump into my van, which is still running, and hit the lock button. Warrior growls as I drive toward the two men, feeling pure fury growing inside.

They stop when they see my vehicle race in their direction. Frozen with arms in the air still holding the bottles, mouths hanging open, they look as if they can't believe that in this gigantic empty parking lot a car would purposely head straight for them.

I screech to a halt, Warrior barks, and I glare at them through our front windshield. Warrior's hair rises on top of his head, neck, and back, as if he's sporting a snake-long Mohawk. He snarls at Jerry and Tony, baring his teeth.

"Wh-wh-wh-whoa," the awkward Tony bleats. "You tr-tr-tryin' to hit us?"

I lower the window slightly. "Do not move." Warrior barks some more. "Easy, boy," I say.

Jerry blurts, "Hey, lady, we don't want any troub—"

"Where'd those scrapes on the side of your SUV come from?" I demand.

"We di-di-didn't do it," Tony whines. "Bobby—"

"Shut up," Jerry hisses.

"Bobby who?" I stare them down, looking back and forth between the two of them. "Was it that guy, Bobby Taylor?" They look at the ground and each other. "It was, wasn't it?" They both nod nervously. "Why was he driving your SUV yesterday?"

"We don't know why he needed our wheels," Tony spits out. "He just said he needed it for a d-d-day to d-d-do something. And that he'd give us some really good weed…"

Jerry glares at Tony. "If we kept quiet about it, moron."

"So he br-br-brought the car back last night," Tony says. "It was dark. We didn't even see the scrapes until this morning."

Jerry pipes up, "Like we said, we don't know why he needed our car—"

I cut him off. "You lend your SUV to just anybody? No questions asked?"

"You know Bobby Taylor?" Jerry asks me.

"No, I do not," I answer.

"If you did, you'd know he's a mean f—. And you don't ask him questions. Like where he's going with your wheels or where the scrapes came from," Jerry says. "We just try to lay low and stay out of his way."

"Where is this Bobby Taylor?" I spit out the name.

"Do not know," Jerry answers with a smug look on his face.

I stare at him, crank the steering wheel to get around the two of them, rev the engine, and drive out of there.

~~~~~

A guy in a black leather jacket on a motorcycle pulls up to my left side as I drive home on a twisty Pennsylvania road. Warrior and I glance over to see him giving me a thumbs-up. I can't see his face because of the helmet…and then he smiles. I know that smile. Helmet-head flips up his visor, and it's Will. My jaw must drop, because he laughs. I open the window and yell, "Hey, I want to speak to you."

"Dairy Queen four miles up the road." He flips down the visor and speeds off. I lose sight of him as he rounds a bend.

What is Will doing here on this quiet country road? This can't be mere coincidence. Three hours before, I left him at the dojo. Oh my god, has he been following me the entire time? I feel a slow boil coming on.

Minutes later, I pull into the Dairy Queen parking lot. The engine off, I jump out, slam the van door shut, and leave Warrior watching me through the windshield. I march over to the smug son-of-a-gun, ready to explode with anger. Will's helmet hangs on one of the handlebars, and he casually leans against his motorcycle seat, licking an ice cream cone. I catch my breath over how sexy he is.

"Will Benson, how dare you follow me without telling me," I practically snarl.

"Why, Mrs. Lake, that's a pretty big presumption to make." His smile is even wider this time and more annoying. "Now, how do you know I don't have business for a different client up this way? You're not the only person I work for, after all." He reaches behind, plucks out another cone that's sitting in a paper cup on the seat and offers it to me. "Come on, lighten up. You look like a woman who prefers chocolate chip cookie dough."

We stare at each other. I don't move. He shrugs and starts to take the ice cream back, and I grab for it. "Not so fast, buster." I have a lick, but I'm still mad. "Seriously, what's going on here? This isn't a coincidence that you and I've run into each other."

He nods his head in agreement. "You're right, Ronnie. I could tell you were upset back at the dojo. I thought I'd keep a friendly eye on you."

I don't like it. "You mean to tell me you've been following me the entire time I've been going all around PA?" I ask, annoyed.

"You bet your ass, Ronnie."

Whoa. "But I never knew you were there," I protest.

He might be at ease, but I'm still not. "That's the point," he says. "I wanted you to have backup in case you ended up in another situation like Bobby Taylor coming at you at the mixed martial arts fight. Remember last night?" He licks his cone again, and I try not to stare.

"For a while I thought you might actually lose it when you lurched from place to place looking for that guy." He grins. "But you calmed down, played it safe from what I could see when you were talking to the two bozos back at the stadium. Good work, Ronnie. You're learning. Not so much bull-in-a-china-shop." Will takes another lick and then bites into the cone.

"Well, just give me a gold star, why don't-cha?" Note to self: Do not watch Will lick ice cream cones. Hard to stay focused on the business at hand.

CHAPTER TWENTY-FIVE

The Great Salt Lake stretches below as the plane circles, ready to land. I stare out the window at the vast open space of the valley, and my mind is on runaway bride Terry Jones. I need to figure out a way to talk to John Palmer, Terry's chess partner at Club Nucleus and her fiancé thirteen years ago, to see if he has information on what became of her. But he's known to be notoriously reclusive. In fact, when you Google him, you don't find much.

Driving by Temple Square in the heart of downtown Salt Lake City, I stare up at a nineteenth-century, multi-spired structure, the largest of all the Mormon temples and the overall hub of this religion. Interesting that Palmer chose this Mormon city as his next business base, but Salt Lake does have a strong work force and an established technology sector. I continue through the bustling center of town with its many office towers and malls.

Once in the eastern foothills of the city, I pass the University of Utah and drive into a nearby tech park. This is where John Palmer has his offices for not only his original Utah start-up, but also a successful parallel investment business. A New York friend tried to arrange a hard-to-get appointment with Palmer under the pretext of my wanting to invest family money in one of his funds, but as it turns out, he has no time in his schedule to see me. Still, at least I know he's here.

I park in a slot a short distance from the main building and open Will Benson's file on John Palmer. I place a recent photograph of Palmer on the dashboard in order to identify him when he comes out. I'm willing to wait.

Clicking through the stations and stopping on Tom Petty's "Runnin' Down a Dream," I discover Salt Lake has great classic rock radio. I unwrap a sandwich purchased at the airport, eat, and wait.

~~~~~

A car door slamming nearby startles me. Oh my god, I fell asleep during surveillance, every P.I. newbie's nightmare. I glance quickly over at the door of the building leading to Palmer's office and then at my phone. It's almost five o'clock, and I have no way of knowing whether or not he's still inside. Did he leave during my unplanned nap? Man, oh, man—I blew it.

I spend the next three hours bored to tears, not sure if this is a total waste of time. People leave for the day, and finally I give up and start my engine.

Then the door to the building swings open again, and this time a familiar-looking man strolls out to a well-lit walkway. Familiar from the photograph, which I grab to compare. I'm certain it's Palmer. He may be successful, but he's still a nerd. In his case, a nice-looking, well-dressed nerd.

When he gets into his top-of-the-line Mercedes SUV, I decide he also looks like a prosperous nerd. He drives out of the tech park, and I follow him at some distance.

With two cars between us, I watch him scoot through a yellow light while I have to stop for the red. I worry I'll lose him as he gets further and further away. Doesn't this light ever change?

Finally it does, and the guy ahead of me takes his own sweet time to move. I see Palmer make a right turn two blocks up. Is he heading for the residential area high above the university? Darting past the slowpoke, I cut in front to make that same right turn.

I catch up, still keeping space between us, as he drives higher and higher into the foothills. I begin to think we'll run out of streets—there aren't many houses up this high—when he stops at a driveway. I see him enter a code on a keypad. A gate opens, and he drives on through. I watch the gate quickly slam shut while I glide by. Now what do I do?

I drive higher into the foothills, pull up to a cul-de-sac with no homes, then stop and turn off my lights. I'm able to look down over the road that ascends from Palmer's gate and winds up a hill to a lit-up, architecturally bold glass-and-concrete house that floats almost like a space station in the evening sky. The views up there must be amazing.

Not sure what to do next, I look out at the Salt Lake Valley, a grid-pattern illuminated by a vast swath of twinkling lights stretching south. I consider my choices.

Option one, I can call it a day and drive down to my hotel, though I'm not yet ready to throw in the towel.

Option two, I can take my small flashlight, get out of the car and try to surreptitiously hike up to Palmer's house and check things out. I flip on the flashlight and look down at my shoes—sneakers when I fly and good for walking, so OK, the footwear is appropriate.

I turn off the light and envision myself carefully hiking through the scrub brush in the dark, trying not to step in holes and fall, probably twisting an ankle. I can just hear Isabella *Sensei* and Will nixing this idea.

Say I get up there, what do I exactly hope to accomplish as Ms. Peeping Tom? Tiptoe around the house and spy on John Palmer? I wonder if he has guard dogs... Or walk up to one of those walls of windows, knock, and expect him to invite me in when I propose discussing his former runaway bride over a cocktail? More likely, he'd hit the panic button, and the police would cart me off before I could get away.

Option three, sit here and do nothing.

So I decide on option three.

Twenty minutes later, John Palmer creates option number four. His headlights wind down the road from his house, stop momentarily as the gate opens up, and continue descending the foothills. I start my engine, and not wanting to attract attention from those living below, don't flick on the headlights until my car is further down the road where there are more houses. Once again, I tail his car.

CHAPTER TWENTY-SIX

This isn't the kind of hip watering hole I expect to find in Salt Lake City, but that shows how much I don't know about this town. The bar is situated in a nineteenth-century bank building that is now a *très chic* hotel. I walk into the dimly lit area surrounding the old bank vault where people sit in intimate scattered groupings of plush chairs.

Reading a newspaper, John Palmer perches on a stool at the bar, and I spot an empty stool right next to him. Man, am I lucky tonight or what?

With my big leather tote bag banging into his shoulder, I slide onto the available seat. "Yikes. Sorry, didn't mean to hit you," I apologize.

"No problem." He picks up his beer, takes a drink, and returns to his paper.

I open the huge tote, rummage around, take out a *Wall Street Journal* and put it on the countertop in front of me.

The bartender comes over, and I gesture toward Palmer's beer. "I'll have one of those, but make it a lite."

"Menu?"

"Sure," I answer, and he hands me one. I peruse it and then sneak a sideways glance to see that Palmer's still reading his paper. I dive into my *Journal* and mark up a tech financial article. We're both quiet and very focused on our newspapers.

Finally, Palmer folds his paper and puts it aside. I ask him, "Are you finished with that?"

"Sure." He pushes it over.

"Thank you." I take the paper. "I'm prepping for a meeting that probably isn't going to happen, but *The Financial Times* will help me get prepared even more, just in case."

He looks at me curiously. "Getting ready for a job interview?"

"Oh, nooo," I laugh. "My sell-by date in the job market was probably a few years ago." Palmer laughs, too. Finally.

I go on. "A friend of mine back East has been trying to set up a meeting for me with a big tech investor out here. He opens up his venture funds every now and then to new investors. So far, she hasn't been able to get the appointment, but I decided to go for it and fly in anyway."

"So you're an investor?" Palmer asks, as the bartender serves him a penne pasta dish. "Thanks."

"That smells good," I say to the bartender. "I'll have one of those, too." Palmer isn't sure if he should start eating his pasta, and hesitates. "You better dig in while it's hot," I urge and see a look of appreciation—then he goes ahead.

I open *The Financial Times*. "Anyway, I guess this big-shot investor is totally booked up, but my friend keeps trying."

Palmer puts down his fork and reaches for a piece of bread. "What do you figure your odds are of getting the meeting—"

"Slim to none!" I burst out laughing, and he does, too.

"So, who's the big-shot investor?" Palmer takes a swig of his beer.

"Some guy named Palmer. Guess he's pretty reclusive—" I stick out my hand, smiling innocently. "By the way, I'm Ronnie Lake."

We shake hands. He doesn't say anything, but has an amused look on his face.

"Hmmm. A mystery man?" I ask.

"It's good to meet you, Ronnie. I'm..." He pauses. "John..." Another pause. "Palmer." His eyes twinkle.

"Nooooo..." I cover my face with my hands and feign horror at my faux pas. "Open mouth, insert foot..." Still, I'm feeling rather smug about my *faux faux pas*. Do I not have a future as a con artist?

"It's OK. Don't worry about it." He takes a bite of penne pasta and signals the bartender for another beer.

"You got it, John," the bartender says.

"So, you come here often." I gesture toward the bartender. "They seem to know you." Palmer nods yes. "But you live in Salt Lake," I say. "You could eat at home."

"Cook is off tonight—" He stops himself. "That sounds pretty spoiled, doesn't it?"

"Yeah, my daughter says the same thing to me when I complain the cook is off." We both laugh.

"I like the company and the place. Friendly, but not nosy," he says. "People leave me alone." He quickly corrects himself. "I don't mean someone like you who doesn't know who I am when—well, you get my drift."

"That's a relief." I root around in my huge, clumsy bag and casually take out a diary, then a phone, and finally my recently purchased copy of the same book about chess that I saw on Juliana's nightstand in her bedroom at Meadow Farm. The same book that *JP*, or probably this John Palmer, had given her many years ago during the dot-com era. I do this rooting-around thing as if I can't find what I'm looking for in the depths of my bag.

Out the corner of my eye, I see the chess book has the intended effect. John Palmer has stopped eating and drinking. He is transfixed by the book.

I look at him and then down at the book, and in a casual tone, ask, "Oh, you play?"

"Yes, I do," he says. "You, too?"

"I'm trying. Again." I pick up the book. "My big brother wanted to teach me when we were kids. My husband also tried but finally gave up." I've made a split-second decision to leave out the *ex* that precedes *husband* in my case. I figure a woman talking about her husband is less likely to be perceived as a cougar-on-the-make. "John, I've heard this one is pretty good." I flip through the first pages of the book and then hand it to him.

"It's excellent." He stares at the cover, smiles and opens to the title page. "The last time I saw this book, I gave it to someone as a gift."

"You have a kid sister you were trying to teach?" I prod.

"No—"

"Oh, your wife," I interrupt.

"Not married, but at the time I thought I was—getting married, I mean." He furrows his brow. "Long time ago— guess it's been about fifteen years, give or take."

"What happened?" I blurt out, and then quickly cover my mouth. "Sorry. I'm just so fascinated by people's stories. My big brother would call it being nosy."

"I'd probably agree with your brother." He shakes his head, and I'm positive I've blown it again. You know, prodded too much. But then he surprises me and chortles. "Did you ever see that movie *Runaway Bride*?" he asks, and I nod yes. "Well, there you have it. I thought I was getting married to the woman I gave this book to, but it turned out she was a runaway bride."

When the bartender serves me my pasta, I take a sip of my beer and pick up my fork. "John."

"Yes, Ronnie?"

"It's been, say, fifteen years since she left you, and I would hope your heart has mended in the meantime." He nods. Then I add with a gleam in my eye, "You also seem like a very nice man, Mr. Palmer."

"Thank you, Mrs. Lake." He laughs.

"John, I promise I'm a wonderful listener, and this sounds like a most interesting story." I fold up the newspaper and tuck it in my bag. "I'm going to forget about prepping for this investment meeting with you that's never going to happen anyway." His eyes convey surprise, and I go on. "Much rather hear all about your runaway bride."

Palmer tries to change the subject, pauses, and then shrugs. He starts out slowly, a little clumsily and hesitantly at first, but then he hits his stride. As I eat my pasta, John tells me the story of Terry/Teresa without using any names. He refers to himself as a geeky kid fifteen years earlier, but I can see by the way he now warmly recounts the past that he outgrew geeky long ago.

He describes with amazement and fondness the dotcom era and his own humble beginnings as a techie who hit it big. He also describes the club, again without naming it, where he met this curious, dark-haired girl who wanted to learn how to play chess. He remembers how their easy rapport grew into a strong connection and that she brought him out of his shell.

"What I really enjoyed was how she wanted to learn about everything. She was like me—her interest in everything was enormous." Palmer pauses, and I see a flicker of sadness cross his face. "We were both too young." He flips through the book again. "Anyway, I gave her this book to use as a reference when she learned to play."

"John, what happened next?" I drink my beer.

"Does there have to be any *next*?" he responds. "She's a lovely memory."

"Hello. You can't expect me to jump from chess student to runaway bride in this intriguing story." I realize I'm being a little too pushy, so I beam a huge smile at him.

"OK, OK. Let's see," Palmer says. "Education was a big deal for her. She told me early on that she'd dropped out of school, and then she got her GED while she was working in Florida. I know she felt self-conscious about not having a college degree, even though no one around the club knew or cared."

The bartender clears our plates and offers dessert menus, which we both refuse.

"May I have a skinny decaf cappuccino?" I ask. The bartender nods yes. I look at Palmer to see if he'd like one, too.

He jumps in. "Don, we'll each have one of those, please." The bartender leaves to get our coffees.

"Well, that's admirable, that this young woman wanted a college education," I say. "Wonder if she ever got her degree?"

"I'm sure she did, because I helped her."

"You did what?" I ask, astounded.

"I set up an account for her, so that she could go to school." He sees my expression. "Don't get the wrong idea. We were friends, not involved...yet. She refused the money, but I told her to take it and get her degree—no strings attached."

"Really? No ulterior motive, John?"

"I told her even if I never saw her again, that I would still want her to have an education." Palmer finishes his beer. "I mean, I'd never met anyone who so thirsted for knowledge the same way I did. So I helped her. It was my own quiet scholarship fund. After all, I had plenty of money."

"So did she go to school on your scholarship?"

"She made plans, registered, and our relationship developed. We got…you know, close. But a part of her life was off limits to me. She was very honest that she had things in her past she wasn't proud of, and I picked up hints that somebody had bothered her at various times."

Don brings the cappuccinos and takes away the beer glasses and plates.

"Did she ever tell you more about that part of her life?" I ask. I pick up the small spoon on the saucer and dip it into the foam at the top of the cup.

"No, and I didn't press her on it." Palmer chuckles shyly. "Hey, I was crazy about her."

"Were you soul mates?" I drink the coffee. "That's corny, huh?"

Palmer smiles. "When I look back at that time, I didn't have a lot of social skills. And here was this young woman who, like me, couldn't get enough knowledge but who had great social skills. She had a lot going for her in general. Well, we made plans to marry." He shrugs his shoulders. "At the last minute, she took off."

I shake my head that such a thing could really happen. "Where'd she go? What became of her?"

"I don't know. I should have tried harder to find her," he says. "But I was shell shocked that she was gone, kind of paralyzed."

We both sip our coffees. "You never heard from her again?"

"Two months later I got a letter with a New York City postmark. She was sorry. Could I please forgive her. She was taking classes at a community college." Palmer stares down at his cappuccino and then looks up.

"A few months after that, we bumped into each other one evening at a restaurant in the Village. It was great, like the split had never happened. The next morning, she was gone." He finishes the coffee. "I kept hoping she'd get in touch. Anyway, after several months more had passed, I called on a guy at my company, a retired NYPD detective. I figured he could track her down. But I'd waited too long. I don't know if she changed her name, since even the detective couldn't find her."

"John, that is an amazing story."

"Haven't talked about it in years," he mumbles. "Not sure why now." He takes a final drink of his coffee, and I can see in his eyes that his thoughts are elsewhere.

~~~~~

John Palmer did squeeze me in for an appointment the next day, and I arrived prepared with plenty of questions about his venture fund. When he told me the minimum dollars required, I tried not to let him see me gulp—even though I already knew the amount from my friend who arranged the meeting in the first place. Big numbers like that always make me gulp.

I told Palmer I needed to confer with my brother, who helps me evaluate all investment opportunities, and thanked him for his time. I couldn't help but wonder why up-by-her-bootstraps Terry-Teresa Gonzalez-Jones had bailed on their wedding so many years before. It certainly didn't make much sense, because John Palmer really is a charming, lovely man. Did threats from Bobby Taylor get in the way? Was he the person bothering her who Palmer mentioned at dinner?

After the morning meeting with Palmer, I text Will Benson to ask him to track down the retired NYPD detective who worked for Palmer during those years. I don't know the guy's name and can't ask Palmer without raising a red flag, but I'm sure Will has ways of finding him.

That detective may be my only hope to learn what might have happened next. Where did Teresa/Terry go to school? What did she study? Did she get her degree? Did she work while she went to school? Did she stay in the city? How could her life get any better than a marriage proposal from the fabulously rich, and most importantly, very nice John Palmer?

CHAPTER TWENTY-SEVEN

"Hi, Rita." I greet Meadow Farm's housekeeper by handing her two boxes with pies. "Picked these up at the farmer's market. How's Frank feeling?"

"Better. Getting there. It's three days since the attack, and I'd say he's at ninety percent." She smiles, takes the boxes, and puts them on a kitchen counter.

"Where is everybody?"

"Well, let's see." Rita ticks everybody off on her fingers. "I think Frank's in the library reading or napping. And Laura's got a break in her tutoring schedule today, so she and Mrs. Wentworth are on the side terrace playing chess."

"Really," I say. "Well, that doesn't totally surprise me, I guess. Laura's been playing since she was five, but I thought she gave it up in college."

"They've been playing out there for quite a while." Rita sniffs the boxes. "Mmm. These smell great, Ronnie. Let me guess. One peach? One rhubarb?" She opens the boxes to look.

"You got it." I take two plates and a pie server. "Think I'll take them to our chess players."

Laura and Juliana don't even look up as I walk out with pie and iced tea on a tray. "Hello, you two. How about a break?"

"In a moment." Laura's eyes flick up at me for a nanosecond. "Need to concentrate here."

"Laura, hasn't it been a long time since you last played?" I ask, slicing the pies.

"Took it up again so I could teach the twins for my nanny job." She's still focused on the chess board.

"Juliana, how about a cool drink and some delicious pie?" I ask. "Is this a good time?" For Frank's sake, I can at least try to be nice, even though I'm having her background checked out and don't really trust her. She also gives me a signal to wait.

My niece makes her move, and Juliana says, "Excellent, Laura! And this is a perfect moment for a break." She looks at the pie. "Ronnie, you're spoiling us—a choice of peach, and let's see, rhubarb? May I please have a sliver of each?" Her voice is friendly, but her eyes aren't. I get the sense that the friendly part is just for Laura's benefit.

"Juliana, who taught you chess? Were you a child like Laura when you learned to play?" I slice the pie and give her the plate. "Frank was always trying to teach me when we were kids, but I never really took to the game."

"No, I started in my mid-twenties." Juliana takes a fork and cuts into her pie. "An old, old friend taught me."

"An old, old friend, huh?" I say. "Hmmm. That sounds like an interesting story. Do you still play with your teacher?"

"We've lost touch." Her eyes quickly glance toward me and then back to the chess board. She moves a piece.

Laura slaps her forehead. "Wow. I didn't see that coming. No offense, Aunt Ronnie, but we need quiet to play. Thank you for the pie and iced tea though." My niece, who got me going with the Juliana investigation, has politely told me to take a hike, so that she can focus on her chess game with, of all people, Juliana. OK.

As I take the tray with the two pies back inside, something on the large, circular, front hall table catches my eye. I quickly deposit the tray in the kitchen and walk back to the foyer.

There on the table is a clear bag that contains Juliana's black pumps. They're polished, and the broken heel has been repaired. Again, something flickers at the edges of my memory, just as it did the other day when Juliana, wearing these shoes, broke the heel.

I pick up the bag and walk into the dining room to where she caught her shoe. It's close to the place on the carpet where I had found her on a different day, on her knees examining the old, faded spot left by a sauce spilled years ago. I look at the shoes through the bag and see they're made by Chanel. I look back at the carpet. I feel the same vague but familiar memory. What is it that I can't recall?

I put the shoes back on the front hall table, but whatever it is that I can't quite remember continues to nag at me. I grab a flashlight from the closet. Jogging up the steps to the third floor of the house, I feel something in the deep recesses of my mind propelling me up toward the attic.

The third floor consists mostly of small rooms that used to be servants' quarters when the house was first built. Those rooms were still used for staff when my parents lived in the house and my siblings and I were children. By the time Frank and Joanie raised their kids here, the space was used for playrooms.

Stepping on several creaky floorboards, I remember as a kid how spooky it seemed on the third floor. I smile, give a slight fake shiver, flick on the light switch, and head for the attic door at the end of a confining dark hallway.

I open that door and walk up the narrow steep flight of stairs into a world of fifty years before when my brothers and I played oh so many games of hide-and-seek. At the top of the steps, I tug on a string hanging from an old light bulb, and it clicks on.

Not a lot of light, but it's enough to make my way to other strings to click on more lights in the vast attic that sprawls from one end of the house to the other. Finally, I stand in the middle and rotate three-hundred-and-sixty degrees to find the space filled to the rafters. Frank and I, with kids, ought to clean this out.

I would bet some relics up here go back to the original owners, mixed among the things that belonged to my grandparents and my parents. I walk around the many ancient steamer trunks and footlockers, using my flashlight to read travel stickers and name tags. I look for a group of cases that I packed with my mother's things after she died.

Even though I gave away a lot of her clothes, I packed up my favorite vintage items of hers thinking I'd get to them one of these days.

Light from a round window at the front of the house illuminates three trunks. Pay dirt. Flipping open the two clasps and lifting the lid of the closest of these trunks, I carefully touch the beautiful clothes by Oscar de la Renta, Valentino, and Dior—and I sigh. I still vividly remember my always elegant mother wearing these dresses. Closing the trunk, I push it aside. This isn't the one I'm looking for.

I open the next trunk and gaze at an amazing mélange of handbags and perhaps two dozen pairs of shoes, all well cared for. When I was in my twenties, I had no interest in these beautiful accessories, but now I often use one of my mother's Hermés pocketbooks, and Laura carries one of her grandmother's Chanel bags.

Sitting cross-legged on the floor, I pull out a half-dozen pairs of beautiful shoes. Then I spot it—a Chanel shoe bag—and I find the pumps with the broken heel. Thinking back to when my mother last wore them, I wiggle the heel, and in an instant I'm back in that moment.

I had been taking some glasses out of a cabinet when my mother entered the dining room carrying a dish filled to the brim with her tomato basil sauce. Suddenly, a little dark-haired girl darted into the room through another door. She was shrieking and laughing as she chased one of our dogs. Was it Glory, our black Lab? This was in the late-1970s, so, yes, the dog probably was Glory.

Gleefully running around the table after the dog, the girl bumped into my mother, who, startled, tried her best not to spill the sauce. I dashed over and caught the dish from my mother, but it still splashed on the carpet.

I should have rushed to my mother's rescue instead as she teetered on the very same Chanel heels I now hold in my hands. "Oh, dear," she cried, as she lost her balance, trying to break her fall against the sideboard and crashing to the floor.

Glory and the little girl stopped running, and the girl stood frozen in horror. As my mother moaned in pain on the floor, the child burst into howling tears, hiding under the table with her arms wrapped tightly around the beautiful black Lab.

"Mother, are you all right?" I dashed over as she sat up to rub her ankle and take off the shoe with the broken heel.

"I'll be fine, Ronnie," she said. "I noticed earlier that this heel felt a little loose. But, you know, they're my favorites. Oh, well, off to the cobbler for repair." I helped Mother stand up and hop to a chair, while the little girl continued sobbing under the table.

Rosa, our housekeeper, entered the dining room, drawn by the commotion. She looked at my mother massaging her ankle, the spilled sauce on the carpet, and the girl glued to the dog under the table. "Oh, Mrs. Rutherfurd. I'll clean this up immediately." She shifted her gaze to the child, who couldn't have been more than four or five. "Maria! What have you done?" she scolded. "Let go of Glory, and go straight to the kitchen."

The small, dark-haired girl released the dog, who rushed over to lick up the spilled sauce. Maria ran out of the room, now crying even harder.

"Oh, Rosa. Don't be so tough on her," my mother said. "It was just an accident..."

Gosh, I haven't thought about Rosa in years. Funny how an old memory can pop up out of nowhere. Obviously, the broken shoe was the trigger. Wonder why my mother never got this shoe fixed?

I put the broken-heeled Chanel back in the trunk filled to the brim with shoes and all those handbags. Mother had so many and all equally gorgeous. I remember, as a little girl, shuffling around in her high heels and feeling so pretty. Definitely where I got my love of beautiful shoes.

As I come down the steps from the third to the second floor, I encounter Juliana standing in the wide hall staring at me with a look that telegraphs *what are you doing up there?* Before I can say a word, she walks into her room and shuts the door. I guess the chess game downstairs is finished.

I get it. She probably wonders whether, if she marries Frank, she'll have her sister-in-law wandering into this house at any hour of the day. If they marry, I'll have to be sensitive to their privacy. But she's not his wife yet.

~~~~~

That evening I join Frank and Juliana for supper at our nearby club. We sit with several friends at a round table on the terrace that looks out over the gently rolling contours of the golf course. Frank gives me a small glance with a quick sad smile, and I'm betting that we're both missing our brother, Peter, who should be with us on this beautiful, balmy evening.

A buzz of lively conversation circles the table, but I sit quietly, distracted by my thoughts, and gaze at the spectacular rolling New Jersey vista beyond the eighteenth hole. I consider how fast things appear to be moving between my brother and his girlfriend and how I need to know more about Juliana Wentworth's life leading up to her years in California. Maybe that's the only way I'll get to the bottom of whether or not she's up to something bad, and therefore bad for Frank.

I discreetly study the two of them, hoping they won't notice me catching the silent looks they give each other. It's as if they have their own unspoken language. And when he or she thinks the other one isn't looking, their adoring glances for each other aren't even subtle.

Frank looks so happy that I would hate to do anything to spoil it. Still, better for him to know the truth now, before the two decide to marry. But what truth am I likely to find?

CHAPTER TWENTY-EIGHT

"O'Sensei is quoted as saying, 'To injure an opponent is to injure yourself. To control aggression without inflicting injury is the Art of Peace.'" Basically, Isabella Romano is reminding the class that when we practice Aikido, we don't try to actually harm each other.

Anyway, a moment ago, two of the men in our class at the dojo became overly aggressive, too in-your-face with each other. What is it with the male ego? Will and another larger classmate had to separate them. This type of thing is a rare occurrence, and we're all taken aback by the incident.

Isabella continues. *"O'Sensei* also said, 'The purpose of training is to tighten up the slack, toughen the body, and polish the spirit.'" All of us sit in *seiza*, or the basic kneeling posture we use throughout class to show respect for the practice and our teachers. "Let's finish with back stretches."

I rise and quickly move to Lizzie, who's smaller than most of our classmates, but tough. She can definitely hold her own on the mat with guys who tower over her. We stand spine to spine and hook arms. I lower my body and fold Lizzie over my back so she gets a terrific stretch. Then she does the reverse, folding me over hers, so that my spine feels as if it elongates by three inches.

Isabella *Sensei* claps to end our class, and we bow out, again sitting in *seiza*. As we thank all our partners on the mat, Will signals for us to meet outside.

Waiting between our cars, Will pulls a slip of paper out of his pocket when I approach. "Here." He hands me the paper with a phone number written on it. "Give this guy a call. His name's Jack Crosby, and he's the retired NYPD detective who worked for ten years at John Palmer's company in the city. These days he lives in Maplewood and does occasional freelance work, mostly around New Jersey."

He catches me gawking, and laughs. "What?"

"It's only been a couple of days, Will, since I asked you to check on this. How'd you find him so fast? I mean, did you miraculously get your hands on an old directory at Palmer's company?" I know I've got a lot to learn, but some tricks of the trade leave me wondering.

"Got a guy who does some work for me here and there." He opens his car door. "I've helped him out, and he owed me one."

"What kind of work does he do for you, Will?" I wave the piece of paper, not sure I really want to know the answer.

"Oh, computers, tech, you know…" He throws a duffel bag into the back seat of his car. "…Database entry, human resources files…" He gives me a hard look, almost daring me to challenge him on this. "…And so on."

"Will, are you breaking the—"

"Don't ask, don't tell, Ronnie." He gets in the car and starts the engine.

"But, Will—"

"Call him, Ronnie," Will says as he pulls away. "See what you can find out." He drives off.

~~~~~

When I contact Jack Crosby, I use a phone purchased an hour earlier and give him the name Reba Long instead of my real name, just in case he's in touch with his old boss, John Palmer. I offer him my usual song and dance, how I'm trying to find someone, someone who's connected to our family. I tell him her name is Terry Jones, and that I believe she used to work at Palmer's company. Crosby says he'll check his old files.

We meet in front of his office in Maplewood. Rather than sit inside, we decide to stroll along the charming village streets toward Maplewood Park and do a walk and talk.

Crosby still has a lot of pep left in him. "I started working for Palmer's company twenty-plus years ago. I wasn't even sixty when I left the NYPD, but a back injury made it tough to stay active on the job."

That means the silver-haired former detective must now be in his late seventies, but he moves as if he's twenty years younger, even with his bad back.

"I took an early retirement," he continues, "and the opportunity at CyTech came along. Worked there for ten years and accumulated some company stock. When Palmer sold the firm, I cashed in and retired out here to be close to my daughter and my grandchildren."

We enter the lovely park and walk along its paths through lush foliage. "Maplewood has such a quaint village center, and this park is beautiful," I comment.

Jack Crosby interrupts my chatter. "Now, Ms. Long, you didn't drive over for a nice walk in the park. What would you like to know about Terry Jones?"

"Ah, where to start, Mr. Cros—may I call you Jack?" He nods yes to me, and I smile at him. "And please, call me Reba."

"Boy, I'd never have pegged you for a Reba," he says.

"Nickname. I'm really Rebecca, but I never liked it." He looks at me curiously, and I change the topic fast. "We've been out of touch for quite a long time. I'm reaching out to family members for a reunion though, and finding Terry has been nearly impossible. So now I'm casting a wider net."

We walk across a small bridge over a stream.

"I know Terry worked at Club Nucleus about fifteen years ago, and she was a good friend of John Palmer's—"

Crosby nods. "I remember seeing her a few times around the office with Palmer. She was a sweet kid." His eyes stare off into the distance.

"Look, I know she was personally involved with Mr. Palmer and played a lot of chess with him around that time. I'd like to get in touch with her, but the trail goes cold after her Club Nucleus days," I say. "I heard she went off to school somewhere, and I'm hoping you have information that could point me in the right direction."

Crosby, I mean, Jack smiles. "Terry wasn't much younger than Palmer. But she had something mysterious in her background, some dark secret that haunted her and that she tried to keep from John."

"Did you discover what it was?" I ask, hopeful.

"No, and whatever it was, I think it popped up in her life again when she was with Palmer. I think that's what caused her to run away. The boss waited too long hoping she'd come back on her own before he asked me to find her. At that point, I tried, but with no success. If he'd asked me immediately, you know, when she first took off, I'd have had a better shot. But then it was simply too late. The trail was cold."

We sit on a bench under a gigantic sugar maple tree. "Did you find out anything? Where she went to school? How she earned a living? Anything, that could help me find her now?"

Jack pulls some papers out of his jacket pocket and unfolds what looks like a computer printout of a report. "I archived some of my old files from CyTech, including this one. The request was such an interesting one from the boss, especially since she wasn't an employee of the company." He thumbs through the several pages and hands them to me. "Here, for you."

I look down at the papers and see the name of the community college where she received an associate's degree. I'm thrilled. "What more can you tell me about the time she spent at school? What did she study? How were her grades?"

"A lot of questions to track her down for a reunion…" He studies me.

"Just friendly curiosity, Jack." I smile sweetly. "Whatever you can tell me would be great."

Maybe he doesn't care what my reasons are. "Well, she worked nights and took classes during the day," he says, "knocking off general ed courses to get her degree. I talked to a couple of the profs from that time who remembered her, and they said this girl had a thirst for knowledge and self-improvement like nobody else. Her grades were pretty good, too." He coughs and takes a package of mints from his pocket.

"What kinds of courses?" I ask.

"Intro to business, history, literature, writing," Jack answers. "She even joined a chess club. Chess was what started her friendship with Mr. Palmer. He liked her curiosity, and he told me she picked up the game really fast."

"So Terry Jones kept up with her chess…" I ponder this.

"That's right." He shakes his head. "I don't know how she had time between a full load of classes, homework, and her job almost every night of the week."

"Where'd she work?" I ask. "What did she do?"

"She worked as a shot girl at Benny's Bar in Soho." Jack sees the surprise on my face. "Ah, ha, Mrs. Long. I mean Reba." He notices my confusion, which is more about momentarily forgetting my new alias, and he smiles. "I see you don't frequent the New York bar scene."

I'm still somewhat baffled. "You've got that right. Is it legal? Being a shot girl, I mean?" I don't know what it is, but it sounds dicey. Hold it. Am I showing my age? But this guy's in his seventies. Why is it that I'm quite a bit younger than he is, and I don't know anything about shot girls?

He laughs as if he knows what I'm thinking. "I wouldn't know about them either, but my work takes me to all sorts of places."

"What do they do? These shot girls, I mean." I raise my eyebrows. "God, it sounds like a real comedown for poor Terry. You know, going from member services at Club Nucleus to working as a shot girl—"

"Actually," he interrupts. "It's not. Nowadays you'll find a lot of press about these shot girls. Most of them are college educated. A lot of them even have advanced degrees. Many shot girls also hold day jobs."

"The money must be great."

"Absolutely," Jack says. "They can take home three- to six-hundred dollars a night."

Wow. "You're kidding." I figure he must be joking, or maybe the girls do more than waitress. "They honestly get paid that much just for serving drinks?" I ask.

"Trust me," he says. "These girls aren't hookers. They walk through the bar carrying trays of novelty drinks, like Jell-O shots. Sometimes they get a cut of what they sell, and the tips are usually pretty good. Of course, good looks, a great figure, and terrific personality are the reason these girls get hired in the first place."

I shake my head in continuing amazement. "Well, in that case, Terry must have been the perfect candidate." I stop. "Wait a minute. They had shot girls fifteen years ago?"

He's still kind of grinning at my naiveté. "Benny's Bar was one of the first, and the girls there made their money from the tips and didn't get a cut of what they sold. I'm not sure they even called them shot girls when the concept first hit." Jack flips to the second page of the report. "One thing that was interesting is that Terry changed her name."

I mentally utter a second WOW. "She what?"

"Well, she still used the name Terry Jones at school, on her transcript," Jack says. "But at work she went by Julie Jones."

Now I take a deep breath at this flash of sudden illumination. "Julie Jones." So Teresa Gonzalez morphed into Terry Jones, who became Julie Jones. I wonder where down the road she made the final switch from Julie Jones to Juliana Jones before she married and became Juliana Wentworth. "It sounds as if she was putting distance between her Club Nucleus days and being a shot girl."

"That I don't know." He gets up from the bench. "Well, we should go now. I don't mean to rush you, but I have a phone appointment at the office in fifteen minutes."

On the way back, I ask, "Do you know of anybody I should call to follow up?"

Jack smiles again. "At the bottom of that report are some phone numbers for you. One of them is the owner of the bar where she worked," he says. "When he and I talked, Terry, a.k.a Julie, had already split. Nobody knew anything about where she'd gone. Then Palmer pulled me off this to work on something else. Maybe she got in touch with Palmer later on. Who knows? Why not give Palmer himself a call?" Already done that, I think to myself, in person, in Salt Lake City.

We return to the center of town near his office. I thank Jack Crosby for his time and say goodbye. As I walk toward my car, I switch back to my regular cell phone, dial and leave a message for my pal. "Will, how would you like to go with me this evening to a bar in New York?" I pause. "Not a date, not that you thought so, anyway. Work related. Bye."

CHAPTER TWENTY-NINE

Standing on a side street in Soho, Will Benson and I take in the black-lacquered front of the building and read the gold raised words above the large front window—Benny's Bar & Grill. We look inside, and I gaze at a world long gone for me, thank god—the New York singles bar scene. It's early evening, only six p.m., but people, some as young as my daughters, are starting to fill up the place.

We walk in and sit at a small table in the corner where we can view the entire room. I ask for a chardonnay and Will an imported beer, and we also order a light supper.

Even though Will may be forty, he could easily pass for a decade younger, so he fits right in. I look around and am painfully aware that I'm probably the oldest person in Benny's Bar. If anyone notices Will and me, like the waiter, for example, well, he probably thinks I'm a cougar out with my...what? My cub?

I look at the name tag and ask our waiter, Tom, if we can buy the owner a drink should he have a moment. Since it's early, I'm hoping Benny Sullivan won't be too swamped yet, managing what promises to turn into a raucous watering hole as the evening progresses. The waiter leaves and speaks with a man at the bar, who looks at us and then back down at his paperwork.

"That's got to be Benny," Will says, stating the obvious.

"Is he blowing us off, or do you think he'll come over?" I ask.

"Hard to say. We'll give him some time," Will tells me. "We can always move ourselves to the bar."

In the meantime, we watch two young women dressed in identical mini-skirts and tops with deep V-necks. Lots of leg and plenty of cleavage. Interestingly, they don't actually look as if they're on the make. Gorgeous hair and not too much make-up. Very natural.

As Tom serves us our beer and wine, I ask, "Are those beautiful young women some of the shot girls that Benny's is so famous for?" Tom gives me a weird look. "Hey, I'm just a housewife from New Jersey..." I cough, adding, "...here with my nephew. What do you expect?" Will barely suppresses a laugh.

"The boss said he'll be over soon," Tom promises me. "Has to finish something first. And yes, Ma'am. Those are a couple of our shot girls, Chrissy and Melanie." He looks amused. "Shall I send one of them over for any other orders?"

"No, no, no. We'll stick with what we have. Thanks, Tom," I say, cutting off Will before he can answer in the affirmative.

"You're welcome, Ma'am." He leaves.

When did *Ma'am* start to sound so old? I mean, I'm wearing expensive, but worn, tight jeans with black boots and a sleeveless fitted black tee-shirt. I've always had good, firm arms, and, OK, I admit I like to show them off. Does the waiter, Tom, think I'm the same age as his mother?

We're well into dessert by the time the boss finally comes over. He gazes down at us through heavy-lidded eyes with dark circles underneath. Must be the hours he keeps. His dark hair is shot through with grey, and a cigarette's tucked behind one ear. His face is unshaven, probably all the time, a sort of permanent five-o'clock shadow. I'm guessing it's his look.

"Hi, I'm Benny Sullivan," he says in a deep, whiskey-stained voice. "Tom told me you'd like to speak with me?" He looks back at the bar for a moment. "Is everything all right?"

I reach my hand out toward him. "Hi, I'm Ronnie Lake." We shake. "This is Will Benson." They shake hands, too.

I cough and shift into my lower register, to match Benny's. "As the owner, you're a busy man, I'm sure." I flash a huge smile at him and hope the effect is a touch seductive. "May we have five minutes of your time? I'm trying to locate a relative, and I think she worked for you almost fifteen years ago."

Benny stares at me for a long moment, as if he's making up his mind. He looks at Will and back at me.

Will jumps in. "Hey, man, let us buy you a drink. We won't take much of your time, and maybe you can help the lady out."

Benny looks around his tavern and back at us. "OK. Things are under control, so I've got five minutes." He sits down, and signals to Tom for the same imported beer that Will is drinking. "Now, who is it you think may have worked for me fifteen years ago?" He takes the cigarette from behind his ear and plays with it, rolling it through his fingers.

"Julie Jones," I answer. Benny looks at me blankly, but then his expression evolves into one of recognition. He stops playing with the unlit smoke. I go on. "Dark haired and beautiful. She took college classes during the day and worked here in the evenings. Curious about everything, always learning as much as she could—"

Benny cuts me off. "I remember Julie." He tucks the cigarette behind his ear again and takes a slow drink from his beer—and Will does, too. "She was as nice as she was gorgeous. Wasn't stuck-up about her looks at all," the bar owner says. "Julie had a lot of sparkle. She was great with the customers."

The sound of laughter distracts all of us, and we watch Chrissy, one of the two shot girls we saw earlier, at a table where she sells a half-dozen Jell-O shots to a group of young professionals. The guys have shed their jackets, loosened their ties, and rolled up their sleeves. Her long, blonde hair and big blue eyes, in addition to the J.Crew-type uniform, make her look more like a college coed than a stereotypical barmaid.

Chrissy's most impressive weapon is her perky personality. She's got the table eating out of her hand. Once she passes around the drinks and collects the money, she flips her blonde mane and walks in our direction tucking the money in her pocket.

She smiles at us, and Will toasts her with his beer glass. He looks at her tray now only half-filled with shots. "I think I'll take one of those," Will says as she comes close. He pulls money out of his jeans.

"Well, thank you." She beams at him.

"Chrissy, I'm conducting an informal survey," Will says, as she hands him the Jell-O shot. "I've heard that most shot girls are college students when they're not working their bar jobs. Is that true in your case?" I don't think Will is on the make, but he does have a gleam in his eye.

"That's right. Many of us are college students," Chrissy answers, "or we have good day jobs."

"And how about you, Chrissy?" Maybe Will is actually flirting with her.

"Halfway through my Ph.D.!" she says with spunk. You know she's proud, and rightfully so.

"What's your subject?"

"Child psychology!" She smiles at Will, flips her hair, and she's off to another table.

CHAPTER THIRTY

"It's all about their personalities," Benny says, watching Chrissy go. "Customers love the positive energy. It makes the evening more fun for everyone, and it's great for business."

"How about Julie Jones?" I ask. "Did her sparkle measure up to Chrissy's pizzazz?"

Benny nods. "Absolutely. We'd been open less than a year, and we hired three girls. They were all terrific, real stars. Julie was part of that original group, although we didn't call them shot girls in those days." He takes another drink from his beer. "Yeah, Julie definitely had a special knack with the customers. Some of them became regulars here because of her."

He then pushes his glass aside and leans forward on the table. "Now, Ms. Lake, what leads you to look for Julie?"

"Please call me Ronnie." Once again, I turn on the smile. "She's part of my extended family, and I'm organizing a reunion."

Benny stares at me hard. "Nah, it's not that simple, Ronnie." A look of concern flashes across his face. "I'm not buying it. What's happened to make you go back fifteen years to try to find her? I was worried about her then, and now I'm starting to worry all over again."

Will gives me a quick glance, and I continue. "Benny, Julie's been out of touch with the family for a long time."

"Maybe she has good reason to be," he responds.

"Don't know her reasons, but on my end it's simply a family reunion." I shrug. "Every time I've tried to track her down, I hit a dead end. So I've pushed further and further into her past, trying to find a moment that would help me link up with her."

I take a deep breath and look at Will, who quietly finishes his dessert. I take another bite of my pie. "Benny, you said you were worried about her then. Why?"

"She only worked here for about six months," he says. "But it was a memorable time. The dot-com era was at its height. It seemed like anything was possible. And as I said, the bar was new, and we all worked hard. The business was taking off—it was exciting, and Julie was part of it. Then one day, she was gone."

"What happened?" I ask.

"Well, she gave one of the other girls who worked with her a note for me saying she was quitting immediately. No notice," he says. "Frankly though, I wasn't surprised."

"Why?" Will asks. "I thought you said she was a star."

"She was, but a guy started turning up and bothering her the last couple of weeks before she left," Benny says. "Billy? Bobby? Yeah. Bobby, uh, Turner?"

"Bobby Taylor?" I throw out.

"That's it," Benny says. "Bobby Taylor. He was some guy she'd known way back when. Sounds as if you know him, too?"

"Well, sort of—"

"This Bobby Taylor started bothering her at work, and it escalated. A couple of times he really made a scene in here. Almost attacked her the last time. Then she took off," he says. "This Bobby guy came back one more time. He threatened me, tried to force me to tell him where she'd gone. Of course, I was in the dark as much as he was. I told the guy if he ever set foot in my place again, I'd call the police. That was it. Never saw him after that."

"Sounds like a lot of drama," Will says.

"But that wasn't the end of it." Benny snorts with a half-laugh. "Some detective showed up a month later trying to find Julie. I guess his boss had been her fiancé." Benny rubs his whisker-shadowed chin. "We couldn't help him either at that point since none of us had heard from her."

I look at Will. "Sounds like another dead end." I push aside my plate.

"Hold on," the tavern owner says, getting up. "Be right back." He walks over to the bar, opens a black leather binder, and flips through the pages. Then he writes on a piece of paper and returns to our table.

"Give Mara Smith a call. She was one of the three original shot girls, and she and Julie became close friends. I remember she heard from Julie sometime after that detective came by. Maybe Mara's still in touch with Julie." He hands me the paper with the number on it. "These days Mara's in Greenwich married with kids. Don't mean to rush off, but I've got to get back to work." He shakes our hands and walks up a stairway, most likely to his office.

Will and I decide to stick around and enjoy people-watching. It turns out to be beer pong night. Several long, rectangular tables have been set up with six-cup triangles at each end.

I smile at the lyrics of a favorite Leonard Cohen song, "Closing Time," coming through the bar's sound system. Two-man teams gather, pour beer into the cups on each edge, and commence aiming at the cups with ping pong balls. A ball dunks in, and the team whose cup it is must drink the beer. People circle around the tables cheering their friends, who shoot a variety of arc, bounce, and fastballs while the rowdiness factor grows.

The teams become increasingly raucous as they swill down the beer and play, and the now unruly crowd cheers them on. Hearing Leonard Cohen's gravelly voice is getting harder.

"Am I showing my age, Will, if I tell you all this noise—not Leonard Cohen by the way—the nonmusic noise is giving me a headache?"

"Decibel level is pretty high," he agrees. "Want to call it a night?" We walk in the direction of the front door, passing one of the beer pong tables.

I notice what sounds like an argument coming from the table, this one about four deep in spectators. A crashing noise interrupts a booming voice yelling, "You mother—"

I stand frozen, watching the group, even though Will is tugging at my arm.

A woman screams, "Watch out! Baby, watch out—"

Suddenly a tall, burly guy in a do-rag, sleeveless shirt, torn jeans, and combat boots comes flying at me through a break in the crowd. All I can think as everything goes slow motion for me is how did this guy get in dressed like that? Benny's has a clearly stated dress code on the website—no do-rags, no sleeveless shirts, and no combat boots.

He's huge, and he's hurtling right toward me. If he hits me, I'm toast. I see the crowd turn to follow the guy's trajectory, and I see Will, out of the corner of my eye, focus on a different big guy, also breaking dress code, who moves toward him.

Just as my guy is ready to slam into me, I duck down, sideways, into a crouch. Since this giant is now connecting with thin air where I once stood, and since he's sailing over my crouched body, he falls. His head bangs into a table, and his body crashes into empty chairs, knocking everything over.

When we practice this in class, the person who attacks moves into a graceful forward roll rather than slamming onto the floor. But this is real life, and the guy is out for a while.

I look over again at Will. Guy number two must think Will is part of the reason his friend is out cold on the floor, and he comes at Will with an overhead strike. I watch my third-degree black belt buddy go on the offensive.

Will gets right into the guy's space on the side, grabbing the striking arm at the elbow, where he can control him. In my mind I hear Isabella *Sensei* telling class how important it is to control your opponent's elbow in certain techniques. In a split second I know that Will plans a *kaitenage*, or rotary-type throw.

Will quickly and firmly grips the man's neck with his other hand and pushes his attacker low to the ground. Simultaneously with this movement, Will also shoves the guy's elbow-held arm into his side throwing the attacker forward and down with a turn of his hips. This guy, just like his friend, crashes into some chairs, finally coming to his own dead stop. He raises himself, dazed, moaning and barely moving.

The beer pong game has stopped, of course, and the crowd watches the two of us in stunned silence. I smile at Will and notice a flash to the side. I turn in time to see a woman in cut-off short-shorts with chains and a hoodie rush at me. From the angle of her arm, I'm certain she plans to attack me with a cross-hand strike.

I'm shocked to see a knife in her striking hand. OK, OK, OK—I've practiced this a thousand times in class (slight exaggeration), and I hope the technique works. Do not panic. Breathe.

Sliding in for a direct entry, I bring my arms up my center, almost as if I'm starting to pray. One of my hands explodes toward her face and shoves her chin back. My other hand clamps overhand between the elbow and wrist of her knife-wielding arm.

My arm that originally went for her face now crosses over my other arm and grabs her wrist overhand. I extend my arms to keep her blade at a distance so that it can't slash me and execute a quick pivot while I push her down to the floor. She screams out a string of profanities as her knee hits the floor first and takes the painful weight of her fall.

Ms. Short Cut-offs is now flat on the floor with her knife-wielding arm straight out, palm up. I quickly pull up her elbow, which positions her wrist at an ugly angle, and she immediately releases the knife. Will kicks it away from all three attackers, and our waiter, Tom, stops it with his foot before someone else can go for it. Other barmen step in to secure the wrists of the three attackers with plastic ties.

Will grabs my arm, pulling me up. "Good job, Ms. *Shodan*, but quit while you're ahead. Let's get out of here."

The beat of Leonard Cohen continues pounding from all directions. Unbeknownst to us, Benny Sullivan, this time with the unlit cigarette hanging from the side of his mouth, has been standing outside his office watching the commotion from the loft space above. He hollers down to us, "Who are you two, really?"

I look up and smile on the way out of the bar and call up to him loudly. "Like I said before, just a housewife from New Jersey."

CHAPTER THIRTY-ONE

"Here to see Mara Smith," I say to the man in the small guard house at the entrance to the very private community of Taconic Harbor.

He peers into my driver's side window and smiles at me. "Yes, Ma'am. Make a left turn, and it's the seventh house on the right." The security guard waves me through, and in my rearview mirror I see him write down my license plate number.

Driving down the curvy road in this exclusive Greenwich, Connecticut enclave, I catch glimpses through walls, gates and hedges of perfectly maintained homes and grounds. My iPod plays Abba's "Money, Money, Money," and I sing along.

I slow my Mustang in order to get a better look at early-twentieth-century grand white elephants that must cost a fortune in upkeep. Scattered among these testaments to new wealth a century before, I catch sight of today's testosterone-produced tributes to hedge-fund excess...uh, success. These massive structures are too, too what—shiny, monstrous, and new?

I make a right at the seventh driveway and pull up to a version of Scarlett O'Hara's Tara on steroids. Oh, dear. While staring at bulging Corinthian columns that reach three stories high to a widow's walk, I sing along to Abba more quietly.

One half of a massive, shiny, black double-door opens, and a slender figure in deep purple yoga clothes springs down the steps, her luscious, thick, red hair bouncing on her shoulders. Two yapping Yorkshire terriers leap down after her, protecting their mistress from unfamiliar visitors.

"Hi, there!" She waves to me.

I step out of my car, and the little dogs swirl around my feet making a racket. "Hush, Trixie, Falco," the redhead orders. "Oh, I'm so sorry," she says to me. "I hope you like dogs."

I squat down and stretch out the top of my hand for sniffs from two cold noses. "It's fine. I've got a German shepherd at home." The Yorkies settle down.

"I'm Mara Smith." I hear a slight Southern drawl in her welcoming voice.

"I'm Ronnie Lake. Thanks for seeing me." We shake hands, and I gaze around the property, hoping I'm displaying a fitting degree of admiration. Mara watches me.

To my surprise, she directs my gaze above her hedge to a lovely old stone mansion with a steep slate roof across the road. "Now, that's where I'd love to live, even though I'm just positive it's a money pit." She giggles. "But since my husband sold his business five years ago, he's become a builder. Said he always wanted to create big, beautiful houses. He built this place and our other homes in Boca

Grande and up on Nantucket. Don't get me wrong. I just love Mike to death, but all our houses are so huge…" She rolls her eyes and giggles again. "…and definitely over the top."

"Oh, no—" I interject.

"Where do you live, Ronnie?"

"Over in Willowbrook, New Jersey—"

"Oh, I thought you were here in Greenwich." She looks at me as if intrigued and then beams a million-dollar smile. "Mike is from New Jersey, too. He grew up in Asbury Park." She walks back up the steps. "Come on, Ronnie. Let's go out back and sit where we have a view of the water."

I follow Mara through a long marble-floored hallway lined with fluted pedestals holding a mix of antique and contemporary sculptures. I discreetly glance through doors as we walk, and the mistress of the house notices my curiosity. She stops at one door, and we look into an enormous empty room, maybe four times the size of the largest room at Meadow Farm. Massive paintings hanging on all the walls are the only adornment. The two Yorkies dash in and chase each other around the expanse as if they were in an Olympic stadium.

"Mike likes to call this the gallery, because he collects art, but it's really our party room," Mara says. "We keep it empty, so that we never have to move out the furniture when we entertain a big group."

Well, now… "That's very practical, Mara," I tell her approvingly.

"Ronnie, guess how many bedrooms in this house." She giggles. But before I can even hazard a guess, she blurts out, "Twelve! In case we have weekend guests for a house party. Can you imagine? Mike planned it that way for the resale value."

"How many do you actually use?" I ask.

"Only a few." She shrugs. "Most of them I never even furnished…just keep the doors closed." She smiles. "Enough of this. Let's go outside."

Mara and I continue walking. This mini museum mile leads to the back of the house, and we step onto a terrace with a spectacular view of the harbor.

We head toward a cluster of oversized outdoor furniture positioned to take in the panorama and sink into their plush cushions. Trixie and Falco hop up on a chaise to better observe what Mara and I are up to.

"I never get tired of looking at the water." Mara reaches for a huge pitcher of lemonade on the glass coffee table.

"With this view, I wouldn't either," I say, as I watch sailboats moored at the yacht club on the other side of the harbor bob in the water.

"Ronnie, I don't mean to brag about my wonderful husband, but Mike made it even more spectacular than when we first bought this property. It was hilly toward the water with giant boulders and too many trees." Mara fills two tumblers and hands me one.

"You don't mean to tell me—"

"Exactly. Mike used some of his earthmoving equipment and got rid of those hills and the boulders. Then he cut down the trees and created this beautiful smooth lawn that swoops down to the water." She grins like a kid getting a pony. "He says he feels as though he's in *The Great Gatsby* when he walks on this perfect grass at dusk with a cocktail and stares out at the lights over there."

"Mara, it is amazing, and it's great how you appreciate and enjoy it all." I can't help but like her.

"The kids are at camp until the afternoon, and my tennis game was cancelled." She takes a drink. "When you called this morning, I really thought you were already in Greenwich. I never in a million years thought you were in New Jersey."

"Oh, it's not that far." I sip the lemonade. "Anyway, as I said on the phone, I've got this deadline looming for a family gathering. And none of us have seen Terry in a long time—I guess you knew her as Julie—so I decided to try to find her." I can't help but notice that Mara, about thirty-five, is one fit lady in her gorgeous yoga clothes. Probably has an enormous gym in the basement of this monster manse where she works out every day.

"So, you're kind of playing detective?" She giggles.

"Yeah, right." I roll my eyes in agreement, and we giggle together. "I kept hitting dead ends, until I got to Benny's Bar. I met the owner, and he suggested I get in touch with you, since you and Ter—I mean Julie—were good friends." From shot girl at Benny's Bar & Grill to housewife and mom living in a Greenwich palace, Mara Smith hasn't done too badly for herself. No siree.

"Mara?"

"Yes?"

"Did Terry ever tell you why she changed her name to Julie Jones when she went to work at Benny's?"

"I think it probably had to do with this guy she had grown up with who was big trouble," Mara says.

"Oh, yeah." I roll my eyes yet again. "Bobby Taylor, right?"

"That's the guy, Ronnie. A real lowlife."

"How long was Bobby around?" I ask as Trixie jumps off the chaise and then into my lap.

"I guess it was only a couple of weeks," she answers as Falco also hops down and squeaks. Mara picks him up. "But he was bad news. I think he hit her and grabbed her hard. One time I saw bruises on one of her shoulders and the other bicep when she took off her sweater, and her cheek was kind of swollen. She told the boss she had been to the dentist, but I knew it wasn't true."

That Bobby Taylor sure had one helluva grip. "That's awful," I say and make a face. "But are you sure it was Bobby Taylor? Maybe it was someone else?" I scratch Trixie's head as she looks at me with deep dark eyes. These Yorkie fur-balls are adorable.

"Absolutely." Mara is certain. "It was Bobby Taylor. One night I caught him pushing Julie around in the alley behind the bar. I hollered at him, pulled out my phone to call the police, and he ran." Mara drinks her lemonade while Falco squirms in her other arm. "Julie begged me not to tell Benny or anyone else at work. She was afraid she'd lose her job."

I act horrified, though I'm not entirely acting, of course. "Did this happen a lot during the two weeks he was around?"

"I don't know. She wouldn't talk about it with me. Then one day she was gone, except for a letter she left me to give to the boss." Mara gets a sad expression on her face. "Just gone. Nobody knew where. I really missed her."

Mara and I sit quietly watching a sail boat pass by. "I think she got pregnant." Her voice is almost a whisper, and my head whips toward her.

"Excuse me?" I say.

"Some time after she took off, I got a few letters and postcards from her. I don't have them anymore, but I remember in one of the last ones she wrote me she was pregnant." Mara shrugs her shoulders and says, "But then she stopped writing, and we lost touch. I don't know how that all worked out…if she ever even had a baby."

"Do you think it happened while she was still at Benny's?" I ask. "And do you think Bobby Taylor could have been the father?"

"Who knows when it happened. But no way was it Bobby Taylor. If he was, then he must have raped her, because she couldn't stand him." We put the Yorkies on the ground, and they chase each other in circles around the terrace. Mara continues, "Look, he may have hit her, but I got the feeling that she could pretty much take care of herself. She wasn't afraid of him—"

"Did she have a boyfriend while she worked at Benny's?" I interrupt. "You would have known, right?"

"Positively, and she did not," Mara says. "She was pretty sad about a breakup she'd had...some guy she was about to marry. She never said his name, but he definitely was the one she cared about." She shakes her head. "I lost touch with Julie after that." A breeze blows, and Mara pushes her hair out of her face. "We both just got on with our lives."

We're quiet for a long moment, as I let these thoughts sink in. A baby. If she was pregnant, that scenario could have played out in different ways. I flash on Francesca with *Tía* Connie in Scranton and do the math. Working at Benny's Bar & Grill could have overlapped the time when Francesca was conceived.

And now I have two candidates as the father. First, that creep Bobby Taylor harassing her at work and, who knows, perhaps raping her. And second, Juliana running into her ex-fiancé, John Palmer, in the city after their break-up and spending the night together. I mean, Palmer pretty much told me so with his 'the next morning she was gone' comment when I was in Salt Lake City.

Finishing my lemonade, I look at my watch. "Mara, thank you for sharing all this with me. Not sure it brings me any closer to finding her in time for our reunion, but I'm not giving up yet."

We walk back through the museum-mile hallway with the Yorkies' prancing at our heels. As we descend the front steps of the house, Mara says, "The one thing I remember is that Julie really wanted to get her college degree. You do know she was taking classes over at Manhattan Community College in Tribeca?" I nod. "Maybe they know where she transferred for her four-year degree," Mara offers. "Don't know if they'll tell you, but it's worth a try."

CHAPTER THIRTY-TWO

While I was traipsing from Salt Lake City, Utah, to Greenwich, Connecticut, and into Manhattan doing my own P.I. work, niece Laura tipped me off that Juliana had disappeared from Meadow Farm several times after my brother headed elsewhere for business meetings. So, once again Warrior sits quietly in the front passenger seat of Daniel's unobtrusive grey van as I drive over to the Keystone State, following Juliana, of course. I wonder if she's picked up on my investigation of her at all. If so, she'd probably accuse me of being a stalker.

We enter a familiar, rundown neighborhood on the outskirts of Scranton, and Juliana slows down in Meadow Farm's inconspicuous Toyota. She turns exactly where I thought she would, onto the same street of ramshackle clapboard houses that I'd visited before, and parks. Slowly, she looks around as if taking in every detail of this impoverished neighborhood. I discreetly pull into an empty slot near a fire hydrant on the block before hers.

Juliana has a brown envelope in her hand, slightly smaller than the one she gave to Bobby Taylor at the

Moosic Café some days ago. Is this one also filled with cash?

She hurries over to the front stoop of the row house I observed last time. The door swings open, and Mrs. de Torres emerges. Juliana runs up the steps where she and the elderly woman embrace, and I take pictures. They go inside the house.

To stay busy, I take pictures of the neighborhood in general, including its residents coming and going. I'm not sure any of it is relevant to my surveillance, but you never know.

Forty minutes later—so boring all this sitting around—Juliana comes out with Mrs. de Torres and I duck down. Both appear to be wiping tears from their eyes. More hugs between the two. The elderly woman goes back inside, and Juliana leaves. I stick around.

Nothing happens for the next ten minutes. I let Warrior out for a drink from his water bowl. We make our way up the sidewalk, as I tell him to *do your business*. Big mistake. First the sound of a car engine alerts me, and then I spot the Meadow Farm Toyota two blocks away heading in our direction.

In a panic at the thought of being spotted, I rush Warrior back to the van and hurry him into the vehicle as the Toyota drives by and stops close to the brownstone. Mrs. de Torres comes out again, and Juliana runs up the steps, glancing in my direction just as I enter the driver's side of the van. She hands the woman two big shopping bags and says something to her. Maybe she forgot to give the bags to her the first time around. They embrace, and

Juliana drives off one more time. Mrs. de Torres enters the brownstone with the bags.

I sit there with Warrior in the front of the van, wondering and worrying: Did Juliana see us?

~~~~~

I worry at the Scranton library during more research on Joe Taylor's drug program, all through my lunch at a nearby diner, and even during a quick drive-by at the Moosic Motel and coffee shop. Did Juliana see us? I head back to New Jersey.

Close to home, my phone vibrates. It's a text from Laura. *Come to MF. Dad & Jules had fight. He's gone. She's upset & leaving too.*

I quickly drive to Meadow Farm and turn onto the dirt road. It's early evening—dusk—and in the distance I see a car I don't recognize coming toward me from the big house. I can't make out who the driver is, but the vehicle is moving too fast on this narrow, winding road. I pull over to the side.

The car whizzes by me and then screeches to a stop. Juliana jumps out. My dog whines with concern, but doesn't growl. "Stay, Warrior," I command and exit the van.

I can feel the anger in her stride as she walks toward me. "I see you're not driving your Mustang." Then she nails me. "I saw you following me today. Why?"

At first, I don't respond—can't think quickly enough. She continues. "Other times I feel you watching me. What is it you think I've done that warrants all this watching and spying?"

"It goes both ways, Juliana."

"What could you possibly mean?" she asks.

"When I drove up to Scranton to meet with Joe Taylor on his school drug program, I'm sure I saw you following me," I state plainly. "When I pulled off the highway, I spotted you in the farm Toyota that has that distinctive dent." I don't give her a chance to deny my accusation. "So what was that about?"

Nothing.

"And you have to admit there've been some strange things going on since you arrived. How do you explain—"

She cuts me off. "I have nothing to explain to you. Frank and I are happy. Leave us alone. Why can't you just leave us alone?"

"Nothing against you, Juliana, but I have a concern this may be too soon after Joanie's—"

"I told Frank we shouldn't leave California," Juliana says. "I didn't want to come here—"

"Why wouldn't you want to come here?" I ask. "This is Frank's home. He's happy here. That's a strange thing to say."

"I have nothing against this place." I perceive a slight tone of defensiveness in Juliana's voice and stance. "It's just that extended families can be, how shall I say, complicated—"

"Who's Bobby Taylor?" There. The question is out. I couldn't help myself.

Everything stops. Juliana stares at me for what feels like an eternity. Her posture straightens; her shoulders drop back as though she means business. "What do you really have, Ronnie? Nothing. Just some crazy suspicions." She holds her head high. "Leave us alone." She turns on her heel and walks to her car.

"Is there still an *us*? I mean you and Frank?" I ask.

Juliana stops, shakes her head, gets in and drives away. I do the same. Coming around the bend, I see the house is all lit up.

My niece runs out the front door when she hears me pull in. "Where have you been?"

I take a deep breath and let it out slowly, still a little shaken after my dramatic encounter with Juliana. "It's a long story. I'll fill you in later," I answer. "First, what's up with Frank and Juliana? Did they break up?"

"Just the opposite." Laura looks at me. "Daddy asked her to marry him!"

~~~~~

My niece and I sprawl on the long sofa in the library at Meadow Farm—my father's favorite room, and Frank's, too—each of us with a glass of Chablis. My dog snoozes near my feet.

"Aunt Ronnie, I didn't mean to listen in on them." I look at Laura skeptically. "Really," she implores. "I was heading to the terrace to join them, and as I came to the French doors in the dining room, I overheard Daddy proposing to Juliana. So I just stood there next to the curtains—"

"You didn't leave," I scold, "and give them some privacy? Come on, Laura."

"Well, I was going to leave…" She sees I'm not buying it. "Honest. But the way Daddy proposed was very sweet, so I had to stay. I mean, he got down on bended knee with a ring." Laura drinks from her glass. "And then Juliana turned him down! She wouldn't take the ring. Anyway, I was shocked…and I froze."

I drink from my glass. There goes the gold-digger theory, out the window. "Laura, what did she say to your father?"

"*Now* are you glad I stayed to listen, Aunt Ronnie?" My niece stares at me, waiting for proper vindication.

"OK, OK. I'm glad. Now, tell me what you heard."

"Juliana said she's honored and that she loves him, but she's not quite ready. And Daddy said he loves her, too. And if they both feel that way then they should go for it. She said she wanted Daddy to please give her more time." Laura pauses, looking sad.

"What?" I ask.

"Daddy said life is too short, and he doesn't want to waste a moment of it—I know he was thinking about Mom when he said that." Her eyes water. My niece blinks quickly, then continues. "And he wants to share the rest of his life with someone he loves, and that he's found her— meaning Juliana."

We sip our wine, and I wonder why Juliana isn't jumping at Frank's proposal. They seem so close, as if they share an unspoken language, what with those secret looks between them at dinner the other night at the club—well, all along they've been that way.

Laura continues. "Juliana got very quiet, and Daddy asked her what was wrong. She said parts of her life are still unsettled and she needs time to take care of that first. Daddy said he wants to help."

"What did she say to that?" I put down my glass.

"Juliana said they're her problems, and she needs to handle them herself, without his help. He started to say something, and I could tell he was getting upset. But she interrupted him, and of course, we know Daddy doesn't like that. And she said one thing, Aunt Ronnie, but it's awkward, because it's about you."

"Go on."

"Juliana told Daddy that she thinks you don't trust her and that you may be looking into her background, like even following her," my niece says. "Oh, Aunt Ronnie, did you hire a private eye to find out about her...you know, the way I suggested when they first came home from California?"

Choosing not to answer her question, I ask, "Does Juliana think I hired an investigator?"

Laura shakes her head. "She didn't say that—only that she thought you were checking her out. Anyway, Daddy asked her for details, and she wouldn't tell him any. Just said that she knows you two are close, and she didn't want to get in the way."

My niece takes a sip of her wine and adds, "Juliana said she doesn't want to marry and have other family members distrust her."

I sip my Chablis. "You really overheard a lot, Laura."

"Yeah. So Daddy stormed off." She looks sheepish. "I'm not proud to admit I slipped behind the curtain as he came through the dining room. I didn't want him to see me so close."

"What did Juliana do?" I ask.

"Nothing. She just sat at the table, and I could tell she was crying," Laura says. "But she didn't run after him."

"So then what happened?"

"I ran outside and caught Daddy as he slammed the door to that loaner car. I asked him if he was all right and where he was going. Daddy said he's fine and that he'd be back in an hour, but I could tell he was pretty upset." Laura looks worried and pours more wine. "I hope he's OK, Aunt Ronnie. He tore out of here really fast. I hope he didn't drive that way on the highway, if that's where he went to let off steam."

"Where did Juliana go?"

"No idea. Next thing I knew, she was upstairs throwing some things in a bag. I could hear her up there crying and getting her things together. Then she ran downstairs and dumped this big satchel she has in that rental car they got for her. I ran after her, Aunt Ronnie, asking Jules where she was going. Like an idiot, I was running after her. Do you believe it? She left maybe ten minutes ago. You just missed her."

I decide not to tell her about my encounter with Juliana on the road. "Laura, what did she say? Anything about where she was going?"

"Juliana said she had to fix some things, and she was going to see some family in Pennsylvania. Of all places. I thought she was from California. Who is she, really, Aunt Ronnie? What do you think?"

I'm mulling over Terry-Teresa Gonzalez-Jones and runaway brides...and worrying about my brother's situation. That's what I think.

Twenty minutes later, Laura and I are in the kitchen putting our wine glasses in the dishwasher when we hear a car pull up. My dog's tail wags.

"Daddy." Laura rushes out.

I close the dishwasher and, with Warrior, follow her outside. Laura has her back to me, hugging her father. Frank looks at me, and his eyes communicate that he is not happy seeing me here.

"Laura, please go inside," he says. She looks back and forth between him and me, shrugs, gives me a quick hug and goes into the house.

I walk down the steps toward my brother. "Are you all right?"

He steps away and puts his arms out to block any possible hug from me. "Ronnie. You need to leave."

"What? Why, Frank?" I'm stunned.

"It seems to me that what started out as sisterly concern about my wellbeing has morphed into nosiness and meddling in my relationship with Juliana." Frank's voice is quiet and take-no-prisoners adamant. He's not loud when he's angry, nor does he argue. "I will not have it, Ronnie."

"But, Frank, what do you really know about her?" I try to stay calm, too. "You have to admit, since you two arrived from California, strange things have been happening. All those mystery hang-up calls, the road-rage accident, someone hitting you on the head—"

"Don't," his voice commands. "Do not say one word against Juliana. Your meddling may have cost me this relationship." He walks up the steps to the front door and turns back to me. "Ronnie, you need to stay away from Meadow Farm. For the time being, you are *not* welcome here."

"But, Frank, don't you see what's happening?" Desperation creeps into my voice. "This is exactly like what happened with Peter. He let a woman break him off from the family. Don't allow Juliana to do this to us. Please."

"You did it to yourself, Ronnie. Juliana did nothing. Stay away from us, and stay away from here." My brother goes inside and slams the door shut. On me. His little sister. And he doesn't even know how much I've *really* done.

"But, Frank, please…" My voice is barely a whisper as tears fill my eyes. Defeated, I take my dog, get in the borrowed van, and leave.

CHAPTER THIRTY-THREE

Sweat is running down my forehead, and I grab a towel off my handlebars to wipe my face. I check the watch part of my heart monitor. My heart rate has spiked into its anaerobic zone. Good.

I turn the knob to reduce the wheel tension and back off the pace slightly to lower my heart rate into an aerobic range. Those anaerobic spikes mean my metabolism should remain revved up for a longer part of the day burning pesky calories. Grabbing a quick swig from my water bottle, I continue pedaling.

Kary teaches a terrific spinning class, even at the bleary-eyed hour of 6 a.m. More importantly, she plays a lot of my favorite classic rock.

"OK, up to two, and one full turn," she yells. That means coming off the seat of the stationary bike, standing up, and turning the knob to increase the resistance. My spin shoes are clipped onto the pedals, and my legs push and pull as I cycle hard. The music is blasting, and I silently mouth Jon Bon Jovi's lyrics to "Runaway," although no one could hear me even if I sang at the top of my lungs.

My attention drifts from class as images float through my mind of a tough thirteen-year-old Teresa Gonzalez on the run from the law in Pennsylvania; of a determined sixteen-year-old Terry Jones changing hotel beds at Disney World; of an eighteen-year-old Terry dressed as Snow White, surrounded by adoring children in the Magic Kingdom theme park; of a helpful twenty-year-old Terry now behind the desk at the Contemporary Resort handling difficult guests; of a love-struck twenty-five-year-old Terry playing chess with geeky dot-com tycoon John Palmer at Club Nucleus in Manhattan; finally, of a heartbroken twenty-six-year-old Julie Jones working nights as a shot girl at Benny's Bar & Grill in Soho while taking college classes during the day.

After my Greenwich visit with Mara, I called Will to ask him to find out what became of Julie while she was at Manhattan Community College. In terms of privacy issues when trying to access information about former students from a school, well, for a pro like Will Benson, that would be a different story. He has years of connections and all sorts of ways to retrieve info, no doubt some legal, and some—how did he put it, "don't ask, don't tell"?

"Let's do jumps on a count of four," Kary hollers. I snap back to spinning class, happy to have another opportunity to spike my heart rate into its anaerobic zone.

My mind now wanders to the explosive Bobby Taylor, who seems to have often—or maybe solely—been the cause of Teresa-Terry-Julie's frequent moves. And all these years later, that creep persists in bothering her in her present life as Juliana.

If Bobby, heaven forbid, is Francesca's father, little wonder Juliana continues paying him off in her quest to keep him away from the girl. I wonder if she even knows who Francesca's father is—Bobby Taylor or John Palmer? I have to admit, though, except for Juliana breaking the law as a misguided juvenile decades ago, I haven't come across anything really terrible in her background.

Then the realization hits me like a bolt of lightning: Jules and I have something in common. We both have family members who are our nemesis—or should that be plural, nemeses? I widen my eyes. Seriously, Juliana's nemesis is right in her face with those constant threats from first cousin, Bobby Taylor. Mine is subconsciously in my face with the ongoing pain I feel regarding the total abandonment by my oldest brother, Peter—his wife being the actual nemesis. Unbelievable.

Nemesis or not, what really bothers me most was hearing Juliana say to Bobby, "You'll ruin everything." That's for sure a loaded sentence, and implies a plan. Maybe even revenge of some kind, considering what was written on the rock.

With a guy like Bobby Taylor lurking around, assuming the worst makes a lot of sense. I still feel protective of Frank, even if he won't speak to me right this minute. After what happened to my other brother, Peter, fifteen years ago, I'm not taking any chances.

I grab my towel from the handlebars to wipe more sweat off my face. I have another decade of Juliana's life left to investigate, which will bring her story up to the present, and I embrace the fascinating opportunity to learn more about her transformation from the scrappy Teresa to the refined Juliana. Whatever is going on with Bobby, I can't help but admire Juliana's sheer determination to create a better life.

But am I missing something more, something dark, something that makes her a danger to Frank—to us all?

"One last sprint," Kary yells to the class. "Three, two, one. Go!" We pick up our speed and pedal as fast as we can.

~~~~~

I figure my brother has had enough time to cool off, so Warrior and I decide to take a little drive to Meadow Farm after spinning class. Before Warrior and I can even make it up the steps to the front door, Juliana appears from around the corner with garden shears. She doesn't even pretend friendliness when we meet.

"What are you doing here?" she demands.

"Excuse me? What are *you* doing here?" I ask. "I thought you left for Pennsylvania."

"Change of plans..." She shakes hair from her eyes. "Anyway, you're not welcome here. Your brother made that perfectly clear to you." She gestures with the shears as she glares at me.

By my side, a low growl starts up. Warrior isn't happy about those shears. "Warrior, sit," I command. He sits, but continues growling. "Juliana, please put down the shears."

She stands as still as a statue with those damn shears pointing at me. Warrior barks two times. "Come on, Juliana. You know dogs. He thinks you're behaving aggressively toward me. Put the shears down slowly, and let me get him into the car."

She does as I've asked, and I take Warrior by his leash and put him in the Mustang. With the shears gone, he settles down, and I pull the top up on my car so that he can't jump out. By the time I turn back, Juliana has planted herself in front of the door and stands there with her arms crossed like a sentry, blocking me from entering the house in which I grew up.

"You're kidding." It occurs to me that this might be a good time to try a little Aikido. "You would seriously prevent me from entering my family house?"

"It's Frank's home, and he told you to stay away." Her voice is icy.

"Well, I think I'll hear that directly from my brother, not some recently arrived visitor. Not some outsider." I snarl the word *outsider*.

Juliana flinches ever so slightly, and then recovers. "You should respect your brother's wishes and leave, Ronnie," she says in a low, even voice. "He doesn't want you here. *We* don't want you here. You're a troublemaker."

"Correction, Jules, darling. You're the troublemaker. Why haven't you called the police on Bobby Taylor?" I ask.

I make a move to step around her to enter the house, but she's too quick for me, and slides in front of me again. Now we're really in each other's faces. Behind me, in my Mustang, Warrior growls as a car approaches the house, but I don't turn around to look. "And who exactly is Mrs. de Torres—" The car stops, and its door opens. Warrior woofs in anticipation. "—And, while we're at it, who is that lovely, young Francesca?" Now I see genuine fear in her eyes.

The car door slams. "Veronica," Frank yells at me, as if I'm six years old. He bounds up the steps and grabs me by the shoulders to pull me from the door. "I told you to stay away." My brother turns me from the house and marches me down the steps.

"But, Frank, you didn't really mean it—" I protest.

"Ronnie, get out of here." He points in the direction of the road exiting the property. "Leave."

"But, Frank, we vowed we'd never let this happen again—"

"This is nothing like what happened with Peter," he insists. "My god, I already said all of this to you before, just yesterday, but you don't listen. Ronnie, you brought this on yourself. You've been pushy, nosy, and annoying. So forget Juliana and me planning a wedding—you'd be such a pain."

I'm relieved by what he says about not planning a wedding, but the momentary reprieve is quickly shattered as my brother continues. "I am so fed up with all of your nonsense that I'm thinking Jules and I will just elope."

Shocked, I plead, "But Frank, what about your fam—"

He cuts me off. "Now go. And don't come back." I've never seen my brother quite this angry. I feel as if I've been stabbed in the heart.

Juliana quietly walks up to Frank and links arms with him. He squeezes her hand. He's made his decision; I feel defeated.

Then I look into Juliana's eyes. One moment I think I see victory, but the next it's confusion and sadness. Confused and sad is certainly how I feel, and Warrior and I take our leave.

~~~~~

Classmate Fred runs at me on the mat as I gesture in a way to invite him to grab my wrists. When I raise my arms a bit higher as he approaches, the energy of his attack changes, and he reaches for me with outstretched arms. Just at the very moment he grabs me (timing is everything in this technique!), I step back and turn in the direction where I intend to throw him. Fred's momentum, along with my help, propels him forward and down, and he safely falls with a perfect roll.

After we've done this four times, we switch, so that I now become the attacker or *uke*. It's Fred's turn, as *nage*, to execute *ryotetori kokyunage* and send me flying into forward rolls. Ever watch football players soar through the air to catch the ball and then land in a forward roll? That's how much energy these rolls require.

We continue to throw each other, but after two more sets, I'm huffing and puffing. I feel a bit wobbly and ask permission to leave the mat for some water.

The class continues practicing while I drink, and Isabella *Sensei* walks over to ask me if I'm all right.

"Feeling tired," I answer. "Should not have taken this class and spinning on the same day. Also, guess I'm a little stressed."

After class, outside by my car, Will invites me to lunch. "You look as if you could use a friend right about now," he says.

Warrior barks out the half-open car window. "Will, have you met my protector and best four-legged pal?" I ask, working hard on *fake it till you make it* so the whole world doesn't see how sad I feel. Putting down the window all the way, I give Will the condensed story of Warrior and my son, Tommy.

Will asks for permission to reach his hand to Warrior so that the dog can smell him. I nod and he does so, and before I know it, Will has worked his way up to scratching the German shepherd's neck. Clearly he's at ease with dogs, and Warrior warms up to him at once.

"OK, time for lunch," Will announces. "Follow me."

We each drive to a nearby diner, where I leave my car windows open for Warrior. Inside, Will and I find a corner booth. I guess I'm in somewhat of a daze, because Will orders for both of us, and I merely nod in agreement. I sit glumly, my hands fisted together covering my quivering mouth.

"Come on, Ronnie. Let it out," Will says.

The tears immediately spill from my eyes. I tell Will everything that happened at Meadow Farm—my confrontation with Juliana; how I feared Warrior would attack her; Frank's talk of elopement, his accusation that our disagreement is entirely my fault, and his telling me to leave Meadow Farm while physically propelling me toward my car, banishing me, maybe forever.

"Oh, Will, I feel as though I'm running out of time," I sob. "What if marrying Juliana turns out to be the worst thing that ever happens to Frank? I'd never forgive myself for blowing this." I sniffle, and Will gives me his handkerchief. I clear my nose, sounding like a foghorn.

Glancing down at his previously unused handkerchief, I ball it up and stuff it in my bag. "I'll wash this and get it back to you next class," I say in embarrassment.

Will laughs and puts his hands over mine on the table. "Now listen, Ronnie…" I sniffle. He smiles. "The best strategy for you is to get back to work and finish this investigation." He reaches for one of two files he brought into the diner.

"Here's Juliana's, or Julie Jones's, community college transcript, plus details of the women's-only residence in New York where she lived while in school. I included the manager's phone number." Will slaps the file on the table. "Make an appointment. The time Julie spent there covers her life through her early thirties." I look inside the file, rubbing my eyes.

"Ronnie, you're close to having Juliana's total story." Will hands me a paper napkin to dab my eyes. "Now get back to work. It'll help take your mind off what happened today."

He reaches for the other file. "Consider this one your homework assignment from me. If you're going to be an accidental detective and snoop around in places that could get you into trouble, you should at least know what you're doing." He beams that fantastic smile at me, and I start to feel a whole lot better. "Now pay attention. Let's call this Surveillance 101, and here are the basics…"

~~~~~

I lean back in the gigantic white porcelain tub that sits in the middle of the bathroom, which I gutted before I moved into my cottage. The only item on the wall opposite the tub is a monstrous blow-up photograph of Sean Connery as James Bond.

When I'm stressed out, I like nothing better than a glass of pinot noir, candlelight, and a soothing hot bath. Looking up at the photo, I stare into Sean Connery's eyes. He's in black tie and holding a gun, of course. A bath-time conversation with 007 is usually a sure-fire technique to unload whatever is bothering me. But tonight it's not working; I keep seeing Frank's angry face instead. So I step out of the tub and nod goodnight to Double O Seven. I turn out the lights and flop onto my bed, asleep almost before I hit the mattress.

> *I'm in our library with my brothers. Frank, Peter, and I joke and laugh and throw popcorn at each other. We're happy as can be.*
>
> *"Peter, please come!" It's a woman's voice elsewhere in the house. "Peter, please hurry." The voice is familiar.*
>
> *Peter gets up to go to her. I realize who it is. Her. The wife. The one we all thought*

we would love when they married. How could we know she had one goal from the beginning—to keep Peter all to herself and completely erase us from his life. We never saw it coming.

"Wait, Peter." Frank stands and puts his hand on Peter's arm, but our oldest brother shakes it loose. Tears fill my eyes.

"Peter, I need you," that wretched voice pleads from somewhere outside the room.

I run up to my brother and hug him as if I'll never see him again. "I love you, Peter."

"I love you, too, Ronnie, and you, Frank." He breaks away and rushes out.

Frank consoles me, but then his cell phone buzzes. He checks the text. "Sorry to do this to you, Sis. Got to go." He dashes out, too.

I run through the house, sobbing and looking everywhere for my brothers. Then I hear the sound of a car engine and rush to a window. Frank pulls away in his Porsche, Juliana sitting next to him.

"No, Frank, no!" I scream and hurry outside. But I'm too late. My brothers are gone, and I'm completely alone.

CHAPTER THIRTY-FOUR

After that nightmare and all the tossing and turning the rest of the night, I feel hung over from a lack of sleep. Instead of driving, I jump on the train into Manhattan early in the morning and now sit at a café where I try to wake up.

I feel like crap and defeated, but my one hope is to finish this investigation of Juliana. Once I've got the whole story, I'll mail the material to Frank's office, if he still won't talk to me. Maybe he'll forgive me then. I drink my coffee and pull the papers from the file Will gave me yesterday.

How Will managed to get a copy of Julie Jones's transcript at Manhattan Community College is beyond me, but I'm happy he did since it sure does make for interesting reading. I flip through the pages listing her coursework and excellent grades. Besides the many required literature and writing classes, I note the strong emphasis in history, philosophy, and psychology.

Juliana certainly was well rounded in her studies. I realize my image of the rough-and-tumble Teresa Gonzalez is transitioning into a picture of the Juliana Wentworth my brother adores. Even though she still went by Julie Jones at this stage of her life, in my mind I now envision a younger Juliana instead of the more grown-up version of the thirteen-year-old Scranton Gang girl.

I read that Juliana, Julie, completed the writing and literature program—attending part-time—and received her two-year degree in 2004, but I notice a ten-month gap in the transcript from late-2000 into 2001. Not a single class. Did Julie take a break to have a baby?

I wonder if one of her professors would remember Julie and, if so, speak to me about her, especially since I'm not a police officer in the midst of an official investigation.

I also see Julie was a member of the chess club at the college. So she obviously continued playing even after she broke off her wedding plans with Palmer. I pull out my tablet, go to the school's website, and send an email, requesting contact information for the faculty member who is the chess club advisor.

I look back at the file. Scribbled on the inside is a note from Will that in 2005 Julie requested a copy of her transcript be sent to UCLA. Finally, we have a connection to her more recent life on the West Coast. This link will definitely speed up my investigation, and perhaps allow me to skip talking with her professors here in New York. I look at my watch, pay for the coffee, and turn off the tablet.

Outside, I hail a taxi and head for my appointment at a ladies-only hotel on West 32nd Street called The Hamilton Residence. I thought apartments exclusively for women were a relic of the 1950s and '60s—you know, all those quaint stories about actresses like Grace Kelly, Candice

Bergen, and Ali MacGraw living at the Barbizon when they first started out. But a bit of online research showed me I was wrong. It's now the 21st century, and a number of these residences are thriving today. As a matter of fact, The Hamilton has a waiting list.

I hop out of the cab and look up at the building. What's not to like? The huge brick edifice is stately and elegant. And safe. It even provides a doorman to sweep visitors through the imposing, colonnaded front door into an enormous lobby that holds clusters of upholstered furniture.

I give my name at the reception desk and sit down on a huge sofa in one corner of the room. Checking my phone, I find a message from the community college with the chess club faculty advisor's contact info. I then compose a quick email requesting an appointment. I may find it useful to talk with him. As I hit *Send*, a woman walks over and greets me in a gracious manner.

"Mrs. Lake, welcome to The Hamilton. I'm Madeleine Avery, the manager."

I stand up. "Hello. So nice to meet you, Mrs. Avery." We shake hands.

She sits down opposite me. "When my assistant scheduled the appointment, she noted that you wished to inquire about a past resident..." An amused smile plays on her face. "...and not that you wanted to stay here."

"That's correct, Mrs. Avery." I smile back.

"We do respect our residents' privacy, but how exactly may I help you?"

"I'm trying to locate a distant family member for a reunion I'm planning." I fold my hands in my lap. "We lost touch with her ten years ago when she lived here at The Hamilton—"

"I've been here thirty years, and I make a point to get to know all our young women at The Hamilton." She tilts her head. "What is her name, Mrs. Lake?"

"Julie Jones. She might have been using her middle name, Terry, instead of Julie." Here we go again with the little white fibs. "My daughter, Jess, was so fond of her growing up."

A long pause and I can see Mrs. Avery going through a mental checklist. Then her face lights up. "You mean the very studious Julie? Of course." She shakes her head. "We have many young ladies who come through The Hamilton, but not many who live here as long as she did. The longer-term residents are easier to remember. Plus, Julie was simply unforgettable."

The manager pauses, as if making a decision. "Since we're talking about a resident who left so long ago, I think I can share with you what I remember about Julie."

"Oh, that's wonderful, Mrs. Avery." I cross my feet at the ankles and sit up straighter, as if I'm being interviewed for approval to stay here myself. "I guess Julie was pretty busy taking classes?"

"I would say that if she wasn't at school, she spent most of her time in this very room studying." She gestures toward the opposite side of the vast lobby. "See that wing chair over there in the corner?" I nod, and she goes on. "If you were looking for Julie, most likely you'd find her sitting in that chair studying, surrounded by her books, papers spread out on the coffee table, her laptop open."

"Sounds as if she was a dedicated student," I say. "Did she make any friends among the other residents?"

"Julie was friendly and helpful to everyone," Mrs. Avery says. "But I remember she was very private. She kept to herself."

"How long did she live at The Hamilton?" I ask.

"Oh, I don't know," she answers. "I'd have to look it up."

"No need—"

"I knew she'd be leaving," she says, and then her tone becomes wistful. "I just didn't think it'd be quite so soon."

I decide to go for the information—gently. "I thought you said she stayed an extended—ooohhh. Right. The baby." Those words hang in the air for such a long moment that I'm worried I've blown it, but then Mrs. Avery sighs.

"I remember when Julie started showing a few months after she arrived. She didn't attempt to hide it." She shrugs. "I tried to quietly offer her opportunities to talk about it, in case she needed moral support, but she absolutely would not discuss it with me."

"I'm sure you did your best, Mrs. Avery." So, Julie/Juliana was definitely pregnant. "She was fortunate to have you here, even if she didn't want to talk to you about it," I say. "How about the father? Did he get involved?"

Mrs. Avery shakes her head quickly. "No. Not at all, as far as I could tell. Julie said nothing about the father and just quietly continued with her studies as her pregnancy progressed."

"Did she have the baby while she was here?" I ask.

"Oh, no. Julie was finishing up a school term and getting bigger and bigger—she was probably about eight months along—when she gave me notice that she'd be leaving in two weeks," Mrs. Avery says and looks at me. "At that moment, I must admit to boldly asking her about her plans. You know, would she keep the baby? Or put it up for adoption?"

"It's a natural question, Mrs. Avery," I reassure the manager of The Hamilton. "Plus, it would have been tough for Julie to support a child. You know, fulltime student, not much money."

"Yes, well, she told me she was still working all of that out." Mrs. Avery taps one of her hands against her leg. She stops. "And then Julie was gone."

"No idea where she went next?" I ask.

"None."

"You never saw her again?"

"That's not the case at all." Now Mrs. Avery smiles widely. "Ten months later Julie returned. She told me she'd had a little girl and said the baby was with someone who could care for her and give her a lot of love. She even showed me a picture of herself holding the little angel in the hospital."

So, Juliana did have a baby. I think back to our conversation in the library at Meadow Farm, when she told me she had four stepchildren. She never volunteered that she had a child of her own or whether she gave it up for adoption. But then why would she respond to my curious— OK, nosy—questions?

The apartment manager gazes out a window fronting the busy avenue. "I remember Julie looked just great. Not at all as though she'd recently had a baby. Anyway, she spent a few more years finishing her degree and working, and then she left for good. California, I think."

"Any forwarding address? I'm really trying to play catch-up here." I suppose my statement sounds sort of weak.

In fact, Mrs. Avery gives me a funny look, and I can practically see the wheels turning. "How is it your family became estranged from Julie?" she asks. "And why have you been out of touch for so long?"

I pathetically make it up as I go along. "I prefer not to go into all the particulars, since Julie broke it off with us when she was pregnant. Certain family members didn't approve and were very critical that she didn't plan to marry the father. She was secretive about all the details, and you know how some people can be quite judgmental. Well, she just washed her hands of us, and I can hardly blame her." I try my best to look regretful.

Mrs. Avery's face relaxes, and she looks at me with sympathy. "Family can be tough, even brutal at times. That poor girl."

"My thoughts exactly, Mrs. Avery. And I want to let bygones be bygones. I thought this family reunion would be a perfect way to knock down any remaining barriers."

"You're so right, Mrs. Lake."

"Plus, I'm dying to meet her daughter," I add, "and bring them both back into the family."

We're quiet, and the silence goes on a little too long. Then the building manager stands up, but before she can speak, I jump in. "While I'm here, may I see a room? I have a niece coming to New York for an internship in the fall. Of course she doesn't want to live in New Jersey with us, but insists on being here, in the Big Apple. The Hamilton could be the perfect solution, providing you have availability in September."

Mrs. Avery smiles broadly. "We will have some turnover at that time. Tell you what. I'll get you a key, and while you look at one of our rooms, I'll put together a packet of information and an application." She heads for the office, still looking at me. "I'll also see if I can find that forwarding address for Julie. Anything to help."

~~~~~

Exiting the elevator on the twelfth floor, I quickly find room 1226 and unlock the door. Even though The Hamilton Residence façade is magnificent and its lobby plush, the rooms are anything but, if this one is typical of the others in the building.

Room 1226 is modest and dark with its one small window facing a brick wall perhaps fifteen feet away. A twin bed, night stand, dresser, desk, and chair all look vintage 1950s and well worn. These pieces of furniture are stuffed in the small room and make the space feel cramped. Still, the room and its adjoining bathroom are spotlessly clean. Plus, though I haven't seen the brochure as of yet, you probably can't beat the price if you're starting your first job in the city or going to school.

I sit on the bed—it feels firm—and imagine Juliana coming back to this lonely little room after working at Benny's Bar & Grill in Soho where she made good money. Living at The Hamilton, with its doorman and front deskman, protected from the Bobby Taylors of the world, probably allowed her to save a lot of money. Her growing nest egg most likely made her move to California possible.

My phone sounds a *ping*, and I find an email from the community college chess club advisor. He writes he can't meet with me for three weeks because of schedule demands. I probably don't need to talk with him anyway. Reading the college transcript and then speaking with Mrs. Avery has yielded plenty of new information about my brother's girlfriend, or is it fiancé?

I wonder if Juliana has told Frank anything about this period of her life and, most importantly, having a baby.

Time to go home. I'm done for the day.

CHAPTER THIRTY-FIVE

Strolling from the dry cleaner to my car, I spot Juliana coming out of the village coffee shop. While depositing my clean clothes in the Mustang and grabbing my hemp shopping bag for the Saturday morning farmers market, I watch her walk in the direction of several boutiques. For a budding P.I., this is a golden opportunity to practice the basic surveillance techniques that Will has been teaching me.

I cross to the other side of the street so I'm now opposite her, which is the preferred strategy when shadowing a target in a residential or uncrowded neighborhood of village shops. I enter a bookstore where I'm able to purchase a newspaper while watching Juliana through the window. She carefully checks out the merchandise displayed in front of the boutiques, but never enters any of the shops.

Juliana continues down the street, and I notice admiring glances from men as they pass her. She could never do surveillance because she stands out too much. No matter how much she'd cover up, I don't think it would ever be enough to help a woman with her immense beauty blend into the background.

She crosses the street at the train station to visit the farmers market. I head into the station parking lot and do the same, losing her in the throng. I have just broken golden rule number one: Never take your eyes off the target.

Turns out the lapse is only for a moment. I soon spot her at a vegetable stand looking over a display of freshly picked tomatoes. Checking baked goods at a different stand, I select and buy two loaves of multi-grained bread and place them in my bag.

I work on doing better with surveillance rule number one and remain discreet, observing Juliana through my sunglasses. Should she spot me, I'm ready with my cover story, which is rule number... What? Two? You must have a reason for being there if you get *made*, or seen, by your target.

I move on to buy flowers at a different stand, while Juliana stays put, having switched her focus to yellow and green zucchinis. As I place the flowers in my bag, I lift my head slightly, watch Juliana pay for the vegetables and glance around the market in general. That's when I see him.

Thank goodness for my shades, which hide where I'm looking, because presently I'm staring straight at Bobby Taylor. He sticks out from others milling about the market who look like ordinary locals. In contrast, Bobby's jeans are worn out and dirty, and he's wearing the same leather jacket that I've noticed before. He pushes at his reflecting shades that hide his eyes and adjusts a grubby baseball cap turned backward over his stringy hair.

I catch a flash of what appears to be a knife handle poking out of Bobby's jeans near his left hip, and it sends shivers up my spine. Juliana's sleazy cousin is hanging back, watching her like prey, and she's oblivious to his presence.

But she's not oblivious to mine. I've been so busy watching him that I again broke rule number one about observing the target. All of a sudden Juliana marches directly up to me, her body language and face full of anger.

"Are you following me? Again?" she hisses.

"Hell, no," I insist. "I always shop the farmers market." Cover story delivered with confidence. Will would approve.

"Right," she says with sarcasm dripping from her voice. "Of course you just happen to be at the farmers market when I'm here. Frank told you to leave us alone."

"Look, Juliana, don't flatter yourself." I show her my market-filled bag. "I grew up here. It's a small community. Friends and neighbors run into each other all the time around town. I promise you, I am not your problem." I nod behind her. "Don't look now, but there's some creep over there with a knife, who's been watching you."

Juliana begins to turn. "Don't move. You'll tip him off," I say. "I believe it's Bobby Taylor." She stiffens, and I continue, "And he looks pissed."

I remember that Will told me a good P.I. is quick thinking and fast to react. In a split second, I come up with a plan. "Juliana, do you have a car nearby?"

"No. Frank is picking me up in an hour." Her voice is shaky, and she glances around.

"My Mustang's right up the street, but don't wait there." Bobby Taylor moves stealthily among the stands, heading in our direction. "There's a bookstore not too far from my car. Go inside and wait for me in the back."

"What are you going to do, Ronnie?" Juliana's hands shake.

"Create a diversion. Now go!" The moment I push her toward the street, I observe a police officer leaning against his cruiser at the train station on the edge of the market.

Bobby Taylor notices Juliana leaving and picks up speed as he makes his way through the stands. I amble toward him with my head down as if I'm shuffling through my bag that holds the flowers and bread.

I time my movements to reach him just as he passes a display of stacked glass jars filled with homemade preserves. At that moment, I pretend to stumble and crash into him big-time, causing him to fall right into the middle of the jam display. The jars all crash down, shattering, and making an amazing racket.

People crowd around us as I apologize to Bobby and the owner. I pull out my wallet as Bobby, swearing at me, stands up and says, "Don't I know you from somewhere—" His feet go out from under him because of the slippery jams and preserves covering the pavement. I couldn't have accomplished the takedown better with my own two hands.

Bobby lands hard on his tailbone and lets out another string of obscenities. He tries unsuccessfully to get up and go after Juliana. But any view of her is blocked by the crowd around us, and I'm confident that she's gotten away.

I once again spot the knife in his waistband and yell, "Knife! Knife!" Panic breaks out, and people scatter. I yell to the policeman, "Officer, help! He's got a knife!"

The minute Bobby Taylor hears me yell for the police, he's out of there. Gone. Nowhere to be seen. I hear a motorcycle start up and screech on by. I see Bobby Taylor speed out of the village in the opposite direction from the bookstore, where I hope Juliana is waiting for me.

After giving the upset jam seller what I consider to be a fair amount of money, I walk to the bookstore. Inside, I wave at Juliana to come with me to the young girl by the register, "Two cups, please," and I pay her. Juliana and I fix ourselves tea at a self-serve counter.

We sit down. She's pale; her hands still shake as she holds the cup. She's hyperventilating slightly. "Calm down, Juliana. Take some deep breaths. Drink the tea," I tell her. "You'll feel better." She says nothing and sips the hot Earl Grey.

Then I barely hear her say in a quiet voice, "Thank you, Ronnie, for helping me back there."

"Juliana," I begin, "why is this creep still in your life? After so many years?" I have a fantasy that she'll 'fess up and tell me the entire story—the Teresa-years all the way up to now.

No such luck. She stares at her steaming mug. "Who is *Tía* Connie?" I ask. Nothing.

I pull out my phone and find a photograph of *Tía* Connie and place it right in front of Juliana, next to her mug. She looks at it and lashes out at me. "What is it with you, nosing around in other people's lives? How often have you followed me? I could go to the police and file a harassment complaint against you—"

"Somehow," I interrupt and take back my phone, "I don't think you'll do that, go to the police, that is." I click onto a shot of Francesca at the small market in Scranton and hold the phone right up to her eyes. "Why don't you tell me about Francesca."

Juliana gets a hard, cold look on her face and swats the phone aside. Her face is now in my space, too close to me, her voice low and controlled. "Ronnie, do not insert yourself into something you know nothing about. Especially when it concerns the safety of a child." She slams her fists onto the table and gets up. Is Juliana behaving like a lioness protecting her cub?

As she leaves, I call out, "If you're in some kind of trouble, I could help you. I'm not your enemy, Juliana."

"Hah!!" The door of the bookstore slams behind her.

CHAPTER THIRTY-SIX

My bags sit unpacked at the Malibu Palm Hotel in a room that opens directly on the beach. Walking onto the warm sand to recline in a chaise under a striped umbrella, I gaze at a quiet ocean with small waves spilling over the sand. If I'm going to investigate Juliana Wentworth's life in California, then I'm going to make the most of it while I'm out here.

I put my ear buds in and turn on my iPod. There it comes—that distinctive Don Felder guitar open. Whenever I play this song, it's just as magical as when I first heard it more than thirty-five years ago.

I know it's trite, but I've always wanted to listen to the Eagles hit, "Hotel California," on a beautiful West Coast beach. Looking up from the chaise, I stare at an unbelievably clear blue sky. I stretch from my fingertips down to my toes while taking in a deep breath, then letting it out slowly. Aaah. Feels good. I settle back and listen to the rest of the song…until one of the last verses makes me pause.

Hah! Am I not a prisoner of my own device (to loosely quote the song lyrics)? Pushing and pushing Frank, until he finally had enough and banned me from Meadow Farm and my family? Whoa, Ronnie, stop thinking like this. Not the time to go there.

I turn down the volume and study the cover of the book in my hands, the same one I saw on Juliana's nightstand at Meadow Farm—*The Tender Bar* by J. R. Moehringer. The author writes about growing up at a neighborhood bar and his climb through the social classes. This is a big part of my prep before visiting Café Casablanca tonight to try to meet the man with the mysterious name of Dragomir. He gave Juliana her copy of this book and even inscribed it, pronouncing her as his *most gifted student.*

Ah, yes, Dragomir, the famous maître d' of Café Casablanca, where the *elite meet*, as I learned in my research while flying to the Coast. Not just Hollywood elite, but old-guard L.A., encompassing the pinnacle of the city's social, political, artistic, and financial worlds.

Café Casablanca is where Juliana worked for three years while she finished a bachelor's degree and then began a graduate program in art history. The café provided a different sort of education, where she was able to polish her people skills under the tutelage of Dragomir and also take the final step in her evolution from Teresa/Terry/Julie with one more name-change, to Juliana. Finally, the restaurant also provided the perfect opportunity for Juliana to meet her future husband, successful investor Carleton Todd Wentworth, an original backer and regular at the café.

~~~~~

The valet hands me a ticket as I step out of my rental car. Before walking through the massive, arched, double doors of the imposing Café Casablanca, I take in the Spanish tile roof; decorative wrought-iron; arched windows; and stucco walls of its Mediterranean façade. I know from my in-flight homework that Wallace Neff, architect to a number of Hollywood stars during the first half of the twentieth century, originally designed this restored Beverly Hills mansion.

Entering, I stare at the vaulted ceiling, which is fifty-feet high and truly grand. A distinguished gentleman in a dark suit interrupts my scrutiny of this classic California architecture and greets me. "Mrs. Lake, we are so happy you have come to Café Casablanca." His brilliant smile is almost blinding. How does he know exactly who I am? But then he must have a great many skills that aren't easily deciphered.

He shakes my hand and executes a quick bow with his head. "I am Dragomir, and Ms. Dugan is at her table," the maître d' continues in heavily accented English. Is the inflection Bulgarian or is it some Hollywood-fantasy Slavic intonation?

"Thank you, Dragomir. I've looked forward to my visit. You and the Café are legendary." We walk past the bar and into the dining room, its décor reflecting an exclusive ambiance, like that of an Old Hollywood private club.

As I discreetly glance at the tables along the way filled with photogenic patrons, I'm relieved my hair got a good blow-dry at the hotel salon and that I guessed right in choosing an outfit for this place. My sleek white pants break at silver sandals, and a slinky, long-sleeved, scoop-necked top with shimmery silver and white stripes finishes off my low-keyed dinner look with a touch of sexiness. At least in terms of my appearance, I feel like a Café Casablanca regular.

I follow Dragomir toward a table at the other end of the dining room where I can see Drea Dugan looking over a menu. She's a girlfriend with whom I shared an office at the beginning of our careers in the TV business. Twenty-plus years ago, Drea moved to Los Angeles and became hugely successful in distribution. Since then, she's made boatloads of money and remains a confirmed workaholic.

Drea spots me and stands up at her corner booth with a view of the entire dining room. "Hi, baby!" She beams and embraces me in an earth-mother hug. It's as if no time at all has passed, and we pick up from where we left off during the last occasion we saw each other, several years before.

We play catch-up over a splendid supper. First, I enjoy a grilled artichoke, and second—I decide to go Hollywood—a black truffle omelet with caviar. While I savor every heavenly bite, I tell Drea the entire story of my investigation into Juliana and how I'm trying to fill in the last few pieces of her life that will take me up to her marrying Carleton Wentworth.

"Ronnie, I remember her," Drea says. "Long, dark hair. Seriously beautiful, kind of like Angelina Jolie. She was Drago's star—he adored her. And then she went off and married that investor guy. There was quite a buzz when it happened."

"How so?" I ask.

"That she really had stepped up in the world. You know, from restaurant hostess to a big life in Bel Air. After they married, they were here for a while and then moved to San Francisco fulltime, and I didn't hear much about her anymore from Drago."

"Drea, it's that inscription in the book from Dragomir that makes me certain he could tell me a lot." I sip my wine. "How do I get him to talk to me, when he's known to be the epitome of discretion, and we've just met for the first time?"

"First, I already told him what a great lady you are and how far back we go. So in his eyes, you're no longer a stranger." Drea's dark eyes twinkle with mischief. "Sweetie, this is the plan. We're going to close down the restaurant, which will be easy, since we have a lot of catching up to do."

"The highlight of being here is seeing you," I say, adding, "definitely not my amateur detective work." We clink glasses.

Drea continues. "Next, we'll time it perfectly as we walk out and stop by the bar, as if we've just decided spur of the moment to finish our night with a Sambuca." She swings back her hair and breaks into a deep, throaty laugh.

"Sounds great," I say. "Then what?"

"I'll invite Drago to have a drink with us," Drea says. "He and I always finish the evening with a nightcap if everyone has left. You leave the rest to me, sweetie."

"Drea, look over toward the right, fourth table down. That guy keeps staring at you. Do you know him?" I ask. "He looks familiar. Maybe New York?"

"Oh my god," she says under her breath. "Do you remember back when we were at MTV?" I nod. "He was at HBO, and on a flight to L.A., I definitely had sex with him…"

~~~~~

It's three hours, one dinner, and two Sambucas later, and Drea, Dragomir, and I are sitting at the bar ordering a third round as the staff resets the tables for tomorrow's lunch crowd. It turns out that because she dines at the Café Casablanca three to four times a week, Drea and the maître d' have become big buddies. It's almost as if Dragomir is Drea's older brother, and the affection is mutual.

Her phone rings, and she checks the incoming text. Then she hops up and gives me yet another warm hug. "Doll, I need to go. You stay here and finish your drink with Drago." Drea turns to him. "Take care of my friend, Drago, and please put everything on my tab!"

I start to protest, but she stops me. "Shhh. Not another word. Ronnie, it's so great to see you!" She hugs me again and departs with a final, "Love ya!"

I lift my glass. "A toast to Drea Dugan, the best friend a girl could have!"

Dragomir clinks my glass. "To great lady." Is it my imagination, or is his mysterious accent sounding a little less pronounced than when I first arrived? "My dear Mrs.

Lake, would you like something else from menu? This is time of evening when I eat light supper."

"No, thank you," I answer, "but you go ahead." He signals the bartender. I continue, "Dragomir, we may have another friend in common." He looks at me with curiosity. "She's a close friend of my brother's and happens to be back East right now. I believe she worked for you."

"Yes?" A look sweeps over his face as if he already knows.

"Juliana Wentworth," I say. "She and my brother Frank Rutherfurd are very close. I dare say she may even become part of our family before long."

His eyes reflect happiness at this announcement. "Dear Juliana. I was very sad when Carleton died two years ago. She was so, so brokenhearted. This news about your brother is wonderful. I'm happy for my sweet Juliana."

I wish I could say I'm as happy as he seems to be. "My brother has also been widowed and grief stricken." I play with, instead of drink, my third glass of Sambuca, as I mostly did with the first two shots. I need to keep my head clear, not to mention that I'll also be driving back to the hotel. "I met her when Frank recently brought her home to meet us in New Jersey. He lights up around her. Dragomir, he's like a new man."

My new friend smiles. "Yes, yes. That sounds like my wonderful Juliana."

The bartender brings Drago an omelet and an order of toast with coffee. Displaying impeccable Continental table manners, he picks up the knife with his right hand, the fork with his left and begins to eat. "She worked here before she married Carleton. As you know, Juliana is so spectacularly beautiful, and she has such a special way with people, that of course I put her out front in restaurant."

I smile as if in total agreement with him, and really, I don't disagree. "She definitely has the gift of making you feel you're the only person in the room," I say. "She must have been wonderful with your patrons."

"I haven't hired anyone since who brought same magic to Café Casablanca." Drago switches from Sambuca to his cup of coffee, and he drinks. "I thought she marry one of A-list Hollywood types who are regulars. Several pursued her." He looks at me to see the effect of his words.

I simply smile. "Most young women would have had their heads turned with all that attention." I keep the tone of my voice kind, not gossipy.

"Not Juliana," Drago declares. "She had eye on education. Getting degree." He lays his fork and knife across the top of his plate to indicate he's finished eating.

"Look what I have!" I feign spontaneity as I dig inside my bag. "Juliana had this book, and it looked so interesting, that I also picked up a copy." I pull out *The Tender Bar* and flip through the pages. "Frankly, I can't put it down."

Dragomir laughs—a hearty laugh. "You want to know more about your maybe-sister-in-law?" I nod enthusiastically. "I pick you up at ten in morning at your hotel, and I give you tour of Juliana's life when she worked for me."

The generous offer is almost more than I could have ever wished for, and I signal my acceptance.

CHAPTER THIRTY-SEVEN

A silver Ferrari Coupe pulls up to the front of the Malibu Palm Hotel. That smile again. It's almost as bright as the shiny car. Guess Mr. Suave-Slavic-Dragomir is just as Hollywood as the next guy in this West Coast car culture. He's also punctual, cheery, and very awake for a night owl working in the restaurant business. Checking out the pricey sports car, I wonder if he's not only the maître d' but perhaps a partner in Café Casablanca.

Radiating my more modest version of a sparkling Hollywood grin, I hop in the passenger side of the coupe. "Dragomir, how are you on this beautiful Malibu morning!" The Ferrari purrs, and I zoom away with this twenty-first century Valentino.

Soon we're in Westwood, and we turn onto a quiet residential street lined with small apartment buildings and multi-unit houses. Dragomir parks along the curb and turns off the motor. Then he reaches behind my seat, pulls out a thermos, and pours us each a mug of coffee. We click our cups and drink. Wow. This man knows how to make a great cup of joe.

"Oh my god, this is amazing coffee," I gush. "Not only is it silky smooth when it goes down, but I taste blueberries." I smell the blend and sip again. "Plus there's something else—"

I can tell my appreciation pleases him. "That's almonds, perhaps honey. This is one of my favorite coffees." He smiles. "Beans grow in Ethiopia."

"Ethiopia? Well, wherever. It's got a great aftertaste." I move my tongue inside my mouth savoring the flavor. "Dragomir, you talk about coffee the way some people talk about wine."

He nods in agreement. "Not only do I enjoy drinking this brew, but it is my business, too. You see, Café Casablanca sells private label coffee," he says with pride.

I take another sip. "So, why are we here?"

"Mrs. Lake, look across—"

"Dragomir, I think it's time you drop the Mrs. Lake formalities." I laugh. "Just call me Ronnie."

"Yes. Ronnie," he says as if he's getting used to the sound of my name. "See white stucco building with black roof on other side of street?"

"Did Juliana live there?" I ask, staring.

"Yes. It is residence for women college students. She could live here safely and inexpensively while finishing degree. I think Juliana saved lot of money in New York, and that helped her get started here. I remember she drove little VW to get around, and also worked part-time in small bookstore." He drinks from his mug. "She was very, very careful about money, but she needed more." I guess the money Juliana received from John Palmer for school wasn't enough to cover all her living expenses, and by that time she was also financially supporting her child. "A board member of this residence is regular at Café Casablanca. She knows I was looking for hostess and sent Juliana!"

We watch as two women with small backpacks, probably students, come out the front door of the house, and he goes on. "When she arrived for interview, I knew in five minutes she was right one for job."

"How could you know that in five minutes, Dragomir? Come on," I say.

"First, she is gracious, and she is calm. For Juliana, it is all about you, not her, and that is secret of success in being hostess of restaurant that has exclusive clientele." He leans forward as if to start the car, but he hesitates while finishing his explanation.

"Second, in ten minutes I know she has keen intelligence and will quickly learn, how you say, lay of land at Café Casablanca. Hostess must know all regulars and understand who should not sit close to each other. Also who wishes to be seen and who wants privacy. Juliana was brilliant in that way."

"Sounds as though you were a good teacher, Dragomir."

"I taught her everything I know," he says with satisfaction. "She became master." He turns on the engine, shifts the car into gear, and we're off again.

It doesn't take long before we're cruising along Sunset Boulevard, and I enjoy the view from inside the sleek coupe, which is turning my adorable Mustang at home into a shabby distant cousin...just for the moment. I do realize that upon exiting this fabulous car, I will once again rebalance my priorities and feel gratitude for my stylish wheels parked back in Willowbrook.

In the meantime, we pass famous landmarks such as the Chateau Marmont, the celeb-favored castle on the hill hotel where John Belushi died, and then Hollywood High, where Drago drives me around the block reciting its cast of famous graduates, everyone from Lana Turner and Mickey Rooney to Sarah Jessica Parker.

We arrive at the West Gate of the exclusive Bel Air neighborhood opposite an entrance to the grounds of UCLA. When we turn off Sunset, Dragomir points out that this campus is where Juliana continued her undergraduate studies, which also confirms Will's note in the folder about Juliana's transcript request from Manhattan Community College to UCLA.

We glide along the residential streets, not able to see much beyond the dense foliage, hedges, walls, fencing, and gates that shield many of the expensive properties from prying eyes. Here and there we glimpse the mix of modest ranch houses and mega-mansions in this neighborhood of no sidewalks. That is, no sidewalks on purpose, to discourage nosy tourists from strolling through.

We slow down near a charming carriage house close to a gate and come to a stop. This time Dragomir idles the Ferrari instead of turning off the motor.

He gestures toward the stone gatehouse. "There. That is where Juliana moved perhaps one year after she came to work for me. One of my clients, Max Chestonville, offered it to her at very good rent, because he travels a lot. His elderly mother lived in big house further back on property, and part of arrangement was that Juliana should check on her when he was away." The Juliana I'm getting to know was operating very true to form it seems. She had no trouble making the most of opportunities that came her way from people who trusted her to do the right thing.

"Dragomir, it's totally charming," I say. "It looks very English and quite cozy. She must have loved living here."

"She did." His fingers tap the steering wheel. "And she had little garden. When Juliana wasn't working at café or in classes at UCLA, she would take Mrs. Chestonville—she call her Mrs. C—outside to terrace for afternoon tea, and Mrs. C taught her everything she knows about gardens. Together, they designed little garden on side of cottage, and Juliana did all planting. They adored each other, and Juliana really took interest in Mrs. C, even after she married Carleton and moved out. Juliana visited Mrs. C two times every week until old woman died."

Amazed cannot begin to describe my reaction to Juliana at this stage of her life, in her early thirties. From California dorm living to Bel Air in less than a year. Not only is she one resourceful lady, but she seems to be a kind one at that. Perhaps I should cut her some slack and stop worrying about her intentions toward my brother. But what to do about her evil Bobby Taylor shadow? Even if he has nothing to do with my brother, was Juliana complicit in a shady episode tied to Taylor well after their Scranton Gang years?

"Dragomir, how could her life get any better than this?" I ask. "When she married, where did she live next?"

He smiles as if he himself had arranged such perfection. "Her new husband, Mr. Carleton Todd Wentworth from San Francisco, is very important investor in technology. He also has old Dolores Del Rio house in Hollywood." He shifts the car into drive. "That's where she moved. Now, I show you."

"Come on, Dragomir," I cajole. "I think you're just looking for an excuse to drive your beautiful car around on this glorious morning. Be honest."

"Oh, yes, yes, yes," he laughs. "And with beautiful woman." The skin on my face all of a sudden feels hot, and I believe I may be blushing in response to Drago's old world charm.

Soon we're motoring among the older Spanish-influenced architecture of houses along Outpost Drive. We arrive at the old Del Rio house where the present owner is doing an A-plus job of maintaining this lovely old villa. Once again we stop, and once again, Dragomir continues his impressive story.

"This is where Mr. Wentworth lived when he is in town. And he dined at Café Casablanca almost every evening. There he met my wonderful Juliana, and even though he much older, they fall very much in love." He smiles. "They invite me to their wedding five years ago." Dragomir says it as though he can hardly believe that he's been included in the inner circle, which Juliana has now joined. "Of course, she stop working for me."

"Of course," I interject.

"They were so happy…" His smile goes away. "…For a short while. Then Mr. Wentworth had heart attack and died two years ago. So sudden. So unbelievable."

"I'm sorry, Dragomir." A tragic turn of events, indeed.

"Happy memories here for Juliana." He looks sadly at the stucco-walled dwelling. "Not long after Mr. Wentworth died, his children sell this lovely house, and she move fulltime to San Francisco."

We leave and drive back to my hotel. It's quiet in the car, as we both probably think about the same woman—his devoted student at the café and my brother's maybe-fiancé. I realize my investigation of Teresa Gonzalez's evolution over the past quarter-century from poverty and crime into her present life as the refined Juliana Wentworth is now complete. I silently acknowledge her focus, spirit of reinvention, and a quiet integrity I've come to admire. But how can I reconcile the Bobby Taylor confusion I've witnessed in her life since she arrived in New Jersey with my brother?

"Did you and Juliana stay in touch?" I ask.

"Whenever she's in L.A., she come to Café Casablanca to see me. Otherwise, we speak on phone every couple of weeks."

The car stops for a long light at a five-way intersection. We have a moment, and I cut to the chase. "Up to Carleton Wentworth's sudden death, it sounds as though Juliana had a good life out here, and that she continued on a path where her life got constantly better and better—"

"Ronnie, she had heart of gold and is very hard worker—" His face beams with pride.

"Definitely, but didn't she have regular problems like the rest of us?" I watch his face closely. "Any difficulties that you know of with family? Relatives?" I pause a moment. "Kids?"

That's when I see it. A cloud of concern passes over his face. He scowls momentarily. "What?" I ask. Silence. "Come on, Dragomir. I can see something is bothering you. I'm a good listener, and I'm discreet." The light changes, and we drive on.

"One time Juliana brought letter with her to café, and during break I saw her reading it. Also I see photograph of little girl, and Juliana crying very quietly. When she saw me standing close by her, she grabbed letter and picture and stuffed them in pocket." He shakes his head and makes a left turn. "She said letter from aunt, and there are problems. She said nothing else. Ever. I always wonder about that child. Who she is."

Another traffic light ahead turns red, and we stop again. "She would be wonderful mother, I know," Drago goes on. He glances at me, tapping the steering wheel as if he's deciding something. Then he tests the water. "But Mr. Wentworth already have grown-up kids. Three sons and one girl." A very pregnant pause follows, and when he can't seem to stand the quiet anymore, Drago dives in. "Mr. Wentworth worship his daughter, but she not nice person and hate Juliana." The light changes, and we drive.

"Did something happen, Dragomir?" I ask.

"One night at restaurant, I hear Marion, that's daughter—I hear her threaten Juliana." My hotel is ahead, and Dragomir turns into the entrance, continuing this saga.

"Marion say she will find out all of Juliana's secrets— because everybody have secrets—and tell her father, Carleton. Marion jealous of Juliana and want to harm the marriage. Marion a vicious person." He stops the car and waves away the valet.

"What did Juliana do to stop Marion?" I ask.

"I think Juliana keep all her secrets very close and careful," he says. "If that little girl in photograph her daughter, nobody ever find out. Even Mr. Wentworth." He shakes his head regretfully.

Then he gets out of the Ferrari and comes around to open my door. "Ronnie, this is private between just us." He smiles. "And I hope you have enjoyed my little tour."

"Thank you, Dragomir," I respond. "You've been so generous with your time and so kind to share with me your impressions and experiences with Juliana. Such a nice way to help me get to know my maybe future sister-in-law." Juliana definitely has trust issues. I guess I would, too, if I had a wicked step-daughter like Marion Wentworth. But I suppose Juliana had problems long before that. "Dragomir, may I ask a favor of you?"

"Absolutely."

"If you promise not to tell Juliana for a little while that I was here, then I promise to call you first when they decide to marry," I say. "She might think I'm being nosy about her life, when my reason for being here really was to see Drea. Meeting you and joining you on this wonderful tour, well that was a bonus." I reach out to shake hands. "Deal?"

He looks at me, breaks out in a huge smile, and shakes on it. "Deal. Ronnie, you have charm the same as my dear Juliana." How interesting that he compares the two of us.

But my plan is to wrap up this meeting on a lighter note. "I have to ask you, where does the name Dragomir come from? It's so romantic and has the sound of mystery and intrigue," I enthuse.

Dragomir laughs. "I was given my Bulgarian grandfather's name. I am happy for this. In L.A., I think I am the only Dragomir!" He sweeps me into a huge hug, and I pat him on the back.

CHAPTER THIRTY-EIGHT

My Mustang idles on the dirt road that leads up to Meadow Farm. The car's canvas top is down, even though it's a cloudy day (unlike yesterday's perfect California blue sky). Warrior sits in the passenger seat, and we both look through the front windshield. The view of the house is beautiful. I should be happy. I'm not. Having never before been exiled from this farm where I grew up, I feel like a miserable outcast.

The music's on, of course, and Warrior, looking at me with big sad eyes, whines along with the crooning of Tom Petty's "I Won't Back Down." It's as if Warrior understands the pain I feel because of the situation with my brother. I lean over and bury my face in my dog's neck, nuzzling his soft coat. I feel cut off from family and forlorn. The first loss was of Peter years ago—not my fault—and now I'm at odds with Frank—this time my fault. How did I make such a mess of things?

Both Frank and Peter told me as far back as I can remember that I was the most stubborn kid sister on the planet. You'd have thought that age and experience would have mellowed me—not a chance. Not when it comes to Frank's welfare and happiness, even if he can't see it, and I'm the only one who can.

Making a quick U-turn, I take off, the wind blowing through my hair and over Warrior's face, and Tom Petty's wailing voice and lyrics boosting my confidence to not back down.

I drive aimlessly along the back roads, narrow and twisty, trying to escape the hurt and worry of a possible permanent break with my brother. I go back to what Dragomir told me about Juliana's true kindness to the old woman at the end of her life. Will Juliana offer lifelong kindness and happiness to Frank? Will she be compassionate enough to not interfere with our sibling relationship?

There aren't many left in my immediate family of origin. Excluding the younger generation and our estranged brother, it's just Frank and me. I suddenly miss our parents deeply and make a quick decision, turning back toward town.

At the outskirts of the village, I pull up to the beautiful stone chapel that is part of the church our family has attended for generations, although my own attendance in recent years has been spotty. The intense feeling that has lured me here has come on so fast I blink back tears, and I want desperately to visit the graves of my parents.

When I park, I feel a sudden wind come up. I notice the sky has turned darker and pull the top up on the Mustang. "Warrior, I'll be right back."

Walking on the stone path to the side of the chapel, I head toward the cemetery around back. Before I turn the corner, though, voices stop me. Familiar voices. I can't understand what they're saying, but I know who they are.

I peek around the corner, and I see Juliana and Bobby Taylor on a bench that happens to be dedicated to my parents. They sit with their backs to me, talking to each other, their faces almost in profile. No voices are raised; no taut body language indicates the two are fighting.

As a matter of fact, this get-together looks a bit too friendly. What is going on here? Anger wells up inside of me, but I resist the urge to dash out and verbally blast at them. Instead, I watch quietly.

The general tone of their conversation sounds friendly enough, even though I still can't catch what they're actually saying. Their faces are close as Juliana and Bobby talk. They look like two people who are relaxed with each other.

Then he does it. Bobby takes Juliana's hand in both of his and kisses it. She shakes her head and her posture droops, as if she's sad.

A few drops of rain plunk down on my head. The two of them look up at the sky. He drops her hand, puts his arm around her and pats one of her shoulders reassuringly.

For an instant, I can hear what Bobby says to Juliana. "It'll all be OK. I'm sorry I've been such a jerk." He pulls his arm back and rubs her neck.

Feeling a huge sense of betrayal on behalf of Frank, I can't watch anymore and silently retreat. I'll save my visit to my parents' graves for another day.

Now, why'd Juliana have to do that, look so cozy with Bobby, exactly when I was beginning to think she might be a good person and the right one for Frank? And to think she met him near my parents' gravesite. This can only be bad.

~~~~~

Will pulls up to my cottage to find Warrior and me in the garden playing catch with a Frisbee. At the moment, my German shepherd sits quietly with the Frisbee in his mouth, looking quite pleased with himself. "Stay," I say.

I turn my attention to Will and wave him over. "Come in through the gate."

Once Will stands next to me, I instruct Warrior to "come." The dog trots across the grass, reaches us and sits, still holding the Frisbee in his mouth. Will and I both squat down, and I take the Frisbee from Warrior.

I rub my dog's head. "Warrior, you remember Will." The German shepherd gives what I call his happy bark, and Will rubs his neck.

The three of us sit on the lawn, horsing around with the Frisbee—sliding it flat but upside down across the grass or rolling it vertically on the lawn. Finally Warrior has had enough, and his head drops between his paws. His big brown eyes grow heavy for a nap, but then pop open to stare at me. "You're such a good boy, Warrior," I tell him. "You, too, Will." We humans laugh.

"On to more serious matters." I recount the scene I witnessed at the church where it looked as though Bobby Taylor was protecting Juliana—from what, I don't know.

"Ronnie, just because the incident looked bad doesn't mean it was, especially if you couldn't hear most of their conversation." Will is using a calm tone, in stark contrast to my tense, upset voice. "It's a mistake to jump to any conclusions."

"You're just trying to make me feel better, Will." I bite my lip. "What do I do?"

Will looks at me as though he's giving this some thought. "First, how much does your brother know about your investigation of Juliana? Does he know anything about you building this timeline of Teresa Gonzalez's life as she transformed into Juliana?"

"Not at all. At least I hope not," I respond.

"So why not drop it if it's upsetting you so much? You haven't really come across any other red flags since her Scranton Gang days, have you?" His eyes meet mine.

"True," I say, and Warrior snores gently. "But Bobby Taylor is a major red flag, and he's dangerous—"

"Let me take care of Bobby Taylor," Will says with sympathy in his voice. "Let me see if I can find any trip-ups since he's been released that we can prove and would get him thrown back in prison." He pauses. "Let your brother and Juliana make their plans, and you stay out of it." I look at him as if he's scolding me. He smiles. "Ronnie, why can't you let go of this?"

"Will, how many brothers and sisters do you have?" I ask.

"There are eight of us. Five boys and three girls." He notes my look of surprise. "Hey, what can I say? On my mother's side, we're a big Irish family." Warrior's asleep, and his legs kick as if he's running somewhere in his dream world.

"Are you close?" I ask. "Do you enjoy being together?"

"Yeah, for the most part, we like seeing each other."

"Bingo. Will, you are blessed with a big family of origin, and you probably have loads of nephews and nieces, too." He nods. "Were you ever married?" I ask.

"For a short while in my twenties," he answers me.

"So you know, Will, marriages can come and go. And then you're left with the family you were born into—"

"And your friends," Will interrupts.

"That's true. But you get my point about your original family, and now it's just Frank and me." My voice gets a bit shaky.

"It doesn't have to be, Ronnie." His eyes are kind and his voice is tender, which surprises me. He reaches across the grass for my hand and holds it gently before speaking. "It doesn't have to be—"

"Will, what are you saying?" I'm suddenly panicked. "You and I, this, this is professional—"

"I know, Ronnie, and you pay me faster than any other client," he says and laughs. "Don't get me wrong. I appreciate it. But you don't have to do this all alone. You can depend on friends—" His voice turns husky. "—Or one special friend."

We don't say another word, but Will continues to hold my hand. I remain speechless. His unwavering, piercing blue eyes cut right through me for what feels like forever.

I snap back to reality, pull my hand away as if I've noticed the heat on the burner of a stove and stand up quickly. I look at my watch and feign surprise. "Sorry, Will. I'm late, uh, and if I don't hurry, will probably, um, miss Warrior's vet appointment. Please stay as long as you like, but I've got to run. Warrior, come. Sorry, Will."

"But, Ronnie—" He looks bewildered.

"Talk to you later," I mumble and flee my house with my dog.

~~~~~

"Good evening, Mr. Bond." I ease into the warm tub with my glass of pinot noir, looking up at the large picture of Sean Connery hanging on the bathroom wall. The candles are lit, and the lighting is low. The mood is just right for a conversation with my favorite spy.

I settle back. "Well, James. What do you think? You know, he's fifteen years younger than I am." I take a drink. "He's kind. He's gentle. He's strong." I laugh. "He's good-looking, and those blue eyes, wow." I take another sip of pinot. "From what I can tell, he's got a great body, too." I chuckle. "What more can I say?"

I stretch out my arm holding the glass and pinch its tricep for droopiness. Then I pat my stomach under the water. "Definitely not as flat as a few years ago, James." I splash a little and take a final drink of my wine. "Anyway, not really sure if he's interested in anything more than being friends…"

I blow bubbles in the water. Can't remember the last time I had sex, what with my marriage coming apart for some time and then finally the divorce.

"What's that you say, James?" I look up at the photograph. "Go for it? Oh, I don't know…"

CHAPTER THIRTY-NINE

Stepping out of the tub, I notice the beautiful dim light of dusk cutting through the grey clouds outside the window. I throw on some clothes, leave the cottage, and walk Warrior up the road that leads to my big house, the one I'm renting to the Lattimore family. When the sprawling white clapboard farm house comes into view, I see the two youngest children playing outside. I flash back for a moment to happier days there when my own kids were still children enjoying one another's company.

I take a left turn well before getting close to the house and walk across a field to a bridle trail that meanders along a stream. This is one of Warrior's favorite walks, and we enjoy the early evening together. I can't get the scene between Juliana and Bobby in the cemetery out of my mind. I also wonder about the mystery of Juliana's baby. How'd she keep that a secret for all those years? It's got to be Francesca, right?

A sudden splash in the stream from a rising trout sends a barking Warrior running over to paw at the water, churning up ripples.

"It's a good thing, boy, that I'm not fishing right here." He runs back to me, and I crouch down to scratch his neck. "Warrior, you've probably scared away every fish in this pool." I hug him, and several large rain drops splatter on the stream and then us. "Ready to run home?"

Once back in the cottage, I sit peacefully on the rug with Warrior listening to the gentle rain. I lean back against my favorite chair and think about Juliana's baby, imagining the child now as a teenager. As Francesca? Does Frankie know who her mother is?

And why the big secret? It's not a scandal to have a child out of wedlock in today's world. Finally, does Frank know about Juliana's daughter, and if he doesn't, would it affect his feelings toward her in any way to suddenly find out? If she hasn't already, I would imagine Juliana probably plans to tell him. I would hope so, anyway, but who can be sure when someone has issues with trust the way Juliana does.

I wonder how Frank and Juliana are enjoying their evening in Manhattan at the theatre, which I happen to know about because Laura called me earlier today. My niece also said she was going into the city to meet friends and that she, her dad, and Juliana would all be back in the morning. So, nobody home at Frank's tonight.

I close up the house. The rain is heavier, and my dog and I make a dash for the car. After I throw down a blanket, Warrior hops in the passenger seat, and we head over to Meadow Farm. If Frank or Juliana turns out to be there, my excuse is that Rita called me to pick up fresh farm eggs.

It's almost dark, but Rita has left a few lights on, as she does every evening when she leaves. All looks quiet, and I park around back near the kitchen.

Usually the doors of the house are left unlocked at all hours of the day, but with everyone away, I know that Rita will have closed up and turned on the alarm. I pull out my key and go in with Warrior through the kitchen door. Frank gave me the security code years ago, and I punch it into the keypad to turn off the alarm.

"Come on, Warrior." We both shake off the rain. "Let's get moving." He follows me as I walk up the stairs, down the hall, and into Juliana's room, where he stretches out and falls asleep. Flipping on the light, I stride over to the now-closed drawer of the bureau and pull it open. I'd like another look at Juliana's old locket, the one with the chain hanging out of the red leather box that I saw when I first snooped among her things.

Finding the box and locket, I turn on the lamp for more light and look at the piece carefully. It's tarnished and scratched the way it was when I first saw it, and it's still attached to a frail silver chain. I pull out my drugstore glasses to get a better look at the hard-to-read inscription.

To MTG, with love, FEB

…could it be *FLB*? Or an *R* instead of a *B*? So, *FLR*?

I remember struggling to figure out the inscription before, and my glasses aren't helping very much. I snap the locket open and stare at the clump of hair I saw the first time. Dark, like Juliana's. Whose is it?

I feel around the edges of the locket with my fingernail, but I can't loosen the small piece of glass holding the hair in place. You never know. It might be handy to have a sample of this for DNA analysis to establish maternity or some other connection. I'm sure Will could handle it for me. Of course, I can't believe it's come to this, as if I'm in the middle of some spy thriller. I put the box and locket back in the drawer. Any more brilliant ideas, Sherlock?

I walk into the bathroom and look around. The small trash can catches my eye. Something odd is sticking out of the top.

I lean over for a look and see it's a wooden handle, a hair brush handle. I peer inside the can more closely and also see the other half of the broken brush. It looks like an expensive one with real boar bristles.

My eyes dart to the long dark hairs that meander through the bristles. For sure this is Juliana's broken brush. Then I notice a loose nest of dark hair to the side of the brush head, as if Juliana had cleaned the bristles after she used it.

DNA! I rush to the kitchen and return with a large baggie and a small plastic garbage bag. Flipping the baggie inside out and putting my hand into it like a glove, I pick up the brush handle (in case I need fingerprints), the brush head, and the nest of hair. I zip the bag shut. Even through the plastic baggie, I can see that some of Juliana's discarded hair strands still have their follicles attached. Pay dirt. I also empty the remaining contents of the trash can so Juliana won't notice the missing broken brush upon her return from the city.

I hear the growl of an engine driving up the road to the house. Sounds like a motorcycle. I don't touch the lights, but creep to a dark bedroom next to this one, clutching the baggie with the broken brush and white garbage bag, with Warrior by my side. My dog barks. "Quiet, Warrior," I say in a stage whisper.

I look out the window and can barely make out a motorcycle stopping a hundred yards from the house. The rider parks his bike behind a bush and walks in our direction under trees when possible, doing his best to stay out of the rain, which appears to be easing up. He avoids a pool of light coming from a front-door lamp fixture.

I watch the figure lurk about the house, trying to see inside. I'm sure he's casing the place to determine whether anyone's at home. The soft rain isn't noisy, and I can hear him mumbling. I guess that's Bobby Taylor down there. While I can't tell in the dark light if his bare arms have those abundant tattoos, I would bet it's that creep and feel a shiver go straight through me.

I reach down to Warrior for reassurance, and he rubs his head against my leg, waiting for my command. I feel him quiver. "Warrior, stay quiet," I whisper.

Warrior does the opposite and whines loudly. The guy's head jerks up, and I back away from the window at once. "Quiet," I repeat softly to my dog, putting my finger to my mouth. "Shhh."

"Who's up there?" Bobby—or so I suppose—growls from below. "Teresa, that you? I know the old guy's not here, so come down and talk to me." Yep, the sound of his voice confirms that it's Bobby Taylor.

I cautiously peek out as he backs up from the house to get a better view of the entire structure. "Aw, Terry," he says. "I thought you were finished with all this. Why'd you want to come back to this house again after all these years?"

Again? I jerk my head back from the window and stare into the room. What's he talking about? I glance outside. He paces back and forth through the pool of light, and even though the rain has stopped, I see his tee-shirt is soaked and now clings to him like a second skin.

"Don't-cha remember?" he says, almost mumbling but I can pick it up by staying very quiet. I think I hear him say, "You swore you'd never come back here...after what happened to you and your mama." And then I feel it once more—a familiar flickering at the edges of my memory. My dog stirs, and I put a finger over my mouth and whisper, "Shhh," to quiet him down.

Bobby walks up the front steps and bangs hard on the door. He slams the heavy brass doorknocker repeatedly, yelling, "Teresa!" over and over.

"Get down here! I wanna talk to you," he demands. "I can help you get revenge."

Revenge? In my mind I hear Juliana's voice saying, *You'll ruin everything, spoil everything*. My radar is on full alert. This revenge factor has always worried me. Revenge for what?

Bobby's getting very worked up now. He jiggles the door knob, attempting to enter the house. Warrior's agitation grows, and he growls. The guy moves over to the windows, trying those, too. My focus is scattered, confused by Bobby's ramblings.

"Teresa! I know you're in there," he yells. Why doesn't he just go away? "Teresa, I can help you, and you can help me. Joe is puttin' a lot of pressure on me for money...for some deal. Terry, I need money." His tone is desperate.

Wait a minute. Joe? Does he mean respectable Joe who runs that model drug prevention program in Scranton? Joe, who says he hasn't seen his brother, Bobby, in such a long time? What kind of deal does Joe have going? If he wants help from Bobby, it must not be very above board.

Bobby bangs his fists against the front door. Oh my god, I'm pretty sure I forgot to lock the kitchen door when I came in.

"If you won't come out, I'm coming in." He rams his body against the big door.

Warrior breaks into a fierce bark, and I make a dash for the upstairs keypad in the center hall. I enter the distress code, which goes straight to the police. In an instant, spotlights turn on and brighten the area around the entire house. Simultaneously, a screeching siren goes off and a digital voice booms from a speaker announcing, "Police notified and sending help."

With Warrior barking ferociously, I dash to a nearby window and peek down below. Bobby Taylor is momentarily frozen, prior to making some kind of a fight or flight decision. It's as though someone has yelled, *Stop or we'll shoot*. His arms are bent out from his sides as if to ward off a blow, and his head turns in all directions, looking for a physical attacker. Then he snaps out of it.

"Teresa, you bitch. You can't hide behind these rich f—s forever," he screams, circling in the pool of light.

Then he comes to a dead stop. "I've got it! I've got a better idea." Huh? What better idea? "You wait! You're gonna love this one," Bobby Taylor threatens. Laughing, he turns on his heels and runs out of the light.

Once away from the house, he cuts behind a bush, and I hear a motor start. He guns the engine, and the motorcycle shoots onto the wet gravel, where he skids into a left turn and speeds away.

Wanting to go after the intruder, my dog continues barking loudly. "Settle down, Warrior," I command. He stops. I can feel my heart thumping away a mile a minute. I open the window and inhale as much of the night air as I can, which finally calms me. Warrior drops to the ground and puts his face down between his paws, his brow furrowed as if he's worried.

I collect my thoughts, which are a confused muddle at the moment. What did he mean: *Why'd you want to come back to this house?* When was Juliana ever here before this visit with Frank?

I can still hear him, and I'm sure he said it—*You swore you'd never set foot here again…after what happened to you and your mama.* What is Bobby Taylor talking about? And how does Joe Taylor fit in? Lastly, what better idea does Bobby have for Juliana?

I turn off the blaring alarm and wait for the police.

CHAPTER FORTY

The police arrive five minutes after Bobby Taylor is gone. Any sooner and they'd have passed each other on the property. But as the cruiser raced up our road to respond to the distress call, I made a snap decision.

I know our local officers—another advantage of small-town life—and tell them I've dropped by to pick up a book at the house, and while here, the attempted break-in occurred. I give them the details as they really happened, except I leave out two major items—one, that I know the identity of the suspect, and two, the suspect's yelling about Teresa. That's the account I stick with when I call Rita right after the police depart Meadow Farm. I leave it to her to pass on the story to Frank.

After Bobby Taylor's outburst, I need to figure all of this out. If I'm to believe what he shouted, then Juliana has already been at my family's farm at some point in the past. This is not her first visit. My mind returns to my memory of the little girl hiding under the dining room table, bawling, with her arms wrapped around our dog, Glory. Is it even possible? But the child I remember was named Maria.

The rolling thunder outside agitates Warrior. *Crack!* My dog and I jump. The lightning seems as if it's right over us. I wonder if these loud noises take Warrior back to Afghanistan when Tommy was shot down.

By now it's four in the morning, and Warrior and I sprawl on the floor of Meadow Farm's library, with me flipping through an old picture album. This one is forty years old, from the 1970s.

"Unbelievable." I stare at a yellowed photograph of myself in 1971, wearing my favorite cork platform shoes and my preppy version of hot pants. Preppy just means they weren't obscenely short and skin tight. I remember clearly how my mother was not happy at all when I showed up in this outfit, and she was even less happy when I came home—next picture—in a purple maxi coat topped by a pink floppy hat after my trip to London with my best friend and her mother.

I stare at the photo and remember how much I loved that purple coat. While Warrior naps on the floor and quietly snores, I continue flipping through the pages of the album, surveying my brothers and me growing up in the '70s.

I stop. Found it. The picture I was sure was in one of these albums. And there she is, the same little dark-haired girl I remembered tearing through our dining room. In this photo, she's slouched over and sitting cross-legged on the floor at the foot of a sofa with her arms draped around our Lab, Glory. Her mother, sitting on the sofa, leans forward with her hands on the little girl's shoulders. The woman smiles for the camera. The little girl looks startled. Scribbled in ink underneath the picture is the caption *Rosa & Maria with Glory.* The year is 1979.

I look closely. I slip the small picture from the photo corners that keep it in place on the page and grab a magnifying glass from Frank's desk so that I can examine it in more detail. It falls from my fingers and floats to the floor, landing face-down. I notice pale writing on the back. Warrior opens one eye to watch me pick it up. The faded words are still clear enough to read—*Rosa & Maria-Teresa Gonzalez.*

Son of a gun! So Bobby Taylor was telling the truth. Maria-Teresa, Teresa, Terry, Julie, a.k.a. Juliana lived at Meadow Farm as a little girl. In my head I hear the echoes of Joe Taylor's voice when I was at his office to learn about his school drug program. *Her mother worked somewhere in New York or New Jersey. I don't remember where.*

At the time, it never dawned on me that Teresa and her mother had lived here, at Meadow Farm. With us. And that's why Juliana knew about our secret tree house; she, we, had all climbed up there as kids.

And now the memories begin to flood back. I remember this adorable little girl and her mother, Rosa. As with Rita today, the Meadow Farm household could not have run without Rosa Gonzalez.

I look for any indication of Juliana's adult face in this beautiful child. It's hard to say. I remember I had thought Juliana reminded me of Angelina Jolie when I first saw her, but I realize now that definitely more than her movie star features were nudging at me.

I flip through the 1980s album and spot other photographs as Maria blossomed into a lovely girl-almost-tween. The full mouth and high cheekbones evolved on the girl's face over the years, and her dark, piercing eyes are the same ones I've seen in Juliana. I note how much, as a tween, Teresa also looks like Francesca in Scranton, like a twin sister who time-traveled a few decades. Then in 1985 the pictures of Teresa and her mother stop. I don't really have to ask myself why.

I close the albums, listening to the rain splatter on the terrace outside the library's French doors, and every painful detail comes back from that time in 1985. It's an understatement to say it was not my finest moment.

I was home for the weekend from my job as a production assistant on some Hollywood-entertainment show in New York. I hated that job. It was tedious, boring, and I couldn't stand the woman for whom I was working.

I arrived from the city in a foul mood, only to discover a pre-teen Maria in my room. I walked in as she pranced in front of my full-length mirror trying on my clothes and jewelry.

I exploded. Blew up. I was nasty, definitely way up in the bitch-decibel level. I demanded Maria get out of my clothes pronto right in front of me. Which she did, scared to death. Tears were running down her face as she ran from my room holding her own clothes in front of her to shield herself.

I cringe when I think of my awful behavior. But I wasn't finished. As I put my things away, I discovered a treasured ring missing. I assumed the worst and tore down the hall after her.

I found Maria in her room crying. She was only twelve, for god's sake, a child. But I didn't let that stop me from accusing her of stealing the missing ring, which meant so much to me because Frank and Peter had given it to me for my birthday.

Rosa intervened and demanded I leave her daughter alone. She insisted she had taken the ring and had sold it. She stuck with this pathetic story, and later, my mother fired her with severance pay...such a sad conclusion to Rosa's seven years of working for my family.

My mother instructed Frank and me to drive Rosa and Maria to the bus station, as Rosa had requested. Rosa wouldn't say where they were going, just that they planned to go where she had family. I still remember how stoic and proud Rosa was as Frank helped them with their shabby suitcases. But the moment was all too much for Maria, who had nonstop tears streaming down her face.

As he placed their suitcases near the bus stop for Pennsylvania, the girl broke away from her mother and ran up to my brother. She pounded at him with her fists, crying out, "I hate you, I hate you, I hate you." Frank, looking sad, just stood there and took her blows, until Rosa pulled Maria off of him.

I waited there without moving and didn't intervene to help my brother. I knew I had made a mess of things and that I was scum. I felt such shame.

Frank and I got into the car and drove home in silence. When we arrived, Mother presented me with the missing ring, which had turned up in a laundry hamper filled mostly with my dirty clothes. The implication was that the ring had been in one of my pockets. My mother looked at me with such disappointment, because I had been so quick to accuse.

It was too late to go after Rosa and Maria; we knew Rosa had too much pride to return. They were gone, and we didn't know where they were in Pennsylvania. We didn't try too hard to find out, either.

Stupid, stupid. How could I have been so very stupid? All little girls want to try on big-girl clothes. When I think back, I can't believe how I let that innocent event snowball into accusations of jewelry theft. It was one-hundred percent my fault.

I know that we all have moments in our past that leave us feeling ashamed of ourselves. Until today, I realize I had successfully buried this memory because I don't think I ever forgave myself.

Then I see the link. I remember their bus was going to Pennsylvania, setting the young Maria on her angry journey toward leading the Scranton Gang a couple of years later.

I also can't get that image of Maria pounding her fists against Frank at the bus station out of my mind. Has Maria Teresa, now as Juliana, been waiting all these years to get her revenge against our family, more specifically, Frank and me? Is Frank walking into a trap? Has another trap already sprung, setting my brother against me so that I'm in exile?

I dial Frank's cell. He picks up, and before he can say anything, I blurt out, "I have something to tell you about when we were kids…you won't believe—"

He clicks off without saying a word. I redial, but he's turned off his phone, and my call goes straight to voicemail. I glance at my watch and groan—it's five in the morning. Of course he hung up; he was fast asleep in Manhattan. I blew it. I'm such a jerk.

CHAPTER FORTY-ONE

"Morning, everybody!" It's later—a respectable nine o'clock—and Warrior and I enter the kitchen at Meadow Farm to find Rita filling my niece's mug with steaming coffee. The wonderful smell of caffeine jolts through me after a sleep-deprived night.

"Oooh. I'll take one of those, too, please," I say to Rita.

Warrior nuzzles his wet face in Laura's lap. She's home from her overnight in Manhattan, and my dog drools over the prospect of breakfast tidbits. "Enough, Warrior," I say. "Now, sit." He does, but his eyes shift from me, the boss lady, up to my niece, hoping for a tiny piece of her toast.

"Breakfast, Ronnie?" Rita asks, pouring my coffee. She's the one who invited me over, wanting complete details about the attempted break-in last night. Plus I'm determined to speak to my brother as soon as he gets home, to tell him what I've remembered about Maria Teresa Gonzalez many years before.

"What are you serving this fine morning, Rita?" I ask.

"Veggie omelets."

"I'd love one. Thank you." I take the steaming mug from her. "So, Laura, when does your father come home from the city?"

Our housekeeper jumps in. "Frank called a half-hour ago," Rita says. "He's at an early meeting and will be back soon, in an hour or so."

"And Juliana with him?" I ask.

"She's already back," Laura says. "The driver delivered her an hour ago. She's upstairs—"

"That's good—" I say.

"Aunt Ronnie, a lot of noise is coming from her room, like maybe she's packing?" Laura puts her cup on the table. "Right before I came down I thought I heard her cell ring, and then it sounded as if she was crying." She looks at me helplessly. "It feels like a repeat of last time when she and Daddy had that fight. Please do something. I'm not sure what to say to her."

I get up from the table with my mug. "How does Juliana take her coffee, Rita?"

"Black." She's already pouring another cup and hands it to me. "I'll wait to make your omelet," Rita says as I head out of the kitchen.

I walk up the stairs and down the hall carefully with two filled mugs. The door to Juliana's room is ajar, and I peek in. I see her pulling clothes off hangers and tossing them into a gigantic suitcase.

"Knock knock," I say, and she freezes with her back to me. "How about a hot cup of coffee to clear away the cobwebs?" She turns and stares at me, as if caught doing something wrong.

I walk in and extend the mug toward her, but she doesn't take it. I put it on her nightstand, next to her books and Kindle. "Juliana, are you OK?"

"Yes." She stands completely still for the longest moment and then wrings her hands.

"I see you're packing," I offer, giving her a chance to talk. She glances nervously at her belongings strewn across the bed. "Are you and Frank going somewhere?" She still says nothing. "Does Frank know you're leaving?" I ask. She seems anxious. "Rita says he'll probably be here soon. Shouldn't you wait until you've talked with him in person?" Does this lady run away whenever a problem arises? I wonder what kind of lovers' quarrel they had this time.

She sits down on the bed, looking defeated. "I don't have enough time," she says. What does that mean?

I take the mug on the nightstand and try again to hand it over. Now, she accepts it and drinks. Feeling a little relieved at this minor thaw, I sit in a chair opposite her. "How can I help?"

She appears surprised and begins to speak, but a half-choked sob comes out instead. Then she starts to cry. I walk over, sit next to her. She scoots away keeping her distance from me.

"Look, I know we haven't gotten off to a great start—" Her huge sob interrupts me. "Just let it out, Juliana. It'll all be OK." She has a long cry and finally breathes deeply as if it's coming to an end. I hand her the tissue box from the bureau.

"You and Frank are close, and my brother is happy when he's with you. I'm sure he wouldn't want you to leave."

She takes a tissue, looking at me as if she's never seen me before. "It's not about Frank."

I try to use a gentle tone. "What's the matter, Juliana?"

"I'd rather not say." She blows her nose and speaks through her sniffles. "I, I can't talk about it…don't know what to do. I have to wait…for the phone call."

My attention is drawn to the old silver locket now lying on the bedside table instead of inside the red leather box where I first saw it. I walk over, pick it up, and read out loud. *"To MTG, with love, FEB*…that's what it looks like." Then I say, "But it isn't *FEB*, is it? It's *FLR*, Frances Livingston Rutherfurd, my mother."

Juliana says nothing. She glances at her phone as if she's willing it to ring.

"OK, while you wait for your call—it's time for true confessions," I continue, and a veil of suspicion drops over her eyes. "Juliana, we knew each other a long, long time ago, didn't we?"

She sits without moving a muscle, not even breathing. The room is so quiet, you really could hear a pin drop. I go on. "It's been bothering me and bothering me, and I finally figured out who you are—how it is that I already know you." I open the locket and then snap it shut again.

"I remember my mother adored you—when you were little, she'd look you straight in the eye and tell you that you could grow up to be anything you wanted. Little Maria

Teresa Gonzalez." I pause because my heart is beating so fast I think it will burst.

"It was *you* who ran through the dining room after Glory." I let out a sigh. "And my mother fell, breaking one of her favorite black heels and spilling the sauce. That's why you were rubbing that old spot on the carpet the day I found you in the dining room. Remember?"

Juliana still says nothing, but her eyes are huge.

"My mother gave you this locket not long before you left Meadow Farm." I put it down on the table. "I looked through some old family albums last night and found pictures of you and your mother. Right up to 1985. That was when you both left, because of my horrible behavior toward you when I caught you trying on my clothes—which my daughters did, too, at your age years later, by the way." I'm running off at the mouth but I can't stop.

"And then my terrible, terrible accusation that you stole my ring. Juliana, what I did was unforgivable." I want to wipe away the pain of what I've done.

She starts pacing the room. I continue, "When Frank and I got home from driving you and Rosa to the bus station, Mother presented me with the missing ring. She'd found it with my dirty clothes in the hamper. I was so ashamed for being such a bitch to you. Of course you hate me, but please don't hurt Frank. Don't seek revenge against him. He's so good—"

She stops pacing and declares, "I couldn't hurt Frank. I love him—"

I bite my lip. "But I remember you pounding on him at the bus station telling him how much you hated him—"

"I was eleven years old, Ronnie, and I took it out on him. Somehow I knew he wouldn't hit back. You, I was scared of."

"Me?" I ask, shocked. "I was that terrible, huh?"

"Yes, you were, Ronnie. And ever since I arrived at Meadow Farm, starting with that cocktail party when Frank wanted you and me to meet—god I was so nervous getting ready—anyway, I've been terrified that you would remember me and try to keep Frank and me apart." Juliana's posture droops even more. Hmmm. Maybe that's why her room looked like a hurricane hit it when I snooped for numbers on her cell phone the evening I first met her— or met her again.

She shakes her head in disbelief. "You think I still want revenge against Frank and your family, for what you did to my mother—may she rest in peace—who was just sticking up for me all those years back?"

"Oh, Juliana, I'm so sorry about your mother." I pause. "How long ago did Rosa die?"

"It's been fifteen years," Juliana says. "It was a heart attack. She didn't suffer." She pauses as if collecting her thoughts, and then I see a hardness in her eyes. "Revenge? Sure I wanted to get back at all of you Rutherfurds— thought of little else all through my teens. It's what drove me forward in life."

Juliana pauses again, and I watch resignation replace the memory of her fury. "Then one day the anger stopped, thank god, because that took a huge weight off my shoulders."

Thank god, I think, too. "If the anger and desire for revenge were gone," I say, "what kept pushing you to go for a better life?"

"Plain and simple," Juliana answers, "it was how your mother inspired me with her kindness, always telling me I could make anything of my life. Her words came back to me many times over the years." Recalling my conversation with Carmela Suarez during my Disney World visit when she told me a mystery person had inspired Teresa/Juliana, it makes my heart melt to learn that the mystery person was my mother. Still…

"So, when you met my brother in California, you weren't even a little bit tempted to seek revenge?" I ask. Juliana emphatically shakes her head no, and I go on. "What was that like? Meeting Frank again? Did you know right away who he was?"

She doesn't answer, but I see a slow, sad smile play across Juliana's face, and then she speaks. "I met friends for golf, and as I walked over to the course, I saw them talking to a tall man with salt-and-pepper hair. I could only see his back," she says. "Then he turned around and looked at me with the kindest eyes—it took my breath away, because I was sure I knew him, but I couldn't place him. Then my friends introduced us and said his name, and I couldn't believe it."

Juliana looks off, and I guess she's reliving the moment. She continues, "Frank Rutherfurd from Meadow Farm. And even more amazing was the instant connection between us…" Her voice drifts off, and she looks back at me. "…The rest is history. So, no, I had no thoughts of revenge. But enough of this, Ronnie, I have more urgent matters to deal with."

"Wait. What about that *revenge* rock that came flying through the living room window when Frank was attacked? Spelled r-A-v-e-n-g-e, by the way. Who spells revenge like that?"

She hesitates, then frowns. "I wasn't the one who threw the rock. But I can't talk to you about this now." She goes on, "I have a bigger problem." Her bottom lip quivers. "I'm waiting for news, a phone call—" A choked sob breaks loose from her throat as tears fill her eyes again. "A family member has, uh, gone m-m-missing." The crying resumes, and she stands up and walks her worry into the rug, back and forth, back and forth.

Her disturbance can only be over one possible person, and I ask, "Is Francesca missing?"

That stops Juliana in her tracks, and she stares at me and says in a shaky voice, "The market where she has her summer job called our *Tía* Connie to ask if Frankie was sick, since she wasn't there for her early shift this morning. Connie is out looking for her, and I was waiting to hear if Connie had found Frankie." She grabs another tissue and dabs the tears from her eyes. "Then this awful cou-, uh, person called to say he's got her…that he grabbed her on her way to work. I don't know what to believe." She glances at her watch. "Enough of this waiting—"

"Francesca isn't just a niece or cousin, is she, Juliana?"

"I don't want to talk about this." Her voice once again has that suspicious tone to it. I back off.

"Is *Tía* Connie your aunt or is she your great-aunt?" I ask, but Juliana says nothing in response. "Remember, I did see you with her, so what's the big secret?"

"Connie's my great-aunt." Juliana sighs and goes back to tossing a few more things into the suitcase. "She has problems because of a nephew who's back in her life."

"So what's the problem with the, uh, nephew? I guess he's your cousin?" I return to my chair, where I can face her and better observe her body language and facial expressions.

"He's an awful man, no shame. Yes, unfortunately he's a cousin..." Juliana glances around the room and then at the huge suitcase on the bed. "...And most of the time I try to stay as far away from him as I can." She stuffs her books and Kindle into the suitcase and then slams it shut. "From what I know of him, I'm sure he's mean to Connie, maybe threatens her, but she won't say." She sits down next to the oversized case.

"Can't you talk to the nephew?" I watch her face closely.

"I tried just yesterday to reason with him, and it didn't do any good." Was that the scene I witnessed at the cemetery? "He's bad news," Juliana says, and her body stiffens. "I don't want to go anywhere near him." Hmmm, I wonder what the truth actually is. She folds her arms across her chest. "I really don't want to discuss this any further."

I switch gears. "Maybe Frank can help you find a solution?"

Juliana stands up, and her voice is sharp. "I don't want Frank dragged into this."

I'm careful what I say next. "You can't run away." The way you did with Mr. Dot-Com, John Palmer, I feel like saying, but resist the urge.

Her cell phone rings, and she looks at the number with relief. "It's Francesca." She quickly answers, "Francesca, are you OK? Where are—"

The voice on the other end interrupts her, and I can make out that it's a *he*, but can't understand what he says. It's certainly not Francesca or *Tía* Connie. Juliana's body tenses; she seems unnerved.

"Don't hurt her, Bobby—" Juliana gasps. "Bobby, wait. I'll do anything you say." She starts to cry again.

The proverbial light bulb goes on. Of course that's what Bobby Taylor meant when he yelled out *I've got a better idea* as he left Meadow Farm last night—he grabbed Francesca. Does he think he's Francesca's father, or is he doing this purely for monetary gain? He said last night that he needs money.

"Where do I bring it?" she asks. "What time?" She glances at her watch. "Noon, OK. I think it's enough time." She hangs up and goes to her big leather satchel that sits on a luggage rack. Rummaging around, Juliana does her best to block my view, but I see a flash of cash.

"What's going on, Juliana?"

"If you want to help me, I could use a hand getting my suitcase downstairs," she says.

Now it's my turn to stand there in paralyzing uncertainty while I try to figure out my next move. She looks at me, assumes I'm not coming, and turns her back on me. She pulls the monster case clumsily off the bed and pushes it by its wheels as she leaves the room, and then I hear the *clunk, clunk* sound of baggage bouncing down the steps.

I run into the hall and dash over to help her carry the piece of luggage. "Juliana, what's happened to Frankie?"

She doesn't look at me and focuses on the steps as we now carry her heavy case downstairs. "I didn't mean to eavesdrop, but that didn't sound like *Tía* Connie's voice on your call."

Nothing from Juliana, except, "Thank you," once we're at the bottom, and she wheels the oversized suitcase across the foyer and out the door.

I follow her. "Was that Bobby?" Silence as she bounces the baggage down the outside steps to her car. "I can help you."

I rush inside and upstairs to her room. I grab her big satchel, but not before glancing inside where I see bundles of cash, like the bundles I saw her give Bobby Taylor that day at the Moosic Café. Holy smoke, she must have ten-thousand dollars in here—a wild guess on my part, but I count about ten bundles of hundred-dollar bills.

Juliana walks in on me holding the satchel handles apart, staring inside the bag at the cash, probably with my mouth agape—definitely awkward. She shakes her head. "I don't have time for this. Please tell Frank I'll phone him when I can." She grabs the satchel and dashes out.

"How can I help you?" I call after her again. Do I call Frank? What about Will? They'd both tell me to stay put and do nothing at all.

Below, I hear a car engine start up. I dash to the window and look outside to see Juliana leave in the rental she's been using. I hurry down the stairs, and as I cross the foyer toward the door, Laura and Warrior come out from the kitchen.

"Aunt Ronnie, was that Juliana who left?" Laura asks.

"Yes," I say as Warrior trots over to me.

"So where are you going now, Aunt Ronnie?"

"To see what I can find out, Laura, and I'll come right back," I answer. "Oh, and when Frank arrives, tell him Juliana said she'll call." I stop at the phone table to write a number on a pad. "And tell him if there's any trouble—"

"What kind of trouble?" My niece sounds puzzled and upset.

"No time to explain, Laura. This is important, so listen to me. If there's any trouble and Frank needs help, he should call Will Benson at this number. Tell your father that Will is, uh, is a friend of mine, and he'll know what to do."

"But Aunt Ronnie—"

I hand her the paper. "Got to go. Just tell him, Laura, and make sure you give him the number."

Warrior and I race outside to my bright red Mustang. I realize the car is hard to miss, a problem if I'm going to successfully tail Juliana. So we detour to the barn, where I find the nondescript farm Toyota, and we hop in. We then hot-rod out of Meadow Farm after Juliana, with Will's and Frank's voices in my head telling me not to go.

CHAPTER FORTY-TWO

Speeding via the most direct route I know to the highway, I catch up to Juliana's rental car as we both enter the on-ramp. Warrior and I once again follow her to Scranton. I'm pretty sure she doesn't notice us tailing her, and I maintain a distance of a half-dozen cars between us. Along the way, I leave a message for Will that my dog and I are probably heading to the Moosic Motel, that I think Francesca's been kidnapped, and can he follow?

I finish up with, "My brother will probably come to Moosic, too, and I gave him your number. Will, if you can't reach me by phone or text, it may be that I've gotten myself into trouble. So call Frank. Perhaps the two of you can help each other. And Juliana, Francesca, and me. Oh, I'm driving the farm Toyota, not my red Mustang." I sign off, leaving Frank's number.

Boy, if that message doesn't get me a lecture, I don't know what will. I can even imagine the conversation when my personal private eye calls back. *Now, Ronnie*, he would caution, *let's agree right here and now that you're not barging into the middle of things the moment you get there.*

You will carefully assess the situation before deciding what to do, check in with me, and follow my instructions.

Then I'll sigh and roll my eyes. And P.I. Benson will continue, *I mean it, Ronnie. We don't know if they have guns. This could be very dangerous, and we don't want anyone getting shot. Do we understand each other? I'm in charge.*

And I would tell him he's in charge, even though I wouldn't mean it. Something in me bristles at being ordered around, even in my imaginary conversation with Will.

Once in Moosic and parked in front the motel with the engine off, I watch Juliana enter the coffee shop. She sits in a booth that's clearly visible through the front window. I check my watch, and five minutes later, at eleven o'clock, crouched low with Warrior in the car, I watch Bobby Taylor saunter out from the far alley of the Moosic Motel. He's playing with his cell phone and doesn't notice me as he walks past the Toyota. Juliana probably doesn't know that Bobby uses the motel, and from her angle in the restaurant, she wouldn't have seen him through the window exiting from that alley.

Bobby enters the coffee shop and sits down in Juliana's booth. His back is to me, but I can observe Juliana clearly. Her side of the conversation appears to grow more and more agitated by the minute. She stands up, pulls her phone out of her pocket, and indicates she's going outside.

When Juliana comes through the door, she locks eyes with my German shepherd, who grows excited when he sees her. "Settle down, Warrior," I say, and he curls up on the seat. Her eyes shift to me, and her brow furrows with worry. She glances back at the restaurant's front window, but Bobby isn't looking in our direction. She glares back at me, and I put my finger to my mouth and shake my head to indicate that I'm not here. I lower my window.

Juliana breaks eye contact with me when she hears a voice on the other end of her phone. What I can't quite hear, I can guess at. "Frank?" She listens. "I'm OK. I'm in Pennsylvania." Another pause. "Please, I need you to trust me, and I'll explain everything later." More listening. "Remember when I told you I had issues in my old life that needed taking care of?"

She nods her head to the phone and then continues. "Well, a deadbeat cousin from my past has kidnapped a family member. He wants money, of course."

She waits a moment. "Yes, Frank, it's my daughter." Her voice cracks. "Oh, Frank, I have what he told me to bring. Ten thousand—I have it here. But he changed his mind. He says his brother wants him to get more money."

Does Bobby Taylor mean his brother, Joe, wants him to get more? So Joe is definitely part of this. I had a bad feeling about that guy when I first met him in his office.

Apparently Frank says something, and Juliana answers, "Now he wants twenty-five thousand." She looks again in the window at Bobby Taylor's slouched back. He turns suddenly, and she gives him a thumbs-up and nods her head. He returns to his coffee, and she looks at me with panic in her eyes while she listens to my brother on the phone.

"Thank you, Frank. I can write you a check or wire it to you from California. I'll tell him the cash will be here in a couple of hours. And Frank, Ronnie's nearby—" I can't hear the rest, because she turns away.

Everything that I was terrified would happen to Frank is happening—he's being dragged into the middle of Juliana's deadly mess. Kidnapping! Ransom! And not just one nasty thug, Bobby Taylor, but it sounds as if his greedy, probably masterminding brother, Joe Taylor, is also involved—the one who just looks like a good guy but wants more ransom money.

OK, focus. It seems my brother is bringing an additional fifteen-thousand dollars to make up the difference and help Juliana meet Bobby's and Joe's new demand. Frank could be walking into a trap. I've got to do something.

My cell phone vibrates, and I pick up. "Ronnie, what do you think you're doing?" my brother asks.

"Helping Francesca and you," I say.

"Not on your life," he responds.

"Frank, you don't know what you're getting yourself into—"

"Leave and go home," he demands.

"I could stay as backup until you get here," I offer, looking in my dog's big brown eyes. I scratch Warrior's head.

"On no account are you to follow Juliana and interfere. Are we clear?" I don't answer. "Are we clear?" Frank repeats.

I hold the phone away from my face and yell, "Frank, can you hear me? I'm having a hard time hearing you—"

"Don't pull that one, Ronnie—" he interrupts. I hang up.

CHAPTER FORTY-THREE

"Warrior, it's time to make my exit," I say to my dog, as I watch Juliana go back inside the coffee shop and sit down with Bobby. "I have an idea where Frankie may be." I pour water into Warrior's bowl and place it on the car's floor.

"If I can release the girl and get her somewhere safe, that takes her out of harm's way, and then my brother won't have to go anywhere near the Taylors. Plus those creeps won't have any more leverage against my brother and Juliana." Even though we're in the shade, it's pretty hot outside, so I've lowered each of the windows a little more than usual for cross-ventilation. I want to make sure Warrior will be fine...should things take longer than I expect.

"Now, Warrior, listen." I look straight into his soulful brown eyes and speak slowly. "If I don't come back, when you see Juliana or Frank, bark. A loud bark, OK?" He puts his head down and nuzzles me. I drop the car keys on the driver's floor mat, kiss the top of his head, and slip out of the Toyota. I scuttle to the side of the motel quickly and glimpse Juliana, who's still in heated discussion with Bobby.

Then I slink down the same alley that Bobby just used—it's as dirty and smelly as the last time I was here. Again, I peek into windows, looking at dumpy, messy rooms with unmade beds or ones that appear to be empty of guests—I guess housekeeping starts later here than at most motels.

I reach the back corner room, passing a window that reveals a huge pile of clothes on a full-sized bed. I slow down before making a left turn into the alley on the back side of the motel, not wanting to repeat that unfortunate run-in with the stoned and malodorous Jimmy, if he should be back there smoking weed again.

I stop and backtrack to the last window. Had something in that mound of clothes moved, or was it my imagination? I see the tip of a navy Converse sneaker twitch. I tap on the window, and a pair of navy sneakers kicks out of the heap of clothing. Suddenly the mass rises jerkily, and pieces of clothing drop away as a dark-haired head emerges from the dirty laundry. The girl squirms around to face the window, her feet tied at the ankles, her arms bound behind her, and grey duct tape covering her mouth.

It's Francesca. Our eyes meet; hers are huge and scared. I again put my finger to my mouth, as a sign to stay quiet, and point to indicate I'm coming to help her. She nods hastily, and I dash around the corner and enter the motel, looking every which way to see if the coast is clear.

A haggard-looking maid with a housekeeping cart stands outside a room several doors down from the one where Francesca is tied up. I walk to the door of what I assume to be Bobby Taylor's room and rummage in my purse as if searching for my key card. Looking up, I meet her eyes. "Morning. Too much to do to get ready for my high school reunion." I give her a big smile, which she returns, and go back to my bag-rummaging.

While digging around in the depths of my handbag, I pull out two twenties and a ten. "I give up," I say, stepping over to her cart and offering her the tip. "I know I should go to the front desk for a new key card, but I'm running so late, I'll miss my appointment. Can you do me a favor and let me in?"

The woman looks suspiciously at the money and then at me. "Please," I say. "You'd really be helping me out."

She takes the money. "Well, good thing you're catching me right as I go on break." She heads over to unlock the door. "You know, so that I never saw you." The lock clicks, and she holds the door open slightly for me.

"Thank you," I say and put my shoulder against the door, so that it doesn't click shut again.

She looks at her watch. "Yep, break time." She pushes the cart into an alcove further down the hall and leaves.

I step inside the room and see the girl sitting on the bed, looking terrified. "Francesca?" She nods. "I'm Ronnie, a friend of—" I stop myself. How much does she know? "Of Juliana's, and I've come to get you out of here." I walk to the bed. "Let's untie you first."

I work on the rope binding her wrists, but don't have much luck. "There are so many knots, this will take forever," I say. "Hold on, I've got something that will cut these ropes."

Digging around in my bag again, I find my small Swiss army knife that big brother Peter gave me when I went off to college many moons ago. I look up at Frankie and show it to her. "This'll work, and I'll be careful, OK?" She nods again. I slide the knife blade under the rope and rotate the blade toward me and away from her skin and slowly cut back and forth. After several moments, the rope snaps, and the girl rubs her wrists and arms.

"Frankie, you take the tape off your mouth, and I'll cut off the ropes around your ankles." I use the same technique to cut those ropes, while she slowly works the tape off her mouth, grimacing as if she were carefully pulling a Band-Aid off a wound. I free her feet at the same moment she gets the tape off her mouth.

"Yuck. That tape is disgusting. The sticky side is gross." She rubs her mouth, making a funny face. I look at her and we both giggle lamely. Nerves?

I tuck the knife deep into my front jeans pocket, the slight bulge hidden by my loose shirt. "Before we leave, I've got something for you in case we get separated." She looks distressed and grabs my arm. "Which we won't. Please don't worry." I reach into my bag one more time. "I always like to have not only a Plan A, but a Plan B and C, if possible. Voilà." I pull out a small black metal canister.

"This is pepper spray." I give Frankie a mock demonstration. "The closer you hold it to your attacker's face, the better the spray will work to burn his eyes. Then you press this button on top and count to three. Pssst."

"What if one squirt isn't enough?" she asks.

"Trust me, one time will work, but you can spray it two times, and then it's empty." I give her the small can. "Stick this in your jeans pocket, and let's see if we can find you something baggy, so if we get caught, the pepper spray won't be noticed in your pocket. OK?"

I dig around an open duffle bag filled with rumpled clothing and my hand hits something sticky. "Ewww." I pull my hand out and it looks like toothpaste—maybe a broken tube that got all over the clothes. I smell mint on my hand, but who can be sure. I dash into the cramped and filthy bathroom.

While washing my hands, my eyes settle on the worn, damp toothbrush in a plastic cup. Bobby Taylor's toothbrush? There's an unused cup in a clear plastic sleeve. I remove the cup from the covering and use the plastic sleeve to bag the toothbrush. You never know—this DNA could come in handy. I'm still wondering about Francesca's paternity.

I return to the room and tuck the wrapped toothbrush in my purse. Frankie has found a large tee-shirt in the pile of clothes that covered her on the bed and sniffs at it. "This smells bad, Ronnie."

"I'm sure it does, Frankie. Turn it inside out, and maybe the creep who tied you up won't notice you have it on if he finds us. If he does, just say you got cold from being scared. OK?" She nods, and I help her pull it over her head. "Let's get out of here." I reach out my hand, Frankie grabs it, and we turn to leave.

Just then we hear the click of the door lock, because someone has used a key card to get in. We freeze. The door opens, and in steps Jimmy, the stoned guy who attacked me behind this motel on my last visit. He's as shocked to see me as I am him.

"What the f— are you doing here?" Jimmy says as he grabs me, while I yell, "Run, Frankie!"

Which she does. I slam my knee up between Jimmy's legs, right into his crotch, hard. Bull's eye! He collapses on the filthy carpet moaning. I turn to leave.

"Hold it, bitch." Bobby stands between the door and me, holding Frankie, with a gun pointed at her head. "I wouldn't try anything stupid."

I stand still. "Don't hurt her," I beg. "What do you want?"

"First, your phone," Bobby says. I hand it to him, and he throws it on the ground, stomping on it and crushing it.

"We're outta here—you first," he says to me. "I'll follow with the kid here. And my gun. So don't get any ideas. Understand?"

"I understand." I try to keep a calm tone, as I look at Frankie, who's shaking she's so scared. "Frankie, we're going to do as he says. I'm here with you, and everything will be OK."

"Jimmy, you stay here," Bobby says, "and call me if anyone else comes snooping around." Jimmy grunts but doesn't get up.

I go out first and glance down the hallway, wondering when the maid will return from her break. Bobby gestures with the gun for me to walk toward the rear of the building, which I do. He and Frankie follow me through the back door, where we see the green SUV with its front windows down. Bobby must have brought it around while I was inside with Frankie.

"The keys are in the ignition, and you're going to drive," he says to me. "This little lady and I will sit in the back seat to make sure you do exactly as I say," he tells me. "Understand?"

"I understand. Where are we going?"

"You'll find out when we get there." Bobby's voice is gruff. "Now move, and remember, I've got the gun."

The two of them climb into the back. I see the scrapes on the passenger side of the SUV that are obviously from the night of the attack on my brother. I make my way around the front to the driver's side, get in, start the car, and drive through the alley. Somebody's got to stop this guy. But first I've got Frankie to think of.

I pull out of the alley between the coffee shop and motel, make a left turn and observe Juliana crouched on the sidewalk-side of the Meadow Farm Toyota that I drove here. A front door is open—maybe she found the car keys—and she's quietly speaking to Warrior, who stays down. I look in the rearview mirror at Bobby, and I'm sure he hasn't seen Juliana next to the Toyota.

The creep is distracted, muttering one obscenity after another, while he jerks roughly on Frankie's seat belt, trying to secure her so she can't move. The girl's clenched jaw and stiff body show me how afraid she is, and she tries very hard not to look at the threatening Bobby recklessly waving his gun around.

As I pass the Toyota, my dog's head pops up to look at us. My eyes meet Warrior's, and I put my finger up to my lips telling him to be quiet. Then my eyes connect with Juliana's, and I think *Call Frank* as hard as I can. A lot of good that'll do...

Driving down the road, I look in the rearview mirror again and see Juliana and my dog pull out in the Toyota to follow us.

CHAPTER FORTY-FOUR

Bobby Taylor directs me to drive to an area filled with industrial buildings. We approach one with an old sign that says *Henderson Manufacturing*. He then instructs me to turn in and park as close as possible to the back entrance of the building. I look up and count six stories high and then glance at the clock on the dashboard. It took us ten minutes, driving west from the motel to arrive here.

"We're getting out," Bobby says. "Don't try to pull any shit on our way to that door, or else someone will get hurt." He brandishes his gun at me. "You hear me, bitch? I don't know your name, so I'll just call you bitch."

Francesca pipes up. "Her name is Ronnie."

"Hey, what did I tell you before?" He shoves Francesca's shoulder. "Stay quiet, you little shit." Frankie looks scared again, and I try to beam thoughts of safety and confidence that we'll be all right from my eyes directly to hers.

The three of us get out of the car and enter the building, only to find the elevator not working. Bobby slaps his hand on the button and then the elevator door and lets out a new string of obscenities.

"Where are we going?" I ask.

"To the roof," he snarls. "And it looks like we're walking up." The door to the stairway is jammed, and Bobby kicks it repeatedly until it opens. "Let's go."

I enter first, followed by Francesca and Bobby. He slams the door behind us.

He sure makes a lot of noise for someone in the midst of a kidnapping. I wonder that he isn't worried about alerting all the other tenants and someone calling the police. "What kind of companies are in this building?" I ask, as I begin the six-story climb to get to the roof. The air is stale in here.

"None of your business who's in this building," he barks. "Now move it."

Frankie runs up faster than Bobby until she's alongside me and can grab my arm and then my hand. I look at her with a smile and squeeze her hand. She squeezes back.

As we pass doors on our way up, I read out the names on the signs showing who's doing business on that floor. Seems to mostly be storage companies of one kind or another, so probably not many people are around who could help us.

"I remember you now," he says with a sneer. "You and your friend were at that mixed martial arts fight by the airport when I worked security there. You're the bitch who almost got me fired." He looks down the barrel of his gun as though he's aiming at me. "Bang!" He cackles—it's a mean sound.

"And you were the creep banging that drunk guy's head on the concrete. What were we supposed to do? Let you kill him?"

"Well, I've got plans for you—"

"Yeah?" I cut him off. "What kind—"

"Ronnie, shhh." It's Francesca, and she's tugging on me. I settle down.

By the time we climb from the sixth floor to the roof, all three of us are huffing and puffing. I push through a heavy metal door, and we walk onto the flat roof. Francesca and I breathe in the fresh air.

The first thing I notice are a lot of cooing sounds coming from a good-sized shed halfway across the rooftop. It's a nonstop chorus. Walkpads on top of asphalt lead straight to the shed.

"What's that?" Frankie asks of no one in particular.

"Those are my brother's pigeons," Bobby says, "and you two are going into their shed." I remember Joe Taylor talking about Teresa's father having homing pigeons and then giving them to Joe and Bobby when he left.

Bobby uses his gun as a pointer indicating we should walk on the pads toward the shed. Keeping his weapon on us, he then unlocks the door and pushes us inside. We stand in a shabby wooden passage that provides access to two pens filled with pigeons sitting in their nesting boxes or perches, or flying about. A third pen is filthy with old pigeon droppings but empty of birds, and Bobby shoves us inside that one. He latches the door with a tight-looped rope over a hook, so we're effectively locked inside the pen.

Bobby's phone buzzes, and he answers, "Yeah?" He shoves the gun into his waistband and listens. "How much longer?" He listens some more. "An hour and a half? You better hope Joe doesn't get here first, 'cause he'll be really pissed."

I whisper to Francesca, "He's talking to Juliana." She nods.

Suddenly Bobby bursts out at the caller, "Don't give me that shit. No excuses. Call me when he's at the coffee shop with the cash, and I'll tell you what to do next. Bottom line, you better have all the money when you come here, or, well, you know—the kid." He looks straight at Francesca when he says the last bit and then ends the call to go outside and sit on a bench by the door to the shed.

Somewhere out there, close by, are Juliana and my German shepherd, but if she knows where we are, I hope she doesn't rush in with Warrior, the way I usually would, and do something stupid. Please let them wait until Frank and Will arrive.

~~~~~

Francesca and I stand by the one small window in our pen and kill time watching the pigeons in an outdoor area that's caged in with wire. I guess it's a safe way for the birds to exercise without getting picked off by a hawk or some other predator. It feels like an hour or more since Bobby stuck us in this disgusting place.

But the door to the roof suddenly bursts open, and we hear Bobby jump up, followed by the sound of footsteps. "Hey, big brother—"

"You idiot," the other voice says. "How could you bring the girl here of all places?" I know that voice. Joe Taylor. I remember it from my meeting with him to learn about his drug prevention program for school kids. Nice guy.

"You mean—here in Moosic, Joe, or here to the pigeon coop?"

"Loft, Bobby. How many times do I have to tell you it's called a pigeon loft, not a coop."

"Things were getting messed up at the motel," Bobby whines. "I didn't know what else to do, Joe."

I hear a string of obscenities from Joe, and the sound of someone kicking a garbage can, probably Joe, too, and the can crashing on its side and rolling around. "This is my special place, Bobby, from Uncle Tony."

"I thought these were *our* pigeons from Uncle Tony," Bobby protests.

"They were ours until you went away to prison and stayed there most of your feeble life," Joe says. "Anyway, Uncle Tony's pigeons died a long time ago, you idiot. But why are we talking about these f—ing pigeons? Where's the girl?" Francesca's eyes look at me with fear, and she grabs my arm.

"I've got them in the empty pen in the back—"

"Them?" Joe asks.

"Yeah. The kid and the broad," Bobby says. "I think her name's Ronnie."

"Mother f—er." Joe slams through the door to the coop—uh, I mean loft—making a racket as he strides to our pen. I shield Francesca with my body, and I feel her shaking.

Joe Taylor peers in, and a look of recognition comes over his face as he stares at me. "You! What are you doing here?" He notices Francesca's arms grabbing mine even though she hides behind me. "How the hell are you connected to the girl?"

Bobby stares at me and then at Joe. "You know her?"

"Mrs. Ronnie Lake." Joe shakes his head at me. "I knew something was off when you came to my office saying you were from that foundation wanting to give my program money."

"I am on the board of that foundation," I insist. "Although, if you're involved in this kidnapping, I would imagine your chances aren't great to get our approval—"

"Shut the f— up," Joe yells at me. "Come on, Bobby. This changes everything. I need to get some air and think about what to do." He drags his brother outside with him.

"Joe, we can still get the twenty-five thousand. Teresa said she'll have it in a little while."

"Bobby, shut up. I need to figure this out." I hear feet pacing back and forth.

"Joe," Bobby whines. "When do you need the money for the deal with Eddie? Isn't the shipment coming in soon—"

"Shut up. I'm thinking."

While Joe and Bobby think, I pull from my pocket the little Swiss army knife—thank god that tattooed dimwit didn't decide to check us for weapons back at the motel—and I stretch it through the narrowly spaced slats at the top of the pen door. I try repeatedly to catch the rope that's looped over the hook, holding the door closed.

After a half-dozen tries, I snag the rope and carefully saw the knife back and forth against the loop. It's slow going and on one of my passes, I drop the rope.

Nothing else to do but try again. I'm getting better at it with my knife and hook it after three tries this time. I start up the sawing again in the deep cut I've already made in the rope. Back and forth I continue.

"Joe what do we do?" Bobby sounds nervous. "This is our chance to be part of some really big money—"

His brother's answer is too quiet to understand. I continue with the knife. Back and forth. Almost got it.

Just as the rope loop gives way with a quiet *snap*, I hear a door creak open. Is it the same one we used to get to the roof? I signal Francesca to stay quiet, as I carefully open the door to the pen that holds us. We tiptoe down the corridor of the loft.

I can hear commotion on the roof outside the shed. "What the f—? Teresa, is that really you?" Joe laughs. "My, my, you've come a long way since we were kids. Just look at you now," he says in a scornful tone. "How did you know to come here? And who's this guy with you?"

The pigeons act up, flying in their pens and cooing. I peek through a crack in the door and see Juliana and Frank side by side facing Joe and Bobby. Francesca crouches low, so that she can get a look-see, too.

"Joe, this is my friend, Frank, and he brought me the rest of the money that Bobby asked for, so that we can pick up Francesca," Juliana tells him. "Where is she? Is she all right?"

"Whoa, Teresa," Joe says and pulls a small revolver from the pocket of his khakis. "…all these people in the know about this transaction. It was just supposed to be you and Bobby. And now, goddammit, Bobby, because, you f—ed up and brought everybody here to my pigeon loft, I got sucked in."

"What do you mean, Joe?" Juliana asks. "It's just the three of us and my friend who brought the money so we can make the trade for Francesca. No need for guns or for anyone to get hurt. Please put the gun away."

Joe motions with his gun and glances toward the loft. "What about the broad back in the pen with the girl?" As he takes his eye off Juliana and my brother, Frank lunges toward Joe to grab the handgun.

But Frank isn't fast enough, and Joe swings his revolver toward him to take a shot. Juliana screams, "Nooooo," and throws her body between Frank and Joe. The gun fires; the shot hits Juliana close range in the chest as she's midway through her air dive to protect my brother. She cries out and crumples to the ground onto her side in a heap. Her head hits the ground last, whiplashing hard against the asphalt of the flat roof.

Next to me, I hear Francesca's quick intake of breath.

Everything stops, and Joe, Bobby, and Frank stare in shock at Juliana's very still body. Francesca and I freeze, too, as we watch blood quickly stain the back of Juliana's top—which means, I pray, that the bullet is a through-and-through injury, and it's not lodged inside of her.

The passage of time since the shot rang out feels like an eternity, but in reality only seconds have gone by.

First, Bobby breaks the silence, yelling at his brother. "Joe, you said nobody would get hurt—"

"Shut up, you worthless piece of shit" Joe yells back.

Frank hastens to Juliana, and then all hell breaks loose.

Will Benson, with his .45 caliber Glock sidearm drawn, explodes through the door from the same stairway we walked up earlier. As Joe swings his weapon toward Will to shoot, Will fires his powerful semi-automatic pistol first and hits Joe in the shoulder. The force of the shot hitting Joe causes his revolver to fly from his hand as he grunts and topples over.

Will runs across the roof to kick Joe's gun out of reach with his foot and secure Joe's wrists with handcuffs to a metal pipe, checking him also for other weapons. Will then retrieves Joe's revolver.

During all this commotion, Francesca moves past me to push open the loft door. She dashes toward Juliana in sheer panic. When she passes Bobby, he grabs her, throws her over his shoulder and makes a run for another door on the other end of the roof. But Francesca kicks with her feet and pounds at Bobby with her fists, trying to wriggle loose. As I scramble into the open, I hear a familiar barking somewhere downstairs. Somehow, I'm certain that dog is Warrior.

I race after Bobby and reach for Francesca's outstretched arms. We connect and hold onto each other as I try to slow Bobby down. He stops suddenly, whips his body around one-hundred-and-eighty degrees, and that breaks the connection between the girl and me.

Even with Francesca now pulling his ears and hair, Bobby manages to take one of his arms and slam his fist into my face, well, my right eye, to be more exact. *Whap!* I drop like a stone, grunting from the pain, which shoots through my entire face.

That's when Warrior comes charging through the open rooftop door and sees me in distress. The decibel level of his barking skyrockets—it's music to my ears—and he runs straight for Bobby and attacks. He clamps his canine jaws onto Bobby's calf, tearing his jeans and biting as hard as he can to slow Bobby down. Bobby screams, releasing his grip on Francesca as he swats at Warrior. Francesca drops and rolls out of the way.

Bobby loses his balance and crashes to the rooftop, his gun falling out of his waistband and clattering across the ground beyond his reach. Warrior never lets go of Bobby's calf, as the thug howls and tries to crawl toward the other roof door to escape.

I see Francesca dig the pepper spray out of her pocket and run over to Bobby—who doesn't notice her because he's in a world of hurt, trying to shake loose from Warrior. Francesca gets low to where Bobby is, swings around the front of him, and presses the button on the canister, aiming for his eyes. *Pssst!*

He howls and his hands go straight to his face. "That's for my mom," Francesca says in a strong voice, and squirts the pepper spray again, this time at his nose and mouth, holding the button down until the can is empty. *Pssssst!* "That's for my *Tía* Connie!"

In a fit of coughing and gulping for air, Bobby manages to gasp out some words. "I, I c—, c—, can't breathe…"

"Thank you, young lady," Will says to Francesca, and he picks up Bobby's gun. I call off Warrior, who releases Bobby's bleeding calf and then trots over to me.

Grabbing a TV cable he spots nearby on the ground, Will quickly uses it to tie Bobby's wrists to a different metal pipe from where Joe is handcuffed. Will also checks Bobby for other weapons.

During all of this, Francesca goes very still—she's stunned, scared, and horrified, all at the same time. Her eyes brim with tears as she looks toward Juliana, who lies almost face down on her side and doesn't move. The child bolts over to Frank—he's beside Juliana and on the phone with 911.

Juliana's hair fans over one side of her face like a curtain, obscuring her features, and Francesca gently brushes it back off her face.

Even though I see stars from Bobby's blow, I try to look clearly in Juliana and Frank's direction, and I, also, feel Francesca's fear…until I finally see Juliana move and hear her moan. As I stumble and make my way over to them with Warrior, I let out a sigh of relief that she's alive. Frank, talking with the 911 operator, discusses Juliana's wounds—whether she may have a collapsed lung and possible concussion—and what to do about the bleeding until the ambulance arrives.

My head pounding from Bobby's wallop to my eye, I kneel down next to Juliana. My brother presses on her wound on the right side of her chest with his wadded up handkerchief. Its white fabric is rapidly turning red, and the exit wound on her back continues to bleed as well.

Frank looks at me with concern and then glances around for something else to add to his handkerchief-compress and to also make a new one for the wound on her back. He notices the baggy tee-shirt Francesca has on over her own clothes, the one from the motel room and motions for her to take it off. I give him my little Swiss army knife to help him tear the shirt in half.

While Francesca pulls off the tee-shirt and gives it to Frank, I gently squeeze Juliana's arm. "You are one brave lady."

Her eyes flicker up at me; she's understandably dazed. "What do you mean?" Her voice is soft, hard to hear.

I lean in. "You know, taking that bullet for my brother."

"Ronnie," she whispers. "Thank you, Ronnie, for protecting my Francesca…"

"Frankie's right here, Jules," Frank interjects and guides Francesca into Juliana's line of sight. "See. She's just fine. Now you have to stay quiet until the ambulance arrives."

"Hey, I'm bleeding," Bobby whines, pulling against the pipe and his ties. "I need help. My leg…I need a doctor."

"Shut up, Bobby," his brother barks. "We're all bleeding. Just shut up, you pathetic bag of shit." And he continues with a long string of obscenities that he hurls at all of us.

"That's enough, you two," Will says. "Quiet, or I'll gag you." The Taylor brothers settle down, even though I hear a continuing buzz of muttering coming from them.

Warrior rubs his head against my arm, and Will, now by my side, gently pulls me away. "Let's give your brother and Juliana some space."

We move off, and my private eye carefully examines my face. "Your dog must have squirmed through one of the partially opened windows in the Toyota that Juliana drove over from the motel," Will says. "Guess Warrior knew you were up here and couldn't stay away."

I hear the sound of sirens getting closer. "Guess so, P.I. Benson, just like you."

"Yeah, well, I did as you instructed in your voicemail," Will says. "I called your brother, who was ahead of me on his way to Moosic. He gave me this location. Now that I have plenty of experience with your M.O., you know, bull-in-a-china-shop, I came as fast as I could."

"M.O.? Is that detective talk?" I ask.

"*Modus operandi* or method of operation. You know, M.O.," he says. "Ronnie Lake, if you plan to do more detective work, you need to learn the lingo." He grins. It's a gorgeous smile.

I try to smile back, but smiles aren't part of my repertoire at the moment, since my face feels as though I ran into a wall. I groan just a little.

"That's one big shiner you can expect to have, Mrs. Lake." He tilts my chin to look more closely at my eye while we wait for the police and ambulance to arrive.

"You're going to end up with a huge black eye in the next couple of days."

I throw my arms around him, relieved and happy he's here beside me. My future shiner looks straight into his piercing baby blues. "Will Benson, you are a sight for sore eyes."

EPILOGUE

One month later

The sound of laughter comes in through the open window of my master bedroom. It's the Lattimore children, whose parents rent my big house. They ride their bikes on the dirt road that passes my cottage, and their laughter sounds innocent and carefree, so much so that I step to the window for a look. Too late—I can only hear their high spirits as they reach the end of my drive, turn around and come back, and then I finally see all five of them ride by as they gleefully pedal back to the big house.

Warrior whines. I look at him curled up on his dog nest near my nightstand, and the minute we make eye contact, his tail begins to thump the floor.

My walking toward him causes his tail to pound faster, and I give the command, "Open, Sesame." Sure enough, his back leg pops up revealing his tummy.

"Good Open Sesame, Warrior." I kneel down and lightly massage his soft stomach. He rolls completely onto his back, goes into a full body stretch and makes a noise that can only mean pure bliss.

I laugh and glance around the room while continuing his tummy rub, my gaze landing on the framed photograph that sits on the bottom shelf of the bookcase. It's the one of my oldest brother, Peter, with his wife and their boys, Petey, Ben, Tim and Jimmy. I feel the usual emotional stab go through my core.

Enough of that. I stand up. This is supposed to be a happy day. I walk to the bookcase and grab the picture. It was my oldest brother who chose years ago to acquiesce to his wife's wishes, which resulted in Peter's divorcing himself from our family. I refuse to pine any longer for what isn't there. I head straight for a closet filled with linens, where I step onto a footstool. Reaching up to the top shelf on my tiptoes, I shove the photo under a pile of blankets and pillows. Then I hop down and close the door firmly.

"Come on, Warrior. We're due for family lunch. Let's go."

~~~~~

We've finished Rita's amazing gazpacho and her delicious spinach salad—almost all the ingredients for both are fresh from the farmers market. Nine of us are spread around the side terrace at Meadow Farm perched on various pieces of lawn furniture, as Rita serves slices of peach pie—straight from the oven—with scoops of vanilla ice cream.

Laura is in the midst of a chess game at a small table with her father. Frank makes a move, and she throws her hands in the air. "Whoa, Daddy. OK, now I think I'm in trouble." He chuckles.

My nephew, Richard, is sprawled in a chaise with his arms wrapped around wife, Susie. "Hey, Sis, need some help?" he asks.

"Did you hear anyone say checkmate? This game is far from over," Laura fires back. "Susie, please keep the peanut gallery quiet over there."

"You tell him," Susie says to Laura, but grinning at her husband.

My daughter, Brooke, comes through the French doors with pitchers of iced tea and lemonade and Warrior following her. She circles around the terrace offering refills. Juliana, reclining in the other chaise, reaches her glass forward and smiles when Brooke gets to her. "Iced tea, please." Warrior nuzzles Juliana's leg and then plops down next to her.

"Juliana, are you OK?" Brooke pours the iced tea into Juliana's glass. "You just take it easy," my daughter coos. "May I get you anything else?"

"Appreciate it, Brooke, but I'm not an invalid," Juliana says. "The doctor told me yesterday that my lung and two ribs have healed, and my concussion was minor. So I'm good as new."

"Yes, the doctor did say that." My brother looks up from the chess board. "He also said that had you been a second faster diving between the bullet and me, well, you wouldn't—" Frank stops himself, swallows and looks at

Juliana. "Well, that our story would not have had a happy ending."

"Don't rush it, Juliana." Will gathers up empty soup bowls and salad plates, stacking them on a tray. "I once had a gunshot wound similar to yours—"

I look at Will with surprise, and he says, "—from a tour of duty in Iraq years ago. Calm down, Ronnie. You don't know everything about me." He smiles, and his blue eyes crinkle at the corners—it's a look that melts me every time.

"Anyway, Juliana," he says. "It took longer to heal than I expected, so take it easy." Will and I haven't made up our minds about where our relationship might go. Doesn't mean something won't happen, but at the moment we're flirtatious friends who enjoy spending time, a lot of time, together.

My thoughts are interrupted as the French doors fling open, and a gangly dark-haired girl comes bursting through. Francesca rushes over to Laura and gazes at my niece as if she's the coolest girl on the planet. "I love, love, love my room, Laura, and that it used to be yours, 'cause that makes it the best room in the house. Thank you for letting me have it." Even though Laura sits at the table with the chess board, Frankie hugs her plus the back of Laura's chair from behind all at the same time.

"Yeah, well, I'm leaving for Australia in a couple of days, and once I'm home I'll probably be living in the city with Brooke." My daughter arches her brows in surprise at this news from her cousin. "Well, most likely...or maybe," Laura says, adjusting her response. "So, Frankie, you may as well have that bedroom. Aunt Ronnie had it first when she grew up here, and she kind of passed it on to me, and now I'm giving it to you." They giggle together.

"Where's *Tía* Connie?" Juliana asks.

"She's unpacking her suitcases in her room and also helping me unpack in mine," Frankie answers.

"And why are you not upstairs helping her?" Juliana asks.

"I was until I smelled peach pie through the window." Frankie dashes over to Meadow Farm's housekeeper. "I know I only ate a little of the salad, but *Tía* Connie finished mine after she ate hers, so I didn't waste it. Please, is there any pie left?"

Rita already has a slice on a plate. "A la mode, Francesca?" She stands ready with the ice cream scoop.

"Oh, yes." Frankie claps her hands. "Thank you, Rita."

I notice Juliana's old silver locket hanging around the girl's neck, the one my mother gave to Juliana more than twenty-five years ago. "Frankie, come on over here, and let me see that beautiful necklace you're wearing." I see that it's no longer tarnished but shiny instead. Someone apparently got out the silver polish.

Francesca beams and proudly walks over to show it to me. "My mother gave it to me, and she told me a very special lady gave it to her when she was younger than me."

"Younger than I am," Juliana says with a smile.

"Younger than I am," Francesca repeats. "Mom told me that I'm named after her."

"Yes, Frances, my mother." I answer, and open the locket to see the strand of hair. "My brother, Frank, is also named after our mother."

"I know that, too." Francesca looks down at the strand in the necklace. "Mom said this is her hair from when she was little, and your mother, Frances, had it put in this necklace. She told me to wear the locket so that I never forget that I am special, because that's what your mom told my mom a long time ago when she gave this to her."

"Checkmate," Frank exclaims. He stands up, leans across the chess board table and affectionately messes his daughter's wild red hair.

"Oh, Daddy, stop." Laura grins.

Frank makes a beeline for Juliana's chaise and sits on the end of it, while Juliana scoots up to him close. He announces, "Juliana and I have news."

Almost in unison, Laura and I declare, "You're eloping!"

Juliana and Frank burst out laughing, and so does everyone else. Juliana winces a bit from her month-old gunshot wound, and Frank gently puts his arm around her. "Well, I can see none of you are surprised that I want to spend the rest of my life with this wonderful woman, especially given everything that's happened." He takes her hand. "So, I've officially proposed—"

"—and I've officially accepted, and we've decided to marry next year in May." Juliana looks at Frank devotedly.

"Why the long engagement, Juliana?" Laura asks. "We already know we want you in the family—you, Frankie and *Tía* Connie."

"Or why not have a shorter engagement, Juliana," I offer. "Laura, Brooke, Susie and I can organize a great wedding for you on very short notice." My daughter, niece and nephew's wife all express agreement.

Francesca pipes up. "I just watched *Maid of Honor* with J-Lo." She sits herself between Juliana and Frank on the chaise. "Mama, I can be your maid of honor when you and Frank walk down the aisle."

"Good idea, Francesca!" Juliana gives her daughter a quick squeeze. "You be my maid of honor...and Ronnie?" Her once inscrutable cat-like eyes are now open and warm. "Would you consider being my matron of honor?"

I break out in a gigantic smile. "Absolutely!" Will, now sitting next to me, squeezes my arm.

Frank, Juliana and I come together for a group hug, while the others break into applause. Will and Richard shake Frank's hand in congratulations.

"Yea!" Francesca jumps up and down clapping. "Yea! Yea!"

Frank hands me a tray, and he takes the other one. We pile them with dirty dishes, as Rita continues slicing the pie and scooping the ice cream. On our way into the house, my brother calls to Francesca, "Look out for your mother, Frankie, and make sure she doesn't lift a finger."

I guess he catches my funny look as we walk through the library, because my brother says to me, "What?"

"I'm still seeing you on the roof of that building, crouched down next to Juliana, calling 911, meeting Francesca for the first time," I say as we cross the foyer and enter the kitchen.

"Hold it, Ronnie," Frank says. "Remember, I've known since not long after Juliana and I met in California that she had a daughter," Frank says. "I already told you that. I just didn't know any details and that it was Francesca." He puts his tray on the counter near the sink, takes mine and places it next to his. "And I also told you that Juliana filled me in on all the details later at the hospital."

"I know, I know. And now when I look at Francesca, I see Rosa's daughter, Maria—your Juliana—chasing Glory all over the house decades ago. Remember?" I ask, opening the dishwasher.

"Yeah, she was a sweet kid back then," Frank answers. "And, despite everything that's happened to her, she's remained a—"

"I can still see her at the bus station pounding you on the chest and crying how much she hated you when she and Rosa left."

"Oh, Ronnie, she didn't mean it," Frank interjects. "She was just a girl—"

"All because of my stupid accusation about my missing ring. I mean, you do realize that's what propelled Juliana into a life of juvie crime." I load the dishwasher with the dirty plates sitting on the trays. "Even back then, Frank, she was a go-getter. She wasted no time dropping the name Maria and morphing into Scranton Gang leader Teresa Gonzalez with those god-awful Taylor brothers. Thank god those two are going away for a long time." I shake my head and place the last plate in the dishwasher rack. "How she grew up to become your beautiful, kind, elegant fiancée is just unbelievable."

My brother hands me the dirty flatware. "I feel like a lucky guy, Ronnie—"

"God, Frank, I know I must have seemed like a pain."

My brother raises his eyebrows at me. "You think?"

"But I was worried to death that Juliana had a vendetta against our family and that she would humiliate you, bring you down somehow." I distribute the flatware in the holder in the washer. "I'm so relieved I was wrong about the revenge thing."

"You know, you're quite a go-getter yourself, Sis. How you poked your nose into all of Juliana's history—even after I expressly told you to stay out of it—well, I see now that Will helped you." He rolls his eyes, and I can see from his expression that he's still somewhat irked by my investigation. "Thank god, you had a professional reining you in."

"Frank, it all comes down to family matters. I'm your sister, and I will always love you."

"I know, and me you. But frankly, Ronnie, I'm amazed Juliana even speaks to you considering how much you snooped into her background, her privacy—"

"Juliana and I have made our peace," I insist.

He puts his hands on my shoulders. "When you presented Jules and me with that pathetic looking toothbrush from Bobby Taylor's motel room and Juliana's broken hairbrush, you did take it to the limit urging her to confirm Francesca's paternity. My god, she had just come home from the hospital. All of that was absolutely none of your business. It was really too much, Sis."

"I know, but—"

"No buts, Ronnie. Jules was already taking steps to resolve all that in her own good time. I didn't know the details, but that's why I took her to the lawyer when she first arrived. That was not your call to try to push along."

"OK, OK. Maybe I did go too far."

"Maybe?" Frank's voice is incredulous.

"OK. No maybe. I did go too far." I try to look repentant.

"I'm glad you understand that, Ronnie." He squeezes my shoulders. "Come on. Let's get back to our party."

~~~~~

In the distance the sound of a car motor quiets all of us on the terrace, and we turn to look. A sporty white coupe zooms down the gravel road toward the house. Everybody moves to the stone wall that edges the terrace to observe the car's approach.

"Who is that?" Frankie asks. "Pretty car!"

Juliana and I look at each other as my brother says, "Now Francesca, remember your mother said she and Ronnie had a surprise for you today?"

"You mean a different surprise from me and *Tía* Connie moving to Meadow Farm?" she asks.

"*Tía* Connie and me," Juliana corrects. "But yes, it is a different surprise. Remember how you told me you hoped one day to meet your father?"

Francesca's eyes turn into big round saucers. She grabs her mother's arm and nestles against her. In a small, shy voice she asks, "You mean—? Is that my real father driving that car?" The automobile is halfway down the drive.

"Yes," Juliana answers. "Ronnie found him, and she went to Salt Lake City—that's where he lives—to talk to him. He's a friend from long ago."

"He wants to meet me?" Frankie asks. Understandably, she sounds nervous. All of us watch the car pull up, and the driver turns off the engine.

My brother nods for me to come close to Frankie, which I do. "He's a good man," I say to her. "His name is John Palmer. Come with us to meet your father."

Palmer gets out of the car, and Juliana and I, with Frankie between us, walk over to welcome him to Meadow Farm.

THE END

A Note from the Author

Thank you very much for taking the time to read *Stunner: A Ronnie Lake Mystery*. Reviews are important to Indie Authors, so please consider writing a review of this title on your favorite eBook retailer or review site.

To be notified of future Niki Danforth books, please sign up at http://nikidanforth.com/ for a quarterly email.

I've lost track of the number of times that my novel has been read and reread. Please email me at nikidanforth5@gmail.com should you spot a typo.

Finally, if you're curious about the elegant martial art that Ronnie Lake practices in *Stunner*, please visit http://nikidanforth.com/ to learn more. You'll also find a complete list of the fabulous, mostly classic rock songs that Ronnie Lake listens to during the course of the story.

ACKNOWLEDGEMENTS

Without the kindness, support and expertise of the following people, *Stunner* would still be a work in progress. Words cannot express the gratitude I feel for their help:

G. Miki Hayden, editor extraordinaire who goes the extra mile for her writers;

Karen De Paola, 5th Dan, SkylandsAikikai.com, consultant for Aikido and fight scenes;

Walter Sutton, senior training manager for The Seeing Eye, Inc., who generously shared his extensive knowledge of the German shepherd breed;

Lt. Vito Abrusci, Mendham Township Police Department, New Jersey, who informed me about gun basics and what might occur during a shootout, as well as how perpetrators can be secured;

wonderful friends who served as an informal focus group along the way;

finally, Jane Ely, Cindy Grogan, and Karen De Paola, the best brainstorming and critiquing partners a writer could hope for.

N.D. August 2013

About the Author

Niki Danforth, daughter of a Cold War covert intelligence officer, has the "thriller/adventure" gene in her DNA. After a career as a successful TV/video producer and director in New York, this empty-nester is picking up her first love of mystery books and recreating herself as an author in the genre. Danforth lives in the New Jersey countryside with her husband and two drama-queen dogs.

Made in the USA
Lexington, KY
24 April 2014